Klaus Mann, the second child of Thomas Mann, was born in Munich in 1906. He began writing short stories and articles in 1924 and within a year was a theatrical critic for a Berlin newspaper. In 1925 both a volume of his short stories and his first novel, *The Pious Dance*, were published. His sister Erika, to whom he was very close, was in the cast of his first play, *Anja and Esther*. He also acted and continued to write prolifically. Klaus Mann left Germany in 1933 and lived in Amsterdam until 1936, during which time he became a Czechoslovakian citizen, having been deprived of his German citizenship by the Nazis. Moving to the United States in 1936, he lived in Princeton, New Jersey, and New York City. He became a U.S. citizen in 1943. He died in 1949, at the age of forty-two, in Cannes, France.

Robin Smyth was the European correspondent for the London *Observer*. He died in 1993.

MEPHISTO

KLAUS MANN

**TRANSLATED FROM THE GERMAN
BY ROBIN SMYTH**

PENGUIN BOOKS

PENGUIN BOOKS
Published by the Penguin Group
Penguin Books USA Inc., 375 Hudson Street, New York,
New York 10014, U.S.A.
Penguin Books Ltd, 27 Wrights Lane, London W8 5TZ, England
Penguin Books Australia Ltd, Ringwood, Victoria, Australia
Penguin Books Canada Ltd, 10 Alcorn Avenue,
Toronto, Ontario, Canada M4V 3B2
Penguin Books (N.Z.) Ltd, 182–190 Wairau Road,
Auckland 10, New Zealand

Penguin Books Ltd, Registered Offices:
Harmondsworth, Middlesex, England

First published in the United States of America
by Random House, Inc. 1977
Published in Penguin Books 1983
This edition published in Penguin Books 1995

3   5   7   9   10   8   6   4

LIBRARY OF CONGRESS CATALOGING IN PUBLICATION DATA
Mann, Klaus, 1906–1949.
Mephisto.
Reprint. Originally published: New York: Random House, c1977.
I. Title.
PT2625.A435M413   1983   833´.912   82–13313
ISBN 0 14 01.8918 1

Printed in the United States of America
Set in Fairfield

Publisher's Note

Mephisto, written in 1936, was the third novel that Klaus Mann—Thomas Mann's son—wrote while living in exile from the Germany of World War II. He wrote this satirical and political novel as the thinly veiled portrait of his former brother-in-law, the actor Gustaf Gründgens. Gründgens, who had been married to Mann's favorite sister, Erika, and had once been a flamboyant champion of Communism, had a magnificent career in Nazi Germany under the auspices of Field Marshal Hermann Göring. Göring, influenced by his actress-wife Emmy Sonnemann, gave Gründgens, who was already in disgrace because of his questionable past, another chance. Gründgens chose the role of Mephistopheles in *Faust*, and Göring was completely bewitched by his breathtaking display of depravity. He appointed him director of the State Theater, and Gründgens became the leader of theatrical life in the Third Reich. Mann wrote *Mephisto* to "analyze the abject type of treacherous intellectual who prostitutes his talent for the sake of some tawdry fame and transitory wealth."

Originally published in Amsterdam, *Mephisto* has been published in nineteen countries. It was published in West Germany in the early sixties, only to be met by the longest lawsuit in the history of German publishing. The suit, brought by Gründgens' adopted son, dragged on for seven years, until the Supreme Court of Germany banned the book in a three-to-three decision.

This translation marks the first appearance of *Mephisto* in English.

All men's failings I forgive in actors;
no actor's failings will I forgive in men.

—Goethe, *Wilhelm Meister*

Mephisto

1936

"I hear over eight hundred workers in one West German industrial center were recently tried, and condemned—all of them—to long sentences. At the same trial."

"I heard there were only five hundred. A hundred more weren't even tried. They were secretly executed because of their opinions."

The two young foreign diplomats were sitting a little apart from the stylishly dressed crowd under the chandeliers of the Berlin Opera House. They spoke in low voices.

"Are wages really so bad?"

"Pathetic. What's more, they're getting worse—and prices keep going up."

"They say decorating the Opera House for tonight cost sixty thousand marks. Add to that at least forty thousand marks for other expenses, not counting the burden on the public purse of keeping the Opera closed for five days while getting it ready for the ball."

"Nice little birthday party."

"Disgusting we have to be part of this."

The two young men bowed with their best smiles in the direction of an officer in full-dress uniform who had glanced distrustfully at them through his monocle. They resumed talking again once they were sure the full-dress uniform was out of earshot.

"The entire general staff has turned out."

"But they all say they want peace, of course," the second diplomat added.

"For how long?" asked the first, smiling brightly at a tiny woman from the Japanese Embassy who glided past, small and delicate, on the arm of a huge naval officer.

"We must be ready for all eventualities."

A gentleman from the Foreign Ministry approached the two young attachés, who promptly began to rave over the splendor and beauty of his decorations.

"Yes, the prime minister takes pleasure in such matters," said the gentleman from the Foreign Ministry with a hint of embarrassment.

"It's all in such good taste," declared the two young diplomats almost in the same breath.

"Of course," said the gentleman from the Wilhelmstrasse unhappily.

"Nowhere else but Berlin can you find a lavish affair like this these days," added one of the attachés. The gentleman from the Foreign Ministry hesitated a second before deciding to let this pass with a polite smile.

The three men fell silent. They looked around them and listened to the sound of many voices. "Remarkable," murmured one of the young men finally, this time with no trace of irony but as if genuinely impressed, almost intimidated by the monumental extravagance of the surroundings. The shimmer of lights through the perfumed air was so bright that it dazzled him. He blinked into the trembling radiance. Where am I? thought the young man, who came from one of the Scandinavian countries. There is no doubt my present surroundings are sumptuous; but there's also something sinister about them. The gaiety of these beautifully groomed people doesn't make one feel at ease . . . They move like marionettes. And there's something hidden in their eyes; one doesn't want to encounter so much anxiety and cruelty in a look. Where I come from, people look at you in a very different way, more friendly, freer. They laugh differently, too, in the North. Here people's faces have something sarcastic and despairing. There's something insolent, provocative and at the same time hopeless—it's horribly sad. No one who feels happy to be alive could laugh like that. You never catch men and women who lead decent, sensible lives laughing like that . . .

The great ball in honor of the prime minister's forty-third birthday filled every corner of the Opera House. The elegant crowd surged through the labyrinth of foyers, corridors and anterooms. Champagne corks exploded from boxes whose balustrades were draped with rich fabrics. The seats had been removed and the great house was jammed with dancing couples. A huge orchestra completely filled the stage, giving the impression that it had been summoned to perform a symphonic poem by Richard Strauss, if not something even grander. In fact, all it was playing was a bold hodgepodge of military marches and jazz—forbidden in the Reich as a product of Negro immorality—which the great dignitary didn't want to deprive himself of on his birthday.

Here was gathered everyone who thought he counted for anything in this country, with the exception of the Führer himself, who had excused himself on grounds of a sore throat and nervous fatigue, and a few eminent party members somewhat too plebeian in origin to have been invited. However, several imperial and royal princes, a good many royal dukes and almost the entire nobility had put in an appearance; so had all members of the general staff of the Wehrmacht, a large collection of influential financiers and industrialists, a sprinkling of members of the diplomatic corps—most of them from embassies of small or distant lands—a number of ministers and well-known actors and even a poet, who looked very decorative and was, what is more, a personal friend of the Führer.

More than two thousand invitations had been sent out. Of these about half were complimentary tickets entitling their holders to the free enjoyment of the feast. Those who received one of the thousand remaining tickets had to pay a fifty-mark entrance fee. This meant that part of the enormous expense could be recouped; the rest of the burden was placed on the average taxpayer, who did not belong to the entourage of the prime minister and therefore was not a member of the elite in the new German society.

"Isn't this a marvelous party!" called the heavy wife of a Rhineland arms manufacturer to the wife of a South American diplomat. "Oh, I'm having such a good time. I can't remember when I felt so good! I just wish everyone in Germany and all over the world could feel as good as I do now."

The wife of the South American diplomat, who had trouble

understanding German and was bored, smiled sourly. Disappointed by this lack of enthusiasm, the wife of the arms manufacturer decided to move on.

"Forgive me, my dear," she said graciously, lifting the glistening train of her dress. "I must go over and have a word with an old friend of mine from Cologne, the mother of the director of our State Theater, you know, the great Hendrik Höfgen?"

At this point the South American woman opened her mouth for the first time and asked in English, "Who is Henrik Hopfgen?" which provoked a cry of astonishment from the industrialist's wife.

"What? You don't know our Höfgen?" She pronounced the name with reproachful care—Herf-gen—rapping out the hard *g*. "It's not Hopfgen, dear heart. And it's Hendrik, not Henrik—he's very particular about that little *d*."

With that she sped forward to block the path of the distinguished lady in question, who was proceeding regally through the room on the arm of the poet who enjoyed the Führer's friendship.

"Dearest Frau Bella, it's been just ages since we last met. How are you, my dear? Do you ever get homesick for our Cologne? Of course, you've got such a splendid position here in Berlin! And how is Fräulein Josy, the dear child? Above all, what is Hendrik doing? Your famous son? Heavens, when you think of what he's become! He's really almost as important as a minister. I assure you, dearest Frau Bella, that we in Cologne all long to see you and your marvelous children again."

If the truth be told, the millionairess had never given a thought to Frau Bella Höfgen when she lived in Cologne and her son had not yet made a great career for himself.

The two women had then had only a very passing acquaintance; Frau Bella had never been invited to the manufacturer's villa. Now, however, the jolly, soft-hearted millionairess clung to the hand of the woman whose son was counted among the closest friends of the prime minister as if she couldn't bear to let it go.

Frau Bella smiled graciously. She was dressed very simply, not without a certain touch of style. A white orchid shone against her black silk gown. Her gray hair contrasted interestingly with a face that had remained young and was made up discreetly. Her large gray-blue eyes looked with reserve and thoughtful friendliness upon the talka-

6

tive woman whose glittering necklace, long earrings and Paris gown were the fruits of Germany's active preparations for war.

"I can't complain, we all seem to be getting on very well," said Frau Höfgen with mingled pride and modesty. "Josy is engaged to young Count Donnersberg. Hendrik is a little overworked. He has so terribly much to do."

"I can just imagine." The millionairess assumed a respectful look.

"May I introduce our friend Caesar von Muck," said Frau Bella.

The author bowed over the bejeweled hand of the wealthy lady, who promptly began to rattle on again. "Oh, I'm so excited. I'm just thrilled to meet you. I recognized you immediately from your photographs. Your play about the battle of Tannenberg really overwhelmed me in Cologne. It was a very good production—but, of course, it didn't get the kind of performance that we're accustomed to in Berlin. It was really very good just the same—without doubt, perfectly fine. And you, Herr Privy Councillor—you've been on such a wonderful trip since then. Everyone is talking about your travel journal. I'm planning on reading it very soon."

"I saw many beautiful and many ugly things abroad," said the poet with simplicity. "I was not, however, traveling merely as a tourist but rather as a messenger and teacher. I feel I can say that I have succeeded in winning friends abroad for our new Germany."

His steel-blue eyes—whose piercing and fiery purity had been commented on admiringly in many an article—appraised the Rhineland lady's fabulous jewelry. I could stay at her house next time I have a reading or a première in Cologne, he thought as he went on. "It's inconceivable how many lies, how many odious misconceptions flourish about our Reich in the outside world."

His face was of a kind that made the expression "rough-hewn" trip easily off many an interviewer's pen: a furrowed forehead, prominent blond eyebrows and a pinched mouth. He spoke with a slight trace of the dialect of his native Saxony. The arms manufacturer's wife was deeply impressed by both his appearance and the nobility of his sentiments. "Ah," she said as she gazed at him entranced, "if you ever come to Cologne you absolutely must come see us."

Privy Councillor Caesar von Muck, president of the Academy of Writers and author of the much performed tragedy *Tannenberg*,

7

bowed with courtly gallantry. "It will give me great joy, dear lady." He went so far as to lay his hand on his heart.

"How heavenly it will be to listen to you for a whole evening, Excellency," the industrialist's wife cried in rapture. "What your life must be like! And by the way, weren't you at one time director of the State Theater?"

This remark showed a lack of tact that chilled both the distinguished Frau Bella and the author of the Tannenberg tragedy. "That is correct," said the poet with a certain sharpness. The wealthy lady from Cologne perceived nothing. She blundered on in a tone of wildly inappropriate roguishness. "Are you sure you are not a tiny bit jealous, Herr Privy Councillor, of your successor, our Hendrik?" She wagged her finger coyly at him. Frau Bella did not know where to look.

But Caesar von Muck now demonstrated that he was truly a man of the world, sophisticated to a degree that verged on heroism. His wood carving of a face lit up with a smile that only in the first instant seemed a trifle sour, and was quickly suffused with mildness, goodness and a touch of wisdom. "I have passed on this heavy burden gladly—yes, with heartfelt joy—to my friend Höfgen, who is qualified as no one else is to bear it."

His voice trembled; he was deeply moved by his own generosity and the beauty of his sentiments. Frau Bella resumed her rapt expression. The helpmate of the arms magnate was so impressed by the noble and majestic attitude of the famous playwright that she nearly wept. With admirable self-control she choked back her tears, dabbed her eyes quickly with a small silk handkerchief and visibly squared her shoulders in a triumph of true Rhineland high spirits. Once again she beamed with pleasure, and crowed joyfully, "Isn't this just a grand party?"

It was indeed a grand party. There was no doubt about it. Such glitter, such noise. It was difficult to tell which shone the brighter, the jewels or the medals. The light pouring down from the chandeliers danced and played over the white backs and beautifully made-up faces of the women; over the stiffly starched shirt fronts and gold-trimmed uniforms of corpulent men; over the sweating faces of the waiters hurrying to and fro with refreshments. Fragrance was everywhere, rising from the luxurious floral arrangements, from the Paris perfumes

8

of the German women, from the cigar smoke of the industrialists and the hair oil of the slim young men in their severe, attractive SS uniforms. It rose from princes and princesses, from the officials of the secret police, from newspaper magnates, from film stars, from university professors who occupied a chair of racial studies or of military science, and from the few Jewish bankers whose wealth and international relations were sufficiently grand to allow even them to be part of this exclusive gathering. Clouds of artificial fragrance had been sprayed in every room, as though to prevent people from inhaling another odor: the stale, sweet stench of blood, which permeated the entire country. Though they loved its pervasive smell, they would have felt a trifle embarrassed by it on such an elegant occasion, and in the presence of foreign diplomats.

"What extravagance!" said one senior army officer to another. "The fat bugger really does things up right."

"Well, as long as we allow him to," answered the other. They put on good-natured expressions, since they were being photographed.

"I hear Lotte's wearing a dress that cost three thousand marks," a film actress confided to the man she was dancing with, a Hohenzollern prince. Lotte was the wife of the prime minister, the powerful man with the many titles who was giving himself a forty-third birthday party fit for a fairy-tale prince. Lotte had been a provincial repertory actress and had the reputation of being a good-hearted, simple, typically German woman. On their wedding day the fairy-tale prince had had two proletarians executed.

The Hohenzollern prince said, "My family never gave this sort of party. When is the august couple going to make their entrance? They must want to build our suspense to the limit."

"Little Lotte knows all about that," a former colleague of the national mother figure said dispassionately.

Yes, it was certainly a magnificent party. All the guests appeared to be enjoying themselves to the fullest, those with complimentary tickets unbending as much as those who had paid their fifty marks. They danced, gossiped, flirted. They admired themselves. They admired one another. Most of all, they admired power, the power which could give such a party. In the boxes and galleries and around the tempting buffets conversation was especially lively. People talked about the women's dresses, the men's wealth and the prizes to be won

9

in the charity lottery. They talked about the most expensive prize, a swastika made of diamonds—a really attractive and expensive thing that could be worn as a brooch or pendant.

Those in the know said there were also going to be some highly entertaining consolation prizes: for instance, tanks and machine guns faithfully re-created in marzipan. Several women declared spiritedly, to much hearty laughter, that they would rather have a deadly weapon made out of such tasty material than the costly swastika.

In lower voices people also spoke of the political aspect of the evening. It caused some surprise that the Führer had sent his excuses and several influential party leaders had not been invited, whereas a larger percentage of noble families were present. This gave rise to a number of rumors, even about the health of the Führer. The foreign journalists and diplomats, as well as the gentlemen of the armed forces and heavy industry, spoke of it in low, urgent tones.

"It appears that it definitely seems to be cancer," a member of the English press corps whispered behind a pocket handkerchief to a Paris colleague. He had, however, chosen the wrong man. Pierre Larue looked like a wily if extremely decrepit gnome; in fact he was filled with enthusiasm for the heroism and beautifully uniformed youths of the new Germany. Besides, he was not a journalist but a rich man who wrote scandalous books about the social, literary and political scenes of various European capitals. His whole aim in life was to collect famous acquaintances. This grotesque and disreputable little man, with the pointed face and plaintive falsetto voice of a sick old woman, loathed the democracy in his own country and would explain to anyone who would listen how he considered Clemenceau a rascal and Briand an idiot, while he viewed any high Gestapo official as a demigod and the rulers of the new German regime as irreproachable gods.

"What infamous nonsense are you spreading, sir?" The little man looked frighteningly evil. His voice crackled dryly, like dead leaves. "The Führer's health gives no cause for any concern. He merely has a slight cold."

The little monster is perfectly capable of denouncing you, the English correspondent thought nervously. He tried to save the situation: "An Italian colleague said something of the sort to me in strictest confidence."

But the emaciated fancier of well-cut uniforms sternly interrupted him. "Enough, sir! I will hear no more. This is nothing but irresponsible tattle!" Looking across the room, he added in a milder tone, "Excuse me. I must go over and say hello to the ex-king of Bulgaria. The Princess von Hessen is with him. I met Her Highness at her father's court in Rome." He went off, his pale, narrow little hands folded on his breast giving him the bearing and expression of a scheming priest.

"Damned snob," the Englishman murmured after him.

A stir went through the hall. There was a change in the pitch of the buzzing voices: the minister of propaganda had arrived. He had not been expected to put in an appearance. Everyone knew of his strained relations with the plump birthday boy who still remained invisible so as to make his entry the climax of the night's entertainment.

The minister of propaganda, overlord of the spiritual life of millions, limped nimbly through the glittering throng which bowed down before him. An icy wind seemed to blow as he passed. It was as though an evil, solitary and cruel god had clambered down among the everyday bustle of pleasure-seeking, cowardly, pitiful mortals. For several seconds the whole company remained as if paralyzed with horror. The dancers froze in the midst of their graceful movements. Hate and humility shone in the timid gazes turned on the fearsome dwarf. The object of attention tried an affable smile, which stretched his thin-lipped mouth from ear to ear, to soften the dreadful spell he cast about him. With a friendly expression in his sly, deep-set eyes, he was at pains to charm and placate. Dragging his clubfoot gracefully behind him, he moved agilely through the room, showing these two thousand slaves, fellow-travelers, swindlers, dupes and fools the profile of a bird of prey. All the while his eyes bore a malicious, abstracted smile as they flitted over the group of millionaires, ambassadors, regimental commanders and film stars. It was when he came to the director of the State Theater, Hendrik Höfgen, privy councillor and senator, that his glance at last came to rest.

Another sensation. Director Höfgen belonged to the circle of loyal favorites of the air force general/prime minister, who had pushed through his promotion as director of the State Theater against the will of the minister of propaganda. After a long and fierce struggle the latter had been compelled to sacrifice his own protégé, writer Caesar von Muck, and to send him on a long trip abroad. But now, with an effusive greeting and exchange of compliments, the defeated minister publicly honored the candidate of his enemy. Was this the subtle propaganda chief's way of demonstrating in the presence of the international elite that there could be no question of disagreement and intrigue among the leaders of the German regime, and that the jealousy between himself and the air force general/prime minister belonged to the ugly realm of invented atrocities? Or was Hendrik Höfgen—one of the most talked-about figures in the city—so supremely cunning as to have managed to establish as close a relationship with the minister of propaganda as he had with the prime minister? Was he playing one power center against the other, while enjoying the protection of both? Certainly, that would be a maneuver to stretch his legendary dexterity to the utmost . . .

In any case, this was a development of overwhelming fascination. Pierre Larue left the ex-king of Bulgaria standing where he was and, driven by his inquisitiveness like a feather before the wind, trotted across the room to witness this sensational encounter as closely as possible. Caesar von Muck's steely eyes narrowed warily. The millionairess from Cologne crowed with excitement and joy over the exquisiteness of the situation. As for Frau Bella, mother of the illustrious man, she smiled graciously and reassuringly upon all around her as though to say: Great is my Hendrik and I am his noble mother. However, there is no need for you all to drop to your knees. He and I are made of flesh and blood—though in other respects we are above the rest of mankind.

"How are you, my dear Höfgen?" said the minister of propaganda smiling cordially.

The theater director responded with a smile that stopped well short of his ears and gave him a pinched look, almost as if he were in pain. "I thank you, Herr Minister." He spoke quietly with a lilt in his voice, lingering over the syllables. The minister was still holding his hand. "May I inquire after the health of your wife?" asked the director. The minister's expression was suddenly grave. "She is somewhat indisposed this evening." With that he let go of the director's hand. Höfgen sighed feelingly, "That makes me very sad."

Naturally he knew—as did everyone there—that the wife of the minister of propaganda was completely ravaged by her jealousy of the prime minister's wife. Because the Führer was still unmarried, the beloved wife of the minister of propaganda had been the first lady of the Reich, and she had fulfilled her God-given mission with decorum and dignity. That was something her bitterest enemy could not deny. But then along came this Lotte Lindenthal, a second-rate actress who wasn't even young any longer, whose marriage to the paunchy air force general/prime minister threatened her rank as first lady. The actress became the center of a cult; it was as though the Kaiser's Queen Louise had risen from the dead. Whenever there was a celebration in Lotte's honor, the wife of the propaganda chief worked herself into such a state that she developed a migraine. This evening she had taken to her bed.

"Certainly, your wife would have enjoyed herself very much here," Höfgen said, still wearing his courtly expression. Nothing in his voice showed any irony. "It's too bad that the Führer couldn't come. The British and French ambassadors weren't able to make it, either."

With these observations, delivered in the gentlest manner, Höfgen betrayed his friend the prime minister, the protector to whom he owned all his prominence, to the jealous minister of propaganda, whom he held in reserve in case of emergency.

"What's the mood here tonight?" the clubfooted minister asked in an intimate tone tinged with irony.

The director of the State Theater answered guardedly, "People seem to be having a good time."

The two dignitaries continued their conversation softly because they were surrounded not only by inquisitive guests, but also by several photographers who were recording the meeting. The wife of the arms magnate whispered to Pierre Larue, who was rubbing his bony little hands together in ecstasy, "Our director and the minister— don't they make a marvelous pair? Both so distinguished! Both so handsome!" She pressed her opulent, jeweled body closer to the spindly form of her small companion. The delicate Gallic admirer of German heroism, strapping German youths, the Führer's great thoughts and aristocratic titles took alarm at the heaving proximity of so much womanly flesh. He tried to draw back a little as he piped, "Exquisite! Utterly delightful! Incomparable!" The lady from the Rhineland confided, "I can tell you our Höfgen is a universal man! A genius of a kind not to be found in Paris or Hollywood. And so utterly German, so straight, simple and honorable! I've known him since he was so high." With her outstretched hand she indicated how small Hendrik was when she, the millionairess, had consistently cut his mother at Cologne charity benefits.

"A magnificent youngster," she declared. And she began casting such soulful, voluptuous glances at Larue that he fled in panic.

Hendrik Höfgen could easily have been taken for a man of fifty. He was in fact thirty-eight—remarkably young for his exalted post. The sallow face with the horn-rimmed spectacles gave the impression of unruffled composure, which very nervous and very vain men can force themselves to assume when they have a large audience. His balding skull was nobly proportioned. What was immediately striking about his puffy gray-white face was the band of strain around his high blond eyebrows and recessed temples—a tense, vulnerable, suffering area that contrasted strangely with the strongly chiseled chin. He jutted that chin upwards to show off the graceful jaw line with its suggestion of resolution and manliness. His broad pale lips were set in an ambiguous smile; it seemed at once disdainful and pleading. His eyes were only occasionally visible behind the large shining lenses of his glasses. It was then one saw with a shock that at moments of tenderness they remained ice-cold despite their sad expression. Their gray-green iridescence made one think of precious but cursed stones or of the greedy eyes of some evil and menacing fish.

Most men and all women considered Hendrik Höfgen to be not only distinguished and gifted but also strikingly handsome. The combination of the calculated grace of his upright bearing and the elegance of his evening clothes did not quite conceal the fact that he was too heavy, particularly around the thighs and buttocks.

"I must congratulate you, too, on your Hamlet, my dear fellow," said the minister of propaganda. "An excellent production. German theater can be proud of it."

Höfgen bowed his head slightly, somewhat lowering his beautiful chin in the process. Above the gleaming white collar a number of wrinkles showed in his neck.

"No one who refuses the challenge of Hamlet deserves to be called an actor," he said modestly. The minister hardly had time to observe that Höfgen showed "the real sense of tragedy" when a great clamor rippled through the hall.

The air force general and his wife, former actress Lotte Lindenthal, had just entered through the wide central doors. They were greeted with applause and ringing cheers. The illustrious pair walked through an avenue of acclaiming guests. No emperor had ever made a finer entrance. The enthusiasm was tremendous: each of these two thousand carefully chosen guests seemed bent on showing each other and the prime minister what a splendid part they were playing not only in the forty-third-birthday celebration of the distinguished gentleman but also in the Third Reich. There were roars of *"Hoch"* and *"Heil"* and "Congratulations." People threw flowers, which Frau Lotte acknowledged graciously. The band played a flourish of trumpets. The face of the minister of propaganda twisted with hate, but no one noticed—with the possible exception of Hendrik Höfgen. He stood motionless, awaiting his patron with a graceful and erect bearing.

There had been bets placed on what kind of fanciful uniform the fat leader would appear in this evening. Through a kind of ascetic coquetry, he decided to surprise everyone with the simplest possible outfit. His bottle-green coat looked like a smartly cut smoking jacket. On his chest blazed a small silver star—his only decoration. In the gray trousers his legs, which he usually like to hide under long coats, had plenty of room to move and looked like stout columns on which he slowly propelled himself forward. The outlandish height and breadth of his monstrous frame were enough to strike terror and awe in all around him—all the more because, despite his ludicrous appearance, there was little reason to find anything comic about him. The smirk of even the boldest onlooker would fade at the thought of how much blood had already flowed at the bidding of the fat giant, and what incalculable rivers of blood might yet flow in his honor. Set on a small bulging neck, his massive head looked as though it had been basted with red gravy—the head of a Caesar flayed of its skin. There was nothing human left to be seen in this face: it was a piece of raw, formless meat.

The prime minister propelled his stomach—an enormous globe that swallowed his chest—majestically through the brilliant gathering. He grinned.

His wife Lotte did not grin; she bestowed regal smiles, playing her queenly role to the fullest. Her dress, whose costliness had been the main topic of conversation among the women present, was simple in its luxury. It was a flowing creation in shining silver ending in a train of royal length. The tiara in her corn-sheaf blond hair, the pearls and emeralds on her bosom, exceeded in size and splendor anything that had ever been seen in these exalted circles. The provincial actress owed her fabulous jewelry to the generosity of a husband who let pass no opportunity for castigating in his public speeches the ostentatiousness and corruption of republican ministers and burgomasters. She was also indebted to the devotion of a few well-placed and privileged hangers-on. Frau Lotte understood how to accept homage of such proportions with a modest good humor that had won her the reputation of being a simple and deserving woman. She was deemed unselfish and of spotless purity. She was the ideal on which German women molded their characters. Her large, round, somewhat protruding cowlike eyes were of a moist, shining blue. She had beautiful blond hair and a snow-white bosom. It must be stated that Lotte also was a little too fat. Good rich food was served at the prime minister's palace. It was said of her, admiringly, that she occasionally pleaded with her husband for Jews in high social positions—yet Jews were still being sent to concentration camps. Lotte was called the Good Angel of the prime minister; yet his cruelty had become no milder since she had gone to work on him. One of her most celebrated roles had been that of Lady Milford in Schiller's tragedy *Intrigue and Love*—the mistress of a man of power, who can no longer bear the sight of her jewelry or the proximity of her prince because she has discovered the price paid for the precious stones.

At her final appearance on the stage of the State Theater she played Lessing's Minna von Barnhelm. Thus, before moving into the palace of the air force general, she had declaimed the lines of a Jewish playwright whom her bridegroom and his colleagues would have harassed and hounded if he had been their contemporary. In her presence the fearful secrets of the all-powerful state were uttered aloud, and she smiled her benign motherly smile. In the morning when she peeked playfully over her husband's shoulder, she saw death sentences lying in front of him on the Renaissance writing table—and he signed them all the same. In the evening she displayed her white bosom and bleached blond hair at opera premières or at banquets of the privileged few considered worthy of her presence. She was imperturbable, untouchable: she was oblivious to the world around her and was sentimental to boot.

She believed herself to be surrounded by "the people's love" because two thousand turncoats, freeloaders and snobs made noise in her honor. She walked through the glittering crowds dispensing smiles—it was all she ever gave. She believed in all seriousness that God was on her side because he had allowed her to accumulate so much jewelry.

Lack of imagination and intelligence shielded her from thinking about a future that might perhaps bear little resemblance to this beautiful present. As she walked on, head held high, suffused with light and admired on all sides, there was no doubt in her heart about the permanence of such magic. Never—she thought serenely—never would this radiance fall from her; never would the tortured be avenged; never would darkness reach out to engulf her.

The trumpets continued their earsplitting fanfares. The jubilant roar still rose from the crowd. Lotte and her bloated escort had now come abreast of the minister of propaganda and Höfgen. The three men raised their arms fleetingly—a nonchalant brief sketch of the Nazi salute. Then Hendrik bowed with a grave, ceremonious smile over the hand of the great lady whom he had so often dutifully embraced on the stage. Here they stood, offered to the burning curiosity of selected members of their public: four powers of this land, four wielders of force, four actors. Here were the publicity manager, the specialist in death sentences and bomber flights, the sentimental wife and the pale-faced intriguer. The chosen public watched as the fat leader slapped the theater director hard on the shoulder, and asked, laughing, "How's it going, Mephisto?"

Aesthetically, Höfgen showed to great advantage. Next to the far too well fleshed couple he looked slim, and in contrast to the deformed propaganda dwarf he appeared tall and comely. His face, too, however pale and gaunt it might appear, contrasted agreeably with the three faces about him. With the sensitive temples and strong outline of the chin, his features seemed to be those of a man who had lived and suffered. The face of his fleshy protector, on the other hand, was a bloated mask, that of the actress a mindless larva and that of the propagandist a grotesque caricature.

The sentimental lady said, glancing soulfully at the theatrical director—for whom she harbored a secret, though not too secret, affection—"I haven't told you yet, Hendrik, how splendid I think your Hamlet is." He silently pressed her hand and, in so doing, moved a step closer and endeavored to look as ardent as his nature allowed.

The attempt misfired; his fishy, glaucous eyes expressed no warmth. So he assumed a serious, almost angry official face and murmured, "I must say just a few words."

The actor's voice had a light, ringing, well-trained timbre that was instantly audible in the furthest corners of the huge hall.

"Herr Prime Minister, Your Highnesses, Your Excellencies, ladies and gentlemen. We are proud—yes, we are proud and happy— that we can celebrate this anniversary today in this place with you, Herr Prime Minister, and your wonderful wife."

At these opening words the loud chatter of two thousand guests was stilled. In total silence, in devout immobility, they listened to the long, trite rigmarole of good wishes delivered by a voice throbbing with feeling. All eyes were fixed on Hendrik Höfgen. Everyone admired him. He belonged to the power establishment and he shared its glamour—while it lasted. Among its representatives he was conspicuously distinguished and gifted. His voice brought to the celebration of his master's forty-third birthday a most unexpected note of jubilation. He held his chin high, his eyes glistened; his gestures had an impetuous verve. He was as careful as possible not to utter a single word of truth. The flayed Caesar, the publicity manager and the cow-eyed actress seemed intent on ensuring that lies and nothing but lies issued from his lips: such was the secret commandment that governed in this hall, as in the country at large.

As he approached the end of his speech, with quickened tempo and elegant turns of phrase, an attractive young woman with a child-like air—the wife of a well-known film director—who had found a spot at the back of the room, whispered to her neighbor, "When he finishes I must go over and shake his hand. Isn't it fantastic? I know him from way back. We got our first parts together in Hamburg. Those were *wonderful* times! What a career he's made for himself since then!"

CHAPTER

1

H. K.

The last year of the world war and the year immediately following the November revolution in Russia were a great period for the avant-garde theater in Germany, despite the country's severe economic difficulties. It was an excellent time, too, for theater director Oskar H. Kroge, who ran a cellar theater in Frankfurt-am-Main. In the highly charged intimacy of this narrow basement room the intellectual society of the city congregated, and a lively young audience was ever eager to discuss and applaud a new production of Wedekind or Strindberg, or the first night of a play by such up-and-coming writers as Georg Kaiser, Carl Sternheim, Fritz von Unruh, Walter Hasenclever or Ernst Toller. Oskar H. Kroge, who himself wrote essays and elegiac odes, saw the theater as a moral training ground: it was from the stage that a new generation would be won over to ideals which in the past men had believed were on the threshold of fulfillment—freedom, justice, peace. Oskar H. Kroge was a solemn, trusting and naïve man. On Sunday mornings before the performance of a play by Tolstoy or Rabindranath Tagore, he would make a speech to his audience. The word "humanity" occurred frequently on these occasions. With emotion quivering in his voice, he would cry out to the young people crowded in the standing room of the pit, "Have the courage to be yourselves, brothers!" And he would reap a storm of applause when he ended with the line from Schiller's "Hymn to Joy": "Embrace each other, oh you millions."

Oskar H. Kroge was much loved and respected in Frankfurt and in other parts of the country where there was an audience for bold theatrical experiments. His expressive face with its high furrowed brow and good-natured, intelligent eyes behind gold-rimmed spectacles was often seen in the avant-garde press and sometimes even in the large, glossy illustrated magazines. Oskar H. Kroge was among the most active and successful pioneers of expressionism in the theater.

Without question it was an error on his part—and he realized it only too soon—to give up his distinguished little Frankfurt basement. The Hamburg Arts Theater, whose direction he was offered in 1923, was certainly larger. That was why he accepted the post. But the Hamburg public proved far less responsive to the excitement of new ideas than the professional and enthusiastic circle that had remained faithful to the Frankfurt cellar club. In the Hamburg Arts Theater, Kroge every now and then had to take his mind off the works in which he was interested in order to produce popular box-office successes. This made him suffer. Every Friday, when the program for the coming week was decided, there was a small struggle with Herr Schmitz, the theater's business manager. Schmitz wanted to include farces and thrillers because they were surefire hits, while Kroge fought for the literary repertoire. Most often it was Schmitz—who through it all had a strong friendship and admiration for Kroge—who gave way. The Arts Theater remained highbrow, and its box-office receipts suffered accordingly.

Kroge complained about both the indifference of the Hamburg youth and the low intellectual level of the general public, which had lost all taste for cultural achievement.

"How quickly it's disappeared," he said bitterly. "In 1919 people still flocked to Strindberg and Wedekind. Now in 1926 they want only musical comedies." Oskar H. Kroge had high standards but no gift for prophecy. Would he have complained about the year 1926, if he could have foreseen what 1936 would bring? "Nothing of the better sort has any appeal any more," he grumbled. "Gerhart Hauptmann's *The Weavers* would have filled the place to the doors not so long ago. And look at the house last night—half empty."

Schmitz tried to cheer his friend up. "Never mind. If need be, our account can still bear the loss." The lines of worry in Kroge's good-natured and childlike old cat's face hurt Schmitz, even though

he himself had every cause for worry and his own plump rosy countenance was even more lined.

"And how," said Kroge, refusing to let himself be comforted,
"how are we going to handle our expenses? We have to invite famous
guest artists down from Berlin—as we did this evening—to get the
people of Hamburg to come to the theater."

Hedda von Herzfeld—Kroge's old associate and mistress, who had
been a director and actress with him in Frankfurt—declared, "You're
looking on the dark side again, Oskar. After all, it's no disgrace to invite
Dora Martin to be a guest star—she's wonderful. And there's no problem about filling the theater when Höfgen's playing."

As she mentioned Höfgen's name Frau von Herzfeld smiled
tenderly. Her broad, heavily powdered face with its fleshy nose and
large, wistfully intelligent gold-brown eyes shone for a moment with a
gentle inner glow.

"Höfgen is overpaid," Kroge said gruffly.

"Dora Martin is, too," added Schmitz. "Granted they have
glamour and distinction and really draw an audience wonderfully. But
one thousand marks a night is really a bit high."

"Berlin star prices," Hedda said, sniffing. She had never worked
in Berlin and had decided to despise the capital and all it represented.

"One thousand marks a month for Höfgen is too much also," said
Kroge waspishly. "Since when has he been getting a thousand? It
always used to be eight hundred, and that was quite enough."

"What can I do?" said Schmitz. "He bounced into my office and
sat on my lap, and he chucked me under the chin." Frau von Herzfeld
saw with amusement that Schmitz was blushing slightly. " 'It's got to
be one thousand marks—one thousand, my darling director, it's such a
nice round sum.' He said that over and over. What could I do, Kroge?
You tell me."

It was Höfgen's artful habit to burst into Schmitz's office like a
minor hurricane when he wanted an advance or a raise. On these
occasions he put on a playfully capricious manner. He knew that the
awkward, fat Schmitz was lost if he rumpled his hair and prodded him
in the stomach with his forefinger. When it came to the thousand-mark
demand, Höfgen even sat in his lap. Schmitz blushed as he confessed
it.

Kroge shook his careworn head angrily. "That's nonsense. Höfgen is basically a trivial creature. Everything about him is phony, from his literary taste to his so-called Communism. He's no artist, he's just an actor."

"What have you got against our Hendrik?" Frau von Herzfeld made an effort to adopt an ironic tone of voice—irony did not come easily when she spoke of Höfgen, to whose winning ways she was only too receptive. "He's our best property. We should consider ourselves lucky if we don't lose him to Berlin."

"I'm by no means so set on him," said Kroge. "When you come down to it, he isn't much more than a routine provincial repertory actor, and at heart he knows that perfectly well."

Schmitz asked, "Where's he hiding this evening?"

Frau von Herzfeld laughed softly. "I'm told he's hiding behind a screen in his dressing room. He's always in a terribly jealous state when Berlin guest artists are around. He's never going to make it to their level, he says to himself, and he goes off to hide behind a screen in a state of sheer hysteria. Dora Martin has a particularly unnerving effect on him. It's a kind of love-hate. This evening he's probably already had at least one crying fit."

"That's where you see his inferiority complex coming out," declared Kroge, looking triumphantly around him. "Or, rather—to put it more precisely—somewhere deep down he has a true appreciation of his real worth."

The three of them were sitting in the canteen called H.K., the initials of the theater's full German name. Above the tables with their stained cloths hung a dusty art gallery of photographs of all those who had appeared on this stage during the past decade. From time to time as they spoke Frau von Herzfeld smiled up at the ingénues and juvenile leads, the old actors, the heroic elders, young lovers, villains and noble ladies.

In the theater below, Dora Martin, who bewitched the cities of Germany with her husky voice, her seductive, boyishly slender body and her childlike, inscrutable eyes, was playing the final scene of a successful middle-brow drama. The two directors and Frau von Herzfeld left their box after the second act. The other members of the Arts Theater group had remained in their seats to see the actress, whom they half admired and half hated, play her part through to the final curtain.

"The cast she has brought along with her is really as bad as it could be," Kroge remarked contemptuously.

"What do you expect?" answered Schmitz. "How could she earn her thousand marks every evening if she had to bring expensive performers on tour with her?"

"But she herself gets better all the time," said the clever Frau von Herzfeld. "She can adopt any mannerism she wants. She can talk like an idiot baby and still be convincing."

"'Idiot baby' isn't bad," said Kroge, laughing. Looking through the window, he added, "It seems they've finished."

People were coming down the alley that led from the theater past the canteen to the gate opening into the street. Gradually the canteen filled up. The actors called out respectful greetings toward the directors' table and teasing remarks to the canteen manager, old Father Hansemann. This thick-set old man, with his waxed mustache and bluish red nose, was for the theater company almost as important a character as the business manager. Advances could be wrung out of Schmitz when he was in a yielding mood; Hansemann had to be approached in writing when money gave out in the second half of the month and advances were not forthcoming. Everyone was in Hansemann's debt; it was said that Höfgen owed him more than a hundred marks. Thus there was absolutely no need for Hansemann to respond to the jokes of his indebted clients. Solemn-faced and frowning, he served cognac, beer and plates of cold meat, which nobody paid for.

Everyone was discussing Dora Martin, each with his own opinion of the quality of her performance. The only point on which everyone agreed was that she was overpaid.

Fräulein Motz announced, "It's the star system that's ruining the German theater." Her friend Petersen nodded grimly. (Petersen played old men and yearned for heroic roles, preferably kings or aristocratic old blades in historical epics. Unfortunately, he was rather too small and plump for such parts—a deficiency he tried to correct through an erect and pugnacious bearing. A full sailor's beard would have suited his face, with its expression of false honesty; but he was clean-shaven, and this—together with his long upper lip and very bright blue eyes that were too small—made him appear overexposed. Fräulein Motz loved him more than he did her; there was no secret about that.)

She went straight over to him and said in an intimate, intense voice, "Isn't it true, Petersen? It's the same kind of mismanagement we've so often talked about."

"Absolutely right, woman," Petersen agreed enthusiastically. And then he winked in the direction of Rahel Mohrenwitz, who was made up like a perverse, demonic girl, with black bangs hanging down to her shaved eyebrows and a large black-rimmed monocle set in a face that was childish, chubby and not yet formed.

"In Berlin, Martin's antics may work," continued Fräulein Motz truculently, "but they can't teach anything to the likes of us. We are far too genuine old hands for that."

She glanced around, seeking approval. Her specialty was comic old women, and sometimes she also played aged dowagers. She liked to laugh long and loud; this had etched deep lines around a mouth in which gold teeth glinted. At the moment, however, she wore a solemn, almost angry expression.

"After all," said Rahel Mohrenwitz, as she toyed haughtily with her long cigarette holder, "no one can deny that Martin is an enormously strong personality. Whatever she is doing onstage, she is always stunningly, intensely *there*. You know what I mean?"

Everyone understood what she meant. But Motz shook her head disapprovingly, while little Angelika Siebert declared, in her high-pitched timid voice, "I admire Martin. She has an aura of magical power. That's how it strikes me." She became very red, because she had managed to produce such a daringly long speech. Everyone looked at her with a certain affection. Little Siebert was charming. Her neat head with its close-cut blond hair was that of a thirteen-year-old boy. Her bright innocent eyes were no less attractive for being short-sighted. Many found that the way Angelika crinkled up her eyes when she looked at you was part of her distinctive charm.

"Our baby has developed yet another crush," said the handsome Rolf Bonetti, laughing rather too loud. He was the member of the company who received the most fan mail; hence his proud though weary look of total disenchantment. But where little Angelika was concerned he was the wooer; for a long time now he had paid court to her. Onstage he had often held her in his arms, because the kind of role he played demanded it. But through it all she remained aloof. With amazing persistence she directed her tenderness only at people who would be certain not to reciprocate and might even repulse her.

She was attractive and desirable; she appeared destined to be greatly loved and spoiled. But the strange obstinacy of her heart made her cold and mocking when faced with Rolf Bonetti's stormy declarations of love, while making her weep bitterly over the icy disdain with which she was treated by Hendrik Höfgen.

Rolf Bonetti said knowingly, "Anyhow, as a woman this Martin doesn't make the grade—she's a weird hermaphrodite. She must have fish blood in her veins."

"I think she's beautiful," said Angelika in a soft but determined voice. "I think she's one of the most beautiful women I've ever seen." Her eyes were full of tears; Angelika cried often, even when she had very little reason to. "It's strange," she went on dreamily. "I feel that there's some kind of secret resemblance between Dora Martin and Hendrik." This was greeted on all sides with astonishment.

"Martin is Jewish." It was young Hans Miklas who chose this way of entering the conversation. Everyone looked with shock and a certain amount of distaste in his direction.

"Miklas is the limit," said Motz, breaking an embarrassed silence, and she gave a forced laugh.

Kroge wrinkled his forehead, puzzled and disgusted, while Frau von Herzfeld could only shake her head; the color had drained from her face. There was a long uncomfortable pause. Young Miklas stood, pale and defiant, leaning with one elbow on the bar counter. Finally Kroge made the sourest face he could muster. "What's that got to do with it?" he said sharply.

Another young actor, who up to that moment had been talking quietly to old Hansemann, said in a firm yet conciliatory voice, "Hey, that went over like a lead balloon. Drop it, Miklas. Things like that happen to all of us every once in a while. But you're all right even so." With that he slapped the culprit on the shoulder and laughed so heartily that everyone was won over. Even Kroge laughed, though his laugh seemed forced.

But Miklas remained grave. He turned his stubborn pale face aside, his lips pressed disdainfully together. "She is nevertheless a Jewess." He spoke so softly that hardly anyone heard him. Only Otto Ulrichs, who had saved the situation by his good-humored intervention the first time, caught the words and punished the speaker with a severe glance.

25

Kroge signaled to Ulrichs. "Ah, Ulrichs, please come over here a moment." Ulrichs sat down at the table with the directors and Frau von Herzfeld.

"I don't want to pry into your private affairs, I really don't." It was clear that the subject Kroge was about to raise was extremely painful to him. "But it happens more and more often that you take part in Communist meetings. You were at one again yesterday. This hurts you, Ulrichs, and it harms us too." Kroge lowered his voice. "You know, of course, how the bourgeois press operates, Ulrichs. We are already under suspicion as it is. If one of our members now comes out into the open politically, it could be fatal for us." Kroge gulped down the last of his brandy; he had become rather red in the face.

Ulrichs answered quietly, "I'm glad you raised this with me, Herr Director. Naturally, I myself have been giving the question a lot of thought. Perhaps it would be better if we parted company, Herr Director. Believe me, it isn't easy for me to propose this. But I can't give up my political activity. So I may have to sacrifice my place with you—and believe me, it really would be a sacrifice, for I'm very happy here."

His voice was pleasant, deep and warm. Kroge looked with fatherly affection at his strong face. Otto Ulrichs was a good-looking man. His black hair was swept back from a high forehead, and his dark-brown eyes were merry and intelligent—they inspired trust. Kroge liked him very much. For that reason he now became almost angry.

"But, Ulrichs," he shouted, "there is absolutely no question of anything like that. You know very well I would never let you go."

"We couldn't possibly manage without you," Schmitz declared. (It came as a surprise that every so often the fat man spoke with a strangely vibrant, ringing beautiful voice.) Herzfeld gave an earnestly approving nod.

"All I ask of you is just a small degree of caution," Kroge insisted.

Ulrichs answered gratefully. "You are all very good to me—really very good—and I shall be as careful as I can not to compromise you too much."

Herzfeld smiled at him confidingly. "It is certainly no news to you," she said softly, "that we go a long way toward sharing your political opinions." The man Herzfeld had married in Frankfurt and whose name she bore was a Communist. He had been much younger

26

than she was, and he had left her. He was now working in Moscow as a film director.

"A long way," declared Kroge, raising his forefinger to drive the message home. "Though not all the way—not in every respect. Not all our dreams have come true in Moscow. Can the dreams, the demands, the hopes of intellectuals ever be fulfilled under a dictatorship?"

Ulrichs answered with great seriousness which sharpened the expression in his narrow eyes, giving them an almost threatening look. "Not only those whom you would call intellectuals have their hopes and demands. Much more pressing are the demands of the proletariat. These can—in the present state of the world—only be fulfilled through a dictatorship."

The face of Herr Schmitz registered dismay. To give the conversation a lighter turn, Ulrichs added with a smile, "At any rate, the Arts Theater was almost represented at yesterday's rally by its most prominent member. Hendrik very much wanted to come—but unfortunately, at the last moment he was unable to make it."

"Höfgen is always unable to make it at the last moment when it is something that might have an adverse effect on his career," said Kroge scornfully.

Hedda von Herzfeld looked at him beseechingly, her face full of misery. But when Ulrichs said with conviction, "Hendrik belongs to us," she smiled with relief.

"Hendrik belongs to us," Ulrichs repeated, "and he is going to give that commitment concrete form. His revolutionary act will be the Revolutionary Theater which is due to open this month."

"It hasn't opened yet," said Kroge maliciously. "So far nothing has materialized except the official notepaper with 'Revolutionary Theater' printed in beautiful big letters. But let's say it actually comes to the point that its doors are opened to the public—do you really think Höfgen will commit himself so far as to put on a truly revolutionary play?"

Ulrichs answered with a certain sharpness. "As it happens, I believe he will. Besides, the play has already been chosen—and you could certainly call it revolutionary!"

Kroge's gesture reflected the weary and disdainful expression on his flushed face. "We shall see then," he said doubtfully. Hedda von Herzfeld saw that it would be advisable to change the subject.

"What was the point of that nasty little observation of Miklas's?" she asked. "Is it true, then, that he's anti-Semitic and involved with the National Socialists?" As she uttered the last two words she screwed up her face in distaste as if she had tripped over a dead rat.

Schmitz laughed scornfully as Kroge said, "That's just the kind of fellow we want!" Ulrichs glanced sideways to make sure Miklas wasn't within earshot before lowering his voice to observe, "Hans is basically a good fellow, I know he is, because I have often talked with him. With anyone so young you have to work hard and patiently. There is a chance he can still be won over to the right side. I don't believe he's already lost to us. His rebelliousness, his utter dissatisfaction have taken the wrong direction—you know what I mean?" Frau Hedda nodded. Ulrichs whispered earnestly, "In that kind of young head everything is turned upside down, everything is unclear. There are millions of youths like Miklas running around in this country. What comes first with them is hatred, which is good because it is directed at the prevailing state of affairs. But then a person like that has the bad luck to fall into the hands of men who pervert his positive hatred. They tell him that the Jews are to blame for all that's wrong in the world, and so is the Treaty of Versailles. And he believes all this rubbish and forgets who the guilty men really are, both in Germany and throughout the world. This is the famous diversionary tactic in operation. With these young scatterbrains who know nothing and can't think straight, it works. So there he sits, a picture of misery, and lets himself be called a National Socialist."

All four looked over at Hans Miklas, who had sat down in the furthest corner of the room next to Frau Efeu, the fat old stage prompter. At the same table were Willi Böck, the little property master, and Herr Knurr, the stage-door man. (It was said of Herr Knurr that he wore a swastika hidden under the lapel of his overcoat and that his home was filled with pictures of the National Socialist "Führer," which he did not yet dare to hang in his porter's lodge. Herr Knurr had violent arguments with the Communist stagehands, who did not patronize H.K. but instead had their own table in a bar across the street where they were visited from time to time by Ulrichs. Höfgen hardly ever ventured near the workers' table; he was afraid the men would make fun of his monocle. On the other hand, he always complained that H.K. was altogether spoiled for him by the presence of the National Socialist Herr Knurr. "That miserable petit bourgeois," Höfgen called him. "There he is waiting for his Führer and redeemer like a virgin for the fellow who'll get her pregnant. I go hot and cold whenever I have to pass the porter and think about the swastika hidden under his lapel.")

"Of course, you must remember that Miklas had a ghastly childhood," said Otto Ulrichs. "He told me about it once. He grew up in some kind of dreadful dark hole in the wilds of Bavaria. His father was killed in the war. His mother seems to have been nervous and slightly mad—she made a terrible scene when Hans wanted to go on the stage. You can see it all so clearly. He is ambitious, hard-working and gifted. He has learned an enormous amount—more than the best of us. To begin with, he wanted to be a musician; he learned counterpoint and can play the piano. He's an acrobat, a good tap-dancer, and plays an accordion—in fact, he can do just about everything. He used to work all day without stopping, which has probably undermined his health—his cough sounds awful. Naturally, he feels he's being slighted and gets bad parts. He blames his lack of success on us—he believes we're in league against him because of his political leanings."

Ulrichs cast another troubled glance across the room at young Miklas. "Ninety-five marks a month," he exclaimed abruptly and looked reproachfully at Director Schmitz, who began to fidget uncomfortably in his chair. "With that kind of money it's hard to stay a decent human being." Now it was Herzfeld's turn to give Miklas a searching glance.

Hans Miklas always made a point of sitting with Herr Knurr and his companions when he felt that he was being discriminated against in a particularly vile way by the theater management, which his political friends had taught him to consider as "Jew-dominated" and "Marxist-oriented." If you believed Miklas, Höfgen was jealous and conceited, a megalomaniac who wanted to play all the roles but who particularly wanted to do Miklas out of any parts that might come his way.

"It's a dirty trick not to let me play Moritz Stiefel," he said bitterly. "When he's directing *Spring's Awakening* himself, why does he also have to play the lead? And for the rest of us there's absolutely nothing. I call that rotten. Besides, he's much too fat and old to play Moritz. He's going to look ridiculous in shorts." Miklas looked angrily down at his own legs, which were lean and muscular.

Willi Böck, whose task it was to take care of the stage scenery, sniggered over his beer glass. It wasn't clear whether the object of his amusement was Hendrik Höfgen as a gymnast or the helpless anger of young Hans Miklas. Next to him the prompter Efeu reacted indignantly. She assured Miklas that it was indeed rotten. The motherly interest the fat old woman took in the young man assured him of her support. Besides, she sympathized with his political views. She darned his socks, invited him to dinner and gave him presents of sausages, bacon and pickles—"so that you'll get fatter, my boy," she would say, looking at him tenderly. Nevertheless, she was attracted by the leanness of his slender, compact, well-exercised body. When the thick dark blond hair at the back of his head stood out too rebelliously, she'd say, "You look like a street urchin," and would take a comb from her handbag.

Hans Miklas really did look like a street urchin, one for whom life wasn't going particularly well and who defiantly hid his wounds. His days were exhausting: he trained continually, making endless demands on his body, which was probably the source of his irritability and the darkly hostile expression on his young face. His complexion was sickly: his cheeks were so sunken that there were dark hollows under the strong cheekbones; the rings around the bright eyes were almost black. But a different impression was given by the bland boyish forehead, which seemed lit by a pale and delicate inner glow. The mouth shone, too, but in an unhealthy way: it was much too red, and the defiantly protruding lips seemed to have drained the face of all its blood. Below the strong seductive lips, from which Frau Efeu could often not take her eyes, the too short and weakly receding chin was a disappointment.

"This morning at the rehearsal you looked so terrible," said Frau Efeu. "And that cough, it sounded so grim, really sad."

Miklas could not bear it when people felt sorry for him. Only the gifts into which such sympathy was transmuted would he accept, though with little sign of gratitude. He took no notice of Frau Efeu's complaints.

There was something he wanted to know from Willi Böck: "Is it true that Höfgen spent the whole evening hiding behind a screen in his dressing room?"

Böck could not confirm this. But the thought of Höfgen's absurd behavior almost restored Miklas's good temper. "He really is a complete clown!" He laughed triumphantly. "And all because of a Jewess whose head is screwed on at the wrong angle." He made himself hunchbacked to show how Dora Martin looked. Efeu found it very funny. "And that kind of trash wants to be a star!" His sneering exclamation could have applied equally to Dora Martin or to Höfgen. Both belonged, in his view, to the same privileged, un-German, reprehensible clique. "That Martin woman," he went on, his malicious, sickly young face sunk in his thin, not too clean hands, "they say she is always mouthing these salon-Communist phrases—her and her thousand marks every night. But there's going to be a clean sweep of that crowd—even Höfgen will have to face up to that before long."

He had been careful in the past to avoid giving open expression to such dangerous notions, especially when Kroge was nearby. Today, however, he let himself go—though not to a point where his voice was loud enough to be overhead. It was a violent whisper. Frau Efeu and Herr Knurr nodded their agreement; Böck merely gave him a watery glance.

"The day will come," Miklas said quietly but with great vehemence. His bright eyes had a feverish glitter. Then he gave way to a fit of hoarse coughing. Frau Efeu slapped him on the back and shoulders. "It sounds dreadful," she said anxiously, "as if it comes from very deep down in the chest."

The crowded restaurant was full of smoke. "Just look at the air in here—you could cut it with a knife," complained Fräulein Motz. "The healthiest man alive couldn't last for long in an atmosphere like this. And think of my voice, children. Tomorrow morning you're going to see me sitting in line once again for the throat doctor."

No one had any wish to dwell on the image of Motz in the doctor's waiting room. Rahel Mohrenwitz went so far as to murmur, "For heaven's sake—our coloratura soprano!" This brought her a withering stare from Motz, who in any case had a grudge against Rahel. Petersen knew why. Only the day before, he had been found in the dressing room of the young *femme fatale*, which caused Motz to weep bitter tears. However, today she seemed determined not to allow her composure to be undermined by a stupid goose, who, to judge by her monocle and her ridiculous hairstyle, was living in some obscure fantasy world. So Motz folded her hands contentedly across her stomach and reacted good-humoredly. "But it's nice here," she said. "Isn't it, Father Hansemann?" She winked at the landlord, to whom she owed twenty-seven marks, which explained why he did not wink back. The next moment she was in a rage because Petersen had ordered steak with a fried egg on top. "As if a couple of sausages wouldn't be enough!" Tears of anger shone in her eyes. There were constant arguments between Motz and Petersen because he was, in the opinion of his companion, far too given to extravagance—always ordering expensive things and overtipping outrageously.

"Of course it has to be a steak and a fried egg," declared Motz scathingly. Petersen murmured something about a man needing to be decently fed. But Motz—completely out of control now—suddenly turned on Rahel and asked with wrathful sarcasm whether it was true that Petersen had given her a bottle of champagne. "Veuve Cliquot, top quality!" shrieked Motz, her voice shaking with indignation and pronouncing the brand name of the champagne with the refinement she had made her own in her dowager roles. Rahel was deeply insulted. "Would you kindly tell me if that's meant to be funny?" she called out shrilly. The monocle fell from her eye. Her chubby face, flushed with anger, suddenly looked anything but demoniacal.

Kroge turned an astounded glance in their direction. Frau von Herzfeld smiled ironically. Handsome Bonetti patted Motz on the shoulder and did the same to Rahel. The two women, spoiling for battle, had moved near each other. "Stop fighting, girls," he said, with more than the usual world-weary and disenchanted lines showing around his mouth. "It gets you nowhere. Let's play cards instead."

Just then there was a sound of muffled cries that rapidly grew louder. All eyes turned to the door, which had opened suddenly to reveal Dora Martin standing in the threshold. Behind her, grouped like the retinue of a stage queen, was her inseparable traveling cast.

Dora Martin smiled and waved to all the members of the Hamburg Arts Theater. And she addressed them in her husky voice with its celebrated emphatic mannerism, which had been copied by thousands of actresses throughout the country.

"Darlings, we've been asked to an *utterly* dreary banquet—*ghastly* bore, but we just *must* go." She seemed bent on parodying her own way of talking, so capriciously did she draw out the length of the syllables. But the sound rang pleasantly in the ears of everyone in the room, even of those who couldn't bear Dora Martin—young Miklas, for instance. There was no denying that her entrance had made a great impact. Her wide-open, childlike yet enigmatic eyes beneath the high, intelligent forehead disturbed and enchanted everyone. Even old

Father Hansemann's face broke into an idiotic, infatuated grin. Frau von Herzfeld, who in earlier days had been a friend of Martin's, called to her, "What a pity, Dora, baby. Can't you sit with us just a little while?" The general opinion of Hedda rose because she was on intimate terms with Martin.

But the famous actress declined with a sideways movement of her smiling face, which, so high did she shrug her shoulders, was all but swallowed up in the raised collar of her brown fur coat.

"Such a shame," she cooed, and as she shook her head her loose red mane of hair swung about. "But we are already far too late."

Suddenly someone behind her pushed his way through the retinue. Hendrik Höfgen abruptly emerged in the doorway. He had on the dinner jacket he wore in drawing-room comedies. Seen up close, it proved to be stained and threadbare. Over his shoulders he had thrown a white silk scarf. He was out of breath, and his cheeks and forehead were flushed. The nervous laugh that shook his body as he hastily bowed low over the actress's hand made a most uncomfortable impression; yet it was not without a certain wild sincerity.

"Forgive me," he stammered. His face, in which the monocle surprisingly remained fixed, was still bowed over her hand and he was still smiling with the same rigid ardor. "It's outrageous—I'm far too late. What must you think of me—an incredible situation . . ." He shook with laughter again and his face grew even redder. "But I didn't want to let you go"—here he straightened up at last—"until I had an opportunity to tell you how much I have enjoyed this evening—how wonderful it's been." Abruptly, whatever it was that had made him almost fall apart with laughter seemed to have vanished altogether, and he turned a completely solemn face on the actress.

It was now Dora Martin's turn to laugh a little, which she did with seductive warmth and charm. "Fake," she cried, drawling the word out as though she never intended to let it go. "You weren't in the audience at all. What you did was *hide*." With that she flicked him lightly with her yellow pigskin glove. "But that's of no importance," she added with a dazzling smile. "I hear you are *so* talented."

This compliment took Höfgen so completely by surprise that the bright color drained from his face. "Me? Gifted? That's an altogether unfounded rumor . . ." He too stretched out his vowels, but his style of speech owed nothing to Dora Martin: while she cooed, he intoned affectedly. He assumed the smile he turned on at rehearsals for actresses

33

when they had a daring scene to play: it showed his teeth and made him look common. He called it his "dirty" smile ("Dirty, you understand, darling? Dirty!" he would tell Rahel Mohrenwitz or Angelika Siebert at rehearsals, baring his teeth as he did so).

Dora Martin showed her teeth, too; and while a sort of baby talk came out of her mouth, and her head ducked coquettishly between her shoulders, her intelligent, sad eyes scrutinized Höfgen's face. "You will give proof of your talent again," she said softly; and for a second, not only her eyes were serious, but her whole face. Indeed the gravity of her expression was almost threatening as she nodded at him. Höfgen, who only a quarter of an hour earlier had been hiding behind a screen, held her glance. Then Dora Martin laughed again and cooed, "We are *far* too late." She waved and vanished with her retinue in her wake.

The meeting with Dora Martin had wonderfully raised Höfgen's spirits; he seemed now to be in an almost holiday mood. He looked around him graciously. And everyone looked back at him almost as captivated as they had been by the Berlin star. Before Höfgen greeted Kroge and Frau von Herzfeld he walked up to Willi Böck. "Listen Böck, old fellow," he said, standing rakishly by the table with his hands sunk deep in his trouser pockets, shoulders slouched and the dirty smile on his face, "You've got to lend me at least seven marks. I want to have a decent dinner and I have a nasty feeling that today old Father Hansemann wants cash." His gleaming eyes darted a distrustful sideways glance at Hansemann, who sat unmoved behind his counter.

Böck rose to his feet. The dismay aroused by the mixture of flattery and nastiness in Höfgen's demand made his eyes even more watery and his cheeks dark red. In speechless agitation he rummaged in his pockets. Hans Miklas surveyed the scene with malignant intensity.

Angelika hurried over to them. "But, Hendrik," she said timidly, "if you need money I can lend you fifty marks till the first of the month."

Höfgen's eyes turned cold. He snapped haughtily over his shoulder, "Don't interfere, child. This is men's business. Böck's a willing giver." Böck nodded nervously, and Siebert withdrew, tears brimming in her eyes. Without a word of thanks, his mind already on other things, Höfgen slipped Böck's silver coins into his pocket. Miklas, Knurr and Frau Efeu glowered at him. Böck looked on in bewildered

34

silence and Angelika followed him with tearful eyes as he walked with a springy step across the canteen, the white silk scarf still draping his shoulders.

"Little Father Schmitz would happily see me starve," Höfgen declared as he turned a triumphantly smiling face toward the directors' table. In answer the directors mustered a few gruff words of greeting. Even Kroge put on a somewhat noisy and not too convincing display of enthusiasm. "Now, you old sinner, how are things going? Have you managed to get through the evening all right?" Deep lines appeared beside his catlike mouth, and his eyes glinted maliciously behind his spectacles. All at once, the look on his face made clear that apart from writing lyrical odes and political and cultural essays, Kroge had been a man of the theater for more than thirty years.

Höfgen and Otto Ulrichs shook hands warmly without speaking. Schmitz made some irrelevant light-hearted remark in his quiet, pleasant voice. Frau von Herzfeld smiled with apparently pointless irony, and her gold-brown eyes misted with tenderness as she fixed them on Hendrik. He allowed himself to be guided by her in the choice of his supper, which gave her an opportunity to draw close to him, bring him near her swelling bosom. His dirty smile did not seem to frighten her off. She was used to it and she liked it.

When Father Hansemann had taken the order, Höfgen began to talk about his production of *Spring's Awakening*. "It's going to be quite good, I think," he said while gravely casting a searching eye around the canteen like a battle commander reviewing his troops. "As Wendla, Siebert can't do too much damage. Bonetti isn't an ideal Melchior Gabor but he'll get by. As for our demonic Mohrenwitz, she'll make a first-class Ilse."

It was not often that he spoke as he did now—without tricks, seriously intent on his subject. Kroge, taken by surprise, listened attentively. It was Herzfeld who broke the spell by remarking in a delicately sarcastic voice, her powdered face close to Höfgen's, "And now, how about the role of Moritz Stiefel? We have just learned from an extremely authoritative source—from Dora herself—that the young actor to whom we have entrusted this part is not wholly without talent . . ."

Kroge wrinkled his forehead, but Höfgen appeared not to have heard Hedda's teasing. Instead, he looked at her broad white face and inquired, "And how will you manage as Frau Gabor, my love?"

This was undisguised, raw derision. It was no secret to anyone that Hedda was a notably ungifted actress; and everyone knew, too, that this caused her pain. It was a constant joke among the cast that the clever lady could not be safely entrusted even with modest mother roles. Overwhelmed by Höfgen's rudeness, she tried to shrug it off with a show of indifference. But Kroge saw the dark red flush spread over her not so youthful face and his heart missed a beat with a pity close to love. Many years ago Kroge had had an affair with Frau von Herzfeld.

To change the subject or perhaps to bring the conversation around to the only subject that really interested him, Ulrichs began to talk about the Revolutionary Theater. It was planned as a series of Sunday morning performances that would be directed by Hendrik Höfgen and sponsored by a Communist organization. Ulrichs, for whom the stage was above all a political instrument, had clung with dogged persistence to the project. The work chosen for the opening performance was marvelously appropriate. "People in the party are very seriously interested in our plans." He cast a conspiratorial glance at Höfgen over the heads of the others, plainly proud that they could hear what he said and confident that he was making a deep impression.

"But the party will pay me no compensation if the good people of Hamburg boycott my theater," grumbled Kroge, who had evidently agreed to the idea of a Revolutionary Theater with some skepticism. "In 1918 one could indulge in such experiments. But today . . ." Höfgen and Ulrichs exchanged another glance of aloof complicity in which there was a great deal of contempt for their directors' petit bourgeois notions. The look lasted long enough for Frau von Herzfeld to notice it and feel hurt. Finally Höfgen turned toward Kroge and Schmitz and said in a fatherly, condescending tone, "The Revolutionary Theater will do us no harm—absolutely none—do believe that, Schmitz, old man. Whatever is really good never compromises anyone. The Revolutionary Theater will be good and it will become absolutely outstanding. A production backed by a real faith, a genuine enthusiasm, will convince everyone—even its enemies will fall silent before this manifestation of our passionate conviction."

His eyes glittered, he squinted slightly and seemed to gaze entranced into a far distance where great decisions were made. His chin jutted up arrogantly and his sallow, delicate features wore an expression of victory. That is real emotion, thought Hedda von Herzfeld. He can't fake that, however gifted he is. It was with triumph that she now looked at Kroge, who could not conceal the fact that he was moved in spite of himself. Ulrichs wore an expression of religious solemnity.

While they all sat spellbound by his enthusiasm, Höfgen underwent one of his abrupt changes of mood. He burst out laughing and pointed to a picture hanging on the wall above the table: it was a heroic father figure with arms defiantly crossed, an unswervingly honest gaze peering from under dark brows and a beard carefully spread over a splendid hunting jacket. Hendrik could not get over how droll the old fellow looked. As he laughed, and Hedda slapped him on the back to prevent him from choking on his salad, he gasped that he had once looked very much like that himself—yes, almost exactly the same—when he was playing old men's roles in the Northwest German Touring Company.

"When I was still a boy," he declared joyfully, "I had this fantastically aged appearance. And on the stage I was always bent double out of sheer embarrassment. In Schiller's *The Brigands* I played old father Moor. I was a wonderfully good old Moor. As it happened, both my sons in the play were twenty years older than I was."

At the mention of the Northwest German Touring Company, his colleagues moved over from the other tables, knowing that now there would be stories told—not stale old anecdotes but new ones, for Hendrik rarely repeated himself. Motz rubbed her hands together expectantly, flashed the gold in her teeth and declared with fierce joviality, "Now it's going to be fun." The next moment she was casting an angry look at Petersen, who had just ordered himself a double brandy. Rahel Mohrenwitz, Angelika Siebert and handsome Bonetti all hung on Hendrik's words. Even Miklas felt compelled to listen, and he chuckled reluctantly at the polished jokes of the man he hated. Efeu, seeing that her wicked darling was amused, became merry herself. Gasping, she drew her stool close to Hendrik's chair. "I hope you good people don't mind my joining you," she murmured, putting her knitting aside and cupping her right hand behind her ear.

It was a delightful evening. Höfgen was in dazzling form. As though he was performing before a large audience instead of a few undistinguished colleagues, he generously and joyfully poured forth wit, charm and a rich store of recollections. There was apparently no end to what went on in this touring company where Hendrik had to play old men. Motz became breathless with laughter. "Children, I can't take any more," she crowed. And as Bonetti, with mock gallantry, fanned her with a table napkin, she pretended not to notice that Petersen had treated himself to yet another brandy. But when Höfgen imitated the shrill voice, fluttering gestures and weirdly crossed eyes of the young leading lady of the touring company, even Father Hansemann's stony countenance broke up, and Herr Knurr had to hide his grin behind a handkerchief.

When the fun had reached its peak and the situation would yield no more, Höfgen broke off. Motz suddenly became serious as she realized how drunk Petersen had become. Kroge gave a sign that it was time to go home. It was two o'clock in the morning. As a parting gesture, Mohrenwitz, who always had strange impulses, presented Hendrik with her long cigarette holder, a decorative but otherwise valueless object—"Because you have been so immensely entertaining this evening." Her monocle glinted at him. Angelika Siebert's nose became white with jealousy and her eyes filled with tears.

Frau von Herzfeld had invited Hendrik to drink another cup of coffee with her. In the empty canteen Father Hansemann was already turning out the lights. The half-darkness was flattering to Hedda. Her large white face with the soft, intelligent, soulful eyes now looked younger, or at least ageless. This was no longer the sorrowful face of an aging woman. The cheeks were not downy but smooth. The smile that hovered on the Orientally indolent half-open lips was no longer ironic but almost bewitching as she gazed tenderly at Hendrik Höfgen. It did not occur to her that she herself looked more charming than usual. She had eyes only for Hendrik's face with its strained temples and noble chin, pale and strongly outlined against the shadows.

Hendrik was resting his elbows on the table and pressing together the fingertips of his outstretched hands. It was the gesture of a man showing off his particularly beautiful, narrow hands. But there was nothing Gothic about Höfgen's hands; in fact, they were unattractively blunt. The backs were very broad and covered with red hairs. The fairly long but thick fingers ended in narrow (and not too clean) nails, which made the hands look almost disgusting.

These shortcomings were, however, veiled by the half-light which emphasized the enigmatic appeal of his dreamy hazel eyes.

"What are you thinking about, Hendrik?" asked Hedda in an intense hushed voice, breaking a long silence.

Höfgen answered softly. "I was thinking that Dora Martin was wrong . . ." Hedda let him talk on in the darkness, his fingers placed together as if in prayer. She simply watched him in silence.

"I shall never prove myself," he muttered in the dusk. "There is nothing there to prove. I shall never be first-class. I'm provincial . . ." He fell silent and pressed his lips together as though shrinking from the self-knowledge and confession that this strange hour had brought him.

"And do you never think beyond that point?" asked Hedda in a tone of gentle reproach. "Do you always stop there?" He remained silent, and she thought, Yes, of course, this is the only thing that occupies his mind; all that about the political theater just now and his enthusiasm for the revolution—that, too, was only play-acting. This discovery filled her with a deep sense of disappointment; but also in some strange way she felt relieved.

His eyes clouded over mysteriously; he gave no answer.

"Don't you see how you are torturing little Angelika?" Hedda asked. "Don't you see that you make others suffer? Somewhere you should have to pay for all that." She gave him a plaintive searching look. "Somewhere you should have to make amends—and love."

She quickly regretted that she had said this. It was clearly too much; she had let herself go. She turned her face away. To her surprise, he did not sneer or make a scornful remark. Instead, his gleaming eyes remained fixed on a point in the darkness, as though searching for an answer to urgent questions, something that would still his doubts, some image of a future destined to make him great.

CHAPTER

2

The Dancing Lesson

Hendrik had scheduled the next morning's rehearsal for *Spring's Awakening* at nine-thirty. The members of the company assembled punctually, some of them on the drafty stage and others in the dimly lighted auditorium. After they had waited about a quarter of an hour, Frau von Herzfeld decided to fetch Höfgen from his office, where since nine o'clock he had been conferring with Schmitz and Kroge.

As soon as Höfgen made his appearance it was clear that he was in one of his most ungracious moods; there was no trace of the affable, brilliant talker of the previous evening. With his shoulders nervously hunched, and his hands sunk in his trouser pockets, he walked quickly through the orchestra asking querulously for a copy of the script. "I left mine at home." He sounded bitter and hurt, as though everyone present was to blame for the fact that he had been absent-minded on setting out that morning.

"Now can I ask for your cooperation?" He managed to speak in a tone that was both subdued and bitingly sarcastic. "Has nobody got a book for me?"

Young Angelika handed him hers. "I don't need my text any longer," she said, blushing. "I know it by heart."

Instead of thanking her, Hendrik snapped back, "I should hope so," and turned away.

Above the red silk scarf he wore, which almost hid his shirt, his face looked more than usually sallow. One eye gazed out scornfully and malevolently from under a half-closed lid; the monocle glittered in the other. When he suddenly called out in a loud, piercing, parade-ground voice, "We'll start now, everyone!" a quiver ran through the company.

While the rehearsal was in progress he prowled around the auditorium. He had Miklas, whose own part gave him very little to do, stand in as Moritz Stiefel, the role he had reserved for himself. This could be interpreted as a particularly spiteful gesture, since poor Miklas would have given anything to play Moritz. Moreover, with provocative arrogance, Höfgen seemed to be serving notice on his colleagues that he himself had absolutely no need to rehearse—as director, he was a cut above the common herd. It was as if his work on his own role could be done privately almost as an afterthought. Not until dress rehearsal would he let anyone discover how Moritz Stiefel, the melancholy student, the despairing lover and suicide, should be interpreted and played.

On the other hand, he was already brimming with suggestions about what could be done with the girl (Wendla), the boy (Melchior), and the motherly Frau Gabor. Hendrik sprang with surprising agility onto the stage and transformed himself instantly into the delicate maiden walking in the garden in the early morning, wanting to embrace the whole world as she thought of her lover. He became the proud youth with his hunger for life, and the wise, careworn mother. His voice could be tender, high-spirited or thoughtful. He succeeded in looking almost childishly young one moment and extremely aged the next. He was a superb actor.

After he had spectacularly demonstrated to Bonetti, whose eyebrows were raised half in anger and half in grudging respect, and to the submissive Angelika, who was fighting back tears, what anyone who had what it takes could begin to do with their roles, he made a weary and contemptuous grimace, fixed his monocle into his eye and climbed down into the orchestra. From there he continued to explain, shape and criticize. No one was spared his sneering disparagement. Even Frau von Herzfeld was given a dressing down, which she took with a twisted ironic smile. Angelika disappeared several times into the wings to wipe her eyes. Angry veins stood out on Bonetti's forehead. But the most passionate indignation was shown by Hans Miklas, whose face seemed to have decomposed with anger. The hollows in his cheeks looked like black holes.

When it was clear that everyone else was suffering, Hendrik's temper visibly improved. In the canteen during lunch hour he kept up a lively conversation with Frau von Herzfeld. At two-thirty he called the cast back to work.

It was toward three-thirty that Bonetti twisted his mouth in disgust, sunk his hands in his trouser pockets like a spoiled child and said sulkily, "Haven't we about come to the end of this drudgery?" Whereupon Höfgen turned pale, cold eyes on him in a withering glance. "When we stop is for me alone to decide," he said, raising his handsome chin at a particularly imposing angle. To some he resembled a noble and temperamental tyrant; to others a waspish old governess; all were intimidated by him. Little Angelika felt delicious shivers run down her spine.

There were a few moments of pained silence. Then Hendrik clapped his hands and threw back his head with vivacity. "Carry on, everyone," he called out in a ringing metallic tone. "Where did we break off?"

They went through the next scene submissively, but they had hardly reached the end when Hendrik looked at his watch. It was a quarter to four. His start of dismay was so strong that he felt a twinge in his stomach: at four he had an appointment at home with Juliette. His smile was a little forced as with a few hurried cordial words he told the cast that that would have to be all for the day. He saw young Miklas moving toward him with a surly expression and he gave him a hasty dismissive wave. He stumbled through the dark orchestra to the exit and ran up the steep path between the theater door and the canteen. Arriving breathless in H.K., he grabbed his brown leather coat and soft gray hat from the stand and left.

As he pulled on his coat in the street he debated the fastest way of getting home. If I go by foot, he thought, I shall arrive a few minutes too late however much I hurry. Juliette will have an unpleasant welcome waiting for me. With a taxi I shall get there all right. If I take a streetcar I shall be more or less on time. But I've only got a five-mark note in my wallet and that's the least I can offer Juliette. So there is absolutely no question of a taxi. But a streetcar's out, too, for that would leave only four marks eighty-five pfennigs, which is too little for Juliette. Besides, it would be in small change, which she had ruled out once and for all.

Turning this over in his mind, he had already gone a good part of the way. It struck him that there was no alternative but to walk: his mistress would really have lost her temper over the broken five-mark note, whereas her rage over his being a few minutes late was almost part of a ritual.

The winter day was clear and very cold. Hendrik was freezing in his light leather coat, which he had neglected to button up, and his hands and feet already felt frostbitten. He owned no gloves, and the sandals he always wore were not suitable for such cold weather. To warm himself up and make better time he walked in long strides that occasionally degenerated into a curious sort of skip and jump. Several passers-by looked back at the odd young man with either a smile or a disapproving glare. In his light eccentric footwear he moved with a nimbleness that was both graceful and clownish. Not only did he skip and jump, he sang to himself as well—interspersing Mozart with musical comedy—and accompanied himself with gestures not often seen on the street. He was also playing catch with a bunch of violets he had discovered fastened in the buttonhole of his coat. It must have been the gift of an admirer in the company—very probably the affectionate tribute of Angelika.

Hendrik thought of this near-sighted and sweet-natured girl as he hopped and sang, unaware of the reactions of those who encountered him. He did not see the one elegant woman shopper nudging another to whisper, "That *must* be someone from the theater," and the other snickering, "That's right—that's the man who plays in the Arts Theater productions. He's called Höfgen. Look, my dear, at the mad gestures he makes and how he's chattering the whole time to himself." They both laughed, and on the other side of the street a group of teenagers laughed with them. But Hendrik—though vanity and the demands of his profession had trained him to observe people's reactions to his every gesture—noticed neither the women nor the schoolchildren. His buoyant progress through the cold and the anticipation of his meeting with Juliette had induced a state of mild intoxication. How seldom did such euphoria now come his way! Earlier—ah yes, in the old days—he was nearly always filled with this feeling of being propelled forward on winged feet—oblivious of his own existence. In his early twenties, when he'd played old men and seasoned heroes with the touring company, he had been truly happy. His high spirits, his pleasure in things for their own sake, were stronger then than his ambition. That was a long time ago—and yet perhaps not so dreadfully far off as it generally seemed to him nowadays. Had he really changed so much? Was he no longer light-hearted and playful? He was still able to cast aside his ambitions—were the notions of ambition and making a great career for himself to rise up before him now, he would have laughed at them. All he felt now was that the air was fresh and the sun shining, and that he himself was still young. Moreover, he was running, his scarf was fluttering and very soon he would be with his mistress.

His elation made him feel benevolent toward Angelika, whom he so often humiliated and wounded. A dear child, a very dear child, he thought almost tenderly—I shall give her some present this evening so that she will be happy for once. Would it be possible to live with Angelika? It would certainly be a much more comfortable existence than with my Juliette, he thought. Despite his generous mood, at this point he had to break into a malicious giggle because he had compared Angelika with Juliette—poor little Siebert with the great Juliette, who in a terrible way was precisely what he needed. For such wickedness he silently implored Juliette's forgiveness as he reached the door of his house.

The old-fashioned villa in which he occupied a basement room was located on one of those quiet streets that thirty years earlier had been among the most respectable in the city. Inflation had impoverished the majority of the inhabitants of the elegant quarter. Their villas, though still adorned with many pinnacles and gables, had a definite air of having come down in the world: they had run to seed like the large gardens that surrounded them. And Frau Monkeberg, the consul's widow to whom Hendrik paid forty marks a month for a large studio room, had found herself in straitened circumstances. Through it all, she had remained an irreproachable proud old lady, who wore with great dignity her strange dresses with puffed-out sleeves and lace shawls. There was never a strand displaced in her smoothly parted hair, and the lines around her small mouth showed irony without bitterness.

Widow Monkeberg was sufficiently superior to the eccentricities and rough ways of her tenants to see their funnier side, rather than to be offended. To her circle of friends—old ladies of a similar refinement and indigence who looked very like her—she gave dryly humorous reports on her lodger's peculiarities. "Sometimes he hops down the stairs on one leg," she would say, smiling. "And when he goes out walking he often sits down suddenly on the pavement. Imagine that now—on the dirty pavement! He is afraid that if he doesn't, he will trip and fall." All the ladies would shake their gray heads, half shocked and half amused, their shawls rustling. And the consul's widow would continue in a forgiving tone of voice, "But what do you expect, my dears, an artist! Perhaps a considerable artist!" And across the faded lace of the teacloth the stiff-backed old patrician lady would make a sweeping gesture with lean white fingers, on which for ten years now she had worn no rings.

Hendrik felt unsure of himself in the presence of Frau Monkeberg. Her distinguished ancestry and past intimidated him. So it was not altogether a pleasure for him to encounter the old woman now in the hall, after he had noisily slammed the door. In her presence he pulled himself together a little, tugging the red scarf into place and fixing his monocle in his eye. "Good evening, dear lady, how are you?" This flourish of civility was delivered in his singing voice with no rising inflection at the end, a technique that underlined the purely formal and gallant character of the greeting. He accompanied this polite speech with a slight and carelessly elegant bow that had an almost courtly air.

Widow Monkeberg did not smile; but the small lines of irony were a little more pronounced around her eyes and narrow lips. "Hurry, dear Herr Höfgen! Your . . . teacher has been waiting for you now for a quarter of an hour."

Höfgen felt the flush mounting in his cheeks at the malicious little pause before the word "teacher." I know I have gone bright red, he thought; but she can hardly see what color I am in this half-darkness. He withdrew with the imperturbable grace of a Spanish grandee.

"Thank you, dear lady," he said as he opened the door of his room.

The dimness of the room was suffused with a rose-colored glow. A single lamp shone on the low round table by the sofa bed. Into this penumbra Hendrik Höfgen called out in a tiny, submissive voice, "Princess Tebab, where are you?"

From a dark corner came a deep, rumbling answer, "Here, you pig, where else would I be?"

"Oh—thank you," said Hendrik, still in a very soft voice, as he remained standing with bowed head by the door. "Yes . . . now I can see you . . . I am glad that I can see you . . ."

"What time is it?" shouted the woman in the corner.

Trembling, Hendrik replied, "About four—I think."

"About four! About four!" scoffed the malevolent voice from the shadowy depths of the room. "Isn't that funny! Isn't that just fine!" The woman spoke with a strong northern German accent. Her voice was rasping, like that of a sailor much given to drinking, smoking and swearing.

"It's fifteen minutes past four," she declared in a voice that had abruptly become ominously soft. And in the same dreadful hushed tone she continued, "Won't you come a little nearer to me, Heinz—just a tiny little bit! But first put the light on."

The name Heinz made him wince as if he had been struck. He allowed no one else, not even his mother, to call him by that name; only Juliette could use it. Apart from her no one in the city knew that his real first name was Heinz. In what hour of bliss and weakness had he let her into his secret? Heinz—that was the name by which he had been known to everyone up to his eighteenth year. Only when it became clear to him that he wanted to be an actor and become famous did he substitute the more aristocratic-sounding "Hendrik." How hard it had been to impose the new name on his family, to get people accustomed to it and to take it seriously. How many letters beginning with "Dear Heinz" had been left unanswered before his mother and his sister had at last gotten used to the new form of address. Links were severed with childhood friends who stubbornly clung to "Heinz." Besides, there would have been no point in continuing to see friends who liked to guffaw over painful memories from a colorless past. Heinz was dead; Hendrik was on the road to greatness.

The young actor Höfgen waged a bitter struggle with agents, theater directors and newspaper critics to ensure that his invented first name was correctly spelled. He trembled with anger and mortification when he found himself named on a program or in a review as "Henrik." The little *d* in the middle of his adopted name was in his eyes a letter of very special magical significance: once he could reach the point where the whole world without exception knew him as "Hendrik," he would have achieved his goal and at last become a complete man. The name was therefore a mission and an obligation to his ambitious dreams. And yet he endured it patiently when Juliette threatened him from her dark corner with the detested "Heinz."

He obeyed her two commands: he reached for the light switch, filling his eyes with a sudden harsh brightness; and with his head still bowed, he took a few steps in Juliette's direction. When he was a yard from her he stopped. But even this did not win the lady's approval. She murmured with a husky and disturbing intimacy, "Come closer, my friend."

When he remained stock-still, she cooed to him as people do when they are coaxing a dog to their feet—a summons as gentle as the punishment to come would be violent. "Just a little closer, honey. Right up close. Don't be scared now." He remained motionless as before, his face still cast down, his arms and shoulders hanging limply forward, the pulse throbbing tensely in his temples. His distended nostrils breathed in a penetratingly sweet cheap perfume which merged in a tantalizing and exciting way with another, gamier odor—the smell of perspiration.

The girl, now bored and irritated by his suppliant attitude, let out a yell that sounded like a roar from the jungle. "Don't stand there as if you'd wet your pants! Hold your head up, man!" With a majestic ring in her voice she added, "Look me in the face."

Slowly he raised his head. In his sallow face his gray-blue eyes widened, either from joy or fear, and the line of tautness in his temples grew more marked. He stared speechlessly at Princess Tebab, his black Venus.

She was black only on her mother's side, but that inheritance had proved stronger than the white from her father. She looked not like a half-caste, but like a pure-blooded black. Her somewhat cracked skin was dark brown; in some areas, such as her low, domed forehead and the backs of her small, sinewy hands, it was almost black. Apart from the natural paleness of her palms, only her starkly angular cheekbones were of a contrasting hue: she had heightened them with bright red rouge. Her eyes were also carefully made up, with shaved, penciled eyebrows and false eyelashes; the upper lids were painted a bold dark purple. The thick pouting lips had been left their natural color. Against the blazing-white even teeth, which she bared in laughter and in rage, the lips appeared as rough as the skin of her hands and neck; they were dark violet, in marked contrast to the red of her gums and tongue.

In a face so dominated by mobile, fiercely intelligent eyes and flashing teeth, one hardly noticed the nose. Only at second glance did one see how flat it was. In fact, it seemed as good as nonexistent: it was a hollow, rather than an eminence, in the middle of this evilly attractive face.

The proper background for Juliette's barbaric head was primeval jungle—not this bourgeois room, with its plush-covered furniture, statuettes and silk lampshades. Not only the backdrop seemed out of place, but also the hair on the head itself was incongruous: it was far from the curly black mane that would have suited the forehead and mouth. Dull blond and surprisingly smooth, it was arranged simply with a part in the middle. The dark lady liked to maintain that she had done nothing to alter its appearance—she had inherited the color from her father, Herr Martens, the Hamburg engineer.

That her father was a man of this name and calling seemed certain, or at least was not questioned by anyone. Martens had been dead for years. His arduous stay in Central Africa had not agreed with him: weakened by malaria, his heart undermined by quinine injections and heavy drinking, he returned to Hamburg, where without attracting any great attention he soon died. He had left in the Congo both the black girl who had been his mistress and the dark-skinned little offspring he had apparently fathered. News of his death never reached Africa. A long while later, after she had lost her mother, too, Juliette set out for the very distant and, in her dreams, very wonderful land of Germany. Once there she hoped that fatherly love would protect her and launch her into the world. As it turned out, no one could even show her the engineer's grave. The bones of her poor father were lost. He had dropped altogether from the minds of men.

It was lucky for Juliette that she was a passable tap-dancer. This was something she had learned at home. Before very long she got herself taken on by one of the best establishments in the St. Pauli night-club quarter of the city. There she could certainly have held her place, and an intelligent and industrious woman might even have managed to better herself considerably, had not a violent temperament and an overwhelming taste for strong liquor fatally weighted the scales against her. She had a taste, which she was unable to control, for taking a riding whip to those of her acquaintances and colleagues with whom she was not in entire agreement. This habit was at first regarded in the St. Pauli area as little more than a humorous and entertaining whim; but in the long run it became rather too singular and, finally, downright annoying.

Juliette was dismissed and sank step by step into the lower depths. This meant displaying her tap-dancing in ever-smaller and more sordid places, which brought her so little money that she soon found herself compelled to resort to additional sources of income. And what other employment was there than that of the evening walks in the Reeperbahn and the narrow streets leading off it? The beautiful dark body, which she held erect as she moved disdainfully along the pavement, was certainly not the worst bargain in the terrible trade that each night invited the custom of sailors on shore leave and of both poor and well-heeled citizens of Hamburg.

Höfgen first encountered his black Venus in a sleazy bar filled with the tobacco smoke and hoarse shouts of drunken seamen, where she showed off her dark smooth limbs and rhythmically tapping feet for three marks a night. On the program of this dingy cabaret the black dancer Juliette Martens was listed as Princess Tebab—a stage name that she laid claim to also in private life. Her story was that her mother, the abandoned mistress of the Hamburg engineer, had been of royal blood. She was the daughter of a real, fabulously rich, proud black king who unfortunately had been eaten by his enemies at a relatively early age.

In Hendrik Höfgen's case, it was not so much her title that impressed him—although he found it thoroughly agreeable—but her ferociously darting eyes and the muscles of her chocolate-brown legs. After Princess Tebab's number was over, he went to her dressing room to make what was perhaps a rather surprising proposal: he wanted her to give him dancing lessons. "These days an actor must be trained like an acrobat," Höfgen had declared. But the Princess displayed no great eagerness to hear his explanations. Without much hesitation she named her price per hour and fixed the first appointment.

That was the start of the relationship between Hendrik Höfgen and Juliette Martens. The black girl was the "teacher," the monitress and ruler; the pale man stood before her as the "pupil," obedient and groveling, who accepted with equal submissiveness constant punishment and scant, grudging praise.

"Look at me," ordered Princess Tebab. She rolled her eyes fearsomely and he, pleading and docile, hung on her commanding gaze.

"How beautiful you are today," he muttered finally, his lips hardly stirring to form the words.

"Stop that nonsense," she bellowed. "I am not any more beautiful than usual." However, she languorously stroked herself across the bosom and tugged into place her tightly fitting pleated skirt, which ended just above the knee. Only a narrow strip of black silk stocking was visible above green boots of supple patent leather which reached above her calves. With the beautiful boots and the short skirt, the Princess wore a gray fur jacket with the collar turned up at the back of the neck. Cheap bangles of gilded metal clattered on her wrists. The most elegant of her accouterments was the riding crop—a gift from Hendrik. It was of bright red braided leather. Juliette drummed the whip ominously against the side of her green boots.

"Once again you are a quarter of an hour late," she said after a long pause, wrinkling her low brow in angry furrows. "How often do I have to warn you, honey?" she said with a wheedling softness that abruptly changed to a crescendo of anger. "I have had enough. I am fed up! Put out your hands."

Hendrik slowly extended his hands, palms upwards. But his hypnotized wide-open eyes never left the enraged and fearfully distorted mask of his loved one.

In a harsh snarling voice she counted: "One, two, three" as she struck. The thong of the elegant whip hissed horribly as it came down on the outstretched hands, raising thick red welts. The pain was so intense that it brought tears to his eyes. He screwed up his mouth. At the first stroke he cried out softly; then he gained control of himself and stood there with a stiff white face.

"That'll do for a start," she said and gave him a tired smile that was altogether against the rules of the game. Her face was emptied of menace and in its place was a look of good-natured mockery and a little pity. She dropped the whip and turned her head to show her face in profile. She stood for a moment in a pose that was beautiful. "Get dressed," she said softly. "We'll get down to work."

There was no screen behind which he could disappear to change his clothes. Juliette watched his every movement through half-closed lids with a total lack of interest. He had to take everything off and

51

display his pale, rather too fleshy body covered with reddish hairs, before slipping into the undignified attire he called his "track suit"— a childish and ridiculous getup consisting of black sneakers, short white socks coquettishly turned down above the ankle, shorts of shiny black satin such as little boys wear at gym classes and a striped sweat shirt that left arms and neck bare.

She cast a coldly critical eye over him. "You have grown rather fatter since last week, honey," she said striking the whip menacingly against a green boot.

"Forgive me," he murmured. His white face with the firm line of the chin, the sensitive temples and fine mournful eyes, were at their most serious and invested the grotesquely clad body with an almost tragic dignity.

The black girl was setting up the gramophone. The blare of jazz filled the room and she said hoarsely, "Go to it." She bared her almost too white teeth and moved her eyes menacingly. This was exactly the expression he had longed to see. Her face reared up before him like the awesome mask of a strange god, a god enthroned in a secret place in the deepest jungle and crying out for human sacrifice. A human body is brought to her and blood poured over her feet; through distended nostrils she breathes in the sweet stench and rocks her majestic torso to the rhythm of the wild drums. Around her the slaves dance in ecstasy: they swing their arms and legs, leap in the air, sway and stagger. Their roar becomes a long moan of joy, and the moaning becomes a subdued panting, and they sink to the ground before the feet of the black god they love and worship with all their hearts, as men can only worship the one to whom they have sacrificed that which is beyond price—blood.

Hendrik had started to dance slowly. But where was the triumphant lightness that the public and his colleagues so admired in him? There was not a trace of it; he now moved his feet in anguish—an anguish that could also be read as joy in the abstracted smile of his pale, compressed lips and glazed eyes.

As for Juliette, she danced without thinking. She let her pupil toil on alone, livening him up from time to time by clapping her hands, giving shrill cries and rhythmically shaking her body. "Faster, faster!" she shouted angrily. "What have you got in your bones? You want to be a man, you want to be an actor and have people pay money

52

to watch you? You wretched little lump!" The whip lashed him over the calves and arms. This time no tears came to his eyes, which remained dry and shining. Only his tightly pressed lips trembled.

He worked without a break for half an hour, as though he was engaged in a serious course of exercises instead of a gruesome form of entertainment. Finally he began to gasp and wheeze; his face was covered with sweat.

"I'm getting giddy," he said in an exhausted whisper. "Can I stop?"

With a look at the clock she answered dryly, "You've got to keep jumping for at least another quarter of an hour."

As the music swelled again, and Juliette began frantically clapping her hands, he tried once more to follow the complicated steps. But the tormented feet in their trim gym shoes and bobby socks refused to obey. Hendrik staggered for a second, then stood still and wiped the sweat from his brow with a trembling hand.

"What do you think you're up to?" she cried "You stop without my permission, that would be just lovely, wouldn't it?"

This time she aimed the red thong at his face. He ducked just in time to avoid the terrible blow. To arrive in the theater in the evening with a blood-red stripe from his forehead to his chin would be going too far—that much was clear to him despite his dazed condition. "Stop that," he said shortly. As he moved away from her he added, "Enough for today."

She understood that the game was over. With a small relieved sigh, she watched him put on his elegant quilted red-silk dressing gown, which was torn in places, and lie down on the couch. This sofa, which at night was transformed into a bed, was covered in the daytime with a throw and colored cushions.

"Turn off that harsh light," implored Hendrik plaintively. "And come to me, Juliette."

She walked toward him through the rose-tinted gloom. When she stood beside him he sighed. "How nice."

"Did you enjoy it?" she asked in an even, dry voice. She lit a cigarette and passed the match over to him. He inhaled through the long cigarette holder given to him by Rahel Mohrenwitz and said, "I am completely worn out." She forced her powerful mouth into a good-natured and understanding smile. "Good," she said, bending over him. He placed his broad, pale red-haired hand on the shining black silk covering of her splendid knee. Dreamily he murmured, "How ugly my wretched hand looks against your marvelous leg, my love."

"Everything about you is ugly, my little pig—head, feet, hands, the lot," she assured him with a rough tenderness. She slipped down beside him. The gray fur jacket was off. Under it she wore a snug shirt of red-and-black checked silk.

"I shall always love you," he said in an exhausted whisper. "You are strong. You are pure." And he gazed through half-closed lids at her firm pointed breasts which thrust through the thin, tightly stretched material of her blouse.

"Ah, that's just talk," she said with a note of scorn in her voice. "You just imagine things. Lots of people are like that. They just have to imagine things like that. Otherwise they can't feel good."

He pressed his fingers against the soft leather of her boots. His eyes were closed. "But I know that I shall always love you," he whispered. "I shall never again find a woman like you. You are the woman of my life, Princess Tebab."

She bent her face close to his. "But even so, I can't go to the theater when you are playing," she declared indignantly.

"But I act only for you," he whispered. "Only for you, my Juliette, you are the source of my strength."

"I'm not going to wait any more to be asked," she said defiantly. "I'm going to go to the theater whether you let me or not. And, what's more, I'm going to sit in the orchestra and I'm going to laugh out loud when you come on stage, my ape."

This drew a sudden cry "You aren't serious!" His eyes widened in alarm and he half raised himself. But a glance at the black Venus seemed to reassure him. He smiled and began to recite in French, " 'Do you come from the distant heavens or rise from the lower depths, O Beauty?' "

"What's that drivel?" she asked impatiently.

"It's from that wonderful book there." He pointed to a yellow-bound edition of Baudelaire's *The Flowers of Evil* lying on the low table under the lamp.

"I don't understand that," she said peevishly.

But he was not to be prevented from giving his ecstasy full rein and murmured on, " 'You walk upon the dead, Beauty, and mock them as you pass. Horror is not the least charming of the jewels that you wear. And murder, among your dearest trinkets, on your proud womb dances lovingly.' "

"How can you talk such crazy nonsense!" She silenced his moving lips with a long dark finger. But he talked on, always in the same melancholy lilting tone: "You never talk about how you lived before, Princess Tebab . . . I mean in your part of the world . . ."

"I don't remember any more," she said abruptly. Perhaps it was only to stop the flow of searching poetic interrogation that she now kissed him. Her wide-open animal mouth with the dark cracked lips and the blood-red tongue slowly approached his own, which was livid, craving.

As soon as she lifted her face from his, he went on murmuring, "I don't know if you understood me just now when I said that I only act for you and through you." As he spoke tenderly and dreamily, she moved her lithe fingers through the pale thinning hair swept back from his temples, on which the lamplight cast a golden sheen. "I meant it quite literally," he continued. "When the public likes me a little—when I have a success—I owe it all to you. To see you, to touch you, Princess Tebab, acts on me like a miracle cure; it's so wonderful—a refreshment like no other I've ever tasted."

"Ah, you and your chatter and lies, you really are the weirdest little shit I've ever met." To stop his talking she had laid her two hands on his face. Her broad bangles jangled against his chin; the pale pink palms of her hands rested on his cheeks. At last he was still. He leaned his head back on the pillows as if to sleep and, in a gesture that was like a plea for help, threw up both his arms and locked them around the black girl. She remained quite still in his embrace, leaving her hands over his eyes as though to prevent him from seeing the tenderly malicious smile on her lips as she gazed down at him.

3

Knorke

The season wore on and it turned out not to be a bad one at all for the Hamburg Arts Theater. Oskar H. Kroge had been decidedly unfair to say Höfgen was being overpaid at a thousand marks a month. Without this actor and director the theater would hardly have managed to get by. His output was enormous. He was as tireless as he was inventive. He played every role he could—from juvenile leads to old men. Not only Miklas but Petersen, too, had cause to be jealous of him; and even Otto Ulrichs would have had reason for complaint had he not been preoccupied with more serious matters that placed him far above the intrigues of the bourgeois theater. Höfgen won the children's hearts as the witty, handsome prince in the Christmas pantomime; women found him irresistible in French drawing-room comedies and the plays of Oscar Wilde; the intellectuals among the Hamburg public discussed his direction of *Spring's Awakening* and his playing of the lawyer in Strindberg's *The Dream* and the farcical lover in Büchner's *Leonce and Lena*. He knew how to be elegant, but he could also be tragic. He could delight his audiences with his high spirits and command respect with his imposingly lifted chin, his authoritative voice and arrogant gestures. And then again he could arouse their sympathy with a display of meekness, a helplessly lost gaze, an unworldly and vulnerable bewilderment. He could be generous or base, haughty or tender, scornful or overwhelmed, exactly as the part required. In

Schiller's *Intrigue and Love* he played on alternate nights the passionate lover and the scheming villain. He hardly needed such displays of virtuosity, so widespread now was his reputation as a masterly performer. In the mornings he rehearsed *Hamlet* and in the afternoons a farce called *Mitzi Does Everything*, which opened on New Year's Eve to considerable success. Schmitz was delighted. *Hamlet* aroused the fury of Kroge, who right up to dress rehearsal wanted to cancel the production altogether. "I haven't yet ever tolerated a piece of shit like that on any stage of mine," declared the outraged old pioneer of the avant-garde theater. "One doesn't throw off *Hamlet* without a second thought as if it were just a thriller." But Höfgen went through with it, and looked very impressive in his high-necked black doublet, with the enigmatic cast in his eye and his mournful parchment-colored face. Next day the Hamburg press decided that it had been an interesting interpretation, perhaps not completely thought through—somewhat improvised, in fact—but even so, filled with impressive moments. Angelika Siebert had been given the role of Ophelia and burst into floods of tears at every rehearsal. The first night she could hardly appear onstage because she was sobbing so bitterly. However, several worthy critics considered her contribution the best part of this questionable production.

Höfgen worked sixteen hours a day and had at least one nervous outburst a week. These fits were always of alarming violence and took different forms. Once he fell to the floor, shaken by silent convulsions. The next time, he remained standing but gave blood-curdling shrieks for five minutes without a break. On the third attack, he announced during a rehearsal, to the horror of everyone present, that lockjaw had set in and he could only murmur, which he proceeded to do. Before the evening performance he called Böck into his dressing room—Böck, who still had not been paid back his seven and a half marks—and had him massage the lower part of his face, while he groaned and muttered through clenched teeth. Onstage a quarter of an hour later his mouth functioned normally.

The day Princess Tebab failed to show up he wept, screamed and had convulsions. It was a particularly spectacular attack; the frightened cast who clustered round him were deeply shaken, though they had seen him in a wide variety of states. Finally Frau von Herzfeld poured water over the frantic man. It was rare for Juliette to give her friend the pretext for such a fit of despair; generally she appeared at his lodgings punctually at the agreed hour and did exactly what was expected of her. He emerged from these exhausting afternoon sessions strengthened and refreshed, more inventive, domineering and stubborn than before. He told Juliette that he loved her, that she was the core of his existence. Sometimes he believed what he said. For was not the black Venus the means by which he atoned for his ambition and humbled his vanity? Did he not truly love her? Sometimes he turned this over in his mind at night on the road home from H.K. And he told himself, Yes, I love her, there's no doubt about it. An even deeper voice whispered to him, Why lie to yourself? But he managed to smother this inner voice. Hendrik had to believe he was capable of love.

Little Angelika suffered, and Hendrik did not care at all. Frau von Herzfeld suffered, and he regaled her with intellectual conversation. Rolf Bonetti suffered because of Angelika, who remained coldly unyielding despite the ardor of his obstinate courtship. The handsome young lover had to fall back on to Rahel Mohrenwitz, which he did reluctantly. The hatred of Hans Miklas continued. He starved, when Frau Efeu was not feeding him bread and butter; and with his political friends he railed against Marxists, Jews and the servants of the Jews; he exercised his body feverishly; he was given small parts; and the hollows under his cheekbones grew ever darker.

Otto Ulrichs saw a good deal of his political friends too. He was embarrassed with them because of the constant postponement of the opening of the Revolutionary Theater. Each week Hendrik found a new excuse. Often after a rehearsal Ulrichs would take his friend aside and implore him, "Hendrik, when *are* we going to start?" And Hendrik would launch into a swift, passionate diatribe against the evils of capitalism, the theater as a political weapon, the need for a vigorous, carefully prepared cultural and political campaign; and would wind up by promising that rehearsals would start on the Revolutionary Theater immediately after the first night of *Mitzi Does Everything*.

However, after the successful launching of the New Year farce, many other first nights followed and the season drew to a close, but there was still nothing more to show for the Revolutionary Theater than the handsome letterhead which Hendrik used for a high-flown and voluminous correspondence with prominent authors who had left-wing leanings. When Otto Ulrichs once again pleaded for some action, Hendrik explained that due to unforeseen and unavoidable circumstances it was too late to begin during the current season. There would, alas, have to be a postponement until the following autumn. This time a shadow of doubt crossed Ulrichs' face; but Hendrik put his arm around his friend's shoulders and spoke to him in that utterly irresistible voice that started in a singing, vibrating tone and then became vehement as he scorched the moral decadence of the bourgeoisie and praised the international solidarity of the proletariat—they parted on a long handshake.

This happened as the finishing touches were being put to the final new production of the season. Hendrik Höfgen was to play the lead in Theophilus Marder's comedy *Knorke*. Marder's satirical play had caused a great stir in the German theater. All the critics praised its highly idiosyncratic style, theatrical craftsmanship and merciless wit. The Berlin critics were coming down for the Hamburg first night. The author himself was expected, too, not without a certain amount of foreboding, for Marder's inexorably high opinion of himself was well known, as was his fierce rudeness and his tendency to start violent quarrels with people at the drop of a hat.

Though a little anxious, Höfgen was delighted at the prospect of the celebrated playwright's arrival. He had little doubt that his interpretation would meet the approval of Marder's acute intellect. I must be good in *Knorke*, Hendrik swore to himself.

In order to devote all his time to the role, he handed over the production to Kroge, an old hand with the comedies of Theophilus Marder. *Knorke* was one of a series of satirical plays that scornfully portrayed the German middle class during the reign of Kaiser Wilhelm II. The hero was a social climber who, with his cynically won fortune, coarse enthusiasm and unscrupulous, vulgar intelligence, won power and influence in the highest reaches of society. Knorke was grotesque, but at the same time impressive. He represented the typical pushing bourgeois bubbling over with life and irredeemably philistine. Höfgen promised to be sensational in this role. He had the ruthless cutting voice and the sometimes almost touching helplessness that the part required. He had everything: the flamboyance of bearing and gesture that was touched with insecurity; the mean and nastily skillful eloquence of someone who strains every nerve to get ahead; the pale, frozen, almost heroic face of a man consumed by ambition; and even the look of horror that he casts back over his own far too precipitous ascent, which could at any moment come to an abrupt end. There was no question about it, Höfgen was going to be sensational in the part.

The role of Knorke's mistress, who was no less unscrupulous than he himself and only weaker in that she loved Knorke, was to be played by a young girl who had been passionately recommended by Marder in insistent, almost angry letters. Nicoletta von Niebuhr had very little actual stage experience, having only made rare appearances in small towns; nevertheless she had an almost intimidating self-assurance. Marder had threatened poor Kroge in the crudest terms with a most terrible scene if Fräulein von Niebuhr was not signed and given the leading role. Kroge, who became small and anxious under the impact of the dramatist's threatening manner, agreed to try her out. She arrived with a great many red-leather suitcases and wearing a man's broad-brimmed black hat and a scarlet raincoat. She had a prominent beak of a nose and bright catlike eyes under a fine broad forehead. Everyone noticed immediately that she was a real character. Motz declared as much in an awed voice in H.K. and nobody felt like contradicting her. Even Rahel Mohrenwitz kept silent, although she was extremely indignant about the new guest artist: it was all too clear that Nicoletta was a *femme fatale*, like herself, and one who needed neither a monocle nor a long cigarette holder to advertise the fact.

Rolf Bonetti and Petersen discussed whether Nicoletta could be called beautiful. Always enthusiastic, Petersen found her "just dazzling," while Bonetti, a more cautious connoisseur, would go only so far as to say that she was "interesting." "There is no question of beauty with a nose like that," he declared disdainfully. "But the eyes are wonderful," protested Petersen, looking around to make sure that Motz was not within earshot. "And how she carries herself! It's almost regal." Just then Nicoletta passed by outside, arm in arm with Höfgen. Her head was that of an Italian Renaissance youth. The likeness was remarked upon with sad perspicacity by Frau von Herzfeld, who followed the couple with an envious gaze.

Nicoletta was in the process of making it plain to Höfgen that she was ambitious, and, if crossed, was not above resorting to intrigue. Her sharply defined, brightly painted lips formed words with a cutting precision: every phrase rang out clearly; the vowels were smooth and even and not a consonant was lost. The most casual remark became a triumph of elocution. "But of course, darling," she said firmly to Höfgen, whom she had known only for a few hours, "we all want to get ahead. You have to use your elbows."

Hendrik glanced at her sideways with curiosity, and wondered if she was sincere at this moment or just putting on an act. It was difficult to decide. Perhaps her devastating cynicism was a mask behind which she hid a very different face . . . and who could tell if this hidden face had such a bold nose and sharp mouth as the one she so proudly showed to the world?

Hendrik could not deny that he was impressed by the woman at his side. Without doubt she was the first one who had excited his interest since Juliette had come into his life. He had confessed this to the black Venus and was given a terrible whipping that had no element of ritual and play-acting about it, for Princess Tebab was in a real fury. Hendrik groaned and groveled with suffering and pleasure. He swore to his princess when it was over that she alone would remain his true mistress and love. But when he saw Nicoletta again he was captivated anew by her trenchant way of talking, her shining, piercing gaze and her proud bearing.

Her legs were not beautiful—being rather too thick—yet she displayed them in black silk stockings with a triumphant ostentation that forbade any doubt as to their beauty, much as Hendrik showed off his inelegant hands as though he had the slender fingers of a Gothic statue. Nicoletta crossed her legs with a radiant enigmatic smile and lifted her dress above her knees. Hendrik of course saw exactly what she was up to, but was all the more enchanted. Besides, he found he could easily imagine these legs, over which Bonetti was already casting an appraising eye, sheathed in green leather boots—a mental picture that made her even more attractive. Hendrik threw his head back and let his shining eyes wander greedily.

He liked what she told him blandly about her origins and her past. Because his own background was so conventionally bourgeois, he was all the more impressed by the eccentricity and shady adventurousness of her story. Nicoletta had never known her parents. "My father was a swindler," she told him with delight and pride. "Mama was a minor dancer at the Paris Opéra. Very stupid, from what I hear. But she apparently had the most divine legs." She looked down at her own, provocatively implying that they were of equal divinity. "Papa was a genius. He always managed to live in great style. He died in

China, leaving seven teahouses and a mass of debts. The only memento I have of him is his opium pipe." In her hotel room she showed Hendrik this relic. With a courtesy that seemed to conceal limitless reserves of mischief, she asked him whether he would like tea or coffee. And she passed on his order to the waiter over the house telephone in a cold inflexible voice as if it were the most terrifying announcement of doom. Then she talked at length about her childhood. "I never really learned much," she said, "but I can walk on my hands and run on top of a rolling ball and screech like an owl." Her favorite reading had been a magazine called *La Vie Parisienne*. She grew up partly in French boarding schools, from which she had been quickly expelled for bad behavior, and partly in the house of Privy Councillor Bruckner, who, she said, was a childhood friend of her father.

Höfgen had already heard about Privy Councillor Bruckner, a historian who had written many books. Though Hendrik had not read them, he know that the councillor was a scholar and thinker who was not only one of the most eminent and talked-about figures on the European literary scene but also one of the most influential in political circles. His friendship with a certain Social Democrat minister was well known. He had links, too, with the army; his deceased wife had been the daughter of a general. His lecture tour in the Soviet Union had aroused a great deal of comment, particularly in the nationalist press, which had made him the object of a strident witch hunt. Ever since, it had become fashionable to attack his work for having a strong Marxist bias. Students sometimes booed when he appeared behind the lectern to address them. But his world-wide reputation and his calm and superior demeanor overawed his critics, and he always emerged victorious from any confrontation with them. He remained invulnerable.

"The old man is wonderful," said Nicoletta, "and he knows something about human nature. For instance, he was very attached to Papa. Which is why he has put up with so much from me—and I on my side have been patient with the distinguished form of boredom he generates."

Nicoletta's best friend was Bruckner's daughter Barbara, who was expected for the opening of *Knorke*. "Such a beautiful creature, and so good!" Nicoletta's gaze softened as she said this, but there was no change in her vibrant, hard-edged voice.

"I wonder if you are going to like her," Nicoletta said, hammering out her vowels. "Perhaps she's not quite your type. Do be nice to her, though, for my sake. She's a bit shy."

Barbara Bruckner arrived on the day of the first night; Marder appeared only toward evening on the Berlin Express. Höfgen met Barbara when he went into the canteen to drink a brandy just before the performance. "This is my dearest friend, Barbara Bruckner," Nicoletta said in a piercing voice, enunciating each word with the utmost precision. She accompanied the introduction with a hieratic gesture of her arms under the stiffly pleated folds of her black cloak. Hendrik was too overwrought to look closely at the young girl. He tossed off his brandy and fled. In his dressing room he found two large bouquets: white lilac from Angelika and pale yellow roses from Hedda. To place himself in favor with the gods by performing a good deed, Höfgen gave little Böck—who always looked somewhat fearful before first nights—five marks. This did not completely clear his debt of seven and a half marks, but Höfgen made it appear a grand gesture.

The first night of *Knorke* went marvelously. Marder's savagely pointed lines exploded across the footlights, arousing the audience to laughter that was half shocked and half delighted. But the greatest success of the evening was the acting of Höfgen and newcomer Nicoletta von Niebuhr—a dazzling partnership from every point of view that did full justice to both the insolence and the pathos of the leading roles. After the second act the two stars were called repeatedly in front of the curtain by the ecstatic audience. In the intermission Theophilus Marder came to Höfgen's dressing room accompanied by Nicoletta.

Marder's restless, piercing gaze moved over everything in the room before finally settling on Höfgen, who was sitting exhausted in front of the mirror. Nicoletta stood in respectful silence by the door. "You're certainly quite a fellow," Marder announced in an imperious voice. His unflinching eyes remained fixed on Höfgen's face.

"Are you satisfied, Herr Marder?" Höfgen tried to disarm the satirist with an appealing glance and a tired smile. But Theophilus only said, "Well, yes . . ." and then continued with calculated rudeness, "Well, yes, Herr . . . ? What do you call yourself?"

Hendrik was hurt, but he gave his name in his singing, shy voice.

"Hendrik . . . Hendrik, that's an odd name if ever there was one—very odd." There was so much concentrated malice in Marder's tone that Höfgen felt cold shivers run down his spine. Then suddenly the writer burst out with a frightening cheerfulness: "Hendrik, but why Hendrik? Why, of course, your name's really Heinz. His name is Heinz and he calls himself Hendrik! Ha, ha! That's really good!" He went off into a long burst of strident mirth. Appalled by the combination of so much venom and accuracy, Höfgen began to tremble. He paled under his terra-cotta stage makeup. Nicoletta turned her bright cat's eyes with amusement from one man to the other. Theophilus's face grew serious again; he seemed sunk in thought, his bluish mouth working silently under his black mustache like some avidly sucking carnivorous plant.

"But you're quite a fellow just the same," declared Marder finally. "Great talent—I can smell that. I've got a damned good nose for that sort of thing. We'll eat together afterwards, talk . . . Come along, baby." He took Nicoletta's arm and swept out of the dressing room, leaving Höfgen in a state of complete consternation.

He did not regain his composure until he was again onstage before the footlights—and then he was fully himself. In the third act he surpassed in style and brilliance all his past achievements. When the curtain fell the house broke into delirious applause. Nicoletta, her arms full of flowers, hung around Höfgen's neck and whispered, "Theophilus has got it right again—you really are quite a fellow." Kroge joined them to murmur his congratulations. He assured Nicoletta that it would be a pleasure to continue working with her and she could call on him in his office the following morning to discuss her future. Nicoletta put on her crafty, reserved expression, bowed solemnly and told the director in a few crisply enunciated words that his suggestion met with her approval.

Theophilus Marder invited Nicoletta and Barbara along with Höfgen to a very expensive, solidly bourgeois restaurant. Hendrik had never set foot inside its doors, which gave Marder the opportunity to point out that it was really the only place in Hamburg where they still served edible food. According to the dramatist, everywhere else one was served rancid fat and rotting meat, but here the customers were sophisticated old *bon vivants* who still knew how to live—moreover, the cellar was good.

In fact the only other customers in this wood-paneled dining room, with its hunting prints and tapestries on the walls, appeared to be gentlemen of great wealth but of an advanced age. More dignified than them all was the headwaiter. There seemed to be a trace of irony

65

in the way he took Marder's order. Marder proposed that they begin with crayfish. "What do you think, my dear Heinrich?" he asked Höfgen in a polite tone that Nicoletta might well have learned from him. Hendrik had no objection. He felt rather ill at ease and embarrassed in the grand establishment. He imagined that the headwaiter had disdainfully inspected his dinner jacket, which was dirty and showed patches of shiny grease stains. Under the searching gaze of the aloof waiter, Hendrik was fleetingly but violently conscious of his revolutionary beliefs. I don't belong in this restaurant for capitalist exploiters, he thought angrily as he watched his glass being filled with white wine. He regretted having so long postponed the opening of the Revolutionary Theater.

Marder was a great disappointment. When you met him face-to-face, this mercilessly lucid and dangerous critic of bourgeois society was revealed as a man with alarmingly bourgeois tastes. He had a loud parade-ground voice and a spiteful look; he wore a far too perfectly tailored dark suit with a carefully matching tie; and when the crayfish arrived he had a much too knowledgeable way of selecting the best ones for himself. He appeared in fact to have a great deal in common with the characters he lambasted in his plays. Now he was praising the good old days when he was young, a period which surpassed in every way the shallow corrupt contemporary scene. All the while he kept his cold and lustful eyes on Nicoletta; and she not only twisted her mouth, but contorted her whole body in its shining lamé evening dress.

Barbara sat quietly by Hendrik's side. Finally disgusted by Nicoletta's provocative flirtation with Marder, and perhaps a little jealous as well, Hendrik turned his attention to Barbara. He noticed her gaze was fixed searchingly on him. Hendrik Höfgen was suddenly afraid. In his heart of hearts he was terrified that he found in Barbara Bruckner an attraction he had not discovered in any other woman. As he looked at her he recalled in swift but precise succession—as though he were drawing a line forever under a long and shabby past—all the women in his life. The sturdy, cheerful Rhinelander who without much fuss or refinement had initiated him into the crude facts of love; the more mature though still lively women—friends of his mother, Bella—succeeded by his sister Josy's young but not very sensitive friends; the seasoned prostitutes in Berlin and the hardly less skilled ones in German provincial towns, who had performed certain services he yearned for and which had caused him to lose the taste for less special pleasures; finally, his actress colleagues, beautifully made-up and always willing, to whom he granted his favors only on rare occasions, and who most of the time had to make do with his erratic friendship, which ran between cruelty and seductive flirtation. The procession of women—the timidly virginal, the somberly pathetic and the sophisticated and intelligent—now filed past in his memory, then were gone—erased by the extraordinary perfection of Barbara. Even Nicoletta, the captivating daughter of an adventurer, with her attractive precise way of speaking, faded into the background. Her formal ways and perversity made her an almost comic figure. Hendrik renounced all interest in her—but what would he not have sacrificed in this fateful and sweet moment of decision?

Was not this long look at Barbara his first betrayal of Juliette, his dark mistress, whom he had called the center of his existence and the great source of power from which his own strength was renewed? He had never seriously betrayed Juliette with Nicoletta, whose legs aroused daydreams of high green boots; the actress would have been at best a substitute for the black Venus rather than a rival. But the rival now sat beside him. She had looked at Hendrik searchingly while he was still preoccupied with Marder and Nicoletta. Now he looked at her, not with his calculatedly seductive gaze but with a defenseless sincerity. She cast down her eyes and turned a little away from him.

Her utterly simple black dress, with its stiff white schoolgirl collar, left her neck and thin arms bare. The sensitive and graceful oval of her face was pale; her lightly bronzed neck and arms had the golden bloom of fine apples ripened through a long summer. Hendrik had to ransack his memory to find what this luxurious color reminded him of and why it moved him even more than Barbara's face. He recalled the women painted by Leonardo da Vinci; and it comforted him to think that while Marder was boasting about his knowledge of old French recipes, he was sitting here silently thinking such cultured thoughts. Yes, in certain pictures of Leonardo you found this rich, soft, virginally sensitive skin color; it was to be seen, too, in the bodies of some of the boys who raised a gentle curved arm from the shadows of Leonardo's canvases. Youths and madonnas in the pictures of the old masters had this kind of beauty. It was on these youths and madonnas that the bewitched Hendrik's mind dwelt as he gazed at Barbara Bruckner. This beautiful slenderness of limb recalled ideally formed boys. But her face was that of a Madonna, as was the way in which Barbara now opened her dark blue eyes, which looked almost black under long, full and completely natural lashes. Their gravely searching expression was touched with a friendly curiosity that seemed almost mischievous. In fact, her face had something boyish, or even roguish, about it. Her rather large, moist lips smiled meditatively but with a touch of humor. The heavy ash-blond hair that fell a bit loosely into a knot gave her a certain hoydenish quality, despite the absolutely straight part down the middle.

"Why are you looking at me like that?" asked Barbara finally, when it seemed that Hendrik's spellbound glance would never leave her face.

"Shouldn't I?" he answered softly.

With a boyish flirtatiousness mixed with timidity she said, "If it gives you pleasure . . ."

Hendrik thought her voice brought to the ear the same pleasure as the color of her skin to the eye. It seemed saturated with tenderness and fullness of tone; it bloomed luxuriously. Hendrik listened to her with the same abandon as he had previously experienced looking at her. He asked questions just to keep her talking. He wanted to know how long she intended to stay in Hamburg. She answered, pulling at her cigarette with an awkwardness that revealed her lack of experience. "As long as Nicoletta is playing here. So it depends on the success of *Knorke*."

"Which makes me delighted the audience applauded so long this evening," said Hendrik. "I think that the reviews will also be good."

He asked about her studies—Nicoletta had told him that Barbara was at the university. She spoke of her sociology and history courses. "I am far too irregular a pupil," she declared gravely but with a hint of sarcasm, and then she placed her elbows on the table and sank her face into her hands. A less besotted onlooker than Hendrik might have found this gesture clumsy and almost vulgar; but it struck him as beautifully and touchingly shy. The stiffness of her bearing revealed the young girl from the provinces, the not very sophisticated daughter of a professor, and contrasted with the intelligence and cheerful candor of her eyes. She had the insecurity of someone who has been much loved and spoiled in a narrowly circumscribed circle and who was now outside its protection. In Nicoletta's presence Barbara had become accustomed to playing a secondary role, and so she was delighted as well as a little amused that this fine actor Hendrik Höfgen took notice of her in such an obvious way. Without reluctance she continued their conversation. "I do all kinds of things," she said thoughtfully. "For instance, I draw . . . I have been very involved in theater designing."

This stirred Hendrik deeply, and in a rush of enthusiasm that brought color to his cheeks he spoke of the stylistic changes in stage scenery and of everything in this field that was to be discovered or rediscovered or improved. Barbara listened, answered, looked at him questioningly, smiled. She made charming awkward gestures with her slender arms, and her voice was alternately teasing and pensive as she delivered quietly intelligent responses.

Hendrik and Barbara continued to talk softly and intently, and there was something close to tenderness in their voices. Meanwhile, Nicoletta and Marder beamed at each other, both bringing all their powers of seduction into play. Nicoletta's beautiful bird-of-prey eyes glittered more brightly than ever, and the precision of her speech took on a tone of triumph. Her little pointed teeth shone between her brightly painted lips whenever she spoke or laughed. Marder responded with a display of intellectual fireworks. His twitching mouth, whose bluish color looked most unwholesome, talked almost nonstop, frequently repeating himself. His most persistent theme was that the modern age—of which he considered himself the best-qualified and most vigilant judge—was the worst, most corrupt and most irretrievably doomed of all epochs: absent was any stirring of spiritual regeneration, any guiding principle or special achievement; above all, what the modern world lacked was men of character—Marder himself was the only one around and he was too little known. What was most worrisome about Marder was that, as observer and savagely critical judge of the decline of Europe, he could propose no alternative to the desolate contemporary scene.

The feverishly animated Nicoletta was not in a mood to be distracted by anything Marder said; had she really listened to him she might have thought it strange that the very man who liked to set himself up as the scourge of the bourgeois era now sang the praises of Rhineland industrialists and the Prussian officers of the old German army, singling them out as examples of superb discipline and bold individualism while pouring scorn on his other contemporaries.

He bellowed so angrily that the old men sitting by their bottles of red wine turned their heads in astonishment. Women, too, had lost all sense of discipline, he declared. They no longer understood anything about love. They made a commerce of the gift of their bodies. They had become as superficial and vulgar as men. Here Nicoletta laughed so challengingly that he added gallantly, "There are, of course, exceptions."

He continued his tirade. German men had lost all sense of order and respect since conscription in the army had been abolished. Today, in a degenerate democracy, everything was false, fake, a swindle. "If it were otherwise, wouldn't I be the man guiding the country?" Marder asked bitterly. "Wouldn't the enormous power and efficiency of my brain be enlisted to settle all the important matters of public life? As it is, however, now that every instinct and yardstick is incapable of measuring true superiority, my voice is no more than the nearly inaudible protest of the bad conscience of the age."

His eyes blazed. His gaunt face, whose paleness contrasted sharply with his black mustache, was contorted. To calm him, Nicoletta reminded him that the works of no other living author were so often performed. He smiled, fleetingly satisfied, then he suddenly roared at Hendrik Höfgen, who was deeply absorbed in his conversation with Barbara, "Have you, sir, done your military service?" Hendrik, surprised and horrified by such a threatening question, turned a dismayed face toward the dramatist. "Answer me, sir!"

Forcing a smile, Hendrik murmured. "No, naturally not . . . Thank God, not . . ."

Marder laughed triumphantly. "There we are, you see! No discipline, no backbone! Have you by any chance any discipline, sir? Have you any character? Everything is fake. Everything is ersatz—vulgarity is everywhere I look."

This was insulting. Hendrik did not know how he should react. He felt a rising anger, but decided to be quiet—a scandal should be avoided for the sake of the women and the respect due Marder's fame.

Suddenly an astounding and distressing change came over Marder, who, in a grotesquely hushed voice, his eyes like those of some mad prophet, murmured, "It will all come to a horrible end."

On what distant landscape, in what deep abyss, was this gaze fixed that was suddenly filled with such visionary power?

"The worst will happen. Think of me, children, when that day comes. I have foreseen it and predicted it. Our age is corrupt. It stinks. Think of me—I smelled it out. I am not deceived. I sense the coming catastrophe. It will be like nothing that has ever happened. Everything will be swallowed up, which will be no loss—except in my case. Everything that exists will fall apart. It is rotten. I have sensed it, tasted it and cast it away from me. When it comes down, it will bury us all. I pity you children, for you will not be able to live your lives. Whereas I have had a beautiful life."

Theophilus Marder was fifty years old. He had been married three times. He had been hated and mocked. He had known success, fame and wealth.

His voice fell silent and he wheezed exhaustedly. The others, lowering their heads, said nothing.

Then abruptly Marder's mood changed. He poured out more wine and became charming. He complimented Höfgen, whom he had just insulted, on his brilliant acting. "I know very well," he said, "that it's a marvelous part and my dialogue is unbeatable. But those miserable souls who call themselves actors nowadays manage even in my plays to be overwhelmingly boring. You, Höfgen, at least have an inkling of what theater is. Among the blind, you give me the impression of being at least one-eyed." He raised his wineglass. "Your health."

"You seem to be getting on not too badly with our Barbara," he said cheerfully. Barbara met his suggestive smile with a grave look.

It struck Hendrik as odd that Marder, who prided himself on his infallible instinct for recognizing superior womanhood, seemed not to notice Barbara at all. He had eyes only for Nicoletta, who for her part carefully avoided meeting the affectionate, concerned gaze that Barbara from time to time turned in her direction.

Marder ordered champagne to accompany the last course, which was now being served. It was midnight. The distinguished restaurant was empty except for the four diners, and had long since locked its doors. But Marder made it plain to the waiters that a substantial tip would be forthcoming if they continued their service longer than usual. The great satirist, the alert conscience of a corrupt civilization, now displayed his talent for light-hearted banter. He told funny stories, mixing Prussian military jokes with Eastern European Jewish humor. Every now and then he looked at Nicoletta as if to say "Beautiful girl! A disciplined creature, an object rarely to be found today!" He scrutinized Höfgen and shouted briskly, "This so-called Hendrik—

quite a fellow—a tremendously funny, talented phenomenon, entertains me no end—I must make a note of it."

Hendrik let him boast on. He didn't begrudge him his triumphs; he hadn't the slightest desire to compete with him. Let Marder dominate this little table; Hendrik would laugh happily at his anecdotes. Besides, there was a special pleasure in the situation: he saw himself, in contrast to the crude and vociferous Marder, as calm and refined—a feeling he seldom experienced. He thought he must be making a good impression on Barbara, who probably didn't much appreciate Marder's flamboyant style. Hendrik was aware of her eyes fixed on him with sympathetic interest. He believed he appealed to the girl—the most wonderful hopes swelled his troubled heart.

They parted very late and in high good spirits. Hendrik walked home, thinking about Barbara. The feeling of being truly in love was a completely new experience and was agreeably heightened by the aftereffects of large quantities of good wine.

What's the secret of this girl? he asked himself. It must be her perfect manners . . . yes . . . she's the person most worthy of respect I've ever seen. *She could be my good angel.*

He stood in the middle of the street. The dark night was warm and scented, and the feel of summer was in the air. He had hardly noticed that spring had come and gone. His heart trembled with a happiness it had never known and for which no training had prepared it.

Barbara will be my good angel.

The thought of his meeting with Princess Tebab the following day filled Hendrik with anxiety. He must ask his dance mistress not to visit him any more—his new deep feeling for Barbara demanded that. But it already hurt him to think of no longer seeing Juliette; he trembled at the thought of her reaction to the news.

Hendrik made a great effort to explain the changed situation to Juliette as quietly as possible. But his voice shook, no "dirty" smile came to his aid; instead, he alternately blushed and paled, and large drops of sweat stood out on his forehead. Juliette raved and screamed that she would tear out the eyes of this girl Nicoletta, who had humiliated her. Hendrik, who expected at any moment to see the whip appear, implored her to control herself and assured her that Fräulein Niebuhr had nothing whatever to do with his decision.

"You told me that I was the center of your life and all that nonsense," Princess Tebab raged.

Hendrik bit his pale lips and looked penitent.

"You lied," shouted the Princess. "I always thought you were lying to yourself—but no, you were lying to me. You can never tell how rotten men can be."

There was no doubt that her anger was real. "But I'm not going to run after you," she said proudly. "I'm not the kind to run after anyone. If you've found someone else who can beat you as I know how to do—then the best of luck."

Hendrik handed her money, which she sullenly accepted. But in the doorway she beamed a triumphant smile. "Don't think that we're through with one another, you and I." She nodded at him. "If you need me again—you certainly know where to find me."

Theophilus Marder left town, but not before having a spectacular quarrel with Oskar H. Kroge. The playwright had wanted to force the director to promise in a legally binding document that his play would be given at least fifty performances. Naturally, Kroge refused, whereupon Marder threatened him with legal proceedings, and when this did not have the desired effect, he accused the director of the Hamburg Arts Theater of being a complete nonentity lacking discipline and character, a cheating racketeer, a cretinous philistine and a typical representative of all this stinking rotten age. Even Kroge, with his calm nature, could not help reacting to so many taunting insults. They shouted at each other for an hour, after which Marder boarded the Berlin Express in the best of moods.

Hendrik, Nicoletta and Barbara met every day. Sometimes it chanced that Hendrik and Barbara found themselves together without Nicoletta. They went for walks or they sailed on the lake; they sat on terraces or visited art galleries. They drew closer to each other; they talked more intimately. Barbara learned from Hendrik what he wanted her to know: with exalted pathos he discussed his beliefs, confided in her his faith in the coming world revolution and the mission of the Revolutionary Theater. He told the story of his childhood in dramatically heightened terms.

Barbara, too, talked about her childhood. Hendrik gathered that the two key figures in her life so far had been her darling father and Nicoletta, the friend for whom she felt such a special tenderness. This eccentric, adventurous friend had already given her considerable cause for concern; but what chiefly worried her right now was Nicoletta's new relationship with Marder. Hendrik had guessed right: Barbara loathed Marder. And from her contemptuous hints Hendrik concluded that before Theophilus had known Nicoletta, he had paid passionate court to Barbara. She, however, had remained cold to his advances; hence his hatred of her. He enjoyed his conquest of Nicoletta all the more as she explained to anyone who would listen to her that Theophilus Marder was the only thoroughly worthwhile and first-rate man— the only man on the contemporary European scene who could be taken completely seriously. Nicoletta talked to him on the telephone almost daily, despite Barbara's obvious disapproval.

For her part, Nicoletta benevolently watched the growing affection between Barbara and Hendrik. It pleased her that Barbara, whose affectionate censoriousness had become a burden, was now embarked on a sentimental venture of her own. Nicoletta did whatever she could to encourage the relationship. She spoke to Hendrik about it when she visited his dressing room one evening.

"I'm delighted that you are getting on so well with Barbara. You'll get married. The girl doesn't know what to do with herself."

Hendrik waved aside such suggestions. But he trembled with joy as he asked, "Then you feel Barbara is thinking along those lines . . . ?"

Nicoletta gave her ringing laugh. "Of course she thinks about it. Don't you notice how completely changed she is? Don't be misled, my dear, if she gives the impression of taking pity on you. I know her— she is the kind of woman in whom affection is always mixed with pity. Marry her! It's clearly the most practical solution for you both. Besides, it will be a good thing for your career—old Bruckner has a lot of influence."

This had occurred to Hendrik, too. The intoxication of his love— which persisted and which he wanted to believe would be long-lasting —could not altogether obscure more mundane considerations. Privy Councillor Bruckner was a great man, and he was not a poor one; an alliance with his daughter would bring other advantages besides happiness. Was there truth in Nicoletta's cynical words? Had Barbara considered the possibility of linking her life with Hendrik's? How far did her interest in him go—was it only a superficial game? Her madonnalike face with its occasional street-urchin mischievousness was inscrutable. Her deep golden-toned voice gave nothing away. But what was the real message of her searching eyes that so often settled on his face with curiosity, pity, friendliness—and perhaps love?

He would have to hurry if he wanted to have an answer. The season was nearly at an end. The last performance of *Knorke* had been presented, and Barbara and Nicoletta were ready to leave.

Hendrik made his decision. Nicoletta had pointedly announced that she intended to go for a long walk with Rolf Bonetti, so Barbara was alone. Hendrik went to see her.

It was a long conversation. Barbara's bewildered look left him in no doubt that Nicoletta's little speech of encouragement had been an error or an impudent trick: marriage with Höfgen had never so much as entered Barbara Bruckner's head.

Hendrik sank to his knees and burst into tears. "I need you," he sobbed, his head in her lap. "Without you I shall go completely to pieces. There is so much that's bad in me. Alone I can't muster the force to get the better of it. But you will make what is best in me strong."

Such were the pathetic and painfully sincere words that his despair wrenched from him. He raised his tear-stained face slowly from her lap. His pale mouth twitched; the piercing glint in his eyes was dimmed. They looked blind with misery.

"You don't love me," he sobbed. "I am nothing, I will never achieve anything, you don't care for me—I am finished . . ." He could get no more words out. What he still had to say came out as a senseless mumble.

Barbara gazed down at his thinning hair. The few strands that were normally combed to conceal the bald patches were now in great disorder. Perhaps it was the sight of this sparse hair that moved her.

Without touching the damp face he lifted toward hers, without raising her eyes, she said slowly, "If you really want it so badly, Hendrik . . . we could certainly try . . . we could try . . ."

Hendrik Höfgen gave a hoarse cry that sounded like a muffled shout of victory.

That was their engagement.

CHAPTER

4

Barbara

Barbara embarked with great astonishment on an adventure for which neither her heart nor mind had prepared her. What had she let herself in for, why had she done it? Did she really feel a deep attachment for this ambiguous, versatile, highly gifted, sometimes touching, sometimes almost repellent creature—this actor Hendrik Höfgen?

Barbara was hardly a woman to let herself be seduced; the most expert ploy left her cold. But she was all the more vulnerable to appeals that awoke feelings of pity and solicitude. Hendrik had been cunning enough to realize this. Since the first evening, when he had played the reserved man of refinement in flattering contrast to Marder's noisy flamboyance, he had renounced any attempt to dazzle Barbara and remained quiet and low-key in her company. Their conversation was confined to subjects that were either elevated or intensely personal: his ethical and political ideals, his lonely childhood, the toil and the magic of his profession. Finally, at a decisive moment, he had showed the girl a face wet with tears and blinded by suffering; and what he still had in mind to say to her was lost in unintelligible mumbling.

Barbara was accustomed to her friends seeking her out when they were in trouble. Not only did Nicoletta come to her with her confused confessions, but also young men and even older men, friends of her father's, confided in her when they were in need of consolation. She was accustomed to dealing with the anguish of others, but since early childhood she had refused to take her own sorrows and dilemmas very seriously, and was reluctant to open her heart to anyone. The result was that people took for granted that her composure was proof against any emotional problem. Her friends considered her the most level-headed, wise, energetic, versatile, mature, gentle and solid creature alive. Perhaps there was only one person close to her who knew how vulnerable she really was—knew of her self-doubt, her nostalgic love for the past and her fear of the future. Old Bruckner loved his child and knew her.

And so the letter the old man wrote to Barbara when he received the news of her engagement expressed not only sadness but a certain concern at the thought that she now wanted to leave home. Had she really taken everything into consideration and properly weighed her decision? Barbara was alarmed by the warning implicit in her father's question. She began to ask herself whether indeed she had properly considered her decision. Each piece of advice that Barbara gave her friends was the long-pondered outcome of careful reflection. But in her own life she seemed to just let things happen to her with a certain detachment, as if it were a game. Sometimes she frightened herself a little, but never enough to cause her to retreat or refuse—curiosity as much as pride would not allow her to go back on any decision. She took things as they came, skeptically with a smiling audacity, never placing her hopes too high where her own welfare was concerned. It was with a smile that she looked at her strange Hendrik, who demanded with such soulful eloquence that she play the part of his good angel. Perhaps that would be a worthwhile activity; perhaps this was where the path of duty led; perhaps there was in him an endangered core of nobility that she—and only she—could protect. If this were so, Barbara would not draw back. She was far more concerned about Nicoletta's abandonment of herself to Marder than about her own surprising fate.

Things began to happen fast. Hendrik insisted that the marriage should take place in the summer. Nicoletta supported him in this. "If you must marry, my love," she said—in the tone of someone who had been utterly opposed to the idea but was resigned to it now that it appeared to be inevitable—"if it must be, then it would be much better to do it immediately. Long engagements are ridiculous."

A wedding date was set for mid-July. Barbara had gone home; there were many preparations to be made. In the meantime Nicoletta and Hendrik gave guest performances at Baltic coastal resorts in a comedy with only two characters. Barbara had to put through numerous expensive telephone calls to Hendrik before she got him to send the documents that were essential for the City Hall records.

Two days before the ceremony Nicoletta arrived—a sensational spectacle for the little South German university town where the Bruckners lived. A day later Hendrik made his appearance after stopping off in Hamburg to collect his new tail coat. The first thing he told Barbara on the station platform was that the dress suit was dazzlingly beautiful but not yet paid for. He laughed nervously a great deal; he was sunburned and wore a light-colored, somewhat too snugly fitting summer suit with a pink shirt and a silver-gray felt hat. His laughter became ever more convulsive as they neared the Bruckner villa. Barbara deduced that Hendrik was frightened at the prospect of meeting her father.

The privy councillor was waiting for the young couple in the garden outside his house. He greeted Hendrik unsmilingly with a bow so deep and solemn that it could have been interpreted as ironic. His appearance was one of such distinction and sensitivity that it was almost frightening. The narrow head—the furrowed brow, the long, delicately arched nose and the firmly molded cheeks—looked as though it had been carved out of rare yellowed ivory. The large space between the nose and mouth was adorned by a gray mustache. Perhaps it was this disproportionately broad stretch between the upper lip and the nostrils that gave the face its special character—made it look somewhat distorted, like a reflection in a fairground mirror or a portrait by a primitive. The chin was bearded. At first one had the impression that the privy councillor had a long pointed beard; in fact the gray hairs hardly extended below the chin and the imperial-beard effect came from the exceptional length of his chin.

The delicate shape of the face, its spiritual quality and its age, gave it a nobility that was intimidating yet somehow sad. What was most surprising about his face were his eyes: they were the deep and soft, almost black dark blue that Hendrik knew so well from Barbara's eyes, but the lids were heavy and often lowered, so that his glance was veiled, while his daughter's was clear and candid.

"My dear Herr Höfgen," said the privy councillor, "I am glad to make your acquaintance. Let me express the hope that you have had a good journey."

His voice was remarkably clear without being at all like Nicoletta's diabolically precise diction. With loving care the privy councillor gave each word the clearest pronunciation, as though a sense of fairness forbade his overlooking a single syllable. Even the most insignificant final syllables, those that are generally swallowed, received a careful, elegant articulation.

Hendrik felt very uneasy. Before deciding to adopt a solemn expression, he laughed a little, absurdly, in the affected way he used to greet Dora Martin in H.K. Although Barbara gave him a troubled glance, the privy councillor did not seem to notice this odd behavior. He remained scrupulously polite and kind, and, with friendly cere-moniousness, invited the two young people inside. He said to Barbara, who was waiting to let him go ahead, "You go ahead, my child, and show your friend where he can leave his smart hat."

They stepped into the cool semidarkness of the hall. Hendrik respectfully inhaled the scent of the room—the smell of flowers stand-ing about on tables and on the mantelpiece mingled with the venerable aroma of leatherbound books that covered all the walls, floor to ceiling.

Hendrik was led through several rooms. He talked feverishly to show that he was not overawed at all. Actually, he was conscious of very little that he saw. A large dog of alarming aspect rose, growling, was stroked by Barbara, and departed with dignity; a portrait of the dead mother loomed above him—a gracious face crowned by an old-fashioned hairstyle. An old governess or housekeeper—small, good-natured and talkative, and wearing a curious long starched apron —curtsied and shook his hand warmly. She then launched into a long conversation with Barbara about household matters. Hendrik was amazed that Barbara concerned herself with so many details of the running of the house and was so familiar with the routine of the kitchen and the gardens.

These imposing rooms with their beautiful carpets, varnished paintings, bronze busts, large clocks and velvet upholstered furniture constituted Barbara's home. She had spent her youth in these sur-roundings. These were the books she had read; she had entertained her friends in this garden. Her childhood had been tenderly and care-fully sheltered by the wise love of her father; her adolescence had been passed in innocence—filled with games to which she alone knew the secret rules. Hendrik was moved almost to awe; but there was some-thing else in his reaction that he did not want to admit to himself—

envy. It was painful to think that the following day he must introduce his mother Bella and his sister Josy to Barbara's father in these rooms. He shuddered as he thought of their petit bourgeois ways. It was fortunate at least that his father couldn't be there.

They lunched on the terrace. Hendrik admired the beauty of the garden, and the privy councillor pointed out the statue of a youth—a Hermes—attractively slender, with one arm raised as if about to fly off among the birch leaves. This work of art seemed to be an object of special pride for the privy councillor. "Yes, yes, my Hermes *is* beautiful," he said. His smile broadened into a grin. "Every day I feel happy all over again that I own him and that he stands so charmingly among my birch trees." He was also clearly delighted that there was such good wine and food at his table. He served himself without excess but plentifully, and praised the dishes. "Raspberries," he announced with satisfaction. "They are in season just now and they do smell so nice." The mood he created around him was a singular blend of solemnity and benevolence, of inaccessible reserve and cheerfulness. His future son-in-law did not seem to displease him too much. He treated him with a cordiality not perhaps wholly free from irony. His smile seemed to say, My dear fellow, the right to exist in this world also belongs to characters like you. It is amusing to observe them; at least one is not bored in their company. Certainly, I have never thought that a person of your kind would ever be sitting at my table as my son-in-law. But I am of a nature to accept things as they are—you have to try to see the best and funniest side of things, and, besides, my Barbara must have good reasons for wanting to marry you . . ."

Hendrik felt he had a chance of succeeding in making a good impression. He could no longer keep himself from using that veiled, shimmering gaze that had worked so well on other occasions. With his head thrown back and an enigmatic smile on his lips, he flashed his seductive glances at the privy councillor. The old man listened attentively as his future son-in-law expounded his opinions in a carefully prepared and impressive speech, condemning in the most devastating terms the bourgeoisie's cynical exploitation of the masses and the criminal folly of nationalism. The old man interrupted only once, raising his lean, beautiful hand to exclaim, "You speak so scornfully of the bourgeoisie, my dear Herr Höfgen, but I also am one of them. It's true I'm not a nationalist," he added in a friendly tone, "and, I trust, not an exploiter, either."

Hendrik—his face above the pink shirt flushed with lively talk and wine—stammered that there were certain kinds of upper-middle-class bourgeois for whom the man with communist tendencies had a high regard, and that the great heritage of the bourgeois revolution and liberalism was kept alive in the "pathos" of Bolshevism—and made other such conciliatory assurances.

With a smile the privy councillor waved these explanations aside. But then—as though determined to convince Höfgen of his political impartiality—he described elaborately and vividly the impression left on him by his journey through the Soviet Union.

"Every objective observer must come to the conclusion—and we must all learn to live with the idea—that a new form of community life is in the process of coming into existence there." He spoke slowly. His blue eyes gazed into the distance as though he were seeing the overwhelming events emerging in that far country. He added with severity, "This state of affairs can only be denied by fools and liars."

Then suddenly his mood changed. He asked for the bowl of raspberries, and while he helped himself to another serving he said almost maliciously, "Don't misunderstand me, dear Herr Höfgen. Naturally, this world is strange to me—only too strange, I fear. But must that mean that I have no feeling for its enormous potential?"

Hendrik was glad to be able to monopolize the conversation again—he was not particularly interested in the account of life in the Soviet Union; he began to talk enthusiastically about the Revolutionary Theater and his persecution in Hamburg by the forces of reaction. He became very vehement, referring to fascists as "beasts," "devils" and "fools," and abusing those intellectuals who, out of opportunism, sided with militant nationalism. "They should all be hanged," exclaimed Hendrik, going so far as to hit the table with his fist. The privy councillor said quickly as though to soothe him, "Yes, yes—I, too, have had some difficulties." This was his only allusion to the well-known and scandalous events of which he had been the victim —the uproar caused by nationalist students in his classes and the crude attacks in the reactionary press.

After lunch, the old man asked his guest to give a demonstration of his art. Hendrik, who was quite unprepared for any such request, put up considerable resistance. But the privy councillor wanted very much to be entertained. Since his daughter was going to marry an actor with a pink shirt and a monocle, he wanted at least to get an amusing performance out of it. So Hendrik stood in the hall reciting poems by Rainer Maria Rilke. Even the old housekeeper and the big dog came to listen. Nicoletta, who had not been at the luncheon, now joined the little audience and was greeted by the privy councillor with a kind of ironic formality. Hendrik took great trouble to show his voice to its best advantage. He did very well and was much applauded. After he had concluded with a fragment from Rilke's dramatic poem *Cornet*, the privy councillor shook his hand warmly; and Nicoletta, letting the words fall from her mouth with pristine clarity, praised his "brilliant diction."

The following day saw the arrival of the two women of the Höfgen family, mother and daughter. Hendrik said to Barbara as they waited on the station platform, "You wait and see, Josy will fall on my neck and say she's gotten herself engaged again. It's awful, she gets engaged at least once every six months and to such terrible men—you can't imagine! We're always delighted every time we get the news it's been broken off. Last time it nearly cost my poor old father his life. The prospective bridegroom was a racing driver. He took Papa with him in his car, and that little spin ended in the ditch by the side of the road. The driver was killed, thank God, and Papa only had a broken leg. Naturally, he was very shaken up, which is why he can't be here with us all today."

It happened just as Hendrik had predicted. Sister Josy, wearing a bright yellow summer dress with red flowers embroidered all over it, jumped lightly from the train, fell upon her brother and excitedly demanded his congratulations. This time it was a man who had an important job at the Cologne radio station.

"I'm going to sing on the air," crowed Josy. "He thinks I'm very talented. We're going to be married in the autumn. Are you happy, Heinz—er—Hendrik?"—she corrected herself quickly and guiltily—"Are you happy too?"

Hendrik shook her off as if she were a tiresome little dog and hurried to help his mother, who was calling out of the compartment window for a porter. Josy meanwhile kissed Barbara on both cheeks. "Wonderful to meet you," she said. "I'm so glad Hendrik is getting married at last. Up to now I've always been the one to get engaged. Hendrik must have told you about how bad it all turned out last time. Papa's leg is still in a cast. But Konstantin really has a very good job with the radio. We're going to get married in October. You're looking wonderful, Barbara, where does your dress come from? It must be a genuine Paris model."

Hendrik had extricated his mother and her face shone with pleasure as she gave Barbara her hand. "My dear, dear child," said Frau Höfgen and her eyes grew moist. Hendrik smiled with tenderness and pride. He loved his mother—Barbara saw it and was pleased. True, Höfgen was often ashamed of her because he didn't think she was refined enough, and there was a middle-class quality about her that he found embarrassing. But he loved her and he showed it by the happy look on his eyes and the way he pressed her arm against his own.

How alike they looked, mother and son. Hendrik had inherited his mother's long, straight, somewhat too fleshy nose, her sensual mouth, her distinguished chin with its deep cleft and her wide gray-green eyes. They had the same arched blond eyebrows and even the sensitive, strained look about the temples.

The difference was that in the stout mother these features, unlike her son's, did not have a tragic cast to them. Frau Bella was an energetic, cheerful, well-preserved woman in her early fifties with a fresh complexion and an attractively open face. She had a comfortably round bosom and wore a flowered straw hat over blond hair set in a permanent wave. Her nose was lightly freckled.

"You've got to have a bit of fun from time to time," she began as the party was driven through town in an open car. She then launched into a long-drawn-out story about a particularly enjoyable charity bazaar held for the benefit of orphans in Cologne. It was an honor to participate, so Frau Höfgen had been happy to take over the champagne counter. Afterwards, however, there was dreadful talk about the whole affair and some crude people had suggested that Frau Bella had been dispensing her sparkling wine not for humanitarian reasons but because she had been paid to do so by the champagne firm. And they had been so low as to add that she had allowed herself to be kissed—think of that—and what was more, kissed on the bosom! Flushed with indignation, she wailed, "It was a low, groundless libel. People are so wicked. No matter how proper your behavior is, they always find something unpleasant to say about you— But now they'll have to stop their nasty innuendos, won't they, Hendrik? Because you'll stop them, won't you?" She cast a proud look at her son and at Barbara. Hendrik had suffered agonies as his mother pursued her tasteless monologue. He blushed, bit his lips and finally took desperately to commenting on the beauty of the street along which they were driving.

The privy councillor received the ladies at the garden gate with the same bright gaiety he had shown to Hendrik the previous day. Barbara took Bella and Josy upstairs to wash quickly and powder their noses. An hour later they drove in two cars to the Registry Office. In the Bruckners' car was the bridal pair, Frau Höfgen and the privy councillor. Josy and Nicoletta followed in a taxi with the old housekeeper and a childhood friend of Barbara's named Sebastian, whose presence caused Hendrik some surprise.

Nicoletta and the privy councillor acted as witnesses. Frau Bella and the little housekeeper wept, while Josy giggled nervously. Hendrik answered the registrar's questions in a muted voice with fixed and slightly narrowed eyes. Barbara turned her softly inquiring gaze to the man standing next to her, who now—astonishingly—was to be her husband. The civil ceremony was over quickly. Good wishes and embraces were exchanged. To everyone's surprise, Nicoletta asked Frau Höfgen sharply for permission to call her Aunt Bella; when this was granted, the actress bowed and, with an expression of diabolic courtesy, kissed the lady's hand. Nicoletta was looking particularly elegant and was in singularly high spirits. She held herself very straight in a stiff linen dress, which sheathed her like armor plate and was cinched at the waist with a bright red patent-leather belt. She said to Barbara, "I'm so happy, my love, everything has worked out so well"—a rather silly remark under the circumstances, but delivered with cutting clarity. Her beautiful cat's eyes gleamed. She took Josy aside to tell her about a wonderful cure for freckles that—she was making this up as she went along—her father had invented and spread throughout the Far East. "You are welcome to use it, dear girl," said Nicoletta with a threatening expression. "Your little nose is really spoiled by them." She looked with severity at the red blotches that spread across Josy's pert snub nose and covered part of her cheeks and forehead like a spiral nebula or Milky Way. "Yes, I know," said Josy miserably. "In summer it's always just terrible." But then, already reassured, she added, "Konstantin likes them very much." And she began to describe once again her future bridegroom's good position with the Cologne Radio.

Barbara's grandmother, a general's widow, made her first appearance at lunch. The old woman made it a matter of principle never to travel by car. She covered the six miles separating her small property from the Bruckner villa in a large old-fashioned carriage, and consequently she was always late for all family occasions. In a beautiful warm voice that went from deep bass to high treble, she bemoaned having missed the ceremony at the Registry Office. "And now let's see what you look like, my new grandson," she said, studying Hendrik with great concentration through the lorgnette that hung around her neck on a long silver chain set with blue jewels. Hendrik blushed and didn't know where to look. The examination lasted a long time. At last the general's widow dropped her lorgnette, and uttered a silvery laugh. "Not at all bad," she said, placing her hands on her hips. She nodded vivaciously at him.

Never in his life had Hendrik encountered such a remarkable old woman. She looked like an eighteenth-century aristocrat: her proud, intelligent face was framed in gray hair rolled into stiff curls over her ears. At the back of her head one expected to see a braid, and it was surprising and a little disturbing not to find it there. In her pearl-gray summer outfit decorated with lace ruffles at her neck and cuffs, the general's widow had an almost military bearing. She wore a wide necklace that was almost like a stiff collar. It was an antique of beautiful workmanship in unpolished silver and blue jewels that matched those on her lorgnette chain.

It was natural for the general's widow to set the tone for whatever group she found herself in. She had never known any other way. She had been considered one of the great beauties of German society well into the first two decades of the twentieth century. All the most celebrated artists of the period painted her portrait. In her drawing room princes and generals mixed with writers, artists and composers. For many years the brilliance and originality of the general's wife were as celebrated as her beauty in Munich and Berlin. Opinions that would have been viewed as eccentric and shocking from anyone else were forgiven her, because her husband had friends in the highest circles as well as a considerable fortune. Even the Kaiser was struck by her beauty, which enabled her to plead for women's suffrage in 1900. She knew Nietzsche's *Thus Spake Zarathustra* by heart and sometimes quoted passages from it, to the consternation of her aristocratic guests, who looked upon it as arrant socialism. She had known Franz Liszt and Richard Wagner; she had corresponded with Henrik Ibsen. Very probably she was opposed to the death penalty. She could do anything because of her remarkable presence, in which insouciance was allied with incomparable dignity.

The general's widow made a far greater impression on Hendrik than had the privy councillor, and he began to fully realize what a dazzling world he had entered. Faced with relations like these, the shopkeepers of Cologne would have to stop their insolent innuendos about the alleged drop in status of the Höfgen family. Barbara, too, rose higher in Hendrik's estimation now as he remembered how close was the link between her and this brilliant grandmother. Barbara had spent her school holidays and almost every Sunday at the estate of the general's wife, who had read Dickens and Tolstoy aloud to her granddaughter; reading aloud was a passion of the general's wife and she did it with great expressiveness. They had often gone out walking together through a countryside Hendrik imagined to be as distinguished and romantic as an English park with woods, small hills, gorges and valleys, cut across with silver streams, opening out onto wonderful vistas. Once again there was an element of envy in the delight with which Höfgen thought about Barbara's childhood. Had not this carefree childhood known the best of both worlds—the perfection of culture as well as almost perfect freedom? When Hendrik compared such a childhood with his own, it was hard for him to suppress a feeling of bitterness.

For in Cologne, at his father Köbes Höfgen's house, there had been no park, no carpeted rooms, no books or paintings. Instead, there had been musty rooms where Bella and Josy chattered on when guests were invited, but where the atmosphere grew sour and slovenly when the family was alone. His father was always deep in debt and complaining about the baseness of a world where his creditors harassed him. Even more painful than his bad moods were the bouts of high spirits which would suddenly overtake him from time to time, often on special holidays and sometimes for no particular reason at all. A little bowl of punch would then be prepared, and his father would ask his family to drink with him. But young Hendrik would refuse. He would sit pale and withdrawn in a corner with one thought in his head: I've got to get away from these surroundings. I've got to leave all this far, far behind me.

Barbara has had an easy life, he thought now as he talked with her grandmother. There has always been someone to smooth her path;

she is a typical product of the privileged few. She would be astounded by the hardness of the life I have known. What I shall achieve, and what I have already achieved, I owe completely to my own strength.

It was not without irritation that he said to his young wife, who had led him to the table where the telegrams of good wishes and wedding presents lay, "The messages of course are all for you. I never get cables." Barbara laughed in a way that struck him as mocking and complacent. "Not at all, Hendrik. Several people have sent congratulations just to you—Marder, for instance." From the high stack of letters, cards and cables she singled out the ones especially for Hendrik. Besides Theophilus Marder, whose message was framed in ambiguously formal and probably mischievously intended terms, there were congratulations from Angelika Siebert, the two directors—Schmitz and Kroge—Hedda von Herzfeld and—which appalled him—Juliette. How had she managed to discover his address and the date? Hendrik's face was pale and he crumpled this last message in his hand. To change the subject, he admired in an ironically exaggerated manner the gifts Barbara had received: porcelain, silver, books and jewelry—a large number of elegant and useful objects chosen with affectionate care by relations and friends.

"What are we going to do with all this loot?" asked Barbara, gazing helplessly at the laden table. Hendrik thought that these elegant objects would fit very well into his Hamburg rooms; however, he did not say so out loud, but shrugged disdainfully.

Sebastian, the young man whose presence had disturbed Hendrik, came up to them and began talking rapidly to Barbara, making many private allusions that Hendrik had difficulty following. Hendrik realized he had taken a great dislike to this man, whom Barbara called her best friend and who, she said, wrote beautiful poems and brilliant essays. He is arrogant and unbearable, thought Hendrik, who felt ill at ease in Sebastian's company despite the fact that the young man treated him pleasantly. But it was precisely this offhand and rather supercilious amiability that was so wounding. Sebastian had thick ash-blond hair that fell in a large lock over his forehead. He had a fine, drawn, rather tired face with a long prominent nose and gray eyes with a hazy unfocused look. His father, too, is probably a professor or something of the kind, Hendrik thought bitterly. It would be just such a pampered brilliant lad who could be the means of my undoing with Barbara.

After lunch they sat in the hall together, for it had become too hot for the terrace. Frau Bella considered it her duty to say something about literature. She said that in the train she had read something very nice, really so exciting. Now, who was the author—the name was on the tip of her tongue. "It was our Russian, our very greatest," cried the poor woman, racking her brains. "How could I have forgotten the name, when he has always been my very favorite writer?"

Nicoletta suggested that it perhaps might have been Tolstoy. "Quite right—Tolstoy," declared Frau Bella with relief. "I did say, didn't I—our greatest—and it was something that he has just written." But it soon emerged that the work that had given such pleasure to Frau Bella had been a short story by Dostoevsky. Hendrik flushed deep red. To change the subject and to show this arrogant audience that he would not forsake his mother in this painful situation, Hendrik engaged her in lively conversation, recalling with delighted laughter many amusing incidents from the past. How comic it had been when they both had gone completely mad at carnival time and startled his father out of his wits. Frau Bella had been dressed as a pasha and little Hendrik (whose name was Heinz in those days, although no mention was made of this) was dressed as a dancing girl. The whole house had been turned upside down; his father could not believe his eyes when he returned home.

"Mama was the first to realize that I must become an actor," said Hendrik, gazing affectionately at his mother. "For a long time Papa resisted every step of the way." Then he told the story about how he had embarked on his theatrical career. It was still wartime—1917—when Hendrik, who was scarcely eighteen years old, found a newspaper advertisement announcing that a company playing to the troops in Belgian-occupied territory was looking for a young actor. "But where I found this fateful piece of newspaper I cannot reveal," said Hendrik. When everyone laughed, he said in mock shame, his face hidden behind his hands, "Yes, yes—I'm afraid you've guessed it—in the john." The general's widow crowed shamelessly and her loud laugh sprang forth in bold coloratura that ranged from deepest bass to silvery soprano.

While the mood of the occasion became ever merrier, Hendrik moved on to anecdotes about the touring company where he had played all the older roles. Now relaxed and expansive, he could shine once more by bringing out all his long-treasured party pieces, for to this audience they were still unknown. Barbara had heard some of them, and for that reason the expression on her face as she listened to her husband was one of surprise mixed with a slight trace of distaste.

In the evening a few friends joined the party and Hendrik showed off his unpaid-for evening clothes. The table was beautifully decorated with flowers. After the main course the privy councillor tapped his champagne glass and rose to speak. He greeted the guests, singling out Hendrik's mother and sister—he called Frau Bella with facetious gallantry "the other young Frau Höfgen"—and went on to speak of the problem of marriage in general, and of the character and artistic merit of his new son-in-law. The privy councillor, choosing his words with amiable deftness, succeeded in presenting the actor Höfgen as a kind of fairy prince who, adopting an ordinary appearance by day, could undergo a magical transformation when night fell. "There he sits" cried Bruckner, pointing with his long index finger at Hendrik, who blushed deeply. "There he sits, only look at him. He appears to be just a slender young man—certainly very impressive in his well-cut tailcoat, but relatively undistinguished. Undistinguished, that is, beside the colorful, magical figure he becomes at night behind the footlights. There he begins to shine. There he becomes irresistible."

And carried away by his theme, the privy councillor compared Höfgen, whom he had never seen on the stage and only knew from the Rilke recitation, to a glowworm that out of artful modesty makes itself invisible by day only to glimmer seductively after dark. At this point Nicoletta let out a strident peal of laughter and the general's widow clattered her lorgnette chain.

The privy councillor ended with a toast to the health of the bridal pair. Hendrik kissed Barbara's hand. "How beautiful you look," he said and smiled intently into her upturned face. Barbara's dress was of a heavy tea-colored silk. Nicoletta had criticized it, complaining that it was not fashionable and looked like a fancy-dress costume run up by the local dressmaker. But it suited Barbara marvelously. Her neck rose light brown and slender above a broad collar made from old lace, which was one of the wedding presents of the general's widow. The smile with which she answered Höfgen was a little abstracted. Her dark blue eyes cast a soft questioning glance over Höfgen's shoulder. Whom was this look intended for? It seemed both troubled and a little mocking. Hendrik felt suddenly annoyed and turned away. He saw Sebastian standing, with his shoulders slumped, only a few paces away. His face seemed sad and strained, and he moved the fingers of both hands in an odd manner as though he were playing the piano in midair. What did this mean? Was he communicating with Barbara in a secret sign language? Why was this odious young man listening? And why the sadness on his face? Did he love Barbara? Certainly, he loved her—very probably he had wanted to marry her. Perhaps years back, there had been a childish engagement between them. Now I have spoiled everything for him, thought Hendrik; and he felt half triumphant and half horrified. How he hates me. He looked away from Sebastian and scrutinized the other friends of this celebrated household. It seemed to him they all looked sad. He saw men with well-defined features full of character. At the moment of introduction Hendrik had not caught their names; but they were certainly professors, writers, well-known doctors. There were a few young men, who all seemed to him to bear a depressing resemblance to Sebastian. The girls wore their evening dresses as though they were in disguise and were used to going around in gray flannel trousers, laboratory assistants' white smocks or green garden overalls. It seemed to Hendrik that the looks they cast in his direction were compounded of envy and mockery. Had they, then, all loved Barbara? Was he taking her away from them all? Was he the intruder—the suspicious, superficial character with whom they consorted only reluctantly because of Barbara's mystifying—and probably fleeting—caprice? Hendrik was convinced he monopolized their thoughts; they were talking about him, smiling about him, making fun of him . . .

He was suddenly so ashamed of himself that he wanted to creep away and hide. Hadn't even the privy councillor tended to make fun of him in his speech? Within a matter of seconds everything that had happened that day took on a hostile and degrading significance. The privy councillor's tolerant good humor that a short while earlier had made him so proud now appeared on closer reflection far more mortifying and humiliating than any outright severity or overt arrogance could have been. Now Hendrik perceived a wounding scorn behind the vivacity of the general's widow. Certainly, she was an imposing character, a great lady in the best tradition; and she looked ravishing as she now approached the young couple, dressed all in white with a gleaming pearl necklace wound three times around her throat, her head held high and her fingers playing nobly and carelessly with her lorgnette. If earlier in the day she had looked like an eighteenth-century marquise in her gray outfit, she now had an air of almost papal splendor.

The earthy high spirits of her speech made a delightful contrast to the grandeur of her appearance. "I must clink glasses again with my glowworm and my little Barbara," she declared in a ringing voice, brandishing a champagne glass.

Nicoletta appeared, flashing her eyes and making a hard thin line of her brightly painted mouth. "*Prost!*" shouted the general's widow. "*Prost,*" shouted Nicoletta. Hendrik first toasted the noble grandmama, and then turning to Nicoletta, suddenly realized that she was strikingly out of her element. Nicoletta owed her existence here to the inquisitive, generous tolerance of the privy councillor, the vigorous self-assurance of the general's widow and to the tender protection of Barbara. Hendrik experienced a very clear and strong feeling of solidarity—a brotherly sympathy for Nicoletta. Of course, her father had been a man of letters and an adventurer whose vitality and cynical intelligence fascinated the bohemian world at the turn of the century, while the petit-bourgeois insecurity of his own father could fascinate no one and was only of a kind to infuriate his creditors. But here, among these highly cultivated and immensely rich people (in fact, most of those present owned very little), among this self-confident and intelligent crowd in whose society Barbara could move with irritating assurance—here he and Nicoletta played the same outsider's role. In their hearts they were both determined to let this society carry them upwards to a point where they could triumph over it. That would be their revenge.

"*Prost,*" said Hendrik. His glass clinked lightly against Nicoletta's. Barbara, who had been chattering and laughing her way around the table, had reached her father. Silently she put her arm around his neck and kissed him.

The beautiful hotel on one of the Bavarian lakes had been recommended by Nicoletta, who accompanied the young couple on their short honeymoon. Barbara was very happy there: she loved the landscape with its meadows sweeping over hillsides, its forests and streams. It was gentle and lethargic, yet hiding beneath its surface was something harder—a hint of a future possibility of heroism, of danger. When the wind blew, the mountains seemed to come up close to the lake. In the light of the sunset their jagged peaks and snow-covered slopes were dyed blood-red. Barbara found them even more beautiful when in the hour before dusk they faded to an ethereal paleness and loomed above her in an icy peace made, it seemed, of some hard yet delicate substance that was neither metal nor stone but a material infinitely more rare, and as yet undiscovered by man.

Hendrik was unreceptive to the charm and magnificence of the landscape. The atmosphere of the elegant hotel made him uneasy. He was suspicious and irritable with the waiters. He claimed that they treated him worse than the other guests. And he reproved Barbara for having started already to encourage him to live beyond his means. But the social standing of the hotel's clientele pleased him. "There is hardly anyone here besides ourselves who isn't English," he said.

Despite Hendrik's nervousness they often had an enjoyable time. In the mornings, the three of them lay on the wooden pier, which stretched far out over the blue water. Every afternoon they welcomed a little white steamboat decorated with strange gilded ornaments. Nicoletta did calisthenics. She jumped rope, walked on her hands and leaned over backwards until her forehead touched the ground, while Barbara lay lazily in the sun. Afterwards, when they plunged into the lake, it was Barbara who made a better showing than the zealous Nicoletta: Barbara could swim faster and farther.

There was no question of Hendrik entering into any kind of athletic competition. He yelled when he so much as put his toes into cold water; and only after a great deal of goading and mockery could Barbara get him to try a few strokes. Fearful of getting out of his depth, his face clenched in anxious lines, Hendrik lumbered through the hostile element. Barbara watched him with an amused eye. Abruptly she called out to him, "You look ridiculously like your mother—the resemblance is even more striking when you are swimming. My God, you've got her face, there's no difference at all!" Whereupon Hendrik giggled so much that he couldn't move his arms any longer, swallowed a lot of water and almost drowned.

But Hendrik got his own back in the evening when they danced. All the hotel guests, and even the waiters, were captivated when he led Nicoletta or Barbara onto the floor for the tango. None of the other men in the hotel could muster such nobility and grace. Hendrik's tango was a theatrical performance; everyone clapped when it was over and he smiled and bowed as though he was taking a curtain call. When he had to be a member of the audience, a man among other men, he felt self-conscious and often bewildered; only when he could stand apart, step out into a bright spotlight and shine, did a sense of security return to him.

One day the newlyweds learned that on this very lake, whose beauty Nicoletta had so warmly recommended, Theophilus Marder had a summer villa. Barbara grew silent and her eyes darkened. At first she refused to visit the satirist. Finally, however, she let Nicoletta talk her into making the excursion. They boarded the white boat with gold ornaments that they had so often seen from the landing dock, and it steamed diagonally across the lake. The weather was beautiful. A light, fresh wind rippled the water, which was as blue as the bright sky. The more excited Nicoletta became, the quieter Barbara grew.

Theophilus Marder was awaiting his guests on the shore. He wore a bold checked sports coat with wide-pleated golf knickers and a white pith helmet that made for a very eccentric effect. He was smoking a short English pipe, which he did not remove from his mouth when he spoke. Nicoletta asked him when he had taken up smoking a pipe, and he answered with an abstracted smile, "The new man has new habits. I am changing mine. I startle myself every morning. For when I wake, I am no longer the same man I was when I went to sleep the night before. During the night my spirit has enormously increased in stature and strength. I make the most tremendous discoveries now while I sleep. That's why I sleep so much—at least fourteen hours a day."

This announcement, which was hardly designed to allay the forebodings aroused by the pith helmet, was followed by a cordial, bleating laugh. Then Theophilus was his civilized self once again. He treated Hendrik and Nicoletta with the most assiduous courtesy while appearing to overlook Barbara's presence altogether.

After lunch, which was served in a large, light and elegant dining room paneled in unstained wood, Theophilus put his arm on Höfgen's shoulder and drew him aside. "Now between us men," said the dramatist with a sly look and a smacking of his bluish lips under his mustache, "are you satisfied with your experiment?"

"With what experiment?" Hendrik asked.

"Now, what else—your marriage, of course," Theophilus whispered hoarsely. "You're really quite a fellow to get caught up in a thing like that. She's hard to make, this privy councillor's daughter. I know because I've tried." His eyes narrowed venomously. "You won't have much pleasure out of that one, my dear fellow. She's a lame duck—believe me, the greatest expert of the century—she's a lame duck."

Hendrik was so astounded by this speech that the monocle fell from his eye. Marder poked him cheerfully in the stomach. "No harm meant," he crowed, all of a sudden in the best of moods. "Perhaps you'll bring it off—one never knows—you certainly are quite a fellow."

During the entire afternoon he complained about the total lack of discipline that was such a sad feature of the century. Endlessly, he announced, "Nowhere are there any characters. There is only me left! However carefully I look around me, I never find anyone but myself." He compared himself to some of the great men of the past, the poet Hölderlin and Alexander the Great, and then praised the "good old days" when he himself was young. In this context he came to speak about Privy Councillor Bruckner. "Of course, he's colossally boring," declared Theophilus, "but certainly solid. Good old school—no charlatan; without question a relatively praiseworthy chap. The present age produces only idiots and criminals."

Then he showed the three young people his library, which contained several thousand volumes, and told them they should "start to learn something."

"You all know nothing," he roared suddenly. "The universal ignorance and imbecility cry out to heaven. A totally dissolute generation. For that reason a European catastrophe is unavoidable and, from the highest viewpoint, justified." But when he wanted to prove his point by putting Hendrik through a test in Greek irregular verbs, Barbara decided it was time to leave.

On the return journey in the steamer, Nicoletta explained that her father, the adventurer, must have been just like Theophilus Marder. "I have no pictures of Papa," she said and gazed pensively out over the water, which was no longer touched by the sun's rays and lay still, giving off a gray mother-of-pearl light in the rapidly falling dusk. "No pictures—only the opium pipe. But he must have

95

had a lot in common with Theophilus. I have a strong instinct that tells me that this is true—which is why I am so deeply linked to Marder."

After a short pause, Barbara spoke, "Your father was certainly much, much nicer than Marder. Marder is not at all nice." Nicoletta's cat's eyes flashed a malicious and amused look in her friend's direction, and she laughed softly to herself.

Almost every day after that, Nicoletta made the trip in the steamer to the opposite bank to visit Marder's villa. She left around noon and returned at night, often quite late. Barbara became ever more silent and thoughtful, especially in the presence of Nicoletta.

Moreover, Nicoletta's unwise and stubborn flirtation with Theophilus was not the only reason Barbara was lost in thought. At night, when she lay alone in her bed—and she did lie alone—she searched her heart to discover whether Hendrik's strange and rather disgraceful behavior, his failure as a husband, was a source of relief or disappointment to her. She finally decided that she was more relieved than disappointed.

Barbara's and Hendrik's rooms had a communicating door. At a late hour Höfgen, decoratively attired in his sumptuous but dilapidated dressing gown, would pay a visit to his wife. His head thrown back, his lids half closed over his gleaming eyes, he would stride across the room assuring Barbara in his singing voice how happy and thankful he was, and that she would always be the center of his existence. He would embrace her too, but only fleetingly, and turn pale as he held her in his arms. Trembling, with sweat breaking out on his brow, shame and anger would make his eyes fill with tears.

He had not been prepared for this fiasco. He had believed he loved Barbara. Yes, he did truly love her. Had his friendship with Princess Tebab corrupted him to such a point? It was true, he could not imagine green boots on Barbara's beautiful legs. He began to have a horror of these pitiable and unsuccessful embraces. He imagined he saw scorn and reproach in Barbara's eyes, when in fact they gazed back at him with no more than a quiet and somewhat amazed interrogation. To extricate himself from this ghastly situation, he chattered on, saying anything that came into his head; he became lively, dashing up and down the room laughing nervously.

"Have you got the same kind of frightful little memories as I have?" he asked Barbara, who lay motionless watching him. "You know, memories of a kind that make one go hot and cold all over when one thinks of them—and one has to think of them often." He stood leaning on Barbara's bed shaking with laughter, his face an unhealthy bright red, and with feverish haste continued, "I must have been eleven or twelve years old when I was allowed to join the boys' choir of our high school. This made me terribly happy, and I imagined I could sing better than all the others. Now comes the diabolical little memory; though it probably won't sound bad at all when I tell it now. There was a wedding, and our boys' choir had to sing for the church ceremony. It was a great occasion and we were all pretty excited. But I was possessed by the devil: I wanted to turn the thing into a great personal success. So when our choir began its pious hymn, I had such an enormously high opinion of my voice that I really thought it would make a charming effect if my shrill tones echoed in the church vaults. There I was, swollen with pride, letting out a piercing yell. The music teacher who was conducting gave me a look that was more sickened than punishing and said, 'Shut up, you!' Do you understand, Barbara"—Hendrik laid his hands on his flushed face—"do you understand how appalling that was? Quite dryly and softly he said to me, 'Shut up, you.' I who took myself to be a caroling archangel . . ."

Now Hendrik was silent. After a long pause he said, "Such memories are like little hells into which we must descend from time to time." With a mistrustful look he asked, "Don't you ever have memories of that sort, Barbara?"

No, Barbara was untroubled by such thoughts. This made Hendrik suddenly annoyed, almost angry, "That's just it," he cried vindictively, and there was a wicked light in his eyes. "That's just it. There has never been anything in your life you really needed to feel ashamed about . . . It has happened to me so often—only that was the first time. So often I've had to be so horribly ashamed—have had to descend into the hell of shame . . . Do you understand what I mean, Barbara?"

5

The Husband

The Höfgens and Nicoletta von Niebuhr returned to Hamburg at the end of August. Hendrik had rented from Frau von Monkeberg the entire ground floor consisting of three rooms, a small kitchen and a bathroom. Privy Councillor Bruckner helped in the furnishing of the three large comfortable rooms by paying for some new, fairly expensive things.

Nicoletta preferred to stay in a hotel. "I can't stand the narrow-minded philistine atmosphere of that house," she said irritably. Barbara suggested soothingly that the consul's wife was in her own way a very worthy, even attractive person. "In any case I get on wonderfully with her," she declared. On her arrival Frau Monkeberg gave her two kittens, one black and one white, and showed her every possible kindness. "I am happy, my child, to have you in my house," the old woman assured her new lodger. "We are part of the same world." The consul's wife, whose father had been a university professor, had in her youth known Dr. Bruckner when he was a lecturer in Heidelberg. She invited Barbara to tea upstairs, showed her family photographs and introduced her to her friends.

Nicoletta scolded Barbara fiercely for having accepted such an invitation. The people Nicoletta entertained in her hotel room were acrobats, gigolos and tarts. Hendrik trembled at the thought that in this unconventional world she might by an unlucky but not improbable chance encounter Princess Tebab. With what pleasure Fräulein von Niebuhr would have entertained the black Venus! For she practiced the inverse snobbery of priding herself on her eccentricity and depravity. "The people my father thought good enough to call his friends are not too bad for me, either," she would say.

There was no doubt at this time that Nicoletta was in splendid form. Everything about her seemed tensed, everything glittered, bewitched, crackled as though charged with electricity. More certain of succeeding than ever, she carried her boyish head high.

Most of the male members of the Arts Theater company were now terribly in love with her. Motz scolded and sobbed because Petersen once again lost all self-control, and in a reckless mood invited Nicoletta to a dreadfully expensive dinner at the Hotel Atlantic. Someone else who was bitterly resentful was Rahel Mohrenwitz, who'd become accustomed to acting as substitute for little Angelika in Bonetti's life, and now saw the stronger, more devastating charm of Nicoletta preferred to hers. To no avail the zealous Rahel painted her lips black violet, plucked her entire eyebrows and smoked long Virginia cigarettes that made her feel sick. Nicoletta's cat's eyes shone, and like those compulsive Indian tellers of folk tales, who bring their entranced audience to see palms growing in empty air and monkeys leaping through trees, she hypnotized everyone into believing she had marvelous legs.

Though Oskar H. Kroge could not stand Fräulein von Niebuhr, he had—on the insistent advice of his colleague Schmitz, who said people wanted to see "that kind of thing"—offered her the leading role in the first autumn production. It was a French box-office success in which Nicoletta played a tragic "kept woman" who at the end of the third act is murdered under the eyes of the audience. Bonetti was the young murderer; his arrogant, disdainful expression perfectly suited the role. The pimp, who looked like a man about town but underneath was a coarse brute, was played by Höfgen. Frau von Herzfeld, who had translated and adapted the piece, was in charge of the production.

"In this bit of nonsense you'll have an even greater success than you had in *Knorke*," Hedda told Nicoletta, for whom she had conceived a motherly affection ever since her jealousy on Hendrik's account had been concentrated on someone else. "That's my opinion too," answered Nicoletta coldly. "A performance the like of which I am going to give tomorrow has probably never been seen in Hamburg."

Schmitz superstitiously knocked on a table. "Touch wood," he said happily, "but it seems to me we are going to have a run of this production for at least thirty performances."

When the opening-night curtain fell, applause swept through the house. Nicoletta was called back over and over again. People would gladly have had her replay her death scene. Her cries and gestures as Rolf Bonetti turned his revolver on her were completely overwhelming. The bullet was fired. The tragic courtesan fell. Her limbs contorted. She screamed, and as she died delivered a long tirade of savage insults at her jealous lover in particular, and the male sex in general. She breathed a prayer, screamed once more and died.

Next day the critics chorused enthusiasm. All the newspapers agreed that Nicoletta was superb. NICOLETTA VON NIEBUHR AT THE START OF A GREAT CAREER was the headline on the front page of the *Mittagzeitung*, the paper with the largest circulation in the city. The Berlin press carried reports of the same kind. People began to queue up in the morning outside the Arts Theater box office—something that had not been seen in years. The next five performances of the spectacular drama of the life and death of a prostitute were immediately sold out.

But at noon on the day after the first night Nicoletta received the following telegram from Theophilus Marder:

DEMAND YOU COME TO ME IMMEDIATELY STOP FORBID YOU CONTINUE PROSTITUTING YOURSELF AS ACTRESS STOP VIRILE SENSE OF HONOR IN ME PROTESTS AGAINST YOUR DEGRADATION STOP DISCIPLINED WOMAN MUST BELONG UNCONDITIONALLY TO MAN OF TOTAL GENIUS WHO WISHES TO RAISE HER TO HIS LEVEL STOP IF IN MOMENT OF SUPREME DECISION YOU REFUSE AND FOR ANY REASON DELAY ARRIVAL CONSIDER SELF DEFINITELY REJECTED BY ME. THEOPHILUS.

Nicoletta imperiously dismissed a few ballet dancers who had come to congratulate her on her success. She phoned Höfgen and announced dryly that she intended to leave for South Germany in an hour's time. Hendrik asked whether she was joking or had gone out of her mind. "Neither," she answered witheringly. Rather, she was renouncing her present engagement with the Arts Theater and her entire career as an actress. The part of the French whore could easily be taken over by Rahel Mohrenwitz, who already knew it. As for her, Nicoletta, only one thing now mattered in the world—the love of Theophilus Marder.

"The disciplined woman belonged entirely and unconditionally at the side of the man of genius who wanted to raise her up to his level." So said Fräulein von Niebuhr over the telephone to the astounded Höfgen.

The horror of it all almost deprived Hendrik of his voice. He murmured, "You're sick. I'm taking a taxi over to see you right away." Ten minutes later he was standing with Barbara beside Nicoletta, who was busy packing.

The noble and sensitive oval of Barbara's face was as white as the wall against which she was leaning. Barbara said nothing. Nicoletta said nothing. Hendrik talked. At first he scoffed, then he beseeched, finally he threatened and raged. "You have a contract! There are legal penalties."

Nicoletta remarked softly but still with the greatest clarity: "Herr Kroge is unlikely to find much pleasure in bringing suit against Theophilus Marder for the possession of my person."

"Your career is ruined," Hendrik warned her. "No theater in the world will engage you again."

"I have already told you," Nicoletta said, "I'm renouncing my career with uttermost joy. What I exchange it for is incomparably more valuable, more fundamental, more beautiful." Now her voice was no longer sharp but filled with suppressed exultation. Hendrik could scarcely conceal his shock. He was mystified. This girl was living proof that there were passions that could take such a powerful hold on people they were ready to throw aside a career—even one that had opened with such enormous promise. Hendrik was incapable of imagining emotions beyond the compass of his own heart. The passions to which he yielded generally had consequences that were beneficial to his career; on no account were they allowed to endanger or disturb it. "And all because of that snotty prophet," he said at last.

At that, Nicoletta drew herself up and hissed, "I forbid you to speak in such a way of my future bridegroom, the greatest living human being."

Hendrik smiled wearily and wiped the sweat from his forehead. "Well," he said, "now I must break the news to poor Kroge."

While he was phoning the Arts Theater, Barbara spoke for the first time in a saddened voice. "So, you want to marry him?"

"If he will have me," said Nicoletta, taking care to avoid her friend's eyes.

Barbara said, "He is thirty years older than you. He could be your father."

"Exactly," said Nicoletta with the light of madness shining in her eyes. "He *is* like my father. I have found in him the man I lost."

Barbara said imploringly, "He is sick."

But, head held high, her friend declared, "He has the superior health of genius."

Barbara could only groan, "My God, my God," and she sank her face in her hands.

By the time Oskar H. Kroge, Schmitz and Hedda von Herzfeld arrived, Nicoletta had packed her many cases and was standing in the hotel lobby waiting for a taxi to take her to the station.

Schmitz screamed at her, threatening police and prison. Oskar H. Kroge spat rage like an old tomcat while Nicoletta thrust back like a vulture. Hedda tried reasonable persuasion, but fell silent under the barrage of Nicoletta's shrill and icy scorn. They all talked at once: Schmitz bemoaned the sold-out houses; Kroge spoke of lack of artistic responsibility and human decency; Hedda described Nicoletta's conduct as the hysteria of delayed adolescence. In the meantime Barbara had left the hotel without anyone's noticing, and without saying good-bye to Nicoletta.

Nicoletta's abrupt departure caused Barbara pain, but also a feeling very close to relief. She received the news of the wedding of Nicoletta and Theophilus Marder "in complete privacy" without any special emotion. Poor Nicoletta. It had turned out just as Barbara had always known it would. And now Barbara must learn to live without the fickle pleasures of a friendship that over the years had absorbed, delighted and tortured her. It was hard to think of a future without Nicoletta. Nevertheless, she loved to cast her mind back over the past and tell herself the story of a friendship that had come into being in strange circumstances and then had developed so peculiarly.

Willy von Niebuhr, the father whose life had followed such a reckless course—if not perhaps quite as adventurously as his daughter made out—had never paid much notice to Nicoletta. The girl was thirteen when he died in China. She had just been expelled with considerable scandal from the school in Lausanne. Niebuhr, who knew he had not long to live, wrote from Shanghai to Bruckner, who had been his friend in student days, "Look after the child." The privy councillor had decided to take the girl in for a few weeks until a suitable new school or some other form of upbringing could be found for her.

It was thus that Nicoletta arrived in the Bruckner household: a solemn, clever and willful creature. Everything about this young guest struck the privy councillor as sinister: the seductive, threatening gaze, the excessively clear, cuttingly accentuated speech, the unnerving correctness of her behavior. He found it fascinating but also painful to have the strange daughter of a longtime friend living in his house and to have to keep his eye on her.

It surprised him—but he made no attempt to prevent it—that Barbara formed such an intense friendship with Nicoletta. What drew his child to this exotic, disturbing girl? Lovingly he wondered if Barbara was seeking in Nicoletta the being most different from herself in every way. However, this friendship was sufficiently disturbing to him so that he began to look for a way of getting Nicoletta out of the house. She was sent to a pension on the French Riviera; but there, too, there was soon a scandal, and Nicoletta returned to the Bruckner villa. Again, she was sent away and again returned; it became an oft-repeated game. Barbara was always waiting, and always welcomed her back. The privy councillor saw it, wondered, worried over it, but tolerated it. After all, his beautiful clever daughter in no way neglected her own life while participating so intensely in the strange existence of her friend. She occupied herself in a playful and thoughtful way with a thousand things: she had other friends, to whose moods and worries she brought a patient sympathy. She was both frivolous and lost in dreams, half-Amazon and half-nun; cold and generous, prudish, and carefully tender. That was Barbara's life, and perhaps it was the fact that she was always waiting for Nicoletta and at any hour of the day was prepared for her unannounced appearance that gave her life a secret meaning, a mysterious center of gravity that it needed.

Nicoletta had always come back. But this time Barbara knew that she would not. This time something decisive had happened. Nicoletta believed that in Theophilus Marder she had found the man who was the equal of her father, or the legendary figure she had made of him. Now she no longer needed Barbara. She dedicated herself to this rediscovered father and new lover with the dramatic fervor that characterized all her actions. Although she held her head high, Nicoletta nevertheless loved to be ordered about, and she subjected herself to Marder's extravagant and neurotic will. What was left for Barbara? Much too proud to impose herself—too proud even to complain—she kept silent and turned an impenetrably serene face to the world. Poor Nicoletta, she thought, now you must manage your life on your own. It will not be an easy life—poor Nicoletta.

In any case, Barbara did not have much time to think about her friend Nicoletta. Her new everyday life in a strange city with a strange husband laid claim to her. She must get used to living with Hendrik Höfgen. Could she gradually learn to love this man to whose pathetic courtship she had yielded partly out of curiosity and partly from pity? Before Barbara even put this question to herself she had to try to answer another which struck her as decisive. Did Hendrik still love her? Had he *ever* loved her? Barbara's intelligence and experience had taught her to be skeptical; and she now doubted whether the passion Hendrik had demonstrated during the first weeks of their acquaintance had ever been genuine. I have been deceived, was the thought that often crossed her mind. I have let myself be duped by an actor. It seemed useful for his career to marry me, and apart from that he needed someone by his side. But he has never loved me. Probably he is incapable of love . . .

Pride, good breeding and compassion prevented her from voicing her mortification and letting her disillusionment show. But Hendrik was perceptive enough to sense what she—more out of pride than kindliness—was hiding from him. It escaped her cleverness that he suffered.

He was filled with anguish by the failure of his feelings for Barbara and by his repeated physical failures. He groaned under his defeat, for the kindling of his emotion, the ardor of his heart had been real, or very nearly real—real to the highest degree possible for him. I shall never feel stronger and purer than in those early summer days after the *Knorke* first night, Hendrik told himself. If I fail this time, then I am condemned to always fail. Then it will be certain that all my life I shall belong to girls like Juliette.

But, as in almost everyone, self-accusation—however sincere and bitter it may be—turns after a certain point into self-justification. Thus he soon began to collect arguments he could use against Barbara and that could ease his own conscience. When he came to think about it, wasn't it Barbara's aloofness that had blunted the ardor of his passion? Didn't Barbara have far too high an opinion of her distinguished origins and intellect? Didn't mockery and arrogance lie in the searching glance she so often turned on him? Hendrik began to fear those eyes, which had seemed to him only a short while ago the most beautiful he had ever seen. Hendrik's irritation and wounded pride made him see double meanings even in Barbara's most casual and trivial remarks. Her little habits, and the quiet imperturbability with which she remained faithful to them, frayed his temper to such a degree that even he had to admit to himself on sober reflection that he was being unreasonable.

As was her habit, Barbara had gone riding before breakfast and when she appeared in the dining room at about nine she brought a breath of fresh morning air with her. But Hendrik sat looking haggard, his head resting in his hands, tired and bad-tempered in his dressing gown, which was even more worn than before. At this hour he could muster no seductive smile, no enticing shimmering of the eyes. Hendrik yawned. "You look half asleep," said Barbara equably and poured a soft-boiled egg into a wineglass. It was in this manner that she ate eggs for breakfast: out of glasses and sprinkled with a lot of salt and pepper, sharp English sauce, tomato juice and a little oil. Hendrik retorted icily, "I'm fairly wide awake and have already done some work. For instance I've had a telephone conversation with the local store which is becoming impatient about our large account with them. Forgive me for not presenting a fresh appearance in the early mornings. If I went riding every day like you, I would no doubt look far more lively. But I fear even you can no longer lure me into such fashionable ways. I am too old to change and I come from a background in which such noble sports are not practiced."

Barbara, who did not want to have her good mood spoiled, decided to take this speech as humorously intended. "You adopt that tone wonderfully," she said with a laugh. "One could almost think that you meant it seriously." Hendrik remained angrily silent; to look more imposing, he rammed his monocle in his eye.

To make matters worse, Barbara annoyed him again, certainly without meaning to. While she ate her seasoned egg with a good appetite she said, "You should try to eat your egg this way. I find that without sharp seasoning it tastes insipid."

After a pause, Hendrik asked with a politeness trembling with irritation. "Can I draw your attention to something, my love?"

"Of course."

Hendrik drummed his fingers on the table, thrust out his chin and pursed his lips, which gave him the air of a governess. He spoke slowly. "Your naïve, demanding way of showing amazement or derision when anyone does anything in a way not customary in the house of your father or your grandmother could astound or even shock people who know you less well than I do."

Barbara's eyes, which a moment earlier were of a joyful brightness, clouded over, and she stared at him searchingly. "What led you to make that observation at this moment?" she asked quietly.

Still drumming energetically on the table, Hendrik answered, "It is usual all over the world to eat a soft-boiled egg out of its shell with salt. In the Villa Bruckner they eat them out of a glass, with six different seasonings. That's certainly original. But I see no reason to make fun of someone who is not accustomed to these refinements."

Barbara made no reply, shook her head in amazement and rose from the table. Hendrik watched her as she went with her indolent, careless step slowly across the room. An irrepressible thought crossed his mind: Strange—now she is wearing high boots, but on her legs they don't give the effect I so much want and need. On her, boots are simply a fitting piece of riding attire. On Juliette they mean something different . . .

It was with a feeling of malevolent triumph that he silently invoked Juliette's name in Barbara's presence; he felt compensated for many slights. You go off on your horse, he thought sardonically. You make yourself cocktails out of boiled eggs. You don't know who I'm going to meet this afternoon before the rehearsal. As Barbara left the room, he felt the vulgar satisfaction of a husband who is being unfaithful to his wife and is proud she has not found him out.

Already, the second week after his return, Hendrik had met the black Venus again. She had waylaid him as he entered the theater one evening. With a shudder of pleasure and horror he had heard that hoarse, familiar voice call out from a dark doorway, "Heinz." That name of which he was so ashamed, and which he had rejected, uttered by the muffled voice of the Negress was a savage caress that did him good. However, he forced himself to say to the black girl, "What do you think you're doing—spying on me." Her answer was a derisive gesture of her powerful, sensual hand. "Forget it, honey. If you aren't careful I'll come into the theater and make a scene." It was no good his whispering, "You're trying to blackmail me." She merely grinned. "Of course," she said, her eyes and teeth glittering. Her broad laugh was of an appalling but irresistible coarseness. He pushed Juliette into the doorway, for he shuddered at the thought that someone could come by and see him in such company. Princess Tebab looked as though she had come down a lot in the world. The little felt hat she wore pulled down over her forehead had the same harsh green color as the high shining boots. Around her neck she wore a small boa of soiled, tousled white feathers. Above this sad finery rose the broad dark face with its protruding rough lips and flat nose.

"How much money do you want?" he asked hastily. "I'm fairly hard up at the moment."

She answered almost impishly, "It isn't done with money, my little sugar monkey. You have to visit me."

"What's come over you?" he stammered through trembling lips. "I'm married."

But she interrupted him fiercely: "None of that shit, my lamb. The lady wife can't give you what you need. I've had a look at her, your Barbara." (How did she know her name? The innocuous fact that she knew Barbara's name filled Hendrik with a special fright.) "That person hasn't got what it takes," said Princess Tebab, rolling her wild eyes. Her threatening tone demanded a prompt and exact answer: "So—when are you coming to see me?"

The macabre exercises that earlier had had as their setting Frau Monkeberg's basement began again in an attic, whose gray bleakness was not alleviated but, rather, was given a touch of the grotesque by a sentimental, garish reproduction of a Raphael Madonna over the bed. Here, twice a week, the young husband breathed once again the exotic but familiar smell that seemed a mixture of cheap perfume and the scent of the jungle. Here once again he obeyed the rasping voice, the clapping hands and rhythmical stamping feet of his mistress. Here once again he declaimed French poetry when, groaning with exhaustion, he had sunk down on the hard plank bed where the king's daughter slept. But now these sinister festivities reached an abominable paroxysm that was new to him. When all was over, and Juliette let her gratified and exhausted pupil rest, Hendrik began to talk about his wife.

What he hid from the discreetly probing and jealous inquisitiveness of his friend Hedda von Herzfeld, and from the comradely interest of his political companion Otto Ulrichs, he disclosed to his black Venus. He confessed to her what he suffered because of Barbara. To her, and only to her, he forced himself to tell the truth. He concealed nothing—not even his private shame. When Fräulein Martens learned of his physical defeat, his marital disgrace, she broke into a peal of harsh laughter—this laughter seemed harder for him to bear than the fiercest blows. The black princess grinned maliciously at him. "Well, if that's so, honey—if that's how you behave, you can't expect your beauty to treat you with any particular respect."

He told her about Barbara's morning rides, which he considered a constant provocation. He complained about all her proud whims. "She makes herself a cocktail out of a boiled egg with ten kinds of sharp sauces, and then looks down on me because I eat my egg out of a shell like a normal human being! Everything in my home has to be done as close as possible to how it's done at her father's and grandmother's. That's why she won't let me hire little Böck as a servant. He is an excellent young fellow, devoted to me, and she could never gang up with him against me. But no—she won't let anyone in our household who is on my side. She says little Böck would never be able to keep the place neat. Which shows she knows absolutely nothing about him. He has been my dresser in the theater for years and I can swear that he is order itself. In place of him we now have some disagreeable old woman who was a housemaid for twenty years in the house of the general's wife—just so that nothing need ever change in the life of my gracious lady!"

The black Venus listened patiently. She was also informed that Barbara visited the homes of good Hamburg families—"Privy councillors and bank managers," said Hendrik spitefully—where he, the actor Höfgen, was not invited, or only in a contemptuous way "invited to come along too," which compelled him to refuse. Barbara visited a number of places that seemed to him strange or definitely hostile—lecture halls and salons. Also her voluminous correspondence got on his nerves. She was always writing or receiving letters. Hendrik did not know many of those with whom she maintained such regular communications, and he complained bitterly about this to the black Venus. He wanted to know if Juliette also thought that in these letters Barbara sent to her father, the general's widow or to her inseparable childhood friend Sebastian there might be wounding references to himself. Princess Tebab could not deny this possibility, nor did she wish to. "Certainly in her letters she must make fun of me," exclaimed Hendrik indignantly. "If she did not have something to hide she would surely show me just once the many answers she receives. But she never shows me anything." Hendrik found this particularly sinister and incriminating, because he often showed Barbara letters he received from his mother. "I won't do it any more, though," he said now with determination to the princess. "Why should I take her into my confidence, when she behaves with such total furtiveness? And besides, she has the nerve to laugh over my mother's letters." What had actually happened was that Barbara had laughed heartily when Hendrik showed her the letter in which Frau Höfgen reported the breakup of Josy's latest engagement. "Naturally we are all very happy that the thing once again ended so well," wrote the poor mama. At this Barbara couldn't contain her laughter, and Hendrik had joined in her glee. At the time he found this passage in his mother's letter quite as funny as it appeared to Barbara. It was only in retrospect that anger overtook him. "Everything is sacred about her family," he cried. "The general's widow and her lorgnette are above criticism. But my mother is fit only for mockery."

It was always at the end of his visits that Hendrik poured forth his confidences and lamentations. Before he laid five marks on the bedside table of Juliette's gloomy attic room and left, Hendrik told his princess he loved her much more than Barbara. "That is absolutely not true," answered Juliette in her quiet, deep voice. "You're lying again." Whereupon Hendrik gave her a pained smile. "Am I lying?" he asked softly. And then, abruptly lifting his chin, he said in a ringing voice, "Well, I must be off to the theater . . ."

The rehearsals for the new production of *A Midsummer Night's Dream*, in which Hendrik played the fairy king Oberon, and the preparations for a large revue were more important and exacting than the complicated and futile problem as to whom he loved more, Barbara or Juliette.

"People like us have no right to let private affairs get in the way of our work," he explained to his friend Hedda. "When all is said and done, one is first and foremost an artist."

Barbara, who spent her time in sports, reading, drawing and letter writing or in the auditoriums of the university, sometimes appeared in the evenings in the theater to fetch Hendrik from rehearsals. Occasionally she spent an hour waiting in the dressing rooms or in H.K.—something that Hendrik did not view with a tolerant eye. He suspected his wife was trying to incite his colleagues against him and was strongly opposed to the establishment of too close a contact between her and the Arts Theater Company. In vain Barbara asked to be allowed to design the stage sets for one of the many new productions that winter. Hendrik invariably promised her he would propose to the directors that she should be given an assignment, but he always came back with the news that although directors Schmitz and Kroge had nothing against the idea, everything foundered on the resistance of Frau von Herzfeld.

The assertion was not a total fabrication. In fact, Hedda sulked and became obstructive whenever Barbara's name was mentioned. Acute jealousy made this bright woman spiteful and unjust. She could not forgive Barbara for marrying Hendrik. To be sure, Frau von Herzfeld had never been so bold as to hope that she herself had a chance with Höfgen. She knew the special tastes of the man she loved: she had been initiated into the dark and painful secret of his relations with Princess Tebab. The role with which she had to be content— and for years had made herself content—was that of the sisterly friend and confidante. But it was precisely this that Barbara now threatened to take from her. For Hedda, it amounted to a triumph that her rival did not appear to be satisfactorily fulfilling her highly enviable task. Hendrik did not say this in so many words, but the sharpened instinct of the jealous woman sensed it all the same.

Frau von Herzfeld knew what had gone wrong: The privy councillor's daughter was too demanding. You had to know how to deny yourself and take second place if you wanted to get on with Hendrik Höfgen. Obviously a man of his kind thought above all of himself. Barbara, however, wanted and expected something from him.

She demanded happiness. This thought drew a sardonic laugh from Hedda. Hadn't the proud Barbara grasped the basic premise of her marriage? The only happiness that a man like Hendrik Höfgen could bestow was the excitement of his presence, the intoxication of his closeness. Little Siebert had made the same discovery. But this charming, tender creature was even more deeply resigned where Hendrik was concerned than the aging Herzfeld. Little Siebert suffered, but she harbored no hatred. She greeted Höfgen's wife with timid respect. When this enviable creature dropped a handkerchief, Angelika quickly stooped to pick it up. Rather astonished, Barbara thanked her and little Siebert blushed and laughed nervously, anxiously narrowing her near-sighted eyes. If Barbara's relations with Hedda and Angelika, the two crestfallen lovers, were complicated and full of stress, she made up for it with the other women in the company. With Motz she talked at length about the price of food, dressmakers and the faults of men in general and the character actor Petersen in particular. Barbara was so understanding a listener to the outpourings of this worthy and temperamental woman that Motz formed the opinion—which she expressed aloud whenever the subject came up—that young Frau Höfgen was "a wonderful person." Mohrenwitz had come to the same conclusion: Barbara, who never wore makeup and had no pretensions to being a *femme fatale,* could never be a threat to the abandoned Rahel.

Both Peterson and Rolf Bonetti called Hendrik's young wife "a good sort." Father Hansemann treated her with gruff kindness, because she paid on the spot for what she consumed. The stage doorman, Knurr, gave her a military salute, because he knew she was the daughter of a privy councillor. The directors, Schmitz and Kroge, liked to talk with her. Schmitz at first confined himself to the joking tone of an elderly uncle; but he soon discovered she took a wise and practical interest in the financial worries of the theater and he would draw her into long conversations about this pressing topic. As for Oskar H. Kroge, he revealed to her his concern about the quality of the repertoire of the Arts Theater. The old pioneer of the avant-garde stage looked on sorrowfully as farces and operettas began to crowd out serious plays in his theater. This regrettable development was not only the fault of Schmitz, who had to judge plays on their probable box-office takings; Höfgen was also to blame for the drop in literary standards—paradoxical as that might appear. He spoke of the Revolutionary

Theater but he put on trivial comedies. The Revolutionary Theater, which had still not been opened, was advanced as the pretext for staging box-office successes.

Kroge, despite his objection in principle to communism, had gone so far as to recommend earnestly that a start be made on the proposed project, which could bring not only a revolutionary spirit but also a literary quality back into his theater. But Hendrik asserted with fine eloquence that it was absolutely essential to humor the public and the press by putting on lighter and more popular shows before he could take the plunge with the Revolutionary Theater. Perhaps Otto Ulrichs, as patient as he was enthusiastic, believed these arguments put forward by his good friend. But Barbara was more skeptical and more worried.

She liked talking to Ulrichs. The intransigence and simplicity of his outlook impressed her. She was always careful to say that she understood nothing about politics—which Hendrik sarcastically confirmed. "You have no concept of the real seriousness of these things," he said, putting on his tyrannical-governess face. "You approach everything playfully, in a mood of detached curiosity—revolutionary faith is an interesting psychological phenomenon for you. But for us it's the most sacred thing in life." Thus spoke Hendrik. Ulrichs, who gave half his time and earnings to the political struggle, appeared much less rigid. His tone with Barbara was one of fatherly didacticism but full of sympathy. "You will find your way to us, Barbara, I know you will," he said. "You know already, I'm sure, that truth and the future are on our side. Only, you are still a little bit afraid to admit it and to face all the consequences."

"Perhaps I'm a little anxious, that's all," Barbara answered with a smile.

She never ceased to be amazed by the patient good nature with which Ulrichs accepted Hendrik's postponements in the matter of the Revolutionary Theater. She herself exerted what pressure she could. She had a small egotistic private reason for doing so—she wanted to design the stage setting for the first production of the revolutionary cycle. "It is none of my business," she said almost daily to Hendrik, "and I am not the one for whom belief in the world revolution is the most important thing in life. But I am ashamed for you, Hendrik. If you don't do something serious about this soon, you're going to look ridiculous."

Hendrik went pale and squinted. He answered with freezing superciliousness: "That is a dilettante way of talking. You are completely ignorant of revolutionary tactics."

His revolutionary tactics amounted to daily thinking up new reasons why a start could not be made on rehearsals for the Revolutionary Theater. However, so that there should be something accomplished in the interests of world revolution he suddenly decided to give a lecture on "The Theater of Our Epoch and Its Moral Duties." Kroge, whose enthusiasm for this theme was limitless, placed the Arts Theater for a Sunday morning at Höfgen's disposal. Hendrik's lecture was an artful blend of the language of its enthusiastic director and the vocabulary of Otto Ulrichs. It was an emotional and uncommitted oration, in which both the liberal-minded audience and the young Marxist revolutionary crowd could find many of their favorite slogans.

At the close everyone applauded, and almost everyone was convinced of Hendrik's sincere artistic and political determination—which was confirmed for him at length by the newspaper critics the following day.

Hendrik had been waiting for just such a confirmation. "Now the situation is ripe, we can proceed," he declared, exchanging conspiratorial glances with Ulrichs. The first rehearsal for the Revolutionary Theater was announced. Certainly the chosen play was not the radical work that had been selected the previous year. At the last moment Hendrik had—for tactical reasons—decided on a war tragedy, which in three somber acts portrayed the misery of the winter of 1917 in a large German city. The play was of a generally pacifist character but in no way discernibly socialist. Barbara designed the sets: a dark back room and a gray alley in which women queued for bread. Otto Ulrichs and Hedda von Herzfeld were to play the main parts.

Höfgen, the director, worked up great ardor at the first rehearsal. With a controlled, simple pathos he declaimed the long tirade that Hedda was to deliver at the end of the third act in her role as the tragic mother. Otto Ulrichs wiped his eyes furtively and even Barbara was impressed. But at the second rehearsal Hendrik was suffering from nervous hoarseness; at the third, he was limping—his right knee had suddenly become stiff, he complained he could no longer bend it. Finally, at the fourth rehearsal he appeared with such a sallow angry face that he frightened everyone—not entirely without reason, as was to emerge later. He was in such a terrible temper that he called Frau von Herzfeld "a stupid goose" and threatened the prompter, Frau Efeu, with instant dismissal.

"You are sabotaging our work," he shouted at her, "and do you think I don't know why? Presumably Herr Miklas's party friends have given you this assignment! But we'll put an end to your activities— you, your Herr Miklas, the charming Herr Knurr and the whole damn gang—just you wait!" In vain Efeu wept and protested her innocence.

After this rehearsal, which left a bad taste in everyone's mouth, Höfgen took to his bed with jaundice. He stayed away from the theater for two weeks. Ulrichs, Bonetti and Hans Miklas shared his leading roles. After his recovery he still looked extremely subdued and exhausted, and his glistening eyes were covered with a yellowish glaze. The opening of the Revolutionary Theater was postponed indefinitely: the doctor had expressly forbidden Herr Höfgen to undertake any work beyond his unavoidable daily tasks.

There was at least one member of the Arts Theater Company for whom this development caused great joy. Hans Miklas glowed with triumph. He had of course known immediately that the whole story of the Revolutionary Theater was an outsize swindle. He said as much aloud in H.K. and the reproving glances of Frau von Herzfeld could not dissuade him from saying it repeatedly. His obstinate face shone with satisfaction. He was in a good humor all day long, whistling and humming; there were no black hollows in his cheeks, he coughed hardly at all and even treated Frau Efeu to a glass of schnapps. Such a thing had never happened before and the good woman said, "Boy, you've quite taken leave of your senses today."

Inevitably, the happy incident caused only a temporary improvement in young Miklas's temper. The following day his face appeared to be once again malevolently clenched; the black hollows had reappeared under his cheekbones and his cough sounded alarming. How he hates us all! thought Barbara, who was watching him. She was not unreceptive to the somber charm of the untamed young man. His face under its mop of unruly hair, his broad forehead, the dark circles under his sulky eyes and the contemptuous, unhealthily dark mouth were much more attractive to her than the arrogance and exhausted appearance of the handsome Bonetti. There was something about the thin, wiry body of young Miklas—this constantly exercised, supple, ambitious body—that moved Barbara and prompted her from time to time to talk with him. At first with dour mistrust he repulsed the overtures of the wife of the hated Höfgen. But gradually Barbara succeeded in winning him around to a more friendly and trustful attitude. Sometimes she invited him to have a beer and sandwich with her in H.K.—a sign of appreciation that pleased Hans Miklas greatly. It was especially when Hendrik had enraged Barbara that it gave her pleasure to talk to the angry young man.

"Shall we treat ourselves to another rebellious evening?" she would ask him. And he accepted gladly: he was always ready for a rebellious evening, particularly when an offer of beer and meat went with it.

With an interest in which there was an element of dread, Barbara listened as Hans Miklas detailed his loves and hates. Never before had she sat at the same table with a man who voiced the kind of opinions that this boy put forward with such fanaticism. It became clear to her that he detested or despised everything that was dear and indispensable to herself, her father and her friends. What was he getting at when he violently attacked "corrupt liberalism" or jeered at "certain Jewish and Jew-loving circles" which according to him were sending German culture to the dogs? Yes, thought Barbara, he means everything I have ever loved and believed. When he says "Jewish rabble," he means spiritual values and liberty. And deep down she felt afraid. Nevertheless, Barbara's curiosity induced her to pursue a conversation that assumed in her mind a weird phantasmagoric quality. It seemed to her that she was suddenly transported out of the civilized world she had always known and set down in a wild and barbaric landscape completely alien to her.

What brought joy to such a mysterious creature as Hans Miklas? What ideas and ideals fired his aggressive enthusiasm? He dreamed of a German culture cleansed of "Jewishness." Barbara could only shake her head in astonishment. When her strange companion contended that "the shameful Versailles treaty" should be torn up and the German nation must once again be "ready for battle," his eyes lit up and even his forehead appeared to shine. "Our Führer will restore the German people's honor!" he cried. "We will no longer tolerate the shame of the republic, which is despised by foreigners. We want our honor back again—every decent German demands that. And there are decent Germans everywhere, even in this Bolshevik theater. They should hear how Herr Knurr speaks when he isn't afraid he is being overheard. He lost three sons in the war. But he says that wouldn't have been so bad if Germany hadn't lost its honor. And it is the Führer—and only the Führer—who can restore our honor."

But, Barbara thought, why does he get so worked up about German honor? What mental picture does he have of this vague concept? Is it so enormously important for him that Germany should once again have tanks and submarines? Surely he should first see that he get rid of his dreadful cough and have a success in a good part and earn more money so that he can eat his fill every day. Certainly he eats too little and works too hard—he has a dreadfully overstrained look. She asked him whether he would like another ham sandwich. He nodded swiftly, but then continued in the same ecstatic vein, "The day will come. Our movement must win."

Barbara remembered hearing a similar statement of exalted belief from another source—from Otto Ulrichs. She had not ventured to contradict Ulrichs, for both emotionally and intellectually she was all but convinced by his ardently well-argued faith. But to Miklas she said, "If one day Germany really becomes what you and your friends want it to be, then I would rather have nothing more to do with it. I would leave the country." Barbara smiled at Miklas in a thoughtful, not unfriendly way. But the young man exulted: "I can believe it. A whole mob of gentlemen and ladies are going to make a run for it— that is, if we let them go and don't put them behind bars. For it will be *our* turn! Then at last the Germans will once again have their say in Germany."

He looked like an excited sixteen-year-old with his tousled hair and shining eyes. Barbara could not deny she liked him, even though every word he said was repellent to her. With an eloquence that frequently tied itself in knots but was of an unflagging vehemence he explained to her that the faith for which he was fighting was basically revolutionary. "When the day arrives and our Führer takes over supreme power, then that's the end of capitalism and the economy of the big bosses. The servitude of usury will be abolished. Big banks and stock exchanges that bleed our national economy white can close their doors, and no one will mourn them."

Barbara wanted to know why Miklas did not join the Communists if he, like them, was against capitalism. Miklas explained as eagerly as a child reciting a lesson learned by heart. "Because the

117

Communists have no patriotism for the fatherland, but are supranational and dependent on Russian Jews. And the Communists don't know anything about idealism—all Marxists believe that the only purpose in life is money. We want our own revolution—our German, idealistic revolution. Not one that will be directed by Freemasons and the Elders of Zion."

When Barbara remarked that the Führer who wanted to dismantle capitalism was in fact receiving a great deal of money from heavy industry and large landed proprietors, Miklas furiously repulsed the assertion as "typical Jewish calumnies."

The two of them argued far into the night. Barbara—ironic, mild and inquisitive—listened to all her fanatic companion had to say and tried to change his beliefs, but he was unshakably stubborn in holding on to his bloodstained faith.

From a corner of the canteen Frau Efeu jealously watched the couple. "Frau Höfgen is keen on my boy," she whispered to the doorman Knurr. "That's all I needed. Frau Höfgen wants to take my baby away . . ."

That same night Hans Miklas quarreled with his Efeu. And Barbara had an unpleasant scene with Hendrik. Höfgen raged—not, as he was careful to emphasize, out of "petit-bourgeois marital jealousy" but, rather, on political grounds. "You don't sit at the same table for a whole evening with a Nazi lout," he shouted, trembling with rage. Barbara said that in her opinion young Miklas was not a lout. Hendrik retorted cuttingly, "All Nazis are louts. You dirty yourself when you associate with one of them. I regret you seem incapable of grasping this. The liberal traditions of your home have corrupted you. You have no convictions, only a gambler's curiosity." He stood stiffly in the middle of the room, accompanying his furious sermon with angular flailings of his arms.

Barbara said softly, "I admit, the young man saddens me a little and interests me a little. He is sick and ambitious and hasn't enough to eat. You treat him badly—you, your friend Herzfeld and the others. He is looking for something to cling to which can raise him up. That's what has brought him to this madness he so proudly calls his political faith."

Hendrik snorted contemptuously. Leaning forward, his hands on his hips, he said angrily, "You have an awful lot of sympathy for this blackguard. So we treat him badly! That's a good one! It's a long time since I've heard anything to match that. Don't you have an inkling of how he and his friends would treat us if their gang got into power?"

Barbara replied slowly without looking at him, "I hope to God these madmen never come to power. If they did I wouldn't want to stay in this country any longer." She shook herself a little as though she already felt the loathsome contact of the brutality and lies that would dominate Germany if the Nazis prevailed. "The underworld," she said with a shudder. "It's the underworld crying out for power."

"But you sit at the same table with it and talk." Hendrik strode back and forth across the room with a triumphant look on his face. "That's noble bourgeois tolerance for you! Always the subtle understanding of the mortal enemy—or what people still call the mortal enemy! I hope for your sake, my dear, that you can come to a firm understanding with the underworld if it comes to power. Your liberalism would have to learn to find a *modus vivendi* with the fascist dictatorship. We alone, the militant revolutionaries, are its mortal enemies —and we alone will prevent its achieving its ambitions." He strutted across the room, his chin in the air. Barbara stood motionless. Had Hendrik glanced at her at this moment he would have been startled by the seriousness of her expression.

"Then you believe that I would come to terms," she said quietly. "You think that I would become reconciled—reconciled with the mortal enemy?"

One evening a few days later, relations between Hendrik and Miklas came to a head-on collision. Hendrik was in brilliant form; bubbling over with Rhineland vivacity and entertaining his admiring colleagues with jokes and funny stories. He had just invented an amusing pastime which involved questions and answers. Since the only part of a newspaper that he read thoroughly was the theater section and the only things that really interested him were those that had some connection with the theater, he knew everything about the casts performing at all the German theaters and in the opera and operetta companies. His capacious memory could turn up the name of the second contralto in Königsberg and the actress newly engaged to play dowager parts at Halle on the river Saale. There was great amusement when Hendrik invited his colleagues to test his specialized fund of knowledge.

Hendrik answered promptly when asked, "Who is the young

character actor in Halberstadt?" And he was not stumped by the question, "Where is Frau Turkheim-Gavernitz appearing at the moment?" to which he answered, "As the comic old lady in Heidelberg."

The unpleasantness with Miklas began when someone asked, "Who is the juvenile female lead of the City Theater of Jena?" Hendrik answered, "A stupid cow—Lotte Lindenthal." Up to this point Miklas had remained apart from the others, but now he entered the game. "Why is Lotte Lindenthal a stupid cow?"

Höfgen answered icily, "I don't know why she is one, but she is." Miklas in a hoarse, soft voice said, "But I can tell you, Herr Höfgen, why you want to insult this actress. It's because you know perfectly well she is a friend of our National Socialist leader, namely, our heroic war pilot . . ."

Here he was interrupted by Höfgen, who had been drumming his fingers hard on the table and whose face had stiffened with distaste. "It's of very little interest to me to learn the name and rank of Fräulein Lindenthal's lovers," he said without deigning to cast a glance in Miklas's direction. "Besides it would have to be a long list. Fräulein Lindenthal doesn't amuse herself just with Air Force officers."

With fists clenched and his head lowered, Miklas stood in the fighting stance of a street urchin ready to hurl himself on his opponent at the start of a first-class brawl. His shining eyes looked blind with anger. "Put up your fists," he grunted. Everyone in the canteen was astonished. "I don't allow anyone to get away with publicly insulting a woman because she belongs to the German National Socialist Workers' party and is the friend of a German hero. I won't tolerate it."

"You won't tolerate it," parroted Hendrik and smiled grimly. "Well, well." Miklas made as if to hurl himself at him but was held back by Otto Ulrichs, who grasped him powerfully by the shoulders and shook him, saying, "You're completely drunk."

"I'm not drunk, very far from it," Miklas shouted back, "but it seems that I'm the only man in this room who still has a vestige of honor left in his body. No one in this Jew-infested place seems to find anything wrong when someone insults a lady . . ."

"That's enough," cried Höfgen, who had drawn himself up to his full height. He spoke with a frightening deliberateness, "I, too, am of the opinion that you aren't drunk. You won't be able to claim any extenuating circumstances. I can assure you that you won't have long to suffer in the Jew-infested circles in which you now find yourself—count on me for that." And Höfgen, walking rigidly, left the canteen.

"I feel cold shivers down my spine," whispered Motz in the awestruck silence that followed. But in the corner there was the sound of quiet weeping. The prompter Efeu let her heavy arms fall forward onto the table, and tears ran through her fingers.

Kroge, who had been absent at the scandalous scene in H.K., was not immediately inclined to grant Höfgen's demand for the instant dismissal of the young actor, but Frau von Herzfeld and Hendrik combined their eloquence to break down his scruples. The director shook his careworn face, wrinkled his brow, paced nervously up and down and grumbled, "Perhaps you're right. I grant you that the behavior of this young fellow has been insufferable. But even so, it goes against the grain to throw out a destitute, sick creature without warning." Hendrik and Hedda worked themselves up into a passion, pointing out that there was a detestable similarity between this indecisive compromising attitude and the cowardly behavior of the parties in power in the Weimar Republic toward the shameless terrorism of the Nazis.

"We must show this gang of murderers that they can't get away with everything!" Hendrik struck the table with his fist.

Kroge was all but won over by the arguments of his two principal collaborators when Miklas, to everyone's surprise, found an advocate in Otto Ulrichs.

"I implore you not to do this," Ulrichs cried. "It seems to me that it's punishment enough for the young man not to be signed on here for next season. The stupid boy wasn't really thinking what he was saying when he went on raving the other evening. It can happen to any of us—we all lose our tempers . . ."

"I am astounded," said Hendrik, directing a withering monocled glance at him. "I am very surprised to hear you—you particularly—speak like that."

Ulrichs impatiently waved this aside. "All right," he said. "Suppose we leave the humanitarian aspect out of it. I admit that it hurts me to hear the poor lad's cough and see the black hollows in his cheeks. But I wouldn't intervene in his favor just for those reasons. You should know me well enough, Hendrik, to realize that. In fact, as always, I am thinking in political terms. We don't want to create martyrs. It would be a great mistake—especially in the present political situation."

Here Hendrik rose to his feet. "Forgive me for interrupting you," he said with crushing politeness. "But it seems to me pointless to continue this certainly very interesting theoretical debate. The case is simple. The choice is between me and Herr Hans Miklas. If he remains at this theater, I shall leave it." This was spoken with a grave simplicity that left no doubt as to the genuineness of his ultimatum. He leaned on the table, the full weight of his torso resting on the open fingers of his hands. His eyes were cast down, modestly, as though he felt it would be unfair to influence the decision of those present with the irresistible power of his gaze.

Hendrik's alarming words made everyone start. Kroge bit his lip. Frau von Herzfeld could not prevent herself from putting her hand on her feverishly beating heart. Director Schmitz paled. It made him almost physically sick to think that the Arts Theater could now lose the irreplaceable Höfgen so soon after having been deserted by the sensational Nicoletta von Niebuhr.

"Don't talk nonsense," whispered Schmitz and wiped the sweat from his brow. The stout director added in a surprisingly gentle and pleasant voice, "You can rest assured—the young man will be fired."

Miklas was fired. Only with great difficulty and the zealous support of Ulrichs could Kroge arrange for the dismissed young actor to be given two months' pay. Nobody knew where he went. Even poor Efeu saw no more of him. Miklas, the victim of his childish stubbornness and his passionately held but superficially reasoned convictions, was gone.

Hendrik Höfgen had quelled insubordination and cleared rebellion from his path: his triumph was complete. He was admired more than ever by all the members of the Arts Theater, from Fräulein Motz to Böck. In their bar across the street the Communist stagehands praised his toughness. The doorman Knurr wore a grim expression but didn't dare say a word; he hid his swastika more carefully than before under his lapel. But when Höfgen walked through the stage door a terrible gaze was directed at him from the semidarkness of the porter's lodge which seemed to say: Just wait, you contemptible culture Bolshevist, we'll get the better of you yet! Our Führer and Savior is on his way. The day of the great takeover is approaching. Hendrik shivered, set his face in an impenetrably proud mask and passed without a greeting.

No one could contest his preeminence. He ruled in H.K., in the manager's office and on the stage. His salary was raised to fifteen hundred marks a month. Hendrik no longer took the trouble to take Schmitz by storm to wheedle a raise out of him; he now demanded the money outright in a few short words. He treated Kroge and Hedda almost as inferiors; he appeared to overlook little Siebert altogether; and in the comradely tone he used when talking to Otto Ulrichs there was now a patronizing, almost disdainful note.

There was only one person close to him whom he had not managed to dazzle and convince. The distrust in Barbara's attitude to Hendrik had sharpened since the Miklas affair. But in the long run he could not bear to have someone around him who did not admire him and believe in him. So now he made a real effort to win her over. Was it merely vanity that impelled him to direct his energies into a new courtship? Or was there another motive for his efforts to charm Barbara? He had called her his good angel. But his good angel had become his bad conscience. Barbara's silent disapproval cast a shadow over his triumph. The shadow must be dispelled so that he could enjoy his triumph undisturbed.

Hendrik was almost as attentive to Barbara as he had been in their first weeks together. He began to take hold of himself in her presence, preparing jokes and interesting topics of conversation for their meetings.

It became important to him that she should see him when his glamour and power were at their most visible. So he suggested she come more often to the theater for the major rehearsals. "You could certainly give me valuable advice," he said in his modestly plaintive voice, letting his eyelids droop a little.

Barbara slipped into the auditorium while Hendrik was directing the first dress rehearsal of his new production of an Offenbach operetta. She sat down quietly in the back row of the dark stalls. On the stage the chorus girls were stepping high and singing shrilly. Along the chorus line skipped Angelika Siebert, dressed as Cupid with ridiculous little wings attached to her bare shoulders, a bow and arrow hanging around her neck and a red nose painted on her pale face. What an unflattering mask Hendrik had forced on her, thought Barbara. A melancholy Cupid. And in her dark corner, Barbara felt a surge of sympathy for poor Angelika, who fidgeted and hopped in front of the footlights. Perhaps it was then that Barbara realized it was because of Hendrik that Angelika wore such a plaintive, anxious expression.

With outstretched arms, Höfgen stood tryrannically rigid at the side of the stage, controlling everything. His feet stamped out the rhythm of the orchestra. His livid face had a look of total determina-tion. "Stop, stop, stop!" he thundered. As the orchestra abruptly faded, Barbara was almost as intimidated as the chorus girls, who stood there in confusion, or as Angelika, a Cupid with a frozen nose fighting back tears.

The director sprang to the front of the stage. "You've got lead in your legs," he shouted to the girls, who hung their heads sadly like flowers in an icy wind. "This isn't a funeral march, it's Offenbach." He nodded imperiously at the orchestra, and when it struck up again he began to dance. They forgot that they were watching a balding man in a gray, threadbare business suit. It was a bizarre transformation on a bright mid-morning. For surely this was Dionysus, god of ecstasy and drunkenness, joyfully cavorting! Barbara was shaken to think that only a few minutes earlier she had been looking at Hendrik Höfgen, the commander in chief—edgy, arrogant, pitiless—marshaling his troops. Now without any transition he had plunged into a bacchic frenzy. Strange grimaces passed over his white face; the gleaming eyes rolled in rapture; hoarse voluptuous cries broke from his lips. And he danced wonderfully. Princess Tebab would have been proud of him.

Where did he get that from? wondered Barbara. And what is he feeling now—if he is feeling anything at all? He is showing the girls how they should kick and that sends him into ecstasies . . .

At that moment Hendrik broke off his frantic demonstration. A young man from the director's office had gingerly crossed the orchestra and climbed onstage. Now he gently tapped the shoulder of the entranced actor and whispered, "Forgive the interruption, Herr Höfgen, but Director Schmitz wants to ask your opinion of this sketch for the poster for the operetta. It's got to be sent off immediately to the printers." Hendrik signaled to the orchestra to stop and with a carelessly relaxed air fixed his monocle in his eye. No one looking at the man who now inspected the outstretched sheet of paper would have thought that only moments earlier he had been shaking his limbs in a Dionysian trance.

Suddenly he crumpled the paper in his hand. "The whole damn thing has got to be redone!" he shouted angrily. "It's unbelievable. My name is misspelled again. Is it too much to ask that I should be called by my right name in my own theater? I am not *Henrik*." He threw the paper angrily on the floor. "My name is Hendrik—get that straight once and for all—Hendrik Höfgen."

The young man from the office bowed his head and murmured something about a new printer whose ignorance was responsible for this unforgivable error. The girls tittered softly like little silver bells stirred by the wind. Hendrik swung round and with a fierce look reduced this delicate peal to dead silence.

CHAPTER

"It's just beyond belief . . ."

Hendrik Höfgen was overcome with painful feelings of envy and jealousy as he read the Berlin newspapers in H.K. An immense success for Dora Martin . . . A new production of *Hamlet* at the City Theater . . . A sensational new play at the Schiffbauerdamm Theater . . . And all this time he was still in the provinces! The capital went on without him. The film companies—the really big theaters—didn't need him. His name was unknown in Berlin. The one time he was mentioned by the Hamburg correspondent of a Berlin newspaper, his name was of course misspelled: "In the role of the sinister intriguer a Herr Henrik Höpfgen made a good impression." A Herr Henrik Höpfgen! His head fell forward in despair. The desire for fame—the real fame that was to be found only in the capital—nagged at him like a physical pain. Hendrik pressed his face between his hands as though he had toothache.

"To have star billing in Hamburg—a fine achievement!" he said miserably to Frau von Herzfeld, when she asked the reason for his downcast looks and now tried to comfort him with compliments.

"The darling of a provincial public—thank you very much. I would rather start all over again in Berlin than go on playing a part in this small-town operation."

Frau von Herzfeld was alarmed. "You don't really want to leave here, do you, Hendrik?" Her mournful brown eyes opened wide, and a tremor passed over her large powdered face.

"Nothing is decided as yet—" Hendrik looked severely past Hedda and shrugged impatiently. "First I'm going to make a guest appearance in Vienna." He said this offhandedly, as though touching on a subject that must have been well known to Hedda. But Hedda had no more idea that Hendrik wanted to appear in Vienna than anyone else in the theater—Kroge, Ulrichs or even Barbara.

"The Professor has approached me and offered me a really nice part," he said polishing his monocle with a silk handkerchief. "At first I wanted to refuse because it's a bad time of year. Who's left in Vienna in June? But finally I made up my mind to accept. One can never tell what such an invitation from the Professor could lead to . . ." He fixed his monocle back in his eye. "Besides, Martin is going to play opposite me."

The Professor was a producer with an enormous international reputation who controlled several theaters in Berlin and Vienna. In fact, it was his staff who had offered Höfgen a mediocre role in the old Viennese farce that the Professor wanted to put on in one of his Viennese theaters during the summer months. Moreover, the invitation was by no means a spontaneous gesture. Höfgen had found a protector in the playwright Theophilus Marder. Of course, Marder was on the worst possible terms with the Professor, as he was with all the world. But the famous producer retained a certain amount of ironic respect for the satirist whose plays he had staged in earlier days with considerable success. From time to time Marder recommended to him a young actress in whom he was interested—invariably in an irritated, threatening tone. But it was extremely rare for him to make the same overtures on a man's behalf. For this reason his tribute to Höfgen's talent made an impression on the Professor, although it was coupled with a number of insults directed at the Professor himself.

"You understand about as little of the theater as you do of literature," wrote the omniscient Theophilus. "I warn you, you will wind up as the manager of a flea circus in the Argentine. Think of me, Herr Professor, when you reach that pass. However, the fabulous happiness that I am now enjoying with my young wife, who is totally submissive to me, puts me in a mood to deal mildly even with you, who for years out of baseness and stupidity have boycotted my works.

"As you well know, in these miserable times I am the only one left who has an unerring eye for real artistic quality. Such is my generosity that I have decided to enrich the wretched totality of your foundering places of entertainment with a personality whose original talent is undeniable. The actor Hendrik Höfgen made an honorable showing in Hamburg in my classic comedy *Knorke*. Without doubt Herr Höfgen is of more value than your whole stable of actors, who obviously are worth very little."

The Professor laughed and then was thoughtful for a few moments, his tongue probing the inside of his cheeks. At last he rang for his secretary and told her to get in touch with Höfgen. "We can but try," he said.

Hendrik told nobody, not even Barbara, that he owed the Professor's flattering offer to Theophilus. Nobody knew that he kept in touch with Nicoletta's husband. It was with a casual air that Hendrik made the arrangements for his guest appearance in Vienna, which he had wangled with so much cunning and energy. "I must go quickly to Vienna to play a star part for the Professor," he said, and ordered a summer suit from the best tailor. He owed so much already—to Frau Monkeberg, Father Hansemann, the Colonial Stores and the wine merchant—that four hundred marks more or less made little difference.

Hendrik's sudden departure left many desolate faces in the good city of Hamburg, where his charm had won so many hearts. Perhaps even more dejected than the ladies—Angelika and Hedda—was Director Schmitz, for Höfgen had given all kinds of capricious excuses for refusing to extend his contract with the Arts Theater for the coming season. Schmitz's florid face turned yellow when Hendrik, at once cruel and flirtatious, stubbornly insisted, "I can't tie myself down, little Father Schmitz. It's repulsive to me to be tied down—my nerves can't stand it. Perhaps I'll come back, perhaps not . . . I don't know the answer myself yet, little Father Schmitz. I must be free. Please understand that."

Hendrik left for Vienna. Barbara had already gone to stay with her father and grandmother. Höfgen had seen to it that in parting from his young wife he made an emotional scene. "We shall be seeing each other again in the autumn, my darling," he said, facing Barbara with an expression both proud and pleading. "We shall see each other again, and then perhaps I shall be a different man from the one I am today. I must succeed, I must . . . You well know, my darling, for whose sake I am ambitious, for whom I must prove myself."

Hendrik bowed a stricken pale face over Barbara's tanned hand. Was this scene mere play-acting, or was there some real feeling in it? Barbara turned this over in her mind during her morning and afternoon rides, or in the garden when she let her book fall back on her lap. Where in this man did the untrue begin and where did it stop?

Barbara discussed the problem with her father, the general's widow and her bright, loyal friend Sebastian.

"I think I have his number," said Sebastian. "He's always lying and he never lies. His falseness is his truth—it sounds complicated, but actually it's quite simple. He believes everything and he believes nothing. He is an actor. And you haven't seen the last of him. He still obsesses you. You still expect something from him. You can't leave him yet, Barbara."

The Viennese public was delighted with Dora Martin, who in the popular farce appeared on alternate nights as a charming young girl and a shoeshine boy. She bewitched everyone with her mysterious, large eyes and her husky, cooing voice. Capriciously she drew out her syllables, ducked her head between her shoulders and moved in a way that was both gauche and magically ethereal. She leaped, floated and strolled about the stage, sometimes like a lean, awkward thirteen-year-old boy and sometimes like a charming elf.

Her success was so great that no one around her had a chance. The play's notices were long hymns to her genius, making only passing mention of her partner Hendrik, who portrayed a grotesque foppish nobleman; in fact, Hendrik was even criticized for overacting and affectation.

"You've been a failure, darling," cooed Dora Martin, waving the newspaper clippings at him maliciously, "a real flop. And the worst of it is everyone calls you Henrik. I'm *so* sad." She tried to assume a crestfallen expression, but her beautiful eyes were smiling under the high forehead she wrinkled so regretfully. "I really am so sad. But you are simply *dreadful* in the part." She said this almost tenderly. "Out of sheer nervousness you flounder around the stage like a harlequin—it mades me *so* sad. Nevertheless, of course I can see that you are enormously talented. I'll drop a word to the Professor that he must let you play in Berlin."

The very next day Höfgen was bidden to an audience with the

Professor. The fat man fixed him with close-set eyes that were thoughtful but sharp. Then he pressed his tongue against his cheek and, with his hands folded behind his back, paced up and down the room. He uttered a few loud exclamations: "Well, aha—so this is Höfgen then . . ." Finally he came to rest in front of his desk with his head sunk forward in a Napoleonic manner. "You have friends, Herr Höfgen," he announced. "Several people who know something about the theater have told me about you. This Marder, for instance . . ." At that he gave a short ringing laugh. "Yes, this Marder," he repeated, serious again, and added, respectfully raising his eyebrows, "And your father-in-law, the privy councillor, spoke to me about you when I met him just recently with the minister of culture. And now Dora Martin, too . . ." The Professor fell silent. Höfgen turned alternately red and pale; the smile on his lips tightened. It was hard to endure the Professor's concentrated, cold, thoughtful gaze. Hendrik suddenly understood why the Professor was called the Magician by his admirers.

Finally Höfgen broke into this painfully silent examination by remarking in his singing, flattering voice. "In life I am inconspicuous, Herr Professor. But on the stage . . ." Here he straightened his shoulders, suddenly flung open his arms and let the metallic ring sound in his voice. "On stage a funny change comes over me." He accompanied this explanation with his "dirty" smile. And he added solemnly, "My father-in-law once found very beautiful words to describe this capacity of mine to transform myself."

At the mention of Bruckner, the Professor again raised his eyebrows. But his voice sounded cold as, after several seconds of meaningful silence, he said, "Well, we can only try to do something with you . . ."

Joyfully Höfgen rose to his feet, but the Professor gave him a warning wave. "Don't expect too much," he said gravely. "It's not a large opening that I shall be offering you. In the role you're playing here you aren't making a comic impression but a fairly miserable one."

Hendrik winced. The Professor smiled amiably. "Fairly miserable," he repeated grimly. "But that is not important. Even so, we can see what we can do. As for the salary . . ." The Professor's smile took on a roguish quality and his tongue moved briskly inside his mouth. "Probably, coming from Hamburg, you have been used to relatively decent earnings. You will have to be content with less when you are with us. Are you very demanding?" The Professor spoke as though the answer to this question was of only academic interest. Hendrik quickly reassured him.

"Money is not important to me—really not." He spoke earnestly in response to the Professor's skeptical grimace. "I'm not spoiled. I just need a clean shirt and a bottle of eau de Cologne on the dressing table."

The Professor gave a short laugh. "You can work out the details with Katz," he said. "I will be in touch with him."

The audience was over. Höfgen was dismissed with a handshake and a "Give my regards to your father-in-law." The Professor was already back to pacing the thick carpet of his office, a small compact Napoleonic figure with his hands folded behind his back.

Herr Katz was the Professor's secretary. He made all the business arrangements in the theaters belonging to the great impresario, and spoke in the same grating voice as his master; and he, too, worked his tongue around inside his cheek. The discussion between him and Höfgen took place the same day. Hendrik unhesitatingly accepted a salary the very mention of which would have caused him to box the ears of Director Schmitz. It was really miserable—seven hundred marks a month, before taxes. Moreover, it was accompanied by no guarantee as to what parts he would play. Must he be content with what was offered? It appeared that he must, for he wanted to go to Berlin, and in Berlin he was unknown. A beginner all over again!

Hendrik sent a large bouquet of yellow roses to Dora Martin—he had to get the hall porter to pay for them—along with a card on which, in pathetic angular capital letters, he had written THANK YOU. At the same time he wrote a letter to Schmitz and Kroge informing them, briefly and dryly, that he was sad to say he wouldn't be able to renew his contract with the Arts Theater because the Professor had made him a very fine offer. As he put the letter in its envelope he imagined for a few seconds the consternation with which it would be received in the Hamburg office. The thought of Frau von Herzfeld's tearful eyes made him snicker. It was in a very light-hearted mood that he went off to the theater.

He called at Dora Martin's dressing room, but her dresser told him that she was busy with the Professor.

"I have done you this strange favor," the Professor was saying as

132

he gazed thoughtfully at Dora Martin's thin shoulders. "The fellow is signed up—this— What does he call himself?"

Dora Martin laughed. "Höfgen. Hendrik Höfgen. You're going to hear something of that name soon, my dear."

The Professor shrugged, disdainfully pressed his tongue into his cheek and made groaning noises. "I don't like him," he said finally. "An actor."

"Since when have you got something against actors?" Dora Martin bared her teeth in a smile.

"I only have something against bad actors," said the Professor, and added, "against provincial actors."

Dora Martin became suddenly serious. Her eyes clouded. "He interests me," she said softly. "He is completely unscrupulous"—she smiled tenderly—"an utterly bad human being." She stretched herself almost voluptuously, throwing back her childlike head. "We may yet have some surprises with him," she said, gazing dreamily up at the ceiling.

A few seconds later she sprang to her feet and shooed the Professor with little fluttering gestures toward the door. "It's high time—out you go," she said, laughing. "Out now, quick. I must try on my wig."

"Can't I see how you try on your wig—not even once?" the Professor pleaded from the doorway. He looked her up and down greedily.

"No, no—absolutely impossible!" Dora Martin quivered with horror. "No question of it at all. My dressing gown might slip off my shoulders." And at that she clutched the brightly colored robe more tightly around her.

Between clenched teeth the Professor murmured, "A pity." As the old wizard, whom all the women of his acquaintance bored with their much too passionate advances, left the dressing room he had a feeling that Dora Martin once left alone would change into a water nymph, a goblin or some other creature so bizarre no one even knew its name.

The refined chastity of the great actress had put the Professor in such a thoughtful mood he scarcely recognized the costumed actor who bowed low before him, smiling and sweeping off a bright feathered hat. Only after he had passed by did he realize that it had been "that Höfgen" who had given him a greeting of such obsequious courtesy.

The surprising new situation in which Hendrik Höfgen was placed had a rejuvenating effect. Provincial fame, with all its comfortable reassurance, was now a thing of the past. He was a beginner all over again and had to prove himself, raise himself to the top this time—right to the top. He discovered with satisfaction that his powers were still intact, ready to be called upon. He punished his body: the fat had almost disappeared, his movements were agile and assertive. Surely a man who knew how to smile and to make his eyes shine as he could must find success. Already his voice had a ring of the triumph that in fact he had as yet in no way achieved.

Barbara returned to Hendrik, as her friend Sebastian prophesied she would. She did not regret it. She observed her husband's new vigor with a thoughtful interest in which a real sympathy was mixed with a detached curiosity. Half cynical and half admiring, she observed this changed, tensely expectant Hendrik, with whom she now shared two cheaply furnished rooms. He pleased her more than the spoiled darling of the provincial theater, already putting on fat as he held forth in the H.K. circle and tried to play the middle-class husband in Frau Monkeberg's refined lodging. After the evening performance she liked to meet him in a dim little café, where an electric piano lamented in the half-darkness, where the cakes looked as though they were made of cement and plaster, and where they were certain not to meet anyone they knew.

It fascinated Barbara to listen to Hendrik's tremulous, harassed reports on the progress of his career. At such moments she knew that he was real. His livid face shone in the smoke-filled twilight of the seedy café with a phosphorescent sheen like rotten wood in the night. The sensual mouth with its strong, finely curved lips smiled and talked; the powerful chin with its deep cleft was thrust imperiously forward; the monocle glittered in his eye. And the broad reddish-haired hands, which by a mysterious exertion of will took on the appearance of handsomeness, played excitedly with the tablecloth, with matches, with anything that came within reach.

Full of feverish eagerness, Hendrik outlined his hopes, plans and calculations. That Barbara shared them, that she no longer disdainfully shut them out of her mind, intensified his zest for life and sharpened his ambition. Certainly, Barbara made herself actively useful to his career—it was not for nothing that she had the face of a crafty Madonna. She slyly fitted herself out in a black silk dress and visited the Professor, to whom she brought greetings from her father. The great ruler of all the theaters in Berlin's Kurfürstendamm graciously received the wife of his young actor because she was the daughter of the privy councillor, whose name was so often in the newspapers and who had recently met with the minister of culture. The palace of the Professor could have been that of a ruling prince. The owner of all this baroque furniture, these Gobelin tapestries and valuable paintings, gazed appreciatively at the light brown arms and the mischievous and yet somewhat melancholy face of his visitor. "Well, and so you are married to—this Höfgen," he said after a long inspection and much pressing of his tongue against his cheeks. "He must really have something."

All this, of course, was of great help to Hendrik. Besides, he was now on excellent terms with the other overlords of the Berlin stage—with Herr Katz and Fräulein Bernhard. With Herr Katz, the business manager, who was far from being as Napoleonic as he sometimes tried to make himself appear, Hendrik played cards; and with Fräulein Bernhard, the influential and energetic secretary—a small sturdy brunette with protruding lips and a pince-nez sitting on her nose—he was on almost as good terms as he used to be with Director Schmitz. Though no one had yet found him sitting on her knee, Hendrik Höfgen had only been with the company two weeks and was calling the forbidding Fräulein Bernhard "Rose." Most actors had not even reached the point of knowing that Rose was Fräulein Bernhard's first name.

His colleagues whispered to one another that it was certainly a fine beginning for a Berlin career. His beautiful wife visited the Professor; he played cards with Katz; and he patted Fräulein Bernhard's chin. This could really lead somewhere.

And it did—as very soon it became plain. First it was only a small part in which he caught the public's eye. But he certainly knew how to make the most of it. The critics began to speak of "the talented Herr Hendrik Höfgen"; and along came a Russian play in which he appeared briefly as a young drunken peasant who staggered about the stage, mumbled tipsily to himself and then danced. But how he mumbled, and, above all, how he danced! The Berlin audiences were enchanted by Princess Tebab's pupil: there was a burst of applause when he stopped dancing. Everyone marveled at the obsessive force with which he moved his limbs and the ecstatic expression on his face. Rose Bernhard, who collected gentlemen of the press and society ladies around her at the bar, remarked, "There's something really Bacchic about this man."

The public, distracted by a thousand cares and pleasures, forgot the name of the frenetic dancer. But insiders—the ones who really mattered—noticed Hendrik's first Berlin success. And the whole city spoke of his second.

This was a sensational play—*The Guilt*—and it was strikingly produced. But Hendrik managed to concentrate the greater part of the interest of both the public and the critics on himself. There was even more discussion of his performance than there was of the playwright, a mysterious unknown whose identity was the talk of the city's cafés, theatrical dressing rooms, drawing rooms and editorial offices. Who was the writer hidden behind the pseudonym Richard Loser, whose tragedy portrayed such a pitiable array of want, misery and tumult? Where was this genius to be found, who led his audience through such a labyrinth of corrupt and tragic happenings, who must have experienced passion of the most depraved sort to be able to depict so much agony and despair? There was no doubt that the author of this dark and absorbing drama, which effectively combined both expressionist and naturalistic elements, must be an outsider—a solitary man, who shunned the world of getting and spending. The literary set, always mistrustful of their own calling, were positive about one thing: this was not the work of a practiced writer. His was a brilliantly spontaneous genius; he had never written a line before; he was a young neurologist, according to some of those most in the know about such things—and he lived in Spain; letters to him went unanswered, all contact with him had to be handled through a number of intermediaries. All this was immensely interesting and was discussed with excitement by those who wanted to keep abreast of events.

A young neurologist living in Spain: the notion was highly probable, and people believed it. Only a neurologist could be so knowledgeable about deformities of the human psyche that could lead to such horrible crimes. How thoroughly versed he was in his subject! All the deadly sins trooped across his stage. It was a society of the damned that schemed and suffered. Everyone who made his entrance seemed to have a sinister symbol branded on his or her forehead. The atmosphere of evil made the ladies from Grunewald and the Kurfürstendamm shiver with delight.

But the most depraved of the depraved was Hendrik Höfgen, which was why he won the greatest applause. With a demonic expression, and lifeless voice, he left no doubt he was evil—a blackmailer of the first order. With a horrible leer he led young people to disaster. One of them committed suicide onstage, and Hendrik—his hands in trouser pockets, a cigarette hanging from his lip and a monocle fixed in his eye—slouched past the body. The audience shuddered—this was the incarnation of evil. Sometimes he himself seemed to take fright at his unrelieved wickedness: his face became white and stiff, the glittering fishlike eyes took on a desolate sheen and the sensitive temples tightened with pain.

Höfgen's personification of decadence caused a sensation among the wealthy of Berlin's West End. He served up depravity as a delicacy for the rich, and they hung on the expression of exhaustion and wariness that played over his face and the suavity of his insidious gestures. "He moves like a cat," exclaimed Fräulein Bernhard. "A wicked cat! Oh, how wonderfully wicked he is."

His husky whisper, which rose from time to time to a hypnotic chant, was quickly picked up by his colleagues in smaller theaters.

"Wasn't I right? He really has something," said Dora Martin to the Professor, who could no longer contradict her. "Well, yes," he growled, clicking his tongue. But in his heart he still could not take "this Höfgen" seriously, just as Kroge had not in earlier days. An actor, he thought.

But a fascinating actor in the opinion of the critics and the Berlin society women; and his colleagues could no longer deny it. *The Guilt* owed its exceptional appeal to a great extent to his performance. It was scheduled for a very long run, and the Professor made good money. Then the unbelievable happened: he raised Hendrik's salary while the season was still in progress, though no contract compelled him to do so. Rose Bernhard and Herr Katz had persuaded their distinguished employer to bend the rules in this exceptional case.

Perhaps the play could have run for a hundred and fifty or two hundred performances, but, little by little, rumors about the author began to gain ground and cause disillusionment. All at once everyone was saying he wasn't an eccentric neurologist living in Spain. Nor was he an outsider who knew only the dark recesses of human nature and was entirely untouched by the banal mysteries of the Establishment. So far from being an untainted newcomer, he was quite simply —Herr Katz. The disappointment was acute. Herr Katz, the sure-footed businessman, had written *The Guilt*? Quite suddenly everyone found that the play was nothing but a chamber of horrors, as tasteless as it was insignificant. People felt cheated and thought the whole affair an impertinence on Herr Katz's part. Since when had Herr Katz become Dostoevsky? Herr Katz was the business adviser of the Professor, which counted as an enviable post, but no one would concede him the right to set himself up as a Spanish neurologist and descend into the lower depths. There was nothing to do but to close the play.

A capricious public let Katz drop. But Höfgen had made his breakthrough and won all hearts with his astonishing wickedness. By the end of his first Berlin season he had reason to be pleased with himself: everywhere he was spoken of as the great actor of the future, the rising star, the white hope. His contract for the next season, 1929–30, looked very different from the one that had preceded it. His salary was almost tripled. Groaning and grumbling, the Professor had to give way, for the opposition was now after Höfgen.

"Well, now you can certainly have all the clean shirts and lavender water you want," the Professor said to his new star. And Hendrik corrected him with a winning smile: "Eau de Cologne, Professor! I only use eau de Cologne."

Summer had come. Hendrik gave up the two dim rooms and rented a bright high-ceilinged apartment in the Reichskanzlerplatz in the heart of the fashionable new West End. He bought a large number of shirts, yellow shoes and brightly colored suits. He took driving lessons and bargained with several companies for a discount on the purchase of the latest model of an open car.

Barbara went back to her grandmother's estate. The successful husband interested her far less than the man fighting his way to the top and trembling with unsatisfied ambition.

Hedda von Herzfeld came to visit Hendrik to help him set himself up in his new apartment. She chose steel furniture with Van Gogh and Picasso reproductions for the walls. The rooms had an air of stylishly fastidious bleakness. Hendrik enjoyed Hedda's worship; he took her love, which seemed to have grown in the interval, as a well-deserved tribute. Hedda had now dropped all pretense of an ironic mask where he was concerned; it was with a wistful craving, a hopeless addiction, that she fixed her soft brown eyes on her cruel idol.

138

"Poor little Angelika looks pale and drawn with longing for you," Hedda reported, without revealing that she herself had once let herself go to the extent of weeping with Angelika. The two of them had bitterly mourned the lost man they had never possessed.

Hedda was allowed to accompany Hendrik to the film studios for the making of his first movie. It was a thriller called *Stop Thief*, in which he had the leading role of a mysterious villain who hardly ever removes his black mask. Everything about the villain is black: the color of his clothing symbolizes the darkness of his soul. The Black Devil commands a gang that forges banknotes, smuggles drugs and occasionally robs a bank. He has also committed several murders. It is not only avarice and a taste for adventure that drives the Black Devil to crime: an unhappy experience with a young woman has turned him into an enemy of humanity and he pursues evil as a matter of principle. This he confesses shortly before his arrest to the members of his gang. They are stunned to learn that their chief has not always been a member of the underworld but was once an officer in the Hussars. In the course of this dramatic scene the Black Devil unmasks. Between his stiff black hat and his high-necked black shirt, his face is of a frightening pallor, aristocratic even in its depravity, and not without a trace of tragic grandeur.

The moguls of the movie business were deeply impressed by this cruel and grieving face. Höfgen was original and versatile; he would be a box-office draw both in the capital and in the provinces. The offers they made to Höfgen exceeded all his hopes. He had to turn most of them down, for he was bound by his contract with the Professor. But once he began making himself unavailable, the film moguls became wild about him. They approached Herr Katz and Fräulein Bernhard with offers of handsome compensation if they could have the use of Höfgen's services for only a few weeks in the season. There were constant telephone calls, exchanges of letters, bargaining sessions. Bernhard and Katz stood firm: even large sums of money could not persuade them to give up their prize. Wooed on all sides, Höfgen sat in his bleak and distinguished apartment among his steel furniture, flashed his "dirty" smile and gave a running commentary on the struggle between stage and screen for his priceless person.

This was success! The great dream had come true. You only had to be able to dream intensely enough, Hendrik thought, and the impossible vision materialized. And it was more wonderful than he had dared to imagine it. In every newspaper he opened he found his name—Fräulein Bernhard was adept at securing such publicity—and now it was always spelled right in letters almost as large as the names of those godlike stage heroes whose fame actors used to follow jealously in the canteens of provincial theaters. One of the big picture magazines had Hendrik's photo on the front cover. What kind of face would Kroge make when he saw it? And Frau Monkeberg? And Privy Councillor Bruckner? Everyone who had cast a skeptical and disdainful eye on Hendrik's chances would now look in awe at the soaring turn in his fortunes.

At the close of the 1929–30 season Hendrik Höfgen's stature was incomparably more imposing than at its beginning. He had almost as much say in the Professor's theaters as the great man himself, who spent little time in Berlin and was most often to be found in London, Hollywood or Vienna. Höfgen held sway over Herr Katz and Rose Bernhard; he had come to give them orders as unceremoniously as he used to do with Schmitz and Frau von Herzfeld. Höfgen decided which plays would be performed; and, with Rose, he doled out the parts. Writers who wanted their works performed flattered him; actors who wanted parts flattered him; society—or, rather, the coterie of wealthy snobs who gave themselves that name—flattered him.

Everything was once again as it had been in Hamburg, only this time it was on a larger scale. He worked sixteen hours a day, interrupted every so often by interesting nervous breakdowns. Once in the elegant nightclub called the Wild Rider, where Hendrik from time to time gathered admirers around him between one and three in the morning, he fell groaning from his high barstool. It was only a minor faint, but it caused all the ladies present to scream. Fräulein Bernhard was on hand with strong smelling salts (there was always a devoted woman present when Höfgen had his fits). He indulged himself fairly often now in his little breakdowns, which could take any form from a subdued attack of twitching or a silent blackout to screaming convulsions. And they suited him. He emerged from his fits as out of healing waters, full of new strength for his ambitious, exhausting and enjoyable life.

Soon he had less reason to resort to his refreshing crises, for once again he had Princess Tebab near him. During his first Berlin winter he had left unanswered the threatening letters—teeming with spelling mistakes—of the black king's daughter. But now Barbara had almost completely left him—she could no longer bear the hustle surrounding her smart husband and withdrew into the peaceful rooms of the houses in which she had been brought up. Her visits to Berlin became increasingly rare and her room in the elegant apartment on the Reichskanzlerplatz remained unoccupied for most of the time. It was then that Hendrik decided to send his Juliette money for the train ticket to Berlin. Life without her lacked zest; the hard-eyed ladies striding through Berlin's red light district in their high leather boots were no substitute. Princess Tebab did not have to be asked twice. She arrived.

Hendrik rented her a room in an out-of-the-way neighborhood where he could visit her at least once a week. Dressed like a murderer revisiting the scene of his crime—scarf drawn up over his chin, hat pulled down over his eyes—he stole across the town to visit his beloved. "If anyone caught me in this outfit," he whispered to himself as he climbed into his track suit, "I would be lost!" Princess Tebab was delighted by his trembling fear. For the pleasure of seeing him shudder and also to squeeze more money out of him, she warned for the hundredth time that she would come to the theater and scream like a wildcat when he appeared on stage. "You watch out, baby," she teased him. "One day I really will do it—for instance, at the big first night next week. I'll put on my colored silk dress and sit in the front row. That'll be a scandal all right." The black girl rubbed her hands together with glee. Then she demanded a hundred and fifty marks from him before she would teach him the new dance step. With his rise to fame she had become more demanding. Now she needed expensive perfumes. She bought an ever greater number of silk scarves, gold bangles and candied fruit; she kept the candy in large paper bags and liked to nibble it from her rough fingers. Hendrik paid gladly. It gave him pleasure to be so exploited by the black Venus.

"I love you as I did the first day," he told her. "I love you even more than on the first day. When you're away that's when I realize what you mean to me. The women of this city are unbearably boring."

"And your wife?" demanded the jungle girl with a resentful laugh. "And your Barbara, what about her?"

"Ah, her!" said Hendrik. There was a mixture of sadness and disdain in his voice as he turned his pale face toward the shadows.

Barbara came less and less frequently to Berlin. And the privy councillor hardly ever showed himself in the capital, where earlier, particularly in winter, he had given lectures and attended formal social functions. "I don't feel comfortable in Berlin any longer," he said. "Yes, I am beginning to be frightened of Berlin. Things are about to happen there that horrify me—and the most horrible part of it is that the people around me seem not to see the danger. They are struck with blindness. They amuse themselves, they quarrel, they take themselves seriously. In the meantime the sky grows darker; but no one casts an eye at the approaching storm that is now almost above their heads. No, I no longer enjoy being in Berlin. Perhaps I avoid the city so as not to have to despise it . . ."

But he did come back once more—not, however, to appear at an imposing social function or to lecture at the university, but to deliver a long speech entitled "The Impending Barbarism," a speech about culture, politics and the state of Germany. It was the privy councillor's intention to warn the intellectuals among the bourgeoisie one last time, to tell of what was to come and what darkness and retrogression lay hidden behind what dared to call itself the "awakening" and the "national revolution." The old man spoke for one and a half tumultuous hours before an audience equally divided into vocal admirers and hostile hecklers.

During his last visit to the capital the bourgeois sage, whose visit to the Soviet Union had made him hated by the Right and even a little suspect to Democrats, talked with many of his friends—politicians, writers and professors. All these conversations ended with strong differences of opinion. There was a hint of sarcasm in the remonstrations of his friends: "Where is your intellectual tolerance, Herr Privy Councillor? Where are your democratic principles? We no longer recognize you. You sound like a run-of-the-mill radical politician and not like a man of superior intellect. There is only one way to counter National Socialism—education. We must exert all our efforts to tame these people through democracy. We must try to win them over rather than fight them. We must convince these young people of the virtues of the republic. And besides, dear Privy Councillor—the enemy is on the Left."

Bruckner had to listen to a great deal about the "healthy and creative forces" that "in spite of everything" were contained in Nazism. He had to listen to talk about the noble national ideals of a younger

142

generation, toward which "we old folk" should not assume an attitude of blind disapproval. He had to listen to more about "the political instinct of the German people and their "healthy common sense," which would always protect it from the worst ("Germany is not Italy, after all")—until, angry and disillusioned, he left the city determined never to return.

Privy Councillor Bruckner withdrew from a society that was at Hendrik Höfgen's feet.

In the Berlin drawing rooms anyone was welcome who either had money or whose name appeared constantly in the popular press. In the fashionable quarters of the Tiergarten and Grunewald black marketeers mixed with racing drivers, boxers and well-known actors. A successful banker was proud to have Hendrik Höfgen at his receptions. Certainly, he would rather have had Dora Martin in his house, but Dora Martin didn't come; she refused or, at most, looked in for ten minutes.

Höfgen, of course, didn't put in an appearance before midnight. After the evening performances he stopped in at a music hall, where for three hundred marks he sang a song that lasted only seven minutes. The fashionable crowd, whom he honored with his presence, joined in the chorus of the song that he had made famous—

> "It's just beyond belief
> It's really just too mad
> Have I utterly gone to the bad?
> My God—what's become of me?"

Waving and smiling, with Herr Katz and Rose Bernhard behind him as loyal satellites, he moved through this society of snobbish Jewish bankers, political radicals, artistically impotent intellectuals and sportsmen who never opened a book and for that very reason have been taken up by the literary set. "Doesn't he look like a lord?" whispered a lavishly bejeweled woman in his wake. "He has such a depraved mouth—and those wonderfully blasé eyes! His dinner jacket is by Knige and costs twelve hundred marks." In one corner of a salon someone said, "Höfgen is having an affair with Dora Martin."

"No, he's sleeping with Fräulein Bernhard," declared someone really in the know.

"And his wife?" asked a somewhat naïve young man, who had

143

not long been in Berlin society. He received a scornful smile in reply. The Bruckner family were no longer to be taken seriously since the old man exposed himself politically in such an offensive and senseless manner. Academics should not get mixed up in things they cannot hope to understand—on this everyone agreed. And besides, it was absurd obstinacy to swim against the current. The Nazi movement, so rich in future possibilities and containing so many positive elements, was already on the way to correcting its disturbing little faults —for instance, the bothersome matter of anti-Semitism.

"That liberalism has run its course, and has no future is a fact so self-evident that it no longer merits discussion," said the intellectuals. And neither the boxers nor the bankers contradicted them.

"How delightful you've found an hour to spend with us, Herr Höfgen," declared the hostess to her guest as she handed him a little plate of caviar. "We all know how busy you are. May I introduce you to two of your warmest admirers. This is Herr Müller-Andreä, who is certainly known to you through his enchanting society column. And this is our friend the famous French writer Pierre Larue."

Herr Müller-Andreä was an elegant gray-haired man with protruding watery blue eyes set in a red face. Everyone knew he lived off the good contacts of his beautiful wife, who came from an aristocratic family. Through her he learned the gossip of the whole of Berlin society out of which he composed his little column for a scandalmongering magazine in which Herr Müller-Andreä chattered away each week under the headline "Had You Heard?" It was precisely to this amusing column that "the interesting magazine" owed its popularity, for it informed the reader that the wife of the industrialist Herr X had made a little journey to Biarritz with the Tenor Y, and that the Countess Z appeared every afternoon at the teatime dance in the Hotel Adlon not because of the good band but because of the charms of a certain gigolo dance partner. Herr Müller-Andreä counted on such revelations to enthrall and instruct his readers. But his fairly luxurious life-style was financed not by the money he received for his published work but from the sums he was paid for keeping certain items out of his column. Many a lady rewarded Herr Müller-Andreä handsomely for not mentioning her name in HAD YOU HEARD? That Herr Müller-Andreä was a common blackmailer was something that even he did not bother to deny; and nobody cared to make a fuss about it.

The other warm admirer of Höfgen was a little gnome of a man. Pierre Larue held out a small white hand to Hendrik and spoke in a petulant soprano voice. "Very interesting, dear Herr Höfgen. May I note your address?" With a well-practiced gesture he brought out a thick notebook. "I hope you will soon lunch with me at the Esplanade," he cooed in a voice that sounded like a moaning flute. M. Larue had a wrinkled, spinsterish pointed face and remarkably sharp and piercing eyes, which sparkled with the excitement of his hunt for people, names and addresses—the overriding impulse of his life. M. Larue would die of sadness the day he could make no new acquaintances. However, such a pitiable situation could always be avoided as long as the little name-dropper remained in Berlin. Foreigners were always welcome in Berlin salons, and a guest who spoke broken German was almost as prized at a party as a boxer, a countess or a film star. And even more welcome was a foreigner with money who arranged interesting dinners at the Hotel Esplanade, had been presented to a number of crowned heads and knew the Prince of Wales. No door was shut to M. Larue: even the venerable German president had received him. He enjoyed the acquaintance of the most exclusive and reactionary families of Potsdam, and was also seen in the company of left-wing radical young people, whom he liked to introduce in the houses of bank directors as "my young communist comrades."

"Just yesterday I was admiring your performance at the Wintergarten," said Pierre Larue after taking down Hendrik's telephone number. And he jokingly repeated the popular refrain, "It's just beyond belief." He gave a little laugh like the rustle of dry leaves in an autumn wind. "Ha-ha-ha," laughed M. Larue, rubbing his pale bony hands over his chest and sinking his head deep into the thick black woolen shawl he wore despite the warm temperature of drawing rooms.

It's just beyond belief—the world has never seen the like! In Germany everything is going along perfectly; it couldn't be better. You can live without care, always be in a great mood!

Is there a crisis? Are there unemployed? Is there a struggle for power? Was there any republic that lacked not only self-respect but even the instinct of self-preservation when challenged by its most insolent and savage enemies before the eyes of the entire world?

And these enemies—are they supported and aided by wealthy citizens, who fear only one thing—a government that might decide to take away some of their money? Are there pitched battles in meeting halls and street fights nightly in Berlin? Is there already a civil war that claims victims almost daily? Do thugs in brown uniforms trample on workers and cut their throats while the great People's Leader—head of "constructive elements," the darling of heavy industry and the army high command—publishes his telegram of congratulations to the murderers? Does this same rabble-rouser, who calls for a Night of Long Knives and openly rejoices that heads are about to roll, swear he wants to come to power "only by legal means"? Can he get away with it? Dare he scream threats and infamies across the world?

It's just beyond belief . . . Cabinets fall and are re-formed and the new are no more effective than the old. Must men become savages again? In the palace of the venerable field marshal, the landed proprietors intrigue against a tottering republic. The democrats insist that the real enemy is on the Left. Police chiefs, who call themselves socialists, give orders to their men to fire on workers. But the baying voice, with its promises of punishment and bloody overthrow for the "system," is allowed to continue daily without interruption.

Hendrik Höfgen—typecast as an elegant blackguard, murderer in evening dress, scheming courtier—sees nothing, hears nothing, notices nothing. He has nothing to do with the city of Berlin. Nothing but stages, film studios, dressing rooms, a few nightclubs, a few fashionable drawing rooms are real to him. Does he not feel the change in the seasons? Is he not aware that the years are passing—the last years of that Weimar Republic born amid so much hope and now so piteously expiring—the years 1930, 1931, 1932? The actor Höfgen lives from one first night to the next, from one film to another, his calendar composed of performance days and rehearsal days. He scarcely notices that the snow melts, that the trees and bushes are in bud or in full leaf, that there are flowers and earth and streams. Encapsulated by his ambition as in a prison cell, insatiable and tireless, always in a state of extreme hysterical tension, Hendrik embraces a destiny that seems to him exceptional but is in fact nothing but a vulgar arabesque at the edge of an enterprise doomed to collapse.

It's just beyond belief—there is no way of counting the outlets for his energy, the many inspirations and surprises he employs to

concentrate public attention on himself. He has not renewed his con-
tract with the Professor's theaters—to the infinite sorrow of Fräulein
Bernhard—so that he can be free to seize all the attractive opportunities
that spread before him.

Höfgen acted in one place and directed in another, whenever his lucrative film work gave him time for the stage. On stage or screen he was to be seen in costumes ranging from the exotic and the sumptuous— the embroidered finery of a dandyish eighteenth-century prince; the regalia of an Oriental potentate; a Roman toga; the apparel of a Prussian king or of a degenerate English lord—to the more mundane, such as golfing knickers, pajamas or a tailcoat. In operettas he sang idiotic numbers in so artfully pointed a manner that stupid people found him brilliant. In classical dramas he acted with such careless elegance that the plays of Schiller and Shakespeare came across as amusing conversation pieces. In popular farces, which in Budapest or Paris were cheap formula stuff, he introduced delicate little effects that obscured their essential shoddiness. This Höfgen could do everything! But if you looked at his achievements individually, you found that none of them was of the very first rank: as a director Höfgen was never the equal of the Professor, and as an actor he could not bear comparison with his chief competitor Dora Martin, who remained the brightest star in a firmament through which he moved like a dazzling comet. It was his versatility that created and renewed his reputation. His audiences always said the same thing: It's fabulous how many things he manages to bring off! And, in more elevated terms, the critics agreed.

He was the idol of the radical bourgeois and left-wing press, as he was the favorite of the spacious Jewish drawing rooms. The very fact that he was not a Jew made him appear particularly attractive in these circles; for among the Jewish elite in Berlin "blond was fashionable." The newspapers of the radical Right, which every day angrily demanded the renewal of German culture through a return to racial purity—Blood and Soil—were distrustful and critical of Höfgen. They saw him as a "cultural Bolshevik." That Jewish newspaper editors liked him made him all the more suspect in their eyes, as did his taste for French plays and the un-German and cosmopolitan frivolity of his appearance. Moreover, the nationalist dramatists hated him because he rejected their works. Caesar von Muck, for example, a typical writer of the rising National Socialist movement, in whose works the strangling of Jews and the executing of Frenchmen took the place of good dialogue, wrote of the new production of a Wagner opera in which Höfgen had made a sensation: "This is the rankest yellow-press art, a corrupt experiment, shot through and through with Jewish influence and insolent degradation of the German cultural heritage. The cynicism of Herr Höfgen knows no bounds. In order to offer the Kurfürstendamm public a new sensation, he dares to diminish the most venerable, the greatest of German masters—Richard Wagner." Hendrik and a few radical intellectual friends enjoyed themselves vastly reading this piece of Blood and Soil drivel.

Höfgen had not given up his relations with Communist or semi-Communist circles. From time to time he played host in his Reichskanzlerplatz apartment to young writers or party officials, to whom he recounted in ever new and effective flourishes of speech his undying hatred of capitalism and his ardent faith in world revolution. He kept up with the revolutionaries, not only because he felt that they could perhaps one day come to power—in which case all his dinner parties would be amply repaid—but also because the contact quieted the stirrings of his own conscience. After all, one asks more from life than just to be a well-paid entertainer who becomes completely absorbed in a profession one claims to despise in one's heart of hearts.

Hendrik flattered himself that his life had a complexity of which his colleagues could not boast. Dora Martin, for instance, the great Dora Martin, who was still more famous than himself—what might be going on inside her mind? She went to sleep thinking of her earnings and awoke with the hope of new film contracts. So Höfgen told himself —Höfgen, who knew nothing really about Dora Martin.

Höfgen's relationship with Juliette, the fierce child of nature, was more than a mere sexual affair; it was complicated and secret. Hendrik set great store by this. At the same time, he believed that his relationship with Barbara—Barbara whom he had called his good angel—was not wholly at an end but could still be the source of marvels and surprises. When he reviewed the determining factors of his inner life, he never forgot to include Barbara—with whom he had in fact more and more lost contact.

The most important item on this list of inner involvements remained, however, his revolutionary faith. Under no circumstances did he want to deny himself this rare mark of validity that so favorably distinguished him from the general run of Berlin actors. For this reason he put a certain amount of zeal and adroitness into maintaining his friendship with Otto Ulrichs, who had given up his post with the Hamburg Arts Theater and ran a political cabaret in north Berlin.

"Now all our strength must be placed at the disposal of the political cause," Otto Ulrichs declared. "We have no more time to lose. The day of decision is near."

His cabaret, called the Stormy Petrel, caused a stir far beyond the workers' quarter. Its sketches were bitingly witty and of the highest quality, and young workers appeared there alongside celebrated writers and actors. Hendrik felt that he could get away with a personal appearance on its narrow stage on the occasion of a gala performance given in honor of visiting Soviet authors. Ulrichs announced to the audience that the celebrated Hendrik Höfgen of the State Theater would appear as a special attraction, but before he could finish his introduction, Höfgen, who was wearing his simplest gray suit and had left his Mercedes behind in favor of a taxi, sprang from the wings. "Forget fame, forget the State Theater," he cried in his ringing metallic voice, throwing up his arms in a fine expansive gesture. "I am your comrade Höfgen." The audience roared with delight. The next day the strongly Marxist critic Dr. Ihrig reported in the *New Stock Exchange Gazette* that the actor Höfgen had in one moment captured the hearts of the Berlin working class.

Such stirring happenings in the proletarian suburbs appeased a conscience that might otherwise have rebelled at the commercial non-sense produced and acted in the West End. He belonged to the avant-garde: it was not only his inner consciousness that told him so but members of the literary set—such as Ihrig—who should know what they were talking about. And the attacks of such laughable figures as Caesar von Muck left no doubt about it. He belonged to the literary vanguard: the new productions of the Wagner operas were bold experi-ments—it was only too understandable that they brought the reaction-aries out in force against him. Moreover, he talked with a renewed interest of an avant-garde "workshop"—a series of the most modern experimental plays. In fact, Hendrik went no further toward following up these ambitious plans than he had with the Revolutionary Theater in Hamburg, but he spoke of the project so often and in such seductive terms that young actors and poets spoke about it for years afterward with enthusiasm and gratitude. He belonged to the revolutionary elite and he paid his way. Through Otto Ulrichs, Höfgen made contribu-

149

tions, which were not large but were joyfully accepted, to certain Communist party organizations.

Who would dare suggest that he lived a shiftless and empty life, never looking beyond the present day? His intensive participation in the great contemporary problems had been proved. Proudly Hendrik compared his own blameless radical commitment with the half-hearted approach of others, such as Barbara, for instance, who in the houses of the privy councillor and the general's widow was leading a futile and self-centered life absorbed in her intellectual games and preoccupations.

But what did Hendrik know of Barbara's cares and pastimes? What did Hendrik understand of mankind as a whole? Where human beings were concerned, wasn't he as much at sea as he was in politics? Had he behaved toward the women whom he called the "center of his life" more lovingly than he had to little Böck, who was now formally employed as his servant, or to M. Pierre Larue, who gave splendid dinners for "my young communist comrades" in the Hotel Esplanade?

Did Hendrik give a second thought to the inner life of his mistress, Juliette? He expected her always to be wonderfully brutal and good-humored. She earned good money swinging her whip. Didn't she have every reason to be content? Höfgen never troubled himself about the dark looks that the black girl now so often directed at him. Was she perhaps homesick for the more beautiful landscape from which a capricious fate had driven her into a seedy civilized world? Had she perhaps begun in her secret heart to love her sallow-complexioned pain-addicted friend? Or had she started to hate him? Hendrik knew nothing of either possibility. For him Princess Tebab was a bewitching barbarian, a handsome wild animal in whose untamed strength he refreshed himself. He guessed as little about Juliette as he knew about Barbara and his mother.

Hendrik passed a rapid eye over the letters of his poor mother, for whom her husband and daughter—two volatile and decidedly light-weight characters—were a source of extreme concern. His father had been totally ruined. "It's the economic crisis," his mother wailed. "Your good father is among the countless victims of the crisis." All his investments and savings had been swallowed up, and shameful disaster would have engulfed the family had not Hendrik been able to cable an eleventh-hour rescue in the form of a large sum of money. His sister Josy still got herself engaged every six months, and Frau Bella breathed more freely when these ties were broken off.

Once Nicoletta appeared in Berlin. But she soon returned home, recalled by a threatening and complaining telegram from her husband. "I am very, very happy with him," Nicoletta declared, taking great trouble to flash her beautiful eyes as in the old days. But then it emerged that Marder had been living for the past two years in a sanitarium; Nicoletta had been spending her time tending him. She smiled softly and warmly when she spoke of the childlike thankfulness with which the man of genius rewarded her.

"Now he is getting along much better," she said. "We can soon be off to the South. He needs sun . . ."

The loving Nicoletta possessed her "center of life," while Hendrik could only falsely boast of having Barbara. Others, too, could lay claim to an abiding faith—like Ulrichs, who patiently awaited "the day." Hans Miklas, too, promised in a voice of joyful certainty, "The day will come." For him, the beautiful day was when the Führer would at last come to power and his enemies would all be destroyed. And destruction would certainly descend on the most pernicious and fearful enemy of all—Höfgen. The overthrow of the object of his hatred, whose career Miklas followed from afar with impotent wrath, would be the most enjoyable event of the Great Day. Hans Miklas— like Otto Ulrichs, his political enemy—was an actor merely to serve the great goal. For a long while he had worked not in the theater but for the Nazi Youth movement. He rehearsed his Führer's young followers for open-air rallies and recruiting-drive demonstrations. Work of this kind satisfied his ignorant but enthusiastic heart. Under his direction, Miklas's comrades roared in chorus that they would triumphantly strike down the French and would always keep faith with their leader. Miklas now looked much healthier and fresher than he had in the Hamburg days. The black hollows had almost disappeared from his cheeks.

The day is approaching. That blazing conviction drives Hans Miklas and Otto Ulrichs forward, consuming them and millions of other young people. But for what day is Hendrik Höfgen waiting? He never waits for anything but a new part. His great role in the 1932–33 season is to be Mephisto in a new production of Faust *with which the State Theater will celebrate the centenary of Goethe's death.*

Mephistopheles—"the strange son of Chaos"—the great role of Hendrik Höfgen. Never had he prepared a characterization with such ardor. Mephisto would be his masterpiece. Hendrik made the Prince of Darkness into a "rascal"—precisely the rascal that the Lord of Heaven in His infinite goodness sees in him and honors from time to time with His company—for Mephisto is, of all the spirits that deny Him, the least troublesome to the Almighty. Hendrik's Mephisto was a tragic clown, a diabolical Pierrot. His shaved head was powdered as white as his face, his eyebrows painted grotesquely high, his blood-red mouth stretched into a fixed smile. The wide space between his eyes and the brows shimmered in a hundred different hues. All colors of the rainbow mingled on Mephisto's eyelids and under the arc of his black brows: red merged into orange, then into violet and blue; silver dots glistened in between, and a little gold was lightly spread throughout. The result was a shimmering landscape that set off the hypnotic jewel-like eyes of this Satan.

Hendrik/Mephisto glided across the stage with the grace of a dancer in a close-fitting costume of black silk. With a teasing precision, the shocking epigrams and dialectical jokes tripped from his incessantly smiling red mouth. Who could doubt this horribly elegant jester's power to turn himself into a poodle and draw wine from the wood of a table or fly through the air on his cloak? The most improbable things could be believed of this Mephisto. He was strong—stronger even than God the Father, whom from time to time he willingly saw and treated with a somewhat disdainful courtesy. Had he not good reason to look down on Him a little? For Mephisto was much wittier, much wiser, and in any case much more unfortunate than the Lord; and perhaps there lay the secret of his greater strength—his greater misfortune. The enormous optimism of the exalted Old Man, who allowed his angels to extol Him and His creation in endless song, and His euphoric good nature made an almost simple-minded and senile impression beside the terrible melancholy into which the once favorite angel, the accursed and the dweller in the abyss, fell from time to time between his bouts of sinister vivacity. A shiver went through the audience in the Berlin State Theater when Höfgen/Mephistopheles intoned:

152

For all that meets our eyes
Is worthy only of a quick demise;
And it were better nothing takes its place.

And then he stood motionless. Was he frozen with misery? Under the greasepaint his eyes now had the steady gaze of despair. Let the angels shout for joy around God's throne: they know nothing of human nature. The Devil knows mankind: he has been initiated into its wicked secrets.

After the *Faust* first night, which ended with a great ovation, the actor Höfgen locked himself away in his dressing room: he did not want to see anyone. Little Böck, however, did not dare turn aside one visitor. It seldom happened that Dora Martin came to performances in which she herself was not playing. Her presence that evening had caused a sensation. Little Böck bowed deeply before her and opened the door to the sanctuary—Hendrik Höfgen's dressing room.

They both looked exhausted—Höfgen, and his colleague and rival. He, overtaxed and spent by the exalted performance, and she by cares of which he had no knowledge.

"It was good," said Dora Martin in a quiet, matter-of-fact voice. She had sat down immediately on a narrow armchair, before he had time to invite her to do so. She sat hunched forward, her face, with its high forehead and the large childlike, thoughtful eyes, sunk deep in the collar of her brown fur coat. "It was good, Hendrik. I knew you could do it. Mephisto is your great role."

Hendrik, sitting at his makeup table with his back to her, smiled at her from the mirror. "You don't say that without malice, Dora."

Still in the same quiet, even tone she answered, "You're wrong, Hendrik. I never take it amiss that someone is what he is."

Hendrik now turned his face from which he had wiped the devil's brows and the rainbow-coloured lids. "Thank you for coming tonight," he said, flashing his eyes at her.

But she waved this aside almost contemptuously as if to say, Let's dispense with these pleasantries. He pretended to overlook her gesture and said tenderly, "What are your immediate plans, Dora?"

"I've learned English," she answered.

His face registered a look of astonishment. "English, but why—why English?"

153

"Because I'm going to act in the American theater," said Dora Martin without turning her still, searching glance from him.

When he persisted in his charade of bewilderment, she explained with a certain impatience. "Because the end has come here, my dear. Hasn't that struck you yet?"

At this he grew indignant. "But what are you talking about, Dora? Nothing will change where you're concerned. Your position is unshakable. You are loved—really loved—by thousands of people. None of the rest of us—as you well know yourself—is as much loved as you are."

Here her smile became so sad and scornful that he fell silent. "The love of many thousands." Her voice was weary and toneless with contempt. She shrugged her shoulders. And after a moment's silence spent looking past Hendrik at the blank wall, she said, "They'll have to find other loves."

He continued to protest in an agitated stammer, "But the theater will stay in business. The theater is always going to interest people, whatever else happens in Germany."

"Whatever else happens in Germany," Dora repeated quietly as she rose abruptly to her feet. "Well, I wish you all the best, Hendrik," she said quickly. "It'll be a long time before we meet again. I'm leaving in the next few days."

He was stunned. "The next few days!"

With her dark eyes still gazing into the distance, she said, "There's no sense in putting it off any longer. I have nothing left to look for here." After another pause she added, "But things will certainly go well for you, Hendrik Höfgen—whatever else happens in Germany."

Under the red-tinted profusion of hair, her face—a rather too large face for the small and narrow body—bore an expression of pride mixed with sorrow as she slowly turned to the door and left Hendrik Höfgen's dressing room.

7

The Pact with the Devil

Woe to this land, for the sky above it has grown dark. God has turned his face away, and a river of blood and tears flows through the streets of all its cities.

Woe to this land, for it is defiled, and no one knows when it can be made clean again. What must be the penance? What mighty contribution to the well-being of mankind must this land make to atone for so boundless an infamy?

The foul lie usurps power in this land. It roars in the congress halls, from the microphones, from the pages of newspapers, from the cinema screen. Its mouth gapes wide, and from its rage comes the stench of pestilence. Many are those who are driven from this land. And for those who are forced to stay, their land has become a prison—a stinking dungeon.

The horsemen of the Apocalypse are on their way. Here they have dismounted and conscripted a hideous regiment. From here they mean to conquer the world—where men today laugh at them, they shall tomorrow lie prostrate before them.

It is night in our fatherland. Wicked men range through its provinces. Wherever they or their base accomplices appear the light of reason is extinguished.

The actor Hendrik Höfgen was out of the country when—thanks to the intrigues in the palace of the revered president of the Reich and field marshal—the man with the screaming voice, whom Hans Miklas and a large number of other ignorant and despairing people called their Führer, became chancellor. The actor Hendrik Höfgen was playing an elegant confidence man in a detective movie whose location shots were being filmed near Madrid. After a strenuous day he returned exhausted to the hotel, bought newspapers from the porter and received the shock of his life. Was it possible? The blustering lout whom his brilliant and progressive friends had so often ridiculed had now suddenly become the most powerful man in the country! This is horrible, thought the actor Hendrik Höfgen. A hideous surprise. And I was absolutely positive that these Nazis were not to be taken seriously. What a fiasco!

He stood in his handsome beige spring suit in the hall of the Ritz Hotel, where an international clientele discussed the portentous developments in Germany and their impact on the stock exchange. Poor Hendrik went hot and cold as he thought about what might lie in store for him in the near future. A large number of people to whom he had always done harm now would perhaps have the opportunity of avenging themselves. Caesar von Muck, for instance. Ah, if only he had behaved a little better to the Blood and Soil writers, instead of rejecting all their works! What unforgivable errors you can make— now you realize it, and it's too late! It was too late, for among the Nazis he had made irreconcilable enemies. Deeply shaken, Hendrik thought even of little Hans Miklas: what wouldn't he now give to wipe out that unfortunate incident in the Hamburg Arts Theater! An actress called Lotte Lindenthal was a trifling pretext for a row that now took on such a deplorable aspect. It was very possible that this same actress had suddenly become someone in a position of influence where she had the power to help or damage a man's chances.

With trembling knees Hendrik walked to the elevator. He canceled an evening appointment and ordered dinner in his room. After he had drunk half a bottle of champagne, his mood became a little more optimistic.

You have to remain cool and collected and stave off the impulse to panic. This so-called Führer was chancellor of the Reich—that was certainly bad. However, he wasn't yet a dictator and would almost certainly never become one. The people who had raised him to power, these German nationalists, would be very careful to see that he did not grow too big for them to handle. Then he thought of the powerful opposition parties—they were certainly still in business. The Social Democrats and the Communists would put up resistance, maybe even armed resistance. This was the conclusion Hendrik Höfgen reached in his hotel room with half a bottle of champagne at his elbow; the thought of the coming struggle sent an almost voluptuous shiver down his spine. No, there was a long way to go before the country became a Nazi dictatorship. The situation might even undergo a sudden reversal. The attempt to hand over the German people to fascism could end in the socialist revolution. Something of the sort was very possible, and then everyone would see that the actor Höfgen had gambled with cunning and foresight. But even if the Nazis remained in power, what had he, Höfgen, to fear from them? He belonged to no party. And he wasn't a Jew. This fact above all others—that he was not a Jew—struck Hendrik all of a sudden as immensely comforting and important. He had never in the past estimated the true worth of this considerable and unsuspected advantage. He wasn't a Jew, and so everything could be forgiven him, even his having let himself be acclaimed as "comrade" in the Stormy Petrel. He was a blond Rhinelander. His father, too, had been a blond Rhinelander before financial worries had turned him gray. And his mother Bella and his sister Josy were impeccably blond Rhineland women.

"I am a blond Rhinelander," exulted Hendrik Höfgen, revived by champagne and his optimistic reflections on the political scene. It was in the best of spirits that he went to bed.

But the next morning his uneasiness returned. How would he be treated by his colleagues—those who had never set foot in the Stormy Petrel and who had never been called "cultural Bolsheviks" by Caesar von Muck? And it did seem to him that they treated him with a certain coldness as they all were driven to the location site. Only the Jewish comedian engaged him in a long conversation, and that might be taken as a worrisome omen. Because Hendrik felt isolated and already a little martyred, he was defiant and bad-tempered as he told the comedian that, in his opinion, the Nazis would very soon run out of steam and appear ridiculous. But the little comic answered anxiously, "Ah, no—once they're in the saddle, they'll remain there for a long time. God grant that they'll adopt a slightly more reasonable attitude and show a little forbearance where we're concerned. But if one behaves very quietly, nothing much can happen." In his heart, Hendrik shared these hopes but he was too proud to say so.

Bad weather, which caused an interruption of several days in the film company's location schedule, confined the cast to Madrid until the end of February. The news from home was disturbingly contradictory. It appeared that Berlin was in an absolute delirium of enthusiasm for its new Nazi *Reichskanzler*. But a very different state of affairs prevailed—if one was to believe newspaper reports and private informants—in southern Germany, particularly in Munich. Forecasts that Bavaria would cut loose from the Reich led to rumors that the Bavarian royal house of Wittelsbach would be reinstated. It was considered wiser, however, not to rely too heavily on what appeared to be tendentious overstatement and to express enthusiastic support for the new regime.

Such was the decision, too, of the German actors gathered in Madrid. The young male star—a handsome man with a long Slav-sounding name—suddenly announced that he had been a member of the German National Socialist Workers party for years—a fact he had been careful to conceal until now. The actress playing opposite him, whose melting dark eyes and slightly hooked nose aroused doubt as to her German racial purity, let it be known that she was as good as engaged to a high official of the same party. Daily the Jewish comedian looked more depressed.

Hendrik for his part had decided to adopt the simplest and most effective strategy: he withdrew into an enigmatic silence. Nobody must guess how many worries were gnawing at him; communications he received from Rose Bernhard and other supporters in Berlin were appalling. Rose wrote that one had to be prepared for the worst. She dropped dark hints about "black lists" that the Nazis had been preparing for years past and on which figured the names of Privy Councillor Bruckner, the Professor and Hendrik Höfgen. The Professor was in London and had decided for the time being not to return to Berlin. Fräulein Bernhard urged her Hendrik to follow his example and to stay away from the German capital for a while. Hendrik shivered as he read this. A moment ago he had been one of the elite—was he now to become an outlaw? It was not easy for him to maintain an expression of calm on the set and to flash his famous smile as though nothing had happened.

But when the company began preparing for the homeward

journey, and even the careworn Jewish comedian packed his suitcase, Hendrik announced that pressing discusssions about possible movie assignments called him to Paris. I must win time, he thought. It did not seem advisable for him to show his face in Berlin at this moment. In a few weeks the situation would probably have quieted down.

But the most sensational upheavals were at hand. The first news that met Hendrik in Paris was the burning of the Reichstag. His long experience as a player of villains, which had given him an understanding of the criminal mind, as well as a certain natural instinct for the intrigues of the underworld, left him in no doubt as to who had contrived and committed the outrage. Precisely those films and plays in which Hendrik liked to star had inspired the infamous, and at the same time infantile, cunning of the Nazis. Hendrik could not deny to himself that the horror aroused in him by the burning of the German parliament was mixed with another feeling—pleasure that was almost sensual. The corrupt imagination of thugs had devised a fraud that could only succeed because there was no one left in Germany who dared to raise his voice against it, and because the rest of the world, valuing its own peace more than the morality of European life, did not seem disposed to get involved in the unsavory affairs of this decadent empire.

How strong evil is, thought Hendrik with an awestruck shudder. How it seizes on everything it wants and escapes unscathed! Things really happen in the world as they do in the films and plays of which I have so often been the hero. This was as boldly as he ventured to put it to himself at the moment. But without wanting to admit as much, he felt for the first time a mysterious connection between his own nature and the appalling mentality that could instigate such base acts as the burning of the Reichstag.

Hendrik was scarcely inclined to brood further on the psychology of the German malefactors. He had more urgent worries to preoccupy him. After the Reichstag fire a number of people with whom he had been closely acquainted were arrested in Berlin, among them Otto Ulrichs. Rose Bernhard had hastily abandoned her job with the Kurfürstendamm theaters and left for Vienna. From there she sent a letter to Hendrik insisting that he must on no account set foot on German soil. "Your life would be in danger," she wrote from the Hotel Bristol.

Though Hendrik thought there was an element of romantic

exaggeration here, he was nevertheless alarmed. He postponed his return journey from day to day. Idle and anxious, he strolled through the Paris streets. He did not know the city, but was in no mood to explore and fall under the spell of its magic or even to notice that it had any.

These were bitter weeks, the bitterest perhaps that he had ever endured. He saw no one. Certainly he knew that some of his acquaintances had arrived in Paris, but he did not dare make contact with them. What would their conversation be about? They would fray his nerves with pathetic outbursts of horror over events in Germany, which were in fact growing ever madder and more ghastly. These people had broken all links with their homeland because they hated the tyrants who now ruled it. They were already emigrés. Am I one too? Hendrik asked himself anxiously. But everything in him fiercely resisted any such admission.

Moreover, during the long lonely hours he spent in his hotel room, on the bridges, in the streets and cafés of Paris, a sullen defiance began to grow in him—the best feeling he had ever mustered. Must I beg this murderous crew for forgiveness? he asked himself. Am I dependent on them? Haven't I already an international reputation? I can survive anywhere—it may not be easy but I shall pull through all the same. What a relief. Yes, what a redemption it would be to withdraw from a country where the air is poisoned and to declare with a loud voice one's solidarity with those who want to fight against the bloodstained regime! How clean I would feel if I could win through to such a decision. What a new meaning, what a new dignity my life would have.

These vehement reflections gave him a melancholy joy but they were quick to fade, and he was aware of a need to see Barbara again and have a long talk with her. His good angel—how urgently he needed her at this moment! But for months he had had no news of her. He had no idea where she could be found. Very probably she was at her grandmother's house with nothing in the world to worry about, he thought bitterly. He had always predicted that she would be able to find interesting aspects to the fascist terror. It had been bound to turn out like this: he was the martyr; it was he who had to wander the streets of this foreign city, while she perhaps was already chatting pleasantly to one of these murderers and torturers, just as she had liked to chatter to Hans Miklas . . .

When his loneliness began to be unbearable he toyed with the notion of summoning Princess Tebab to join him in Paris. How refreshing and invigorating it would be to hear her sulky laugh again and to touch her strong hand with its skin that was as rough as the bark of a tree . . . To turn one's back on Germany and to begin a new wild life with Princess Tebab—ah, how beautiful and good that would be. Could it then not happen? Wasn't it within the bounds of possibility? All that was needed was a cable to Berlin and the next day the black Venus would arrive with her long green boots and the red braided whip in her luggage. Hendrik had delicious daydreams about Princess Tebab. He imagined in raw exciting colors the life that they would lead together. They could begin to earn a livelihood as dance partners in Paris, London or New York. Hendrik and Juliette—the two best tap dancers in the world. But dancing was unlikely to satisfy them for long. Hendrik considered bolder possibilities. From dance partners they could develop into a team of confidence operators. It would be amusing to play in real life the part of a society crook that he had so often portrayed in movies and plays, with all the dangers and the consequences. Side by side with this splendid wild animal, cheating and humiliating a hated society that had now unveiled in fascism its real ghastly face—what an intoxicating performance that would be! For several days the idea obsessed Hendrik. Perhaps he would really have taken the first step toward its fulfillment and dispatched a cable to the black princess had he not received a piece of news that instantly altered his whole situation.

The momentous letter came from little Angelika Siebert. Who would have guessed that it would be this girl, always so horribly and arrogantly ignored by Hendrik, who would now play such a decisive role in his life? It was a long time since Hendrik had given a thought to Angelika, and he now tried to bring her face to mind—the gentle and anxious face of a thirteen-year-old boy with short-sighted, close-set bright eyes. It seemed as though that face had always been wet with tears. Had little Angelika not wept almost interminably? And had he not often given her cause? Hendrik remembered all too clearly how meanly he had treated her most of the time. Her obstinate heart had, however, remained true to him through it all. This amazed Hendrik, and with good reason. He reached conclusions about others from his own behavior and he always expected others to behave with outrageous selfishness. Good behavior, the honest charitable action, left him speechless. In his grim hotel room, whose walls and furniture he already knew so well that he had begun to hate and fear them, he burst into tears after reading Angelika's letter. There was nervousness and overstrain lying behind his sobbing, but also something more—he was genuinely moved. What a blessing, what a compensation for so much suffering it would have been for Angelika had she been able to see this. Höfgen, on whose account she had shed so many tears, now wept himself, and it was her love finally that drew the salty drops from his cold eyes.

Angelika reported in her letter that she was in Berlin to do a bit of film work and things were going passably well for her. A successful young director had decided that he wanted to marry her. "But naturally I don't have any ideas of that kind," she wrote. Hendrik could not help smiling as he read this. Yes, that was Angelika, all right—always chaste and recoiling from every attempt at courtship however attractive it might appear, always with her eyes firmly set on the unobtainable, lavishing her passion wherever it would be ignored and slighted.

On the film set recently she had run into the actress Lotte Lindenthal, who used to play lovelorn young girls in the Jena repertory company and was the companion of a Nazi air force officer. Hendrik, who followed developments in Germany in the newspapers, knew that the air force officer now belonged to the powerful inner circle of the new Reich. As a result, Lotte Lindenthal had become an extremely influential character.

In gushing terms the letter described the superior charm, intelligence, sweetness and dignity of Lotte Lindenthal. One could be sure, Angelika felt, that this kind and delightful woman would in every way have the best influence on her powerful friend, particularly in all things to do with the theater. The great man had a marvelous interest in plays, operettas and opera. His mistresses—or, rather, the ladies who had enjoyed his particular admiration—had been for the most part plump young actresses who played ingénue roles. He had willingly done everything he could to please them, as long as nothing serious was involved, amusing minor favors such as the advancement of an actor's career.

Angelika had informed Lotte Lindenthal that Hendrik Höfgen was sitting in Paris and did not feel happy about returning to Germany. At this the favorite of the powerful man had laughed good-naturedly. What had this man to fear? Lotte had opened her eyes wide with an air of bewilderment as she asked the question. Höfgen was certainly not a Jew, he was a blond Rhinelander. And he had never belonged to a party. Besides, he was an important artist— Fräulein Lindenthal had seen his Mephisto. "We really can't afford to lose people like that," said the splendid lady, and she promised to talk to her powerful friend that very same day about the whole affair.

"Hubby is a thoroughgoing liberal," insisted the actress from Jena, who was surely the one to know—and all those present felt an awestruck shiver because she had condescended to talk of the feared giant in such a lovingly intimate way. "He bears absolutely no grudges. In the past this Höfgen may well have lent himself to a number of excesses and little stupidities. Hubby is understanding of that kind of thing when it concerns an artist of a certain stature. The main thing when all is said and done is that a man is sound at the core." Lotte had spoken in rather a scatterbrained way, but with emphatic conviction. And she did what she had promised when the powerful man paid his evening call. "Hubby, be a love," she had implored. She was quite determined, she told him, that Hendrik Höfgen be her co-star in the comedy in which she was to make her debut at the Berlin State Theater. "No one so exactly fits the role as he does —after all, it matters to you, too, that I should have a good partner when I appear before the Berlin party colleagues for the first time." The general had inquired whether Höfgen was a Jew. When he learned that, on the contrary, he was a bona-fide blond Rhinelander, he swore that no harm would come to "this fellow," whatever he may have been up to in earlier days.

Lotte had immediately told her little colleague Angelika about her friendly discussion with Hubby; and Angelika could scarcely wait to inform Hendrik of the happy turn of events.

And so the gloomy ordeal in Paris was at an end! No more lonely walks down the Boulevard St.-Michel, along the banks of the Seine and up the Champs-Elysées. Had Hendrik ever indulged in bold and rebellious dreams in a bleak hotel room? Had he ever felt a strong need to purify himself and the obscure pleasure that went with it—the desire to break free and escape into a new, turbulent life? He no longer knew whether he had or not; all was forgotten in the time it took to pack his cases. Humming with contentment and much tempted to make sudden leaps in the air, he hurried to Thomas Cook

& Son, the travel agent at the Madeleine, to reserve his sleeper on the train to Berlin.

On the way back to his hotel off the Boulevard Montparnasse, Hendrik came to the Café du Dôme. The weather was mild and many people were sitting on the open terrace. Hendrik was hot from the long walk and felt an impulse to sit here for a quarter of an hour and drink a glass of orange juice. But he remained standing; and while he cast a supercilious glance over the chattering crowd, he changed his mind. Who knew what kind of people you might encounter here? Perhaps old acquaintances whom he would much rather avoid were among them. Isn't this Café du Dôme a meeting place for the exiles? No, no, it would be much better to walk on. He was just about to turn away; when a group of people sitting silently at one of the little round tables caught his eye. Hendrik staggered backwards; he received such a shock that he felt a shooting pain in his stomach and for a few seconds was unable to move.

First he recognized Frau von Herzfeld. Then he noticed that next to her sat Barbara. Barbara was in Paris. All this time she had been close to him. He had yearned for her; he had needed her as never before, and she had been living in the same city, in the same *quartier*, perhaps only a few houses away from him. Barbara had left Germany and there she sat on the terrace of the Café du Dôme. There she was, next to Hedda von Herzfeld, with whom in Hamburg she had been in no way on friendly terms. But now hard and exceptional circumstances had brought these two together . . . They sat at the same table, both with the same melancholy, thoughtful gaze that seemed to look straight through their surroundings and to be fixed in the far distance.

How pale Barbara was! To Hendrik it was as though they were not really sitting there opposite him but were the product of his own agitated brain—a vision of his own making. If they were real, why did they not move? Why did they sit there so bereft of speech and motion?

Barbara's small, pale face was cupped in her hands. Between her tightly drawn dark brows ran a furrow that Hendrik had never seen before. Perhaps the result of strenuous embittered reflection, the wrinkle gave her face a brooding, almost angry expression. She wore a gray raincoat and, under its turned-up collar, a bright red scarf. Her clothes and the painfully strained expression of her face lent a wild and almost frightening quality to her appearance.

Hedda was pale, too. But there was no threatening line in her face, only a look of bland melancholy. Apart from Barbara and Hedda, there was another young woman at the table, whom Hendrik had never seen before, as well as two young men—one of whom was Sebastian. Höfgen recognized the sloping shoulders, the veiled thoughtful eyes and the lock of ash-blond hair falling over his forehead.

Hendrik wanted to shout something, call out a greeting, fling his arms around Barbara, talk to her. But thoughts chased each other through his head. How would they receive him? They would ask him questions. How would he answer them? He had a sleeping car ticket to Berlin in his breast pocket. Through the intervention of two kind blond women he was already as good as reconciled with the regime that had driven out these people—the regime against which he had, in Barbara's presence, so often sworn undying enmity. With what a contemptuous smile Sebastian would greet him. And how could he endure Barbara's gaze, her dark, mocking merciless stare? . . . He must take flight—no one appeared to have noticed him, indeed they were still all staring in the same strange way into empty space. He must extricate himself at all costs, for this meeting was beyond his strength . . .

The people around the table did not stir. They seemed to gaze straight through Hendrik Höfgen as if he were thin air. They sat immobile, as though turned to stone by a great sorrow, while Hendrik hurried away with small stiff steps, like a man who escapes from danger in great anxiety but is determined not to give the appearance of running away.

"It's such a shame that the general is so terribly busy now," Lotte Lindenthal said to Höfgen after the first rehearsal. "As soon as he can manage it, he will certainly look in at a rehearsal and watch us at work. You can't imagine what wonderful advice he sometimes gives us actors. I believe he understands as much about the theater as he does about his airplanes—and that's saying something."

Hendrik could imagine it, and he nodded respectfully. Then he asked Fräulein Lindenthal if he could drive her home in his car. She gave her consent with a gracious smile. Offering her his arm, he said softly, "It is such a great, great joy for me to be able to act with you. In recent years I have suffered far too much from the manner-

165

isms of my partners. Dora Martin has corrupted German actresses with the bad example of her convulsive style—that was no theatrical diction but mere hysterical Yiddish jabbering. And now at last I hear again from you a clear, simple tone that is radiant and warm."

She looked at him gratefully with her rather protruding, violet-blue eyes. "I'm so happy you say that to me," she whispered and pressed his arm a little closer to her. "I know that you are not flattering me. A man who takes his calling with such dedicated seriousness as you do, does not flatter in artistic matters."

Hendrik, for his part, expressed horror at the very thought. "But, please . . ." He laid his hand on his heart. "Me—and flattery! My friends are apt to accuse me of being far too ready to cast unpleasant truths in people's faces." Lotte Lindenthal was delighted to hear this. "I have a lot of time for candid people," she said simply.

"What a pity that we are already there," said Hendrik, who had stopped his car in front of a silent imposing house in the Tiergartenstrasse which was Lotte Lindenthal's home. He bowed to kiss her hand, drawing back the gray leather glove a little to allow his lips to brush her milk-white skin. She appeared not to notice this small piece of audacity, or at any rate not to take it amiss, for her smile remained as radiant as before. "A thousand thanks for allowing me to accompany you," he said, still bowed over her hand. As she walked to the door of her house, he thought, if she turns around one last time, all will be well—but if she waves, then it's a triumph, and I can really go far.

She crossed the street holding herself very straight. As she stood before the door of the house, she turned her head with a dazzling smile; and then, to his joy, waved her hand. Hendrik shivered with delight, for Lotte Lindenthal called out gaily, "Bye-bye." That was more than he had dared to hope. With a great sigh of relief he leaned back against the upholstery of his Mercedes.

Hendrik had known even before setting foot again in Berlin that without the protection of Lindenthal he was lost. Angelika, who met him at the station, did not have to make a special point of it: the situation was perfectly clear. He had terrible enemies, among them as influential a character as the writer Caesar von Muck, whom the propaganda minister had made director of the State Theater. The dramatist had prepared an icy reception for the actor, who had so regularly rejected his plays. His face, with its steely eyes and pinched mouth, bore an expression of haughty severity and dignity as he said, "I don't know whether you will manage to settle down among us again, Herr Höfgen. You will find that a very different spirit now reigns in this house from the one to which you have been accustomed. The days of cultural Bolshevism are over." At this point the author of the Tannenberg dramas straightened his shoulders menacingly. "You will no longer have an opportunity of appearing in the works of your friend Marder, or in the French farces you like so much. We now produce neither Semitic nor Gallic works, but German art. You will have to furnish evidence that you can be of assistance in such elevated work. To speak frankly, there didn't seem to me to be any particular reason to call you back here from Paris." At the word "Paris," Caesar von Muck's eyes blazed frighteningly. "But Fräulein Lindenthal wanted you as her partner in the little comedy in which she is to make her debut here." Muck said this with a certain amount of disdain. "I did not want to be disobliging to the lady," he continued with a false respect creeping into his voice. He ended scathingly, "However, I am certain that the part of the elegant hanger-on and seducer will present you with no difficulties." With an abrupt military gesture the director closed the interview.

This was a disturbing beginning. Hendrik knew that behind the vengeful and ambitious poet stood the propaganda minister. In cultural matters he was virtually all-powerful; and he would have been so altogether had not the air force officer promoted to prime minister got it into his head that he too wanted his little say in matters affecting the State Theater. The interest of the fat prime minister was already strong because of Lotte. And so it came to a jurisdictional duel between the two giants—the overlord of propaganda and the overlord of airplanes. Hendrik had not yet seen either of these two demigods face to face; but he knew that he could survive the enmity of one of them for a while only if he was in secure possession of the protection of the other. The way to the prime minister led through the actress. Hendrik had to conquer Lotte Lindenthal.

In the first weeks of his new Berlin career he had only one thought in his head. Lotte Lindenthal must be made to love him. No one had so far failed to succumb to his flashing eyes and "dirty" smile, and Lotte was, after all, only human. This time he knew that everything was at stake, and he must bring all his wiles into play: Lotte must be stormed like a fortress. No matter how full-bosomed and cow-eyed she might be, no matter how provincial and homespun she might look, with her double chin and her blond permanent wave, for him she was as desirable as a goddess.

And Hendrik struggled. He was deaf and blind to everything that went on around him. All his will and intelligence were concentrated on that one aim. Little Angelika had made a grave miscalculation if she believed that out of gratitude Höfgen would now honor her with his attentions. Only in the first hours after his return did he bother to be nice to her. Hardly had she introduced him to Lotte Lindenthal than Angelika seemed to have dropped out of the world as far as he was concerned. She was reduced to crying her eyes out on the shoulder of her film director.

Did he notice how the streets of Berlin had changed? Did he see the brown and black uniforms, the swastika flags, the marching youths? Did he hear the warlike songs that rang out in the streets and from the radio and the film screens? Did he listen to the Führer's speeches with their threats and boasting? Did he read the newspapers, which glossed over, hushed up, lied and still disclosed enough to give an idea of the horror of the new Germany? Did he care about the fate of men whom he had earlier called his friends? He did not even know where they were to be found. Perhaps they were sitting at some café table in Prague, Zurich or Paris; perhaps they were being tortured in a concentration camp; perhaps they were hidden in a Berlin attic or cellar. Hendrik saw no reason to inform himself about these depressing matters. I really can't be of any help to them—this was the formula with which he warded off any thought of the sufferers. He was himself in danger—who knew whether tomorrow Caesar von Muck would not succeed in having him arrested? Only when he himself was finally rescued could he perhaps be useful to the others.

It was against his will and with half an ear that Hendrik listened when people spoke of the rumors circulating about the fate of Otto Ulrichs. The Communist actor and agitator, who was arrested just after the Reichstag fire, had had to endure several of those grim proceedings known as "interrogations" but which in reality were merciless torture sessions. "Someone told me about it who was in the Columbiahaus in the next cell to Ulrichs." So in an anxious hushed voice reported the theater critic Ihrig, who up to January 30, 1933, had belonged to the radical Left and had been an aggressive champion of a strongly Marxist literature exclusively designed to serve the class war. Now he was in the process of making his peace with the new regime. He, the most vigilant and rigorous high priest of Marxist orthodoxy, who had hurled his anathemas at all writers suspected of a bourgeois-liberal or nationalist outlook, who had damned and annihilated them, denouncing them as aesthetic hirelings of capitalism! The Red Pope of literature had not been given to making subtle distinctions. His maxim was: Who is not with me is against me; whoever does not write according to the formula that I hold to be the valid one is an enemy of the proletariat, a fascist—and if he does not yet know it, then he will learn it from me in my newspaper column. Although Dr. Ihrig's categorical judgments appeared in the pages of a strongly capitalist financial newspaper, all those who considered themselves to be members of the left-wing avant-garde took them as holy writ. For in those days financial papers enjoyed treating themselves to the joke of having a Marxist columnist; it added a pungent note and could not seriously disturb anyone. The serious side of life prevailed in the commercial section, but in the pages where no serious businessman ever cast an eye, a Red Pope could be allowed to let off steam.

Dr. Ihrig had let off steam for years and had become a decisive factor in everything connected with Communist art criticism. When the Nazis took power, the Jewish director of the newspaper resigned. But Dr. Ihrig was able to stay on because he could prove that all his forebears on both his father's and his mother's side were "Aryans" and that he had never belonged to any of the socialist parties. Without wavering too long, he began writing his column in the same fierce nationalist spirit that now inspired the political commentaries and was already apparent in the foreign-news reporting. "In any case I have always been against the bourgeoisie and the Democrats," said Dr. Ihrig slyly. He could now continue to thunder against "reactionary liberalism" as before—only the key signature of his antiliberal compositions had changed.

"Ghastly, this business of Otto," said the worthy Dr. Ihrig with a woebegone expression. In many of his former articles he had described the Stormy Petrel as the only theatrical enterprise in the German capital that had a future and was at all worthy of consideration. Ulrichs had belonged to the critic's inner circle. "Ghastly, ghastly," murmured the doctor and nervously removed his horn-rimmed spectacles to polish them.

Hendrik, too, was of the opinion that it was ghastly. Apart from that, the two gentlemen had little to say. They felt rather uncomfortable in each other's company. They had chosen as their meeting place a secluded café which had conveniently few customers. They were both compromised by their past; both were probably still under suspicion of harboring hostile convictions, and it might be taken almost as a sign of conspiracy if they were seen together.

Silently they gazed thoughtfully ahead of them with unfocused eyes, one through his horn-rimmed spectacles and the other through his monocle.

"As I need hardly say, there is absolutely nothing I can do for the poor fellow at the moment," said Hendrik finally. Ihrig, who was about to say the same thing, nodded. Then they were both silent again. Hendrik toyed with his cigarette holder. Ihrig cleared his throat. Perhaps each was ashamed in the presence of the other. Each knew what the other was thinking. Höfgen thought of Ihrig and Ihrig of Höfgen: *Yes, yes, my friend, you're just as great a bastard as I am.*

Because the silence had become unbearable, Hendrik rose to his feet. "One must have patience," he said softly, adopting his sallow governess face for the benefit of the revolutionary critic. "It's not easy. But one must have patience. Good-bye, my friend."

Hendrik had every reason for contentment. Lotte Lindenthal's smile grew ever sweeter, ever more promising. When they rehearsed a love scene together—and the comedy *The Heart* was made up almost entirely of an intimate dialogue between the wife of a successful businessman and the amorous friend of the family—Lotte would sigh, press her bosom against her partner and direct melting glances at him.

Hendrik maintained a reserve intended to convey the impression of a melancholy self-discipline restraining a feverish desire. For the most part he addressed Fräulein Lindenthal formally as "Dear lady," on rare occasions changing to "Fräulein Lotte," and only at work did he once in the shared ardor of their rehearsals slip into the intimate "thou" form of address which was normal among theatrical colleagues. But his eyes always seemed to be saying, Ah, if only I could, how I would like to! How I would embrace you, you angel. How I would press you to me, you beauty. To my great regret I must restrain myself out of loyalty to a German hero who calls you his . . . Such were the lustful thoughts fettered by a virile resignation that were to be read in the soulful eyes of the actor Höfgen. In reality he was thinking: Why in God's name did the prime minister, who can have any woman he likes, have to choose her? She may be a fine person and a superb hostess, but she's really horribly fat and ridiculously affected. And on top of it all, she's a bad actress . . .

At rehearsal from time to time he had a great desire to shout at Lotte. He would have said straight out to any other actress, "What you are doing there, my dear, is the worst form of provincial repertory. Just because you are playing an upper-class lady there is no excuse for talking in such a piercingly high and affected voice, and for grotesquely raising your little finger as you do the whole time. Upper-class ladies dropped this habit long ago. And how did you get the idea that the wife of a wealthy businessman, flirting with her house guest, should hold her elbows far away from her body as though she had spilled some disgusting liquid on her dress and was afraid of getting it on her sleeves. Please drop these absurdities!"

Naturally, Hendrik was very careful not to say anything of the sort to Lotte. Even so, she seemed to sense that she was making a fool of herself at the rehearsals. "I still feel so unsure of myself," she said, putting on her innocent little-girl face. "It's the Berlin atmosphere—that's what makes me feel confused. Oh, I know I'm going to flop dreadfully and get miserable reviews." She behaved as though she was some little unknown beginner who had real cause to fear the Berlin critics. "Oh, please, please, Hendrik, tell me"—she made a little childlike clapping gesture with her raised hands—"will they treat me absolutely horribly? Will they attack me and tear me apart?" With a ring of true conviction Hendrik could assure her he believed this was absolutely out of the question.

While Hendrik and Lotte were still rehearsing *The Heart* it became known that *Faust* would once again be included in the repertory of the State Theater. To his dismay, Hendrik learned that Caesar von Muck—certainly with the backing of the propaganda minister—had decided to give the role of Mephisto to an actor who had for years been a member of the Nazi party, and that several weeks earlier the man had been summoned to Berlin from the provinces. This was the revenge of the Tannenberg author for the plays that Hendrik had rejected. Hendrik thought: I shall be finished if Muck carries through his appalling scheme. Mephisto is my greatest part. If I am not allowed to play it, all the world will know that I am in disgrace. It will be plain that Lotte Lindenthal is not intervening on my behalf with her prime minister, or that she does not have the kind of influence with which she is generally credited. In that case there is nothing left for me but to pack my trunk and return to Paris . . . Perhaps I should have stayed there in the first place. Here everything is really ghastly. My position is wretched, especially in comparison with the one I had before. Everyone looks at me distrustfully. They know that the director and the propaganda minister hate me, and they do not yet have the smallest proof that I am really in the good graces of the air force general. A fine mess I have got myself into! But Mephisto could still save the day—everything depends on him . . .

Before the beginning of a rehearsal Höfgen approached Lotte Lindenthal with a firm step, and for once the vibrato in his voice was not affected. "Fräulein Lotte—I have a great, great favor to ask you."

She smiled a little anxiously. "I'm always happy to help out my friends and colleagues—if I can."

Gazing hypnotically into her eyes, he said, "I *must* play Mephisto. Do you understand, Lotte?" His urgent gravity alarmed her, and she was agitated by the closeness of his body, to which she had for some time not been indifferent. Blushing softly, her eyes cast down, she whispered, "I will see what I can do." She spoke in the tone of a young girl receiving a proposal of marriage who promises to talk to her parents. "I'll talk to *him* today."

Hendrik gave a great sigh of relief.

Next morning the secretary of the director of the State Theater rang to inform him that he was expected to attend that afternoon's preliminary rehearsal for the *Faust* production. This was victory. The prime minister had intervened in his favor. *I am saved*, thought Hendrik. He sent a huge bouquet of yellow roses to Lotte Lindenthal; with the beautiful flowers went a card on which he had written THANK YOU.

It seemed only natural to him that Director von Muck should invite him to visit his office before the beginning of the rehearsal. The nationalist poet greeted him with the most heartfelt cordiality, which

172

was a far more remarkable feat of acting than the air of aristocratic reserve assumed by Hendrik.

"I am delighted to see you as Mephisto," said the dramatist, letting a warm light kindle in his steel-blue eyes as with virile sincerity he grasped the hand of the man he had wanted to destroy. "I am as happy as a child to see you in this eternal, profoundly German role." It was clear that the director had decided to make an immediate and radical change in his attitude toward Höfgen. Naturally, Caesar von Muck still had the inexorable intention of not allowing this dangerous fellow to climb too high, but he thought it advisable to pursue his struggle against his old enemy from now on in a more stealthy and cunning manner. Herr von Muck certainly had no desire to fall out with either the powerful prime minister or Lotte Lindenthal over Höfgen. As director of the Prussian State Theater he had every reason to maintain just as good relations with the Prussian prime minister as with the minister for propaganda.

"Between ourselves," continued the director with an air of comradely connivance, "you have me to thank for this chance to play Mephisto again." It was perhaps his desire to reinforce the vigorous honesty in his voice that made his Saxon accent particularly strong. "There were certain doubts on the subject"—he lowered his voice and grimaced in regret—"certain doubts in ministerial circles. You understand, my dear Höfgen—people feared that you might introduce into our new interpretation the spirit of the former *Faust* production, which, people complained, was somewhat contaminated with cultural Bolshevism. But now I have succeeded in refuting and dissipating these fears." And with that the director heartily slapped the actor on the shoulder.

On this otherwise successful day, Höfgen had to weather an unpleasant shock. As he walked onstage for the rehearsal he bumped into Hans Miklas, to whom Hendrik had not given a thought for several weeks. Miklas had been engaged by the State Theater to play the schoolboy in the new *Faust* production. Hendrik was completely unprepared for this meeting. He had had too much on his mind to worry about the casting of the smaller parts. Now in a split second he asked himself how he should react. This intractable youth still hated him. If that had not been immediately evident, the malevolent glance he now cast at Hendrik amply confirmed it. Miklas had not forgotten; and he could damage him if he had a mind to do so. What prevented him from telling Lotte Lindenthal why they had quarreled in H.K.? Hendrik would be lost if Miklas got that idea into his head. But he wouldn't dare—it was unlikely that he would ever go to those lengths. Hendrik decided to ignore the young actor and to intimidate him with his disdain. Then Miklas would think he was once again securely on top of the world and that it was he, Hendrik, who had all the trumps in his hand. He fixed his monocle in his eye, made a mocking face and said with a nasal twang, "Herr Miklas—well, I never—so you're still around."

Hans Miklas clenched his teeth and remained silent, keeping his face expressionless. But once Hendrik was out of sight it contracted with hate and pain. No one took any notice of him as he stood brooding and alone in the wings. No one saw that his fists were clenched and his bright eyes filled with tears. Hans Miklas's small wiry body trembled—the body of an undernourished street urchin and an over-exercised acrobat.

Perhaps Hans Miklas had begun to see that he had been betrayed—betrayed to a horrible, immense and no longer reparable extent? Ah, perhaps he had not yet reached the point where he could take it all in, but he was aware of the first hints. And these stirrings were tightening his fists and filling his eyes with tears.

In the first weeks after the government takeover by the National Socialists and their Führer, Miklas had felt he was in heaven. The great and beautiful day, the day of fulfillment, awaited so patiently and with so great a longing, had at last arrived. It was an explosion of joy. Young Miklas had sobbed and danced with happiness. In those days his face had shone with wild enthusiasm and his eyes had glowed.

During the torchlight procession in honor of the *Reichskanzler*, the Führer, the Savior, how he had roared in the streets and moved his limbs like a man possessed, swept along by the frenzy which seized not only a city but also a whole nation. Now all promises would become facts. Without any doubt a golden age was about to dawn. Germany had its honor restored, and soon its society would be transformed and wonderfully renewed in the form of a real people's community. For so the Führer had promised one hundred times, and the martyrs of the National Socialist movement had sealed this promise with their blood.

The fourteen years of shame were over. Everything up to now had been only struggle and preparation; now life began in earnest. Now at last men could work together for the construction of a healthy and powerful fatherland. Hans Miklas got himself a badly paid job at the State Theater; a well-placed party official had arranged it for him. Höfgen was in Paris, Höfgen was an emigrant—and Miklas had a job in the Prussian State Theater. The magic of this situation was so potent that it enabled the young man to overlook many things he might otherwise have found disappointing.

Was it really a new, a better world in which he now moved? Had it not many of the old world's shortcomings that he had so bitterly hated—and even some new faults unknown till then? Hans Miklas did not yet dare admit such things to himself. But from time to time his young face assumed the clenched, sorrowful expression of defiance that it had worn in the Hamburg days. Arrogant and angry, the rebellious youth turned his head away when he saw the director Caesar von Muck surrounded by flattery in an even more flagrant manner than the Professor had been. And how Caesar von Muck bent himself double, seemingly on the point of dissolving in servile fawning when the propaganda minister visited the theater! It was extremely painful to watch. The state of affairs that Nationalist agitators used to term the "boss economy" had not disappeared, either, but had taken even worse and more extravagant forms. And among actors there were still "celebrities" who looked down on the smaller fry, drove to the stage door in sleek limousines and wore fabulous fur coats. The great goddess was no longer called Dora Martin but Lotte Lindenthal, a bad actress, who had made up for it by being the mistress of a powerful man. In defense of her honor, Miklas once had almost got himself into a brawl—how long ago was that? And on her account he had lost his job. But she knew nothing of all this, and he was too proud to allude to it. He angrily clenched his teeth, put on his hostile face and allowed himself to be ignored by the great lady.

Germany had its honor restored, for Communists and pacifists sat in concentration camps and some of them had already been executed; and the world became really frightened of a nation that acclaimed such a Führer. But the renewal of German social life had not yet begun: of socialism there was still no sign. Everything can't be achieved instantly, thought Hans Miklas, who had believed with too much fervor to succumb so soon to disenchantment. Not even my Führer can manage to do that. We must have patience. First Germany must recover from the long years of humiliation.

Hans Miklas still trusted. But he received the decisive shock when he read on the rehearsal cast sheet that Hendrik Höfgen was to play Mephisto. There he was again, the old enemy, the supremely adroit, totally unscrupulous cynic, who always survived and made himself loved by all—Höfgen, the eternal adversary! The woman for whose sake Miklas had almost fought with him had herself called Höfgen back home because she needed him to star opposite her in a drawing-room comedy. And now she had gone even further by securing for him the classical role that could bring him his greatest chance of success . . . What if he went to this Lotte Lindenthal and told her what Höfgen had said about her in the canteen? What prevented him? But was it worth the trouble? Would he be believed? Wouldn't he make himself look ridiculous? And, after all, had Höfgen been so completely wrong when he called Lindenthal a stupid cow? Wasn't she just that?

Miklas turned his head toward the shadows so that no one should see the tears in his eyes.

An hour later he had to rehearse his scene with Höfgen/Mephistopheles. In a deferential manner he had to approach the scholar, who was in fact the devil, and declare:

> "I've just arrived, Sir, in this town,
> Drawn by your wisdom and renown,
> I question you with great respect
> Amazed by such great intellect."

The voice of the schoolboy sounded hoarse, and it became a groan as the boy had to answer all the bewildering aphorisms and mocking sophisms of the masked fiend:

> "I'm tied in knots by what you've said—
> It's like a mill-wheel in my head."

The prime minister, accompanied by his friend Lotte Lindenthal, attended *Faust*'s opening night at the State Theater. In fact, the performance started a quarter of an hour late because the great man had not yet appeared. A telephone call from his palace said that a consultation with the defense minister had detained him; however, the actors in their dressing rooms whispered mockingly among themselves that it was just that once again he had not finished dolling himself up in time.

"He always needs at least an hour to change his clothes," declared the actress playing Margaret, who was so blond that she could get away with small acts of irreverence. When they did arrive, the distinguished pair managed their entrance with studied decorum. The prime minister remained at the back of his box while the house lights were on. Only the people in the front rows of the boxes could catch a glimpse of him. They gazed respectfully at his braided uniform, which had a purple collar and broad silver cuffs, and at the blazing diamond tiara of his full-bosomed Aryan companion. Only when the curtain rose did the minister take his seat, letting out a soft groan as he did so, for it was an effort to lower the mass of fat that was his body into the narrow armchair.

During the prologue in Heaven the illustrious spectator assumed a dutiful look of concentration. He seemed to find rather boring the scenes that followed, up to the moment when Mephistopheles slips into Faust's study disguised as a poodle. During Faust's first long monologue he yawned several times, and the Easter parade scene did not appear to please him, either—he whispered something to Lotte that was apparently of a critical nature. However, as soon as Höfgen/Mephistopheles came into his own, the potentate began to take an interest. When Faust called out, "So that is then the poodle's core! A wandering scholar? Now I see—and laugh," the minister laughed too, so loudly and heartily that everyone in the theater was aware of it. As he laughed he heaved his bulk forward, resting both his arms on the red velvet balustrade of the box, and from then on he followed the proceedings with amused attention. And what caught and fixed his eye was the dancer's agility, the mischievous grace and wicked charm of Hendrik Höfgen's Mephistopheles.

Lotte Lindenthal, who knew her man, realized immediately that this was love at first sight. Höfgen had conquered her fat lover, and she understood why only too well. The fellow was truly bewitching, and in the black costume with the diabolical Pierrot mask he managed to be more irresistible than ever before. He was both comic and imposing. He leaped charmingly like a dancer; and yet his eyes occasionally turned deep and baleful or blazed frighteningly, as when he said,

> "What you may call the realm of sin,
> And nothing there but evil see,
> Is where I live and have to be."

At this point the prime minister nodded significantly. Later, during the scene with the schoolboy—in which Hans Miklas was appropriately stiff and tongue-tied—the great man appeared as amused as if he were watching the most hilarious of farces. His good humor became even more pronounced during the burlesque proceedings in Auerbach's Cellar in Leipzig, when Höfgen, with malevolent exuberance, gave a superb rendering of the song "The King and the Flea" before drawing Tokay wine and bubbling champagne out of the wood of the table for the drunken louts around him. And the fat onlooker was beside himself with pleasure when in the darkness of the witch's kitchen, Höfgen allowed the sharp jangling voice of the Prince of Hell to ring out:

> "Death's head, foul witch, have you quite lost your eyes?
> Do you not know your liege and lord?
> I know a lesson that you'll recognize—
> I'll crush you and your monkey horde.
> Does not my scarlet doublet raise your awe?
> This cock's feather does not pierce your slumber?
> I did not hide my face: what more?
> Must I then give my rank and number?"

This disposed of the witch, the midnight hag, who collapsed in a terrified heap. The air force general slapped his thighs with delight. The blinding self-assertion of the spirit of evil, the pride of Satan in his hideous supremacy, amused him all too much. The silvery laughter of Lotte Lindenthal accompanied his greasy, grunting laugh. After the witch's kitchen scene came the intermission. The prime minister invited the actor Höfgen to his box.

Hendrik went quite white and had to close his eyes for several seconds when little Böck gave him the important summons. The great moment had come. He was about to meet the demigod face-to-face. Angelika, who happened to be in the dressing room with him, brought him a glass of water. After he had hastily drunk it, he felt restored enough to give a ghost of his "dirty" smile . . . He went so far as to say, "This is all going splendidly according to plan," as if making a joke of this decisive development. But the teasing words came from pale lips.

When Hendrik walked into the box of the distinguished spectators, the fat general was sitting in front, stroking the red velvet of the balustrade with his thick fingers. Hendrik stood at the door. How ridiculous that my heart should be beating so hard, he thought; and he remained standing there a few seconds longer. Then Lotte Lindenthal saw him. "Hubby," she cried, "let me introduce my distinguished colleague Hendrik Höfgen." The giant turned in his direction. Hendrik heard himself addressed in a fairly high, oily but grating voice, "Aha, our Mephistopheles . . ." This was followed by a burst of laughter.

In his entire life Hendrik had never felt so disturbed, and the shame of this agitation only increased his anxiety. To his blurred gaze even his colleague Lotte seemed to have undergone a fantastic change. Was it only the dazzling jewels, which gave her an intimidatingly regal appearance, or was it the fact that she was in such affectionate proximity to her lord and protector? Whatever the cause, she suddenly appeared to Hendrik as a fairy queen—a well-fleshed and charming fairy queen, but one that was not without a certain menace. Her smile, which had always struck him as good-natured and somewhat stupid, now seemed obscurely treacherous.

But so great was his anxiety that Hendrik registered almost nothing of the stout giant in his colored uniform, the demigod. A veil seemed to hang in front of the great man's face—that mystic veil that has always hidden the faces of the prophets and the gods from the frightened gaze of mere mortals. Only one medal blazed through the mist; the frightening contour of a bulging neck was just discernible. And then the sharp and oily parade-ground voice said, "Come a little closer, Herr Höfgen."

Members of the audience who had remained chatting in the orchestra became aware of the group in the prime minister's box. They whispered and craned their necks. No movement that the prime minister made escaped the curious congregating between the rows of seats. They saw that the expression of the air force general became ever more benevolent and amused. Now he was laughing. The people below watched with fascination the huge man guffawing. Lotte Lindenthal let her pearly coloratura laugh ring out; and the actor Höfgen—decoratively swathed in his black cape—displayed a smile that on his Mephisto mask had the appearance of a triumphant and painted sneer.

The conversation between the man of power and the entertainer became increasingly animated. The prime minister was having a good time. What wonderful stories Höfgen must be telling for the air force general to appear almost drunk with good humor! Everyone in the orchestra tried to glean the words that Hendrik's blood-red lips were forming. But Mephisto spoke softly; only the potentate caught his delectable jokes.

With an expansive gesture Höfgen threw wide his arms under his cloak, making it seem that he had grown black wings. The man of power slapped him on the back. A respectful murmur went around the orchestra. Then, like the music at a circus before the most dangerous act, it fell silent in deference to the extraordinary happening that followed.

The prime minister had risen. There he stood in all his magnitude, his shining bulk, and stretched out his hand to the actor. Was he congratulating him on his magnificent performance? It looked more like the sealing of a pact between the potentate and the actor.

In the orchestra people strained their eyes and ears. They devoured the scene in the box above as though it was the most exceptional entertainment, an entrancing pantomime entitled "The Actor Bewitches the Prince." Never was Hendrik so passionately envied! How happy he must be!

Did anyone watching have an inkling of what was really going on in Hendrik's mind as he bowed deeply over the fleshy, hairy hand of the grandee? Was it happiness and pride alone that made him tremble? Or did he feel something else as well—to his own astonishment? In fact what he felt was something close to nausea.

Now I have contaminated myself, thought Hendrik. Now there is a stain on my hand that I can never wash off . . . Now I have sold myself . . . Now I am marked for life . . .

Over the Bodies of Corpses

Next morning the whole city knew that the prime minister had received the actor Höfgen in his box and chatted with him for twenty-five
minutes during intermission. The performance had continued after
considerable delay. The audience had to wait; and they did so with
pleasure: the scene in the ministerial box was far more absorbing than
Faust.

Hendrik Höfgen, who had introduced himself as "Comrade" at
the Stormy Petrel, who had almost been numbered among the dregs of
the nation—namely the emigrants—sat in the box for all to see, side by
side with the fat mighty man of the regime. He talked and joked with
the prime minister, who more than once slapped him on the shoulder
and in parting appeared unwilling to relinquish his hand. The State
Theater audience was deeply stirred by this performance. And later
that same night the sensational development was passionately discussed in the cafés, drawing rooms and newspaper offices.

Höfgen's name, which for months had been pronounced only
with skepticism or a regretful shrug, was now invested with a new
aura. A gleam of the enormous radiance that surrounds power had
shone on him. For the massive air force officer, newly promoted to
general, belonged to the very highest summit of the authoritarian and
all-powerful state. Above him was only the Führer—a man hardly to be
numbered any longer among mortals. Like the Lord of Heaven with

his archangels, so was the dictator surrounded by his paladins. At his right hand stood the agile gnome with the profile of a bird of prey, the deformed prophet, the eulogist, the insinuator and propagandist, who had the cleft tongue of a snake and invented lies at the rate of one a minute. To the left of the Master stood the obese giant, resting on his executioner's sword, blazing with medals and gold braid, every day tricked out in a new fancy dress. While the little man on the right of the throne created the lies, the fat man daily thought up surprises—for his own diversion and that of the people—entertainments, executions. He amassed medals, fantastic articles of clothing and resounding titles. Naturally, he also amassed money. He gave a contented grunt of a laugh when he learned of the many witticisms to which his ostentatiousness gave rise. Sometimes, when he was in a bad mood, he would have someone who had ventured too far in impudence locked up and whipped. Most of the time, however, he grinned benevolently. To be the butt of public mirth seemed to him a sure sign of popularity. He could not gabble as hypnotically as his rival, the demon of the advertising department, so he had to make himself known through massive and enormously expensive extravaganzas. He was pleased with his fame and with his life. He bedecked his swollen body; he rode to hounds; he guzzled and gorged. He had pictures stolen from art galleries and hung in his own palace. He consorted with wealthy and distinguished people; he had princes and great ladies at his dinner parties. Not long ago he had been poor, which made him enjoy all the more the fact that he now had as much money and as many beautiful things as his heart could desire. Isn't my life like a fairy tale? he often thought. Because he had a romantic nature, he loved the theater and voluptuously sniffed the air backstage; and it was with pleasure that he sat in his velvet-lined box, where he could be admired by the audience before he himself had something nice to look at.

His life seemed pleasant enough to him as it was, but his taste for adventure and excess would be fully satisfied only by another outbreak of war. In his eyes, war was an amusement of a more intense kind than all the other pleasures that he now enjoyed. He loved war as a child loves Christmas; and he saw it as his most essential task to prepare for war with care and cunning. Let the publicity department's dwarf throw all his energy into buying up dozens of foreign newspapers, paying millions in bribes, organizing a network of spies and provocateurs spread over the earth's surface, pouring out insolent threats and even more insolent protestations of peaceful intentions—he, the Fat One, would attend to the all-important aircraft. Germany must have aircraft above all else. Ultimately the poisoning of the atmosphere through lies was only a softening-up process. One day—which he earnestly hoped would not be too long delayed—it would be possible to poison the air of European cities in a way that was not merely metaphorical. Working toward that day was his chief preoccupation, for he by no means spent his whole time sitting in theaters or dressing himself up.

There he stands on legs like pillars, thrusting out his enormous belly and beaming. On him and on the propaganda chief falls almost as much light as on the Führer who stands between them. The Führer's eyes are abstracted and dull like those of a blind man. Is he looking inward, straining his ears to hear something inside himself? Perhaps. Perhaps he is listening to the same message that his propaganda minister and all the newspapers he controls never tire of repeating: that he is the one sent from God who need only to follow his own star and Germany and then the whole world will prosper under his leadership. Perhaps, for his bloated petit-bourgeois face bears an expression of ecstasy. This face hides no secret that can challenge or fascinate us for long. It has never been touched by the dignity of the spirit, nor has it been ennobled by suffering.

Let us leave him standing on Olympus. Who are all those people crowding around him? A beautiful array of gods indeed! A group of grotesque characters before whom a Godforsaken people writhe in a delirium of worship. Arms folded, the beloved Führer looks grimly at the throng murmuring prayers at his feet. The propaganda chief crows and the air force general grins. What makes the corpulent giant appear so brisk and jovial? Is he thinking of new and unheard-of methods of extermination? See, he slowly raises his massive arm! The eye of power has fallen on one of the throng. Will the unhappy man be led away, tortured and slaughtered? On the contrary—mercy comes his way and, more, good fortune. Who is this then? It is an actor. He steps forward modestly but with a firm tread. Let it be admitted that he is not badly suited to this society: he has its false honor, its hysteria, its cynicism and desire for devil worship. The actor raises his chin, his eyes glisten. Now the fat man stretches his arms out to him almost lovingly. The actor has approached the cluster of gods. Already he can bathe in their glamour. And with the perfect grace of a nobleman and courtier he bows his head and knee before the fleshy giant.

In Hendrik's apartment in the Reichskanzlerplatz the telephone never ceased to ring. Little Böck sat beside it with a notebook to write down the names of those who called. They were the directors of theaters and film companies; they were actors, critics, tailors, motor car salesmen and autograph hunters. Höfgen spoke to none of them. He lay in bed hysterical with happiness. The prime minister had invited him to an intimate dinner at his palace. "There will be only a few friends," he had said. Only a few friends! So Hendrik was already reckoned among the happy few! He wriggled and rejoiced among the silk cushions and quilts. He sprayed himself with perfume, shattered a small vase and threw a slipper at the wall.

"It's just beyond belief . . ." he exulted. "Now I shall get really big. Fatty will allow me to get very, very big."

Suddenly he assumed a worried look and called out to Böck. "Böckie—listen, Böckie!" he drawled with a wry glance at his servant. "Am I really a very great bastard?"

Böck's watery blue eyes were bewildered. "How do you mean—a bastard?" he asked. "Why a bastard, Herr Höfgen? You have nothing but success."

"I have nothing but success," Hendrik repeated, and he gazed bright-eyed at the ceiling. He lingered over his words with sensuous pleasure. "Nothing but success . . . I shall use it well. I shall do good, Böckie—do you believe me?"

Böckie believed him.

This was the third ascension of Hendrik Höfgen. The first had been the soundest and the most deserved, for in Hamburg Hendrik had done good work; he had earned the gratitude of the public for many a fine evening. The second time around—the triumph over the "system" in Berlin—already had had a feverishly exaggerated tempo and many signs of unwholesomeness about it. This third ascent had the character of an apotheosis; it came suddenly, like all the deeds of the National Socialist government. Literally overnight, he had joined the ranks of the great. A sign from the fat minister and it was accomplished.

The director of the State Theater immediately made him a large offer. Perhaps he did not do it altogether spontaneously, perhaps not altogether willingly; nevertheless he put on a good face, stretching out his hands to the newly engaged artist and speaking in his richest Saxon dialect: "Splendid that you are now to be a full member of our circle, my dear Höfgen. I must take this opportunity to tell you how very much I admire your evolution. You have grown from a somewhat frivolous creature into a wholly serious, wholly qualified artist."

Caesar von Muck knew very well why he came to have so favorable an opinion of the kind of development he had described in such discreet terms. He himself had had a similar evolution. Certainly his "frivolous" past was more remote than the sins of Höfgen. Before Caesar von Muck rose to be a friend of the Führer and a literary star of National Socialism, he was already famous as the author of dramas full of pacifist and revolutionary feeling. Maybe the dramatist, who had abandoned such a reprehensible outlook in favor of a heroic conception of the world—and a director's post—was thinking of the literary sins of his own wayward youth when he spoke of his respect for Hendrik Höfgen's development.

It was with a warm glance that he now added, "Besides, I shall have an opportunity this evening of presenting you to the propaganda minister. He has announced that he will visit the theater."

By the end of that evening Hendrik felt that he was getting to know the demi-gods and discovering that they were quite as easy to get on with as any Oscar H. Kroge. And relations were much easier than they had been with the awe-inspiring Professor. They really aren't so bad, thought Hendrik.

So this nimble little man was the master of the enormous publicity machine of the Third Reich, the man who liked to call himself in front of the workers "your old doctor," who with his energy, his eloquence and his armed bands had won over to the National Socialist cause the lively and skeptical city of Berlin, which did not easily allow anyone to pull wool over its eyes. So this was the brain of the party who laid all the plans: when there should be a torchlight procession, when people should turn on the Jews and when on the Catholics. While the theater director spoke Saxon, the minister spoke with a Rhineland accent, which made Hendrik immediately feel at home. This elastic little man, whose mouth seemed somewhat frayed from all his ranting, appeared to be full of interesting and modern ideas. He spoke of the "revolutionary dynamic" and of the "mystic law of existence determining race"; and then he talked quite simply about the press ball, at which Höfgen was to recite something.

This formal occasion was the first at which Hendrik appeared openly in the circle of the demigods. He had the privilege of escorting Fräulein Lindenthal into the ballroom, for the prime minister was once again delayed. Lotte wore a wonderful gown of purple and silver thread. At her side Hendrik appeared almost sick under the weight of such distinction. In the course of the evening he was photographed not only with the air force general but also in conversation with the propaganda minister, who had himself given him the signal to come and be pictured at his side. The minister broke into his famous irresistibly charming smile, which he also flashed at those who would be thrown to the wolves a few months later. It was true that he did not altogether succeed in dousing the spark of malevolence in his eyes. He hated Höfgen—the creature of the opposition. But the propaganda chief was not a man to give way to his emotions and allow them to determine his acts. He remained cool and calculating enough to think: If this actor is going to have a place among the great cultural heroes of the Third Reich, then it would be a tactical error to allow my fat friend all the credit for his discovery. So I must clench my teeth and place myself beside him grinning into the camera lens.

How easily everything went! Hendrik felt that he must have been born under a lucky star. All this fine patronage has simply fallen into my lap, he thought. Should I have refused so much splendor? No one else would have done so given the same opportunities; and if someone were to claim otherwise, I should denounce him as a liar and a hypocrite. Living in Paris as an emigrant wouldn't have suited me. In all the bustling excitement of the life that now surrounded him he thought fleetingly and with intense disgust of the loneliness of his walks through the squares and boulevards of Paris. Thank God, now he was once again in the company of his fellow men.

What was the name of the elegant gray-haired man with the prominent blue eyes who was talking to him so eagerly? Yes, it was Müller-Andreä, the famous gossip writer of "the interesting magazine." Did he still make as much money from his telltale column "Had You Heard?" It appeared not: "the interesting magazine" had foundered. Herr Müller-Andreä, however, had survived; he was even going strong, as cheerful as ever. Back in 1931 he had published a book called *The*

Faithful of the Führer—in those days he used a pseudonym. But in the meantime he had come out into the open as the author, had been noticed in high places, and had prospered as a result. The Propaganda Ministry paid well and it was for the Propaganda Ministry that the happy man worked.

And here was the little fellow who waved his notebook like a flag—of course it was Pierre Larue. Now there were no more "young Communist comrades" at his side; they had been replaced by trim sturdy lads in their seductive and intimidating SS uniforms. M. Larue found the parties and receptions of high Nazi functionaries even more amusing than the entertainments of Jewish bankers he had enjoyed in the past. He thrived—there were so many interesting people for him to get to know: very nice murderers who now occupied high positions in the secret police; a professor recently released from a mental hospital and now minister of culture; jurists who considered justice a liberal prejudice; doctors who considered the art of healing a Jewish swindle; philosophers who considered "Race" to be the only objective truth. Pierre Larue invited all these distinguished people to dine with him at the Esplanade. Yes, the Nazis knew how to appreciate his hospitality and his tender nature. He was even permitted to indulge in a bit of intrigue on their behalf among the embassies, and in return he was allowed to speak at rallies. At first people laughed when the pale little bag of bones mounted the podium and chirped something about the deep understanding of "the real France for the Third Reich," but then they became more serious, for their "old doctor," the propaganda minister himself, indignantly called them to order. And then Pierre Larue would declaim a sort of amorous hymn in honor of Horst Wessel, the fallen partisan and martyr of the new Germany, whom he saw as the guarantor of an eternal peace between the two great nations, Germany and France.

M. Larue almost fell upon the neck of Höfgen, so delighted was he to see him again. *"Oh, oh, mon très cher ami! Enchanté*—charmed to see you again." There was shaking of hands and cordial laughter. Wasn't it a pleasure for M. Larue to live in the new Germany? Wasn't his new love in his well-fitting SS uniform much prettier than any of those dirty Communist youths in days gone by? *Bonsoir, mon cher,* I am utterly delighted—long live the Führer. That very evening, Larue insisted, he would send a report to Paris saying how happy and peace-loving everyone was in Berlin. No one has any wicked, aggressive thoughts. How charming Fräulein Lindenthal looks. Here comes Dr. Ihrig. Cheers!

Further handshaking on Dr. Ihrig's arrival. He too seemed in excellent spirits, for which he had good cause. His relations with the Nazi regime, so tense at the outset, were improving from day to day. Höfgen and Ihrig laughed companionably like two city fathers. Now they could once again appear publicly together without compromising each other. They no longer felt uneasy in each other's company. Success, that sublime and irrefutable justification of every infamy, had made both of them forget their shame.

Smiling broadly, all four of them—Larue, Ihrig, Müller-Andreä and Höfgen—bowed their heads, for the prime minister, swaying in waltz time with Lotte Lindenthal on his arm, was dancing past and had nodded at them.

The relationship between Hendrik and Lotte Lindenthal was becoming increasingly close. They both had a great success in the comedy *The Heart*. Lotte's fears about the severity of the Berlin press had proved unfounded. On the contrary, all the critics were full of praise for her "feminine grace," her unpretentiousness and the truly German warmth of her acting. No one was unpleasant enough to ask why she always lifted her little finger in such a comic fashion. Dr. Ihrig, in his long review, expressed the opinion that Lotte Lindenthal was "the actress who most truly represents the new Germany."

"Above all it's you I have to thank for that," said the good-natured blonde. "If you hadn't worked with me so hard and been such a good friend, this beautiful success would not have come my way." Hendrik knew that she owed her success far more to another, but he kept quiet about it.

He and Lotte took *The Heart* to several cities—Hamburg, Cologne, Frankfurt and Munich. Throughout the country he was seen as the partner of "the actress most truly representative of the new Reich." In conversations together during the long railway journeys, the great lady allowed him a closer look into her inner life than she ordinarily felt was wise. She spoke not only of her happiness but of her worries. Her fat lover was often so violent . . . "You can guess what I sometimes have to endure," said Lotte. But all told, she declared, he was a good man: "Whatever his enemies say about him, at heart he is goodness itself. And so romantic!" Lotte had tears in her eyes when she reported how sometimes at midnight her prime minister, dressed in his bearskin coat with a drawn sword at his side, stood in homage before the portrait of his deceased wife. "She was Swedish, of course," said Lotte, as though this explained everything. "A Northerner—and she drove Hubby in a motorcar all over Italy in the old days, after he was wounded in the Munich *Putsch*. Of course, I can understand that he should be so attached to her—he being so hugely romantic. And finally he's got me . . ." Her tone was slightly bleak as she came to her part in the story.

The actor Höfgen was allowed to take part in the private life of the gods. While sitting with Lotte in her beautiful home in the Tiergarten after the evening performance, playing cards or chess, sometimes the prime minister would burst unannounced into the room making a great din. Did he not then seem the most amiable man in the world? There was no sign either of the hideous transactions he had just concluded or of those he was planning for the following day. He joked with Lotte and drank his glass of red wine; he stretched his enormous legs out in front of him and spoke with Höfgen about serious things. His favorite topic was Mephistopheles.

"You're the first person to make me understand this character," said the general. "He really is splendid! And isn't there a little of him in us all? I mean, hidden in every real German isn't there a bit of Mephistopheles, a bit of the rascal and the ruffian? If we had nothing but the soul of Faust, what would become of us? It would be a pushover for our many enemies! No, no—Mephisto, too, is a German national hero. But it's better not to go around telling people that."

Hendrik was able to use these hours of intimacy in Lotte's house to obtain from his protector, the friend of the fine arts and the bomber squadrons, all kinds of things he wanted. For instance, he had set his heart on appearing on the stage of the State Theater as Frederick the Great of Prussia. It was one of his obsessions. "I don't want always to play dandies and criminals," he explained sulkily to the fat general. "The public will begin to identify me with these types if I go on playing them unceasingly. Now what I need is a great patriotic role. This bad play about old Fritz that our friend Muck has just accepted will do nicely. This could be a great thing for me!" In vain the general pointed out that Höfgen bore absolutely no physical resemblance to the great Hohenzollern; Hendrik stood his ground, insisting on his patriotic caprice, supported by Lotte. "But I can do faces with makeup," he cried. "I have done more difficult things in my time than arrange to look a bit like old Fritz."

The fat man had the greatest trust in his protégé's power to create masks. He ordered that Höfgen should play the part of old Fritz. Caesar von Muck, who had already cast the part differently, first bit his lips—but then shook both Hendrik's hands and expressed his heartfelt endorsement in deepest Saxon. Hendrik won his patriotic role, fitted himself out with a false nose, leaned on a stick and spoke in a grating voice. Dr. Ihrig wrote that Höfgen was developing more and more into the truly representative actor of the new Reich. Pierre Larue reported in a fascist magazine in Paris that the Berlin theater had achieved a perfection that it had never approached in the fourteen previous years of shame and conciliation.

Hendrik now began to obtain things of a very different kind from his powerful protector. One particularly genial evening—Lotte had prepared a wine-and-fruit punch, and her fat lover had told stories about his war experiences—Höfgen decided that the time had come to speak openly of his wicked past. It was a considerable confession, but the powerful man took it with good grace. "I am an artist," cried Hendrik with gleaming eyes as he paced the room distractedly. "And like every artist I have done crazy things." He stopped, threw his head back, opened his arms a little and declared pathetically, "You can annihilate me, Herr Prime Minister. Now I am going to confess all."

He admitted that he had not been untouched by the demoralizing Bolshevist currents of the age and had flirted with the Left. "It was an artist's whim," he exclaimed with mortified pride. "Or an artist's folly— if you want to call it that."

Naturally, the fat man had already known this—and a lot more— for a long time, and had never got worked up about it. The country must be ruled by an iron discipline, and as many people as possible must be executed. But in dealings with his immediate entourage the great man was tolerant. "Well, well now," he said. "Everyone can go off the rails. They were bad, disorderly times."

But Hendrik had by no means finished. Now he went on to explain to the general that other deserving artists had committed the same follies as himself. "But they are expiating sins for which I have received such a magnanimous pardon. And, Herr Prime Minister, that haunts me. I am making an appeal for a particular man. For a comrade. I can swear that he has reformed. Herr Prime Minister, I appeal to you for Otto Ulrichs. People say that he's already dead. But he's alive and he deserves to live in freedom." As he said this he made an irresistibly graceful gesture, raising his two outstretched hands.

Lotte Lindenthal trembled. The prime minister growled, "Otto Ulrichs—who's that?" When he realized that he was the director of the Communist cabaret the Stormy Petrel, he said peevishly, "But that's a fairly nasty customer."

Hendrik implored the general not to see it like that. His friend Otto had been a bit reckless—he had to admit that—a bit thoughtless. But not a bad sort at all. And besides, he had certainly changed in the interval. "He has become an entirely new man," insisted Hendrik, who for months had been without any contact with Ulrichs.

Because Lotte Lindenthal threw her weight behind Hendrik in this delicate matter, the fat general finally conceded the impossible: Ulrichs was set free. And he was also offered a small job with the State Theater—even this most improbable concession had been won by the joint efforts of Hendrik and Lotte.

But Ulrichs said of the theater project, "I don't know if I should have anything to do with this. It sickens me to receive a pardon from these murderers and to play the repentant sinner—in fact, I'm sickened by myself altogether at this moment."

"But, Otto," Hendrik exclaimed. "Your grasp of things seems to have suffered. How do you expect to bring anything off nowadays without resort to ruse and pretense? Follow my example!"

"I know," said Ulrichs with a good-natured but distressed glance at Hendrik. "You're more cunning. But I find these things so terribly difficult—"

"You must force yourself," Hendrik broke in sternly, "I had to force myself, too." He informed his friend how much self-discipline he had exerted to bring himself to the point of howling with the wolves as now, alas, he did. "But we must insinuate ourselves into the lion's den," he declared. "If we stay outside we can only shout insults without achieving anything. But I'm right inside. And I'm getting things done." This was an allusion to the fact that Hendrik had obtained Otto's release. "If you get a job with the State Theater you can make contact once again with your old friends and politically do much more useful work than from some obscure hideout." This argument appealed to Otto. He nodded.

"And besides, how are you going to live?" A sharp note of irony entered Hendrik's voice. "Do you imagine that you can reopen the Stormy Petrel? Or do you want to starve?"

They were in Höfgen's apartment in the Reichskanzlerplatz. Hendrik had rented a small room in the neighborhood for his friend, who had been released a few days earlier. "It would be unwise for you to live with me," he said. "That could only harm us both."

Ulrichs agreed to everything. "You will arrange things for the best," he said. His gaze was sad and distracted, and he had grown much thinner. He complained often of pains. "It's my kidneys. They really went at me hard."

When Hendrik's somewhat unhealthy curiosity prompted him to ask for more details, Otto waved him away and was silent. He did not like to talk of what he had endured in the concentration camp. When he did disclose a particular incident, he appeared suddenly to feel ashamed and to regret that he had spoken. Walking with Hendrik in the Grunewald park once, he pointed to a tree. "The tree looked like that—the one I had to climb. It was hard to get up it. When I reached the top they threw stones at me. One hit me in the forehead—the scar is still there. From the top I had to shout a hundred times 'I am a filthy Communist swine.' When at last they let me climb down, they were waiting for me with whips."

Whether out of exhaustion and apathy, or because he was convinced by Hendrik's arguments, Otto Ulrichs allowed himself to be signed up at the State Theater. Hendrik was very happy. I have rescued a man, he thought proudly. That is a good deed. With such reflections he stilled a conscience that was not yet completely dead, despite all the burdens placed upon it. Besides, it was not only pangs of conscience that troubled him from time to time but another feeling as well—fear. Would this whole adventure in which he was so deeply involved last forever? Might there not eventually be a day of upheaval and great wrath? In case that happened it would be wise—and indeed necessary—to take out insurance. The good deed toward Ulrichs constituted a particularly valuable insurance policy. Hendrik congratulated himself on it.

Everything was going beautifully. Hendrik had good reason to be contented, but unfortunately there was one matter that caused him some anxiety. He did not know how he was going to get rid of Juliette.

In his heart he had no desire to be rid of her; and had he been free to choose he would have kept her beside him always, for he still loved her. Perhaps he had never had such a violent longing for her as he did now. He realized that no other woman could ever completely take her place. But he no longer dared visit her. The risk was too great. He had to reckon with the likelihood that Herr von Muck and the propaganda minister had put spies on him. This was very probably the case, though the theater director spoke to him in his most deeply sincere Saxon accent and the propaganda minister allowed himself to be photographed at his side. If they ever discovered that he had a liaison with a Negress and, into the bargain, was being beaten by her, he would be lost. A Negress—that was at least as bad as a Jew. It was precisely what was now known as "profanation of the race" and was the most abject act imaginable. A German must breed children from a blond woman, for the Führer needed soldiers. On no account should he go to a Princess Tebab for dancing lessons! No party comrade who had any self-respect did things like that. And Hendrik could no longer allow himself to do them either.

For a while he clung to the mad hope that Juliette would not discover his presence in Berlin. But naturally, she learned of it the day of his return. Patiently she waited for his visit. When she received no sign, she took the offensive. She telephoned him. Hendrik had Böck explain that he was not at home. Juliette raged, called again, threatened to appear in person. What could Hendrik do? Writing her a letter seemed unwise, for she could use it for blackmail. He finally decided to summon her to the quiet café that had been the scene of his discreet rendezvous with Dr. Ihrig.

Juliette wore no high green boots and no short jacket; instead she appeared in the café at the appointed hour in a very simple gray dress. Her eyes were red and swollen. She had wept. Princess Tebab, the king's daughter from the Congo, had shed tears because of her unfaithful white friend. She had wept from anger, thought Hendrik. For he did not think Juliette capable of feelings other than anger, avarice, greed or sensuality.

"So you're dropping me," said the black girl, keeping her lids lowered over her darting intelligent eyes.

Hendrik tried to explain the situation in cautious but insistent terms. He showed a paternal concern about her future, and in a gentle voice advised her to leave for Paris as soon as possible. There she would find a job as a dancer. Moreover, he promised to send her some money each month. With a persuasive smile he placed a large bank-note on the table in front of her.

"But I don't want to go to Paris," said Princess Tebab stubbornly. "My father was a German. I feel myself to be entirely German. And I have blond hair—really, it isn't dyed. Besides, I can't speak a word of French. What would I do in Paris?"

Hendrik laughed at her patriotism, which made her angry. Now she opened her wild eyes wide and let them roll. "You won't be laughing long," she screamed at him. She lifted her rough dark hands and stretched them out in front of him, screeching reproaches as she did so. Hendrik looked with horror in the direction of the woman behind the counter.

"You've never taken anything seriously," Juliette cried in a voice of pain and fury. "Nothing, absolutely nothing in this world apart from your filthy career! You haven't taken me seriously, or your politics which you were always spouting at me. If you had really been on the Communist side, would you now be getting along so well with the people who have had all the Communists shot?"

Hendrik went as pale as the tablecloth. He stood up. "Enough," he said softly. But she gave a mocking laugh that echoed through the café, which, fortunately for Hendrik, was empty. "Enough," she mimicked and bared her teeth. "Enough—yes, that word suits you beautifully—enough. For years I have had to play the wild woman, though it gave me no pleasure. And now suddenly you want to be the strong man! Enough—enough. Yes, now you don't need me any more—perhaps because there's so much beating up going on in this country right now. So you get your money's worth without me. Ach, you're a bastard! The lowest form of bastard!"

She buried her face in her hands and her body shook with sobs. "I can understand why your wife—why that Barbara couldn't endure life with you," she murmured between her damp fingers. "I had a look at her. She was far too good for you."

Hendrik reached the door. The note was still lying on the table in front of Juliette.

But Princess Tebab was not going to let herself be disposed of easily. She would not retreat without a fight. She realized very clearly that if she gave way now, she would have lost him completely, her Hendrik, her white slave, her master, her Heinz—and apart from him she possessed nothing. When he married Barbara, the upper-class girl, Juliette had remained optimistic and without fear. She had known that he would come back to her, his black Venus. But now it was different. Now his career was at stake. He was sending her to Paris. But she was called Martens, wasn't she? And her father would today have been a highly respected National Socialist if he hadn't caught malaria in the Congo.

The poor girl harassed and badgered him for some time with letters and telephone calls. Then she lay in wait outside the theater. When he left the stage door after the performance—by good luck, alone—there she was standing in front of him with her green boots, short dress, upward-jutting bosom and fiercely blazing eyes. Hendrik made panic-stricken flailing gestures with his arms as though warding off a ghost and ran to his Mercedes. Juliette laughed stridently. "I'll be back," she screamed as he set the car in motion. "From now on I'll be here every evening," she called in a tone of savage gaiety. Perhaps she had gone mad with grief and disappointment over his betrayal. Or perhaps she was only drunk. But in her hand she held the red whip, the emblem of her union with Hendrik Höfgen.

Such a dreadful scene must on no account be repeated. Hendrik felt he had no choice: he must once again place himself in the hands of his fat sponsor. He alone could help. Certainly it was a risk: the potentate could lose patience and withdraw his favor altogether. But something decisive had to be done, or a public scandal would be unavoidable.

Höfgen asked for an audience, and once again made an extensive confession. Fortunately, the general showed a surprisingly tolerant and almost amused understanding for the erotic exploits that now threatened his protégé with such extreme unpleasantness. "None of us are exactly pure angels," said the fat man, whose generosity on this occasion deeply impressed Hendrik. "A Negress prowls around the State Theater brandishing a whip!" The prime minister laughed heartily. "That's really a good tale. Now what are we going to do about it? The girl must go—that's clear . . ."

Hendrik, who did not exactly want Princess Tebab to be liquidated, murmured, "But without doing her any real harm!" At this the statesman gave him a teasing look. "Now, now," he shook a threatening finger. "You still seem to be somewhat enslaved by the beautiful lady." Then he added in a fatherly, reassuring voice, "You leave it to me."

That same day two discreet but relentless gentlemen called on the unfortunate Princess Tebab and informed her that she was under arrest. Princess Tebab yelled, "What do you mean?" But the two gentlemen said in quiet hard voices that left no room for contradiction, "Follow us." She could only say, sobbing, "I haven't done anything wrong . . ."

In front of the house was a police van, which the two gentlemen with somber politeness invited Juliette to enter. During the journey, which took a fairly long time, she sobbed and protested. She asked questions; she wanted to know where she was being taken. When she received no answer, she began to scream. But she stopped abruptly when she felt the crushing iron grip of her escort close on her arm. Then she understood: all words, all complaints were useless, and screaming could perhaps endanger her life. Or was her life already lost? Hendrik had unleashed all the power of the Reich against her. Hendrik was making use of the merciless regime to clear her, a defenseless girl, from his path . . . She stared ahead with eyes wide and blind with horror.

What followed were long days of silence. Was it ten days, or fourteen, or only six? She had been locked into a half-dark cell. No one told her where she was, or why, or how long she must stay there. She had stopped asking questions. Three times a day a silent woman in blue overalls brought her something to eat. Sometimes Juliette wept. But most of the time she sat motionless and stared at the wall. She waited for the door to open and someone to appear who would take her on her last walk, someone who would lead her to an incomprehensible, bitter—but liberating—death.

When one night she was awakened from a heavy dreamless sleep, she felt immediately and almost with relief: *This is it.* But before her stood not the man in uniform with orders to kill her, but Hendrik.

His face was very pale and had the strained look of pain about the temples. Juliette looked at him as though he was a ghost.

"Are you happy to see me?" he asked softly.

Princess Tebab gave no answer. She stared at him.

"You are silent." He looked worried. And in a grieving, singing voice he said, "I, my love, I have been looking forward to this moment. You are free." He struck a pose, flinging open his arms.

While Princess Tebab remained motionless staring at him, he

explained to her that she was authorized to leave immediately for Paris. All was arranged. The French visa was already in her passport; her trunk was waiting at the station. At the end of every month she would find a sum of money waiting for her at an address that would be given to her.

"There is only one condition attached to this great favor," said Hendrik the rescuer. His mild eyes became suddenly hard. "You must keep quiet! If you can't hold your tongue"—here a raw, brutal note entered Hendrik's voice—"then it's finished for you. Even in Paris you wouldn't be able to avoid your fate. Do you promise me, my love, that you will not say a word?" His voice became imploring and he leaned tenderly toward his victim. Juliette made no protest. Her defiance had been broken by the long days in the half-darkness of her cell. She nodded silently.

"You have become reasonable," declared Hendrik with a relieved smile. And he thought, My harsh treatment has made her submissive. I have nothing more to fear from her. But—what a shame, what a dreadful shame that I must lose her . . .

Princess Tebab had gone. Hendrik could breathe freely. There was no longer a dark cloud to mar his happiness. No frightening telephone calls woke him from his sleep. But with the relief there was something else, too . . .

Juliette had disappeared from his life. Barbara had disappeared from his life. To both he had sworn eternal love. Had he not called Barbara his good angel? "She was far to good for you," Princess Tebab had said. What could the savage black girl know of him and the intricate workings of his soul? But his conscience did not always let him off so lightly. Sometimes he was ashamed. He remembered Juliette's despairing gaze directed at him across the dimly lit cell. Now that he had abandoned and betrayed her, there were moments when Hendrik felt a compulsion to think again about his black Venus. He had used her as a wicked inanimate force to refresh and renew his energies. He had made an idol of her before whom he could intone in a trance: "Do you come from the distant heavens or rise from the lower depths, O Beauty?" And in his self-centered ecstasy he had cried to her, "You walk upon the dead and mock them as you pass . . ." But perhaps she was not a demon, after all? Viewed in the cold light of day, he saw that it was not her style to walk on bodies. Now, quite alone and weeping bitterly, she had left for a foreign city. And why? Was it because someone else had been capable of walking on the dead . . . ?

"He walks on corpses—he'd stop at nothing" happened to be one of the phrases used by Hans Miklas to describe his celebrated colleague Hendrik Höfgen. The rebellious youth was unimpressed by the fact that his old enemy was now under the special protection of the prime minister and the great Lindenthal. No thought of prudence held him back. He railed not only against his colleague Höfgen but also against distinguished gentlemen who were far more highly placed. Was he unaware of the risks involved in his insolent and thoughtless tirades? Or did he see the danger and not give a damn? Had he decided to stake everything on one turn of the wheel and ceased to care what number came up?

From the look on his face it was easy to believe that such ideas were running through his mind. Not even in the Hamburg days had he worn such a malevolent expression as he did now. In the past he still had hopes and a great faith to sustain him. Now he had nothing left. He went around saying, "It's all shit. We've been betrayed. The Führer wanted power and nothing else. What has improved in Germany since he took over? The rich have only become worse. Now they talk patriotic bilge while they make their deals—that's the only difference. The intriguers are still on top." Miklas was thinking of Höfgen.

"A decent German can die without anyone worrying about him," he said, driven by a tide of pain and scorn. "But look at Fatty, how he lives it up in his golden uniforms and luxury cars. And how can the Führer stand by and let all this happen—so many dreadful injustices? The rest of us were fighting for the movement when it hardly existed, and now they want to push us aside. But an old cultural Bolshevik like Höfgen is once again the big star . . ."

It was no wonder the members of the State Theater began to avoid Miklas. The director called him into his office one day to reprimand him. "I know that you have been in the party for years," said Caesar von Muck. "This is precisely why you should have learned discipline. And we are justified in making exceptionally high demands on your political good sense."

Miklas put on his obstinate face. He lowered his sulky brow, pushed out his unhealthy red lips and said in a quiet husky voice, "I'm leaving the party."

As Muck angrily turned his back on the young actor, Miklas was convulsed by a fit of coughing that shook his thin body. Then he left the office—his face was gray and his eyes gleamed dangerously. The director looked after the young man with anger, but with astonishment, too, and a little pity. He is doomed, thought Caesar von Muck.

Yes, you are doomed, poor young Hans Miklas! After so many exertions, so much wasted faith, what is left for you now? Only hate, only sadness, and the wild desire to hasten your own destruction. You are weak, young Miklas, and have no protector. The power you have loved is cruel. It allows no criticism, and whoever rises up against it is crushed.

Is there no one to weep over this fall, over this end to such a great and glowing and bitterly betrayed hope? You were almost always alone. It is years since you last wrote to your mother, who has married a strange man. Your father is dead, killed in the Great War. There is no one to weep over your wasted life and your lamentable, lamentable death? It is better to close your eyes so that they no longer stare at the sky with dumb accusation, with immeasurable reproach. Perhaps you will be more indulgent in death, poor child, than a hard life allowed you to be. Perhaps you will be able to forgive us—your enemies—for being the ones, the only ones, to bow our heads over your body.

For your destiny was accomplished. The end came fast. You provoked the climax—you summoned it. If it had been otherwise, perhaps you would have gathered around yourself other youths—even more ignorant and younger than you were—and played at being conspirators with them.

Everything was betrayed. And one morning, youths in uniform appeared in your room. You had worked with them in earlier days—they were all known to you, and they invited you to get into a car waiting below. You did not put up a long resistance. They drove you a few kilometers from the city into a little wood. The morning was chilly. You were freezing, but none of your old comrades gave you a blanket or a coat. The car stopped and you were ordered to walk a few steps. You walked the few steps, conscious of the smell of the grass and of the morning wind that played on your forehead. You held yourself upright. Perhaps those others would have taken fright at the expression of unutterable disdain on your face. But they did not see your face, they saw only your back. Then the shot rang out.

At the State Theater, from whose stage Hans Miklas had been banned for weeks past, it was announced that he had been the victim of a car accident. The news was received calmly; no one felt disposed to question its accuracy. Fräulein Lindenthal said, "How terrible—such a young fellow. I have to admit that I never had any particular feeling for him. He had rather a disturbing appearance—didn't you think so, Hendrik? Such malicious eyes . . ."

This time Hendrik did not answer his influential friend. He was repelled by the thought of summoning up the image of young Hans Miklas's face. But it did appear to him, welcome or not. There it stood before him quite clearly in the twilight of the corridor. The eyes were closed, there was a brightness about the forehead. The sulkily protruding lips were moving.

Hendrik turned and fled, escaping into the glare of the day to avoid hearing the message brought by this severe face transfigured by death.

CHAPTER

In Many Towns

The months slipped by and the year 1933 was over. A great year if one believed the journalists, whose views were dictated by the propaganda ministry. It was the year of accomplishment, of triumph, of victory, the year of the German nation's glorious awakening, when the country found its Führer and itself.

In any case, it had been a gratifying, brilliant year for the actor Höfgen. There had been a few troubles at the start, but it ended in grand style and the ingenious Hendrik was able to face 1934 with good humor and confidence, certain of the favor of those in power, able to count on the patronage of the prime minister. The great man looked on Höfgen/Mephisto as a sort of court jester, a brilliant rascal, an amusing plaything. He had long ago forgiven the actor for his unsavory past, putting it down as the extravagance of an artistic temperament. Hendrik had been rescued from the clutches of the Negress with the whip. Now he could play many fine theatrical roles.

Hendrik was often received by the prime minister. The actor entered his offices and private apartments almost as casually as if he were a paying a call on Director Schmitz or Rose Bernhard.

> "I come to chase your cares away
> Accoutered as a noble earl . . ."

It was with this quotation from *Faust* that Hendrik unceremoniously greeted the prime minister. The great man could think of no more pleasant relaxation after the day's splendidly bloody labors than to dally with his court buffoon. Fräulein Lindenthal almost had cause for jealousy. But she was a kindly creature and in any case had a soft spot for Hendrik Höfgen. And what prestige this much discussed friendship with the awe-inspiring man conferred on Hendrik!

> The admiration of the child and ape,
> If that is really to your taste . . .

This couplet sometimes ran through Hendrik's head as he saw himself surrounded by flattery on all sides. He was showered with obsequious compliments by everyone he met—colleagues, writers, ladies of the new society, even government officials. Had he really acquired a taste for the cloying tattle of the German National Socialist M. Pierre Larue? Did he really enjoy the ponderous compliments of Dr. Ihrig and the snobbish affability of Herr Müller-Andreä? When he was with his old friend Otto Ulrichs, he spoke with scorn about this "damned gang." But at the same time, wasn't he revelling in all these marks of deference and adoration? And whatever he might say to Otto did not keep him from sipping champagne at the table of Pierre Larue at the Hotel Esplanade in the company of handsome young SS officers and finding it very agreeable to the palate.

Hendrik had many friends, and among them several figures of fun. There was, for instance, the poet Benjamin Pelz, whose obscure, rhapsodic verse had delighted to the point of ecstasy a generation of young people who were now for the most part outlaws.

Benjamin Pelz, a stocky little man with cold light-blue eyes, pendulous cheeks and a thick-lipped sensual mouth, told his intimate friends that he adored National Socialism because it was going to completely wipe out the mechanized structure of a civilization he found intolerable. He loved National Socialism because it was leading straight to the precipice, because it had the smell of death about it and would spread immeasurable suffering over a continent in the process of degenerating, on the one hand, into a faultlessly organized factory and, on the other, into a sanitarium for weaklings.

"Life in the democracies has ceased to be dangerous," declared Benjamin Pelz scornfully. "Heroism was something that was being

202

ruled out of our lives. The spectacle we are witnessing today is the birth of a new type of human being—or, rather, the renaissance of a very ancient one, which is archaic, magical and warlike. What a breathlessly beautiful spectacle! What an exciting process! Be proud, my dear Höfgen, that you are able to take such an active part in it!"

Pelz cast a fond look at Hendrik, and then continued: "Life again begins to have a certain rhythm and charm. It awakes from its torpor and soon it will rediscover—as in the times of our buried past— the violent movement of the dance. For people who don't know how to use their eyes and ears, this new rhythm must seem like the well-drilled stamp of marching feet. Fools allow themselves to be deceived by the outward severity of the ancient militant life-style. What a crude mistake! In reality, we are not marching forward, we are reeling, staggering. Our beloved Führer is dragging us toward the shades of darkness and everlasting nothingness. How can we poets, we who have a special affinity for darkness and the lower depths, not admire him? It is absolutely no exaggeration to call our Führer godlike. He is the god of the Underworld, who has always been the most sacred of all for those initiated in black magic. I have a boundless admiration for him, because I have a boundless hatred of the dreary tyranny of reason and the bourgeois fetish concept of progress. All poets worthy of the name are sworn enemies of progress. Poetry itself is in any case a reversion to the sacred primitive state of humanity, before it became civilized. Poetry and slaughter, blood and song, murder and hymns—they are inseparable. Yes, I love catastrophe." Pelz pushed forward his melancholy face with its pouchy cheeks and smiled as though his thick lips were tasting sweets or kisses.

"I am hungry for doomed adventure, for the depths, for the experience of extreme situations that place a man beyond the pale of civilization, in that region where no insurance company, no police, no comfortable hospital can protect him against the merciless power of the elements or a beast of prey. We are going to experience all this, believe me. We are going to be gorged with horror. And, as far as I am concerned, it can never be too horrifying. We are still too soft. Our great Führer can still not do everything he would like. Where is the *public* torture? Why don't we burn all those humanitarian gabblers and rationalist imbeciles at the stake?" Whereupon Pelz tapped impatiently with his spoon on the side of his coffee cup as though summoning a waiter.

"Why the false shame that hides the beautiful festival of tortures behind the walls of a concentration camp?" he demanded. "Up to now we have—to my knowledge—burned only books. That's nothing. But our Führer will soon hand over to us something more. I have every confidence in him. Fires blazing on the horizon; rivers of blood in all the streets; and the frenzied dancing of the survivors, of those who are still spared, around the bodies of the dead!"

A cheerful optimism beamed from the face of the poet as he evoked the horrors in store for the near future. It was with meticulous courtesy, his hands folded piously on his chest, that he assured Hendrik, "And you, my dear Herr Höfgen, you will be among those who will leap most gracefully over the bodies. You have just the face for it. I can see that clearly. You are a very charming son of the Underworld. It's no accident that the prime minister has singled you out. You have the authentic and fertile cynicism of the radical genius. I value you very highly, my dear Herr Höfgen."

Hendrik listened to these strange backhanded compliments with a fixed smile and an uncommunicative gleam in his eyes. Not everyone had such deep and ingenious reasons as Pelz for their newfound love of National Socialism. Others, such as Joachim, the fat character actor, simply said, "I am and will always remain a German artist and patriot no matter who rules my country. I would rather live in Berlin than anywhere else in the world and I have not the smallest desire to become an expatriate. In any case, I couldn't earn as much money anywhere else."

With Joachim, at least, Hendrik knew where he stood. The character actor would have emigrated and become a fanatical antifascist if only he had received a tempting enough offer from Hollywood. Alas, no such offer was forthcoming. Joachim, who had been one of the most celebrated German actors, was no longer quite at the top. So one night, looking around his circle of friends, he said, with an air of bluff honesty, "Where else can you find such good beer as here in our German beer cellars? Can anyone tell me that?"

His large expressive face with its flabby cheeks and suspicious little eyes had the misleading good temper of a bear, which seems so comic and lumbering but of all beasts of prey is the most savage. Sycophants assured him that he bore a marked resemblance to the prime minister, which brought a broad satisfied smile to his face. When he heard that someone had said he was half Jewish, he went

204

into a fury. "Let the scoundrel come out into the open," cried Joachim, his red cheeks going purple. "Then we'll see if he dare repeat such an insolent lie to my face! What an outrage! A barefaced attempt to deprive a German citizen of his honor!"

But the frightful rumors about the character actor persisted. There were whispers that something had been discovered about one of his grandmothers. Joachim put detectives on the trail of his slanderers. Several people were sent to a concentration camp for having cast doubts on his ancestry. "Dirty lies are no longer allowed to go unpunished here," declared Joachim with satisfaction.

He visited his most influential friends and colleagues to assure them yet again, man to man, that he could vouch for the racial purity of his ancestors.

"Hand on my heart," said Joachim to Hendrik, whom he visited one Sunday morning with a certain amount of solemnity. "As far as I'm concerned, everything is in order. All is as it should be. I have absolutely nothing to reproach myself with." He glanced upward with the faithful-dog look he always used when playing rugged fathers with hearts of gold, who after quarreling with their sons have a tearful reconciliation.

"If anyone says anything to the contrary, I shall unhappily be forced to have him put behind bars," concluded the German patriot. "For now we live in a law-abiding state."

Hendrik could only concur with this opinion. He offered cigars and an excellent brandy to his colleague, who was defending his honor with such commendable zeal. The morning meeting between the two actors developed a mood of light-heartedness and trust. When he left, Joachim hugged his friend Höfgen with the clumsiness of a bear whose embrace squeezes the life out of its enemy, and begged him to give his warmest regards to Fräulein Lindenthal.

These were the kind of friends Hendrik had now—some of them interesting, like Pelz, and some merely good-natured, like Joachim.

From Paris, Barbara had written asking for a divorce. The legal formalities were completed easily and quickly without the presence of the couple. There was no need to invoke any particular grounds for dissolving the marriage: judges were perfectly willing to admit that a man with Höfgen's status and views—an eminent member of the State Theater and a personal friend of the prime minister—could not remain the husband of a woman who lived as an exile, made no secret of her antigovernment opinions and, worse still, as had been recently discovered, was racially impure. Even the professional liars of the National Socialist press had not dared go so far as to accuse her father, the privy councillor—politically compromised though he certainly was—of having Jewish blood. But what they did reproach him with was perhaps worse and even less pardonable: he had committed "racial profanation." His wife, the general's daughter, had not been an irreproachable "Aryan." It was not a mere coincidence that Barbara's grandfather, a high-ranking officer whose military prowess was suddenly an unmentionable subject, had always shown suspicious liberal tendencies. And the intellectual liveliness of the general's wife, which had been far above the normal and admissible level in military circles, was now explained in the most simple but distressing way. The general had not been one of the ethnic German family, but an *Untermensch*, a Semite. Wilhelm II had magnanimously ignored this fact; but an anti-Semitic broadsheet in Nuremberg had now brought it to light. The general's wife was also half Jewish: the anti-Semitic paper could prove it. Of what use now was her brilliant past, her noble beauty and her dignity? A scribbling smear merchant, an unwashed thug, who in his whole life had never been able to write a sentence in correct German, was able to proclaim that she did not belong to the national community.

Barbara was therefore more than 30 percent racially impure: this alone was sufficient ground for divorce in the eyes of the German courts. Blond Rhinelanders had the right to a wife of irreproachable race. However, Hendrik would not have been expected to tolerate a wife like Barbara, even had she been a bona-fide Aryan, for her behavior was a public scandal.

She had been in Paris since February 1933. It was plain to everyone who had known her before that she had changed. All the dreamy side of her character had disappeared and she seemed to have lost her taste for light-hearted pastimes. Her face now wore a look of determination; a permanent frown knitted her brows and wrinkled her forehead. Even her ambling walk was now brisk and purposeful, the stride of a person who would never rest until she had achieved her one object in life.

Barbara, who formerly had occupied her time with amateurish sketches and heavy books, who had worried over the problems of her friends or been absorbed in light-hearted distractions, was now a militant dissenter. She worked on a committee that took care of political refugees from Germany. And with her friends Sebastian and Hedda von Herzfeld, she also produced a political review devoted to the ignominy and dangers of German fascism.

Sebastian and Frau von Herzfeld were responsible for the editorial content. Barbara looked after the commercial side. To her surprise, she found that she was not without a certain talent for handling business affairs. The little magazine was not subsidized in any way and had to be self-supporting. It was a weekly, printed in both German and French. Originally it had been sent out only to a very small circle of subscribers and was stenciled, not printed. After six months the few sheets had become a magazine with supporters in most European cities outside Germany.

"In Stockholm we have fifty subscribers, thirty-five in Madrid, a hundred and ten in Tel-Aviv," declared Barbara during an "editorial conference" in her hotel room. "I am pleased with the results from Holland and Czechoslovakia. In Switzerland things could be better. If only we had a good agent in the United States! Our circulation there is too small. What we have to say should have an audience numbering hundreds of thousands. But we are so poor . . .

"Our enemies lay out millions to spread their lies—and we hardly know how to pay for our postage." She clenched her small brown fists. Her eyes took on a menacing expression, as they always did when she thought about the hated enemy.

Sebastian, too, had changed. In the past he had been interested only in the most sophisticated and abstruse matters, but he now forced himself to think and write with the utmost simplicity. "Combat has other laws than the noble rules of art," he said. "The law of battle demands that we renounce all sorts of nuances to concentrate solely on one objective. My duty at the moment is not to study or create beauty, but to act effectively—within the means at my disposal. It's a sacrifice for me to do so—a hard one." Sometimes he became tired and would say, "I'm fed up. There's no point. The others are far stronger than we are. The luck is all on their side. It's a bitter and, in the long run, a ludicrous game to play at being Don Quixote. I long for an island so far away that once you reach it everything that plagues us here will fade away and no longer seem real . . ."

"There's no such place," cried Barbara. "Your island doesn't exist, and it has no right to exist, Sebastian. Besides, right now our enemies are not so terribly strong. They are even a little afraid of us. Every word, every truth we publish does them a little bit of harm and brings them a millimeter—yes, a millimeter—closer, Sebastian, to their final collapse, which will come one day."

Such was Barbara's confidence, or in any case the appearance of confidence she managed to give when her friend Sebastian felt discouraged. "Just think of it," she said. "We have two new subscribers in the Argentine. It's marvelous—they've even already sent the money." Barbara spent half her days writing reminder letters to libraries and distribution centers in Sofia or Copenhagen, Tokyo or Budapest, concerning small outstanding payments.

Between Barbara and Hedda von Herzfeld a bond had developed that was not quite friendship but was something more than the mundane relationship between two people who work together. Barbara respected Hedda's energy and courage. Hedda was quite alone: her work was all she had. She clung to the political review that she edited with Sebastian like a mother to a child. When the first number had been printed and she saw the completed copies with their handsome layout, Hedda almost wept with joy. She embraced Barbara, and although there was no one else in the room, whispered softly in her ear how grateful she was to her for everything. Barbara took a long look at Hedda's large, downy, powdered face and noticed that her features were sharper and more strongly marked: they spoke of inner struggles, of violent and bitter spiritual experiences that Hedda had undergone during this year they had spent together. In the first weeks of exile she had once run into the man to whom she had been married many years before. Perhaps she had secretly begun to set great store by this encounter. Then it emerged that he was living with a girl in Moscow. Nothing could have been more natural, and Hedda was reasonable enough to accept the situation. Nevertheless, she was struck by the revelation as by something totally unexpected that she had had hopes she had scarcely dared admit to herself until then.

Once, but only once, did she mention Hendrik's name to Barbara. "I wonder if he's getting on well," she said softly. It was late at night and they had been working side by side all day. "I wonder if he's enjoying it all—if he is happy with his new fame?"

"Who are you talking about?" asked Barbara without looking up. Hedda blushed a little as she tried to assume an ironic smile, "Now—

who else? Of your esteemed ex-husband . . ." Barbara responded dryly, "Is he still alive? I didn't know that he was still around. For me he died long ago. I don't like ghosts from the past, especially such dubious ghosts as that." They never spoke of him again.

From time to time Barbara visited her father, who lived alone in a town on the French Riviera. He had left Germany immediately after the Reichstag fire, much to the rage and disappointment of a horde of Nazi students who found his house empty when they invaded it to show "the red privy councillor" what "the true German youth" thought of him. They were determined to beat up the world-famous old gentleman and then pack him into a car and deliver him to the nearest concentration camp. The gang roared with fury when they found no one in the villa but a trembling housekeeper. In order to achieve something for the Nazi cause and to give the nocturnal expedition some point, they shook up the poor old woman a little and shut her in the cellar while they enjoyed themselves above in the library. True German youth trampled on the works of Goethe and Kant, Voltaire and Schopenhauer, Shakespeare and Nietzsche. "Marxism—the lot of it," declared the uniformed youths with disgust. And when they threw the works of Lenin and Freud in the fire, they danced with joy. On the drive home the young team decided that, after all, they had spent two very pleasant hours in the house of the privy councillor. "And if the old swine himself had been there," they shouted exultantly, "then we would really have had a time!"

The privy councillor had managed not only to escape but also to take away with him in his luggage his most important papers and a small but particularly treasured part of his library. After he had spent several weeks traveling in Switzerland and Czechoslovakia, he settled in the South of France. He rented a small house; there were a few palms and beautiful flowering bushes in the garden, and he had a view of the sea.

The old man went out very seldom, and most of the time was alone. For hours on end he wandered through his garden or sat in front of the house watching the ceaselessly changing colors of the sea.

"It is a great comfort to me," he said to Barbara. "It pleases me so much to look out at this beautiful stretch of water. It's so long since I've been here. I had forgotten how blue the Mediterranean can be. All Germans worthy of the name have yearned for it; and they have all venerated it as the sacred cradle of our civilization. Now suddenly it has to be hated in our land. The Germans want to free themselves from its power and grace. They think they can do without its beautiful clarity; they howl that it disgusts them. But it is their own civilization they are rejecting. Do they want to disown all the greatness that they themselves have given to the world? Ah, these Germans! How much they are still going to have to suffer, and how horribly they are going to make everyone else suffer!"

The National Socialist regime confiscated the house and possessions of the privy councillor, and Bruckner learned through a paragraph in a French newspaper that he was no longer a German citizen. A few days after he read this, he began to work again. "It is going to be a great book," he wrote to Barbara. "And it will be called *The Germans*. In it I shall collect everything that I know about them, that I fear for them and hope for them. And I know a lot about them, I fear a lot for them, and—even now—I have a lot of hope."

Suffering and musing, he spent his days on the foreign coast he loved. Sometimes weeks passed without his speaking a word, except to exchange a few French phrases with the young servant who looked after his house. He received many letters. People who had earlier been his pupils and were now refugees or remained despairingly in Germany turned to him for encouragement and spiritual advice. "Your name remains for us the symbol of another, better Germany," someone dared to write to him from a Bavarian provincial town, though taking the very natural precaution of disguising his handwriting and giving no address. The privy councillor received such pledges of trust with deep emotion and a certain bitterness. All these people who think and write like this have gone along with the pack, he thought; it is because they have tolerated what was going on and made themselves accomplices of the others that our country has become what it is today. He laid the letters aside and opened his manuscript. It grew slowly, nourished on love and knowledge, on grief and defiance, on deep doubt and a confidence that still, despite countless reservations, remained strong.

Bruckner knew that Theophilus Marder and Nicoletta were living in another small Riviera town not fifty kilometers from his own villa. The two men had once met and greeted each other in the course of a walk. However, they made no attempt to converse or arrange to meet again. Marder was as little disposed as the privy councillor to conversation and sociability. The satirist had lost his cheerfully aggressive insolence. His horror over the German catastrophe had reduced him to silence. Like Bruckner he sat for hours in a small garden among palms and flowering bushes, gazing at the sea. But Marder's eyes did not have a still, meditative gaze: they were restless; they fluttered and wandered, helpless and inconsolable, over the broad shining expanse of water. His bluish lips had retained their sucking, smacking motions, but now they formed no words, only soundless moans.

Theophilus, who used to carry his head so high, now sat hunched in on himself. His lead-colored hands lay on his wasted knees and looked too tired to move ever again. He sat crouched and motionless; only his eyes wandered and his lips pursued their plaintive dumb monologue. Sometimes he started, as though a far too dreadful face had frightened him. Then he raised himself up with difficulty and cried out in a voice no longer snarling but querulous with old age. "Nicoletta, come here! Please, come immediately." And Nicoletta would come to him from the house.

In Nicoletta's face there was now an expression of weariness and melancholy endurance which hardly suited the boldly arched nose, the sharp mouth and the domed forehead. Her cheeks had become broader and softer; her beautiful large eyes had lost the look of challenging brightness that people had found so fascinating and disturbing in the old days. Nicoletta seemed no longer to be the willful and disdainful girl she used to be, but a woman who had loved much and suffered. She had sacrificed her youth; obsessed by an emotion in which hysteria was allied with genuine ardor, she had given her youth to the man who now sat, a miserable wreck, in the chair before her.

"What do you want, Theophilus?" she asked. She had kept her impeccable diction, whatever else she might have lost over the years. "What can I do for you, my love?"

He groaned as though in a nightmare. "Nicoletta, Nicoletta, my child . . . It's so hideous . . . It's far too hideous . . . I hear the shrieks of those who are being tortured in Germany. I hear them quite clearly, the wind is bringing them in over the sea . . . The torturers play the gramophone during the horrible proceedings. That's their obscene trick. They put cushions in the mouths of their victims to stifle their cries . . . But I hear them all the same . . . I have to hear everything. God has thus punished me . . . I am the conscience of the world and I hear everything. Nicoletta, my child!" He clung to her.

His tormented eyes wandered over the Southern landscape, whose peace was for him filled with visions of terror. Nicoletta laid her hand on his hot, damp forehead. "I know, my Theophilus," she said with quiet precision. "You hear everything and you see through everything. You must give the world some account of your knowledge. That would be very helpful to you and the world. You must write, Theophilus. You must write."

For the past year she had been imploring him to work. She suffered under his paralysis. She could not bear his despairing day-dreaming inactivity. She admired him: she held him to be the greatest of living men; and she wanted to see him not on the sidelines of world events but at their center—active, intervening, calling the world to its senses, sounding the alarm.

"What can I write now? I have said everything. I have predicted everything. I have unmasked the whole swindle. I have smelled the rot. If you only knew, my child, how unbearable it is to have been so terribly right. My books are forgotten just as if they had never been written. My complete works have been burned. My prophecies seem to have been blown away on the wind. And yet everything that's happening today, the whole unspeakable calamity, is no more than a trifling epilogue to my prophetic work. Everything is contained in my work. Everything is anticipated there, including what is yet to come —the worst, the final catastrophe. I have suffered it already through and through. I have already given it a form. What then is there left for me to write? I bear the suffering of the world. In my heart all the debacles are running their course, those of the present and of the future. I—I—I . . . ."

On these three syllables—on this "I" in which his bewildered spirit became entangled as in a trap—he fell silent. His face, which suffering had improved—it now looked somewhat delicate, more sensitive and stronger than before—sank forward. He had suddenly fallen asleep.

Nicoletta returned to the house. She remained standing in the dark, cool hallway. Slowly she raised her arms and placed her two hands over her face. She wanted to sob, but no tears came. She had wept too much. Into her hands Nicoletta whispered, "I can't take any more. I can't take any more. I must get away from here. I can't hold out any longer."

The people Hendrik had called his friends were living spread out over many different countries and many towns. For some, things were going well enough: the Professor, for instance, had nothing to complain about. A world-wide fame such as his never wears itself out. He could count on being able to live the rest of his life in castles with baroque furniture and Gobelin tapestries, or in the most luxurious apartments of the leading international hotels. Because he was a Jew, his productions were no longer wanted in Berlin? Good—or, rather, so much the worse for the Berliners. The Professor moved his tongue majestically in his cheeks, groaned and snarled angrily for a few days, and finally came to the conclusion that he had quite enough work on his hands as it was. Let the Berliners manage without him; and let "this Höfgen" present comedies to his Führer. Before the end of the season he still had to direct an operetta in Paris, two Shakespearean comedies in Rome and Venice and a sort of religious musical in London. In addition, he had to arrange a tour of Schiller's *Intrigue and Love* and Strauss's *Fledermaus* through Holland and Scandinavia; and in the spring he must be in Hollywood, where he had signed a big film contract.

Rose Bernhard and Herr Katz ran his two theaters in Vienna. There was no need to worry about the welfare of these two. Sometimes Katz thought with nostalgia about the happy days when he had taken in the Berliners with his abysmal drama *The Guilt* and had posed as a Spanish neurologist. "Jokes were still on the grand scale in those days," he said and worked his tongue around his mouth almost as majestically as his lord and master. Now there was no resuscitating the soul of Dostoevsky. Herr Katz was finally relegated to the nether regions of business.

Fräulein Bernhard, too, became wistful when she looked back on the Kurfürstendamm days, particularly when she thought about Höfgen. "What marvelously wicked eyes he had," she would recall dreamily. "My Hendrik—he's the thing I most resent leaving to the Nazis. They really don't deserve anything so beautiful." However, there was now a dashing young Viennese—not so demonic as Höfgen, it had to be admitted, but more gallant and undemanding—who called her Rose and stroked her chin.

In London and New York, Dora Martin was enjoying a second career, a new triumph that overshadowed all her Berlin successes. She had learned English with the intensity of an ambitious schoolgirl and had been able to translate into the new tongue all those wayward turns of speech with which she had earlier surprised and bewitched Berlin. She cooed, moaned, giggled, crowed with joy, sang. She was still as shy and awkward as a young boy and as weightless and fey as an elf. She seemed always to be carelessly and capriciously improvising; but in fact her great intelligence was brought to bear on every detail of the small but carefully placed effects with which she drew laughter or tears from her entranced public. She was cunning. She knew what the Anglo-Saxons liked. Purposely she was a little more sentimental, a touch more feminine and gentle than she had been in Germany. She made less use of the rough husky tones in her voice, and resorted more often to her innocent, helpless wide-eyed look.

"I have altered my act a tiny, tiny little bit," she would admit, coquettishly sinking her head between her shoulders. "Only just the amount needed to please the British and the Americans." She traveled back and forth between London and New York playing the same part hundreds of times in each city. In the daytime she made films. Her physical endurance was astounding. Her small childlike body was tireless, as though possessed by a superhuman energy. The American and English newspapers saw in her the world's greatest actress. When she appeared after a performance for a quarter of an hour in the Savoy Hotel, the band sounded a fanfare and everyone stood up in her honor. The society of the two Anglo-Saxon capitals paid homage to the Jewish actress who had been driven from Berlin. The queen of England received her; the Prince of Wales sent roses to her dressing room; young American writers wrote plays for her. Sometimes journalists who came from Vienna or Budapest to interview her asked if she ever felt a desire to act once again in Germany. "No, not any more," she answered. "I am no longer a German actress." Nevertheless, she wondered now and then what the people in Berlin were saying about her new success. She hoped it made them a little angry. She knew there would be no one there to rejoice over her victories. A hundred thousand people had professed a burning love for her, and she wanted them to feel a little angry about her now so that they wouldn't altogether forget her.

A British film in which she starred was shown in Berlin, but only for a few days before the scandal broke. The propaganda minister ordered a display of "spontaneous indignation." Members of the SS, dressed in civilian clothes, were sent to the cinema. When the face of Dora Martin appeared in close-up on the screen, the youths dispersed among the audience whistled, hooted and threw stink bombs. "We don't want any more damned Jewesses in a German cinema," they yelled. The house lights had to be turned on and the performance broken off. The inquisitive and the daring who had gathered to see this forbidden entertainment ran from their seats in panic. Those among the audience whose features appeared to have a Jewish cast—and there were a fair number of Jews who turned out to see Dora Martin—were arrested and beaten up.

The minister of propaganda let it be known in London that a liberal-minded German government had allowed the film to be shown, but the Berlin public would not tolerate such things any more. The public anger had been immediate, violent and very understandable. From now on, every film in which the actress Dora Martin appeared would be banned.

They lived in many towns. They sought refuge in many countries. Oskar H. Kroge had settled temporarily in Prague. There was no place for him in the new Germany. He was not a Jew and not a Communist, but an old literary pioneer. He believed in the theater as a moral institution and in the eternal ideals of justice and freedom. Despite so many disappointments, he would not be separated from his starry-eyed optimism. He was determined to regain contact with the noble traditions of the old days in Frankfurt. On arrival in Prague he immediately went in search of people who would understand his enthusiasm and place several thousand Czech koruna at his disposal, for he planned to open a theater workshop in a suburban cellar. He found the donors, though they gave very little. He found the cellar and a few young actors and a play in which there was a good deal about "humanity" and "the dawn of a better era." He worked with the young actors and the play was produced. Schmitz, who had remained faithful to his friend, took care of the financial side. Kroge, the uncompromising idealist and dogged searcher after the highest and most beautiful, wanted to remain undisturbed in the pure air of the summits of Art.

Alas, Schmitz could not always leave him there: they lacked even the bare necessities of life. Never had Kroge, an old bourgeois bohemian who had certainly often known money difficulties but never actual want, never had he thought it possible that even the most modest theater could be kept going with such laughably small sums. Somehow they scraped through, at least for the time being, despite the political difficulties that were added to their economic headaches. The German legation in Prague plotted with the authorities against the emigré Hamburg theater director, whose pacifist obduracy they found troublesome. Kroge and Schmitz defended themselves; they refused to yield. But they both became thin; Schmitz no longer had pink cheeks, and deeper lines marked Kroge's forehead and the corners of his mouth.

In many towns and in many lands . . .

Juliette Martens, known as Princess Tebab, had found a job in a small cabaret in Montmartre. Between midnight and three in the morning she showed off her beautiful body and her supple dancing to Americans (who came to Paris in smaller numbers since the fall of the dollar), a few drunks from the French provinces and a few pimps. She appeared almost naked, dressed in a small brassière of green glass beads and a brief triangle of green satin with a large tail of green feathers at the back. To explain these feathers to the audience she would repeat several times, "I am a little bird and have flown across the ocean to build a nest here in Montmartre."

In fact, the resemblance between Juliette and a bird was very slight. Nor was her dismal room in the Rue des Martyres in any way reminiscent of a nest. It was dark and looked out onto a dirty courtyard. The one ornament on the bare stained walls was a photograph of the actor Hendrik Höfgen. One day in a fit of rage and pain, Juliette had torn it up; but later she had carefully stuck the pieces together again. Hendrik's mouth was now set a little sideways, which gave his face a rather sardonic look; and there was a streak of glue running diagonally across his forehead like a scar; but otherwise his beauty was almost unimpaired.

On the first of every month she collected the small sum of money sent by Hendrik from the hall porter of a house whose occupant she did not know. Her wage from the Montmartre cabaret and the allowance from Berlin just enabled her to live without walking the streets. She saw few people and had no lover. She spoke to nobody about her Berlin adventure, partly from fear of losing her life—or at least her small monthly allowance—and partly from an unwillingness to create difficulties for Hendrik. Her heart was faithful to him, although she had forgotten nothing and forgiven nothing.

At least once a day Juliette remembered with hate and terror the dim cell in which she had suffered so much. She thought of revenge, but it had to be a delicious outsize revenge—nothing shabby and mean would do. For long hours of interminable days Princess Tebab lay on her sordid bed and dreamed. She would return to Africa, collect all the blacks around her and become the queen—the warrior princess of all the black races. And she would lead her people in a great rebellion, a great war against Europe. The white continent was ripe for destruction: this was something Juliette knew without a shadow of a doubt since she had received her visit from the Berlin secret police. The white continent must perish: Princess Tebab wanted to march in a victory procession with her black brothers through the capitals of Europe. A bloodbath of huge proportions would wash away the shame with which the white continent had covered itself. The insolent overlords must become slaves. In her dreams the king's daughter saw Hendrik prostrate at her feet as her favorite slave. How she would torment him! Ah, how she would mock him! She would crown his bald forehead with flowers, but he would have to wear his crown kneeling. Humiliated, and adorned like the most valuable piece of loot, the vile, despicable lover would have to stagger in her wake.

So dreamed the black Venus, and her nimble rough fingers played with the red whip of braided leather.

During one evening walk Juliette saw Barbara coming toward her in the stream of people moving from the Madeleine to the Place de la Concorde. Hendrik's wife, who for so long had been the object of Juliette's reflections, either jealous or sympathetic, was walking fast, deep in thought. Juliette very lightly touched her sleeve with her fingertips and said in her deep husky voice, "*Bonsoir, madame,*" bowing her head a little as she spoke. When Barbara looked up in surprise, the Negress had already passed by. Barbara saw only her broad back, which was quickly lost among other backs and other bodies.

Nicoletta von Niebuhr, Nicoletta Marder, found herself one day again in Berlin. With her red hatboxes, which had become very battered, she appeared in Hendrik Höfgen's apartment in the Reichs-kanzlerplatz. "Here I am," she said making her eyes flash as brightly as she could. "I couldn't hold out any longer down there. Theophilus is wonderful, a genius, and I love him more than ever. But he has placed himself outside time and reality. He has become a dreamer, a Parsifal. I can't endure that. Do you understand what I mean, Hendrik? I can't endure it."

Hendrik understood. He was utterly against dreamers; no one was more careful to maintain the necessary contact with his epoch and its realities.

"Emigration is for weaklings," he said severely. "These people in their Riviera bathing resorts present themselves as martyrs, but they're only deserters. We here are in the front line, while they out there are malingering in the base camp."

"I am absolutely determined to act again," said Nicoletta.

"I can force through almost anything I like in the State Theater," Hendrik said. "Caesar von Muck is still the director, but the prime minister doesn't like him, and the propaganda minister supports him only for prestige reasons. It's been whispered around that our Caesar is a dreadful theater administrator. The plays he chooses are boring— what he would like most would be to put on only his own works. He doesn't understand anything about actors, either. The only thing he can do is pile up an enormous deficit."

Nicoletta could count on getting a job with the State Theater, but first Hendrik wanted to make a guest appearance with her in Hamburg. He chose the two-character play in which they had toured the North Sea resorts just before his marriage. The Hamburg Arts Theater was proud to welcome back as a guest its former member, who in the meantime had become so famous and who was a friend of the country's leaders. The new director, Kroge's successor, a gentleman called Baldur von Totenbach, was on the station platform to meet Hendrik and his companion. Herr von Totenbach had been a regular army officer; his face was covered with scars and he had steel-blue eyes like Muck's. "Welcome, *Kamerad* Höfgen," he called out in a thick Saxon accent, as though Hendrik shared with him an honorable past as an army officer, instead of a shady record as a cultural Bolshevik. "Welcome," called out various other people who had accompained Herr von Totenbach to the station to greet their colleague Höfgen. Among these was Fräulein Motz, who embraced Hendrik with tears of real emotion in her eyes.

"What a long time it's been," cried the staunch lady, showing the gold fillings deep inside her mouth. "And how much we have all experienced!" Nicoletta and Hendrik quickly learned that she had a child—a small girl, the late and rather surprising fruit of her liaison with Petersen, the player of old-man roles. "A tiny German maiden," she said. "We have called her Walpurga."

Petersen had not changed at all. His face still looked somewhat bare and in need of a sailor's beard. From his wandering eye it was clear that he had not lost his habit of squandering hard-earned money and pursuing young girls. It seemed likely that Fräulein Motz loved him more than he did her. Rolf Bonetti appeared in a black SS uniform and looked dazzling. He let it be known that he now received many more love letters from the public than ever before. Rahel Mohrenwitz was no longer with the theater. "She's got Jewish blood," hissed Fräulein Motz behind her hand, and was then shaken with a vicious little laugh as though she had said something obscene. Bonetti put on a disgusted face, perhaps at the thought of all the race profanation of which he had formerly been guilty with Rahel. The young girl—according to what Hendrik was told—had attempted suicide when the impurity of her blood was made known, and finally had married a Czech shoe manufacturer. "Where material welfare is concerned, things will go well for her over there—abroad," said Motz disdainfully. She pointed her thumb over her shoulder as though "abroad" lay behind her in some unspeakable far distance.

The new members of the company were blond youths and girls who worthily combined a sturdy cheerfulness with a taut military discipline. They were introduced to Hendrik and showed him every sign of devotion. He was the fairy prince, who took envy and admiration as a tribute that was his due. He had condescended to climb down to their level for a moment, return to the lowly spot from which he had set out. And he behaved in a very affable way, even going so far as to put his arm around Fräulein Motz's shoulders. "Ah, you haven't changed at all," she said, delightedly pressing his hand. Petersen exclaimed, "Hendrik was always a wonderful comrade." At which point Herr von Totenbach closed the conversation by declaring with a certain sternness, "In the new Germany there are only comrades, whatever their station in life."

Hendrik expressed a desire to greet Herr Knurr, the stage-door man who had always hidden a swastika under the lapel of his coat and whose lodge Höfgen, the cultural Bolshevik, had slipped past with such a bad conscience. Would the old party member not tremble with pride when he now shook the hand of the friend and favorite of the prime minister?

To his astonishment, Hendrik received a fairly cool reception from Herr Knurr. There was no picture of the Führer to be seen in the porter's lodge, although this would now be allowable, indeed desirable. When Hendrik asked after Herr Knurr's health, the porter murmured something between his teeth that had an unfriendly ring, and the look he cast at Hendrik was venomous. It was plain that Herr Knurr had been deeply disappointed by his Führer/Redeemer and by the whole nationalist movement. Like so many others, he felt that his hopes had been betrayed. And so for Hendrik, friend of the air force general, it was still as painful as it had ever been to pass the porter's lodge.

Hendrik was relieved to find that not a single one of the Communist stagehands, with whom he had willingly exchanged a clenched fist salute in the old days, still remained with the theater. He dared not ask what had become of them.

The theater was sold out every evening. The Hamburg public acclaimed their old favorite, who had made such a great career for himself in Berlin. But Nicoletta caused general disappointment. She was found to be rigid, unnatural and even a little sinister. In fact, she had almost forgotten how to act. Her bearing had become stiff, and her voice had a strange, hollow plaintive ring. It was as though something in her had frozen. The public even took exception to her large nose, whispering in the stalls about whether she might not have Jewish blood. But other people pointed out that this was impossible, for if it had been true, Höfgen would never have consented to be seen with her in public.

The following morning Hendrik had the curious idea of paying a call on Frau Monkeberg. She, too, must see him in his glory—she who for years had humiliated him with her refined patrician poise. He remembered how Barbara, the privy councillor's daughter, had immediately been invited to tea in the drawing room, while he had been held off with aloof and mocking smiles. Now he wanted to drive up in his Mercedes to visit the old lady.

To his intense irritation, he was met at the villa by a strange caretaker, who told him that Frau Monkeberg was dead. That was just like her: rather than face a meeting that would have been painful she had taken refuge in flight. These upper-class people of the old school, these gentry without money but with a noble past—why were they totally out of one's reach?

Apart from this disappointment, Hendrik was extremely satisfied with his Hamburg visit. Herr von Totenbach had said on parting, "I and my whole company are proud to have had you with us, *Kamerad* Höfgen." And Fräulein Motz had held out her little Walpurga in her arms with the insistent demand that he should bless the howling infant. "Bless her, Hendrik," cried Fräulein Motz. "Then she will turn out well. Bless my little Walpurga." And Petersen added his voice to her entreaties.

On his return to Berlin, Hendrik learned from Lotte Lindenthal that he was the subject of a violent altercation that had broken out in the highest circles. The prime minister—"my bridegroom," as Lotte now described him—was thoroughly dissatisfied with Caesar von Muck. So much was common knowledge. What was not so well known was the name of the man whom the air force general had chosen to succeed him as director of the Prussian State Theater—it was Hendrik Höfgen. The propaganda minister was up in arms against this, supported by all those high dignitaries of the party who prided themselves on being "one hundred per cent National Socialist." They were fiercely opposed to any compromise, especially in cultural matters.

"It is inadmissible to place in such a prominent and exemplary position a man who is not a member of the party and has the worst kind of cultural Bolshevistic past," declared the propaganda minister.

"It doesn't matter at all to me whether an artist is a member of the party or not—all that matters is that he should be capable," countered the prime minister, who in all his might and splendor often allowed himself to indulge in alarmingly liberal whims. "Under Höfgen the Prussian State Theater will show a profit. The administration of Herr von Muck is too great a luxury for the taxpayer to bear." When it was a question of the career of his protégé the general even gave a thought to the taxpayer, something that very seldom happened otherwise.

The propaganda minister protested that since Caesar von Muck was a friend of the Führer, a seasoned comrade-in-arms, it would be unthinkable simply to show him the door. The air force general jovially proposed that the author of the Tannenberg dramas should be made president of the Academy of Writers. "There he will be no trouble to anyone." He also suggested that he should for the time being be sent on a very fine journey abroad. The propaganda minister put through a telephone call to the Führer, who was resting in the Bavarian Alps, and implored him to prevent the installation in the highest theatrical post in the country of an obviously talented and efficient but morally ill-qualified actor. The prime minister had already sent an emissary to the Bavarian Alps two days earlier. The Führer, who was always looking for ways of getting out of making decisions, answered that the case did not interest him: he had larger and more important things to occupy his mind, and would his ministers kindly settle the matter between themselves.

The gods wrangled. The whole affair became a power and prestige contest between the propaganda minister and the prime minister, between the lame and the fat. Hendrik waited, scarcely knowing which outcome of the battle of the gods to hope for. On the one hand, the prospect of the directorship appealed to his vanity and his search for outlets for his energy. On the other hand, if he occupied a high public post in the state, he would identify himself entirely and forever with the regime. He would link his own fate for better or for worse with that of the bloodstained adventurers. Was that what he wanted? Had this been his aim? Were there not voices in his heart warning him against such a step? The voices of a bad conscience and with them the voices of fear?

The decision was taken. The fat man won. He summoned Höfgen and formally offered him the administration of the State Theater. When the actor responded with an emotion closer to consternation than delight, the prime minister became angry.

"I have staked my whole influence on your behalf, so no nonsense from you." And he added, lying to overwhelm the actor's resistance, "Besides, the Führer is also very much in favor of your becoming the administrator."

Hendrik hesitated, partly because his inner voices would not leave him in peace and partly because he enjoyed being courted by the mighty. They need me, he thought with exultation. I was very nearly an emigré, and now the powers beg me to save their theaters from ruin. He asked for twenty-four hours to think it over. The general grumblingly dismissed him.

That night Hendrik talked it over with Nicoletta. "I don't know— should I or shouldn't I?" He sighed and, under half-closed lids, gazed into empty space. "It's all so horribly difficult." He threw his head back and turned his noble profile toward the ceiling.

"But of course you should," said Nicoletta in a sharp cajoling voice. "You know perfectly well that you should, that you must. This is the victory, my love." Not only Nicoletta's mouth but her whole body made sinuous movements. "It's the ultimate triumph. I have always known that you would achieve it."

With his cold, shining gaze still directed at the ceiling he asked her, "Will you help me, Nicoletta?"

She crouched before him among the sofa cushions. Gazing radiantly up at him with her beautiful catlike eyes and carefully forming every syllable, she said, "I shall be proud of you."

The following day the weather was beautiful. Hendrik decided to go to the prime minister's palace on foot. This unusually long walk would underline the festive character of the occasion. For was not the day on which Hendrik Höfgen placed his talent and his name wholly at the disposal of the bloodstained regime worthy of celebration?

Nicoletta accompanied her friend. It was a pleasant walk. They were both in a confident and cheerful mood. Close to the Tiergarten, an old lady with a strikingly erect bearing and a beautiful, pale proud face was taking the air. With a pearl-gray costume of somewhat old-fashioned but elegant cut, she wore a three-cornered hat of shining black material. Under the hat her hair was arranged in tight round curls on her temples. It was the head of an aristocrat of the eighteenth century. She walked very slowly with small determined steps. Her frail but rigorously disciplined bearing had the melancholy dignity of a past epoch.

"It's the general's wife," said Nicoletta in an awed whisper, stopping suddenly. A little color rose to her cheeks. Hendrik blushed, too, as he raised his light-gray hat and bowed deeply. The general's wife raised her lorgnette, which hung on a long chain of blue semi-precious stones. Through the glasses she coolly and unhurriedly examined the young couple, who were now only a few paces from her. The face of the handsome old lady remained expressionless. She made no response to their greeting. Hendrik wondered if she knew where they were going, and what contract Hendrik was about to sign in an hour's time. Perhaps she guessed it, for she had followed their careers. The chain rattled slightly as she let the lorgnette fall back into place. The old lady turned her back on Hendrik and Nicoletta and moved away from them.

10

The Threat

The director was bald—he had shaved off the last silken strands of hair that nature had left him. He felt no need to be ashamed of his nobly shaped skull. It was with dignity and self-confidence that he displayed the Mephistophelean head that had so taken the fancy of the prime minister. The cold jewel-eyes shimmered as irresistibly as ever in the sallow, slightly bloated face. The tightening of pain about the temples aroused a respectful compassion. The cheeks had become a little slack, but the cleft chin still retained its masterful handsomeness. When the director raised his chin, as was his custom, the result was both aesthetic and imposing; but when he lowered his face, creases formed in his neck and it became apparent that in fact he had two chins.

The director was handsome. Only people who looked very closely, like the general's wife through her lorgnette, thought they could detect that his handsomeness was not quite genuine, that it was more an illusion that was willed than a gift of nature.

"He manages his face as he does his hands," said observers who were malicious and overcritical. "The hands are broad and ugly but he knows how to show them as if they were graceful and gothic."

The director was very dignified. He had exchanged his monocle for glasses with thick horn rims. His bearing was straight, controlled, almost stiff. The magic of his personality made people overlook the fact that he was putting on weight. He spoke most of the time in a soft, veiled singing voice that was discreetly colored as the mood took him with commanding, cajoling, plaintive or thoughtful tones. Sometimes on festive occasions his voice was suddenly loud with a surprisingly bright metallic ring.

The director could also be cheerful. In the armory of wiles with which he cast his spell on people his own playful version of Rhenish high spirits played an important part. The director certainly knew how to be light-hearted when he needed to disarm ill-tempered stagehands, stubborn actors or haughty representatives of the regime. He brought sunshine into grim conference halls; he brightened somber morning rehearsals with a natural mischievousness that careful training had brought to perfection.

The director was loved. Almost everyone took to him and praised his comradely spirit and said he was a fine fellow. Even the political opposition, which could only express its opinion in secret meetings behind locked doors, was indulgent where Hendrik was concerned. Those who were against the regime thought it a distinctly positive development that a self-declared non-Nazi should occupy such an important post. Among these conspirators there were people who felt that the head of the State Theater was managing to force concessions from the prime minister. He had got Otto Ulrichs a job with the theater—a highly risky and praiseworthy achievement. Recently he had even engaged a private secretary who was a Jew, or at least a half-Jew. The young man was called Johannes Lehmann. He had soft, rather unctuous golden-brown eyes and had attached himself to the director with the devotion of a faithful dog. Lehmann was a pious convert to Protestantism. Apart from his German studies and his lecture course on theatrical history, he had also studied theology. He was not interested in politics. "Hendrik Höfgen is a great man," he declared. And he spread the message assiduously, both in the Jewish circles to which he was connected by birth and the religious opposition to which his piety gave him access.

Hendrik paid the devoted Johannes out of his own pocket. He did not begrudge the expense of having a member of the pariah race in his service, so deeply did this impress opponents of the regime. The upkeep of an "Aryan" private secretary would have been paid for by the State Theater; it was unlikely that the director could put in a claim for the support of a non-Aryan, though the prime minister might have forgiven him even this whim. But Hendrik thought it important that he himself should make the financial sacrifice. The two hundred marks it cost him each month was a hardly noticeable fraction of his present budget and was well worthwhile. Johannes Lehmann was a considerable credit item in the balance sheet of Hendrik's insurance policy. He needed it; without it his whole position would be hardly bearable—his good fortune would be overwhelmed by a bad conscience that could never be quite smothered and a fear of the future that sometimes pursued the great man even in his dreams.

The theater was not altogether the refuge it might have seemed. In theory, he could behave there like a man in power. But in practice, he found it unwise to be too unguarded. The propaganda minister and his newspapermen kept a close eye on him. It had to be considered a victory if he could hold out against the worst forms of artistic disgrace, if he could prevent the production of totally empty plays and the engagement of entirely untalented actors who had nothing to recommend them but their extreme blondness.

Naturally, the theater was guaranteed "Jew-free"—from the stars and assistant stage managers down to the movers of scenery and doormen. Naturally, no play could be put on unless the family tree of the author could be shown to be stainless at least four or five generations back. And there was no question of putting on plays that could be suspected of tendencies the regime would find objectionable. Under such circumstances it was not easy to build a repertory at all, for one could not even rely on the classics. In Hamburg a performance of Schiller's *Don Carlos* had given rise to a demonstration of enthusiastic, almost subversive applause when the Marquis of Posa demanded freedom of thought from King Philip of Spain. In Munich a new production of *The Brigands* was completely sold out until the government closed it down. Schiller's youthful work had been recognized and applauded as a modern revolutionary drama. So Hendrik did not dare to put on either *Don Carlos* or *The Brigands*, although he would gladly have played both Posa and the bandit leader Franz Moor. Almost all the modern plays that had been produced in good theaters up to January 1933—the works of Gerhart Hauptmann, Wedekind, Strindberg, Georg Kaiser, Sternheim—were now rejected as the most demoralizing products of cultural Bolshevism. The talented younger dramatists had almost without exception emigrated or were living in a state of virtual banishment inside Germany's frontiers. What could Director

Höfgen produce in his beautiful theaters? The National Socialist bards—enterprising youths in black or brown uniforms—wrote things from which anyone who knew anything about the theater recoiled in horror. Hendrik commissioned works from any of these militant lads in whom he saw hope of even a spark of talent. He had paid out several thousand marks to five of them before the first play emerged. And the results were lamentable. The experiment elicited patriotic "tragedies" that in reality were nothing more than the essays of hysterical school-boys. "It really is no small achievement in our Germany to run an even slightly presentable theater," declared Hendrik in the inner circle of his most trusted supporters. And there was an expression of disgust on his sallow face as he buried it in his hands.

The situation was difficult, but Hendrik was adroit. In the absence of modern comedies he revived old farces and had a great success with them. For months he drew full houses with a moth-eaten French comedy that had amused the grandfathers in his audience. He himself played the lead, wearing a magnificently embroidered eighteenth-century outfit. His lavishly painted face with a black beauty spot on the chin looked so ludicrous that the women in the stalls giggled as if they were being tickled. His gestures had an abandon and his diction a verve that made the farce come across the footlights with the impact of a sparkling modern comedy. Hendrik also turned to Shakespeare. The critics who now set the tone hailed Shakespeare as the great Germanic writer and the popular genius par excellence.

Lotte Lindenthal, the darling of a demigod and the exemplary actress of the new Germany, could get away with appearing in *Minna von Barnhelm,* though the author was as much frowned upon for his Jewish connections as for his wholly outmoded love.of reason. Because Lotte Lindenthal slept with the air force general, people decided to forget the unfashionable opinions of Gotthold Ephraim Lessing. *Minna von Barnhelm* filled the theater. The takings of the State Theater, which had been so meager under the administration of Caesar von Muck, swelled rapidly, thanks to the skill of the new director.

Caesar von Muck, who at the special behest of the Führer undertook a lecture and propaganda tour throughout Europe, had watched his successor's triumph with rising anger. However, he concealed his indignation, even writing picture postcards to his "friend Hendrik" from Palermo or Copenhagen. He never grew tired of re-peating on these cards how wonderful it was to be able to roam freely across the world. "We writers are all vagabonds," he wrote from the Grand Hotel in Stockholm. He had been well supplied with money. In his lyrical yet militant articles, to which all the newspapers had to give much space, there was a great deal about luxury restaurants, reserved theater boxes and ambassadorial receptions. The creator of the Tannenberg dramas was discovering he had a taste for high living. But at the same time he considered his spree to be a "spiritual welfare mission" and to say that he did not want to work for the Third Reich by bribing people with money, as perhaps his limping boss might do, but with tender love songs. In Oslo, for instance, he received a call from the northernmost telephone box in Europe. A worried voice asked from the Arctic circle, "How are things going in Germany?" At which the spiritual-welfare globe-trotter fervently tried to compose a bouquet of a few sentence that would bloom up there in the darkness like a handful of spring flowers.

Everywhere was fine except Paris, where the German bard felt ill at ease. The militaristic warmongering spirit there offended him. "Paris is dangerous," the poet warned his readers.

Nevertheless it was in Paris that Herr von Muck managed to do a little intriguing against his friend Hendrik Höfgen. Through certain spies there—agents of the secret police or members of the German Embassy—the writer learned of the existence of a black woman who had carried on some kind of immoral and unsavory relationship with Höfgen and was still being supported by him. Caesar overcame his innate aversion to Gallic immorality and took himself off to the shady establishment in Montmartre where Princess Tebab appeared as a little bird. He ordered champagne for himself and the black lady. However, when she discovered that he came from Berlin and wanted to know something about the erotic past of Hendrik Höfgen, she responded with a few coarse and scornful words. She stood up, flounced her beautiful green-feathered behind in his direction and accompanied this gesture with a noise from her tightly pouting lips which had regrettably apt associations. The whole audience burst out laughing. The German writer was shown the door in the most ridiculous and shameful manner. He flashed his steely eyes, made a few outraged remarks in a strong Saxon accent and left. That same night he reported to the propaganda minister that somehow all was not well with the love life of the new theater director. Without doubt there was a dark secret here, a chink in the armor of the prime minister's favorite. The propaganda minister effusively thanked his friend the poet for this most interesting piece of news.

But how hard it had now become to nail something on the leading theatrical personality of the Reich, the darling of the men in power and of the public! Hendrik was esteemed by everyone; he was too firmly in the saddle to be dislodged. And his private life made the most favorable impression, for he had brought his parents and his sister Josy from Cologne to live with him in Berlin in a large castlelike villa in Grunewald. For the time being, Nicoletta was staying in a Reichskanzlerplatz apartment, whose lease still had a few months to run. The villa had a park, a tennis court, beautiful terraces and large garages. It gave the young director the aristocratic background he now wanted. How long ago it now seemed when he had cut an almost comic figure as he hurried through the streets in sandals and unbuttoned leather coat with his monocle fixed in his eye! Even in the Reichskanzlerplatz he had been bohemian, though certainly a luxurious one. But now in Grunewald he was the lord of the manor. Money was of no importance. The gods of the Underworld were not closefisted when it came to rewarding one of their protégés. Hell paid up. Hendrik, who had not demanded anything from life but a clean shirt and a bottle of eau de Cologne on the dressing table, could now treat himself to race horses, a host of servants and a fleet of cars. No one—or hardly anyone—begrudged him the pomp in which he lived. The beautiful surroundings where he recovered from his energetic labors were to be seen in all the illustrated papers: HENDRIK HÖFGEN FEEDING HIS CELEBRATED PEDIGREE GREYHOUND HOPPI IN THE GARDEN OF HIS HOME . . . HENDRIK HÖFGEN BREAKFASTING WITH HIS MOTHER IN THE RENAISSANCE DINING ROOM OF HIS VILLA.

Hendrik had bought Hendrik Hall, as he christened the villa, for a relatively small sum from a Jewish bank director who had emigrated to London. At Hendrik Hall everything was of the highest distinction, certainly as grandiose as it had been in the Professor's palace in the old days. The servants wore black livery with silver braid. Only little Böck was allowed to go around looking a little slovenly in a dirty blue-and-white striped jacket. Sometimes he appeared in the brown SA uniform. The stupid youth with the watery eyes and crewcut hair enjoyed a special privileged status at Hendrik Hall, kept on by the lord of the manor as a comic little souvenir of old times. Little Böck's basic contribution to the household was to be in a constant state of astonishment and delight over the incredible transformation of his master's life. At least once a day he exclaimed, "How beautiful and rich we've become! It's just beyond belief! When I think that we once had to borrow seven marks fifty to pay for our supper." Such memories filled Böck with awe and he would giggle respectfully.

"A worthy creature," said Hendrik. "He has been faithful to me in bad times." His feelings toward Böck contained an element of vengeful satisfaction—was it not Barbara who had objected to his having Böck in the Hamburg apartment? He had been forced to make do with a maid who had served a ten-year apprenticeship with the general's wife so that nothing would change in the life of the privy councillor's daughter! In all his present glory Hendrik could never forget even the smallest defeats of the past. "Now I am the master in my house!" he said.

His family, whom he allowed to share in the splendor of his existence, came to sense his moods. From time to time Hendrik organized pleasant evenings at the fireside or charming Sunday mornings in the garden. More often, however, he put on his livid affronted-governess look and hid himself in his suite of rooms, letting it be known that he was suffering from a dreadful migraine—"because I have to work so hard to get money to support you, you idlers," a reproach he did not voice but was clearly to be read in his pained and exasperated manner. "Don't take any notice of me," he would tell his family, and then took it extremely amiss if an hour or two passed without anyone's looking in on him.

It was his mother who best understood how to handle him. She behaved to her "big boy" very tenderly but not without a certain gentle firmness. With her he seldom dared put on too many airs. Besides, he was genuinely attached to her and was now proud of his distinguished mama, for she had changed very much for the better and showed herself fully equal to her new status. She understood how to run her famous son's large household with dignified tact and efficiency. Anyone seeing this elegant matron would never have guessed that she had once been the object of mocking gossip for her silly stories of the old days. Frau Bella had become an unobtrusive but far from negligible figure in Berlin society. She had been presented to the prime minister and frequented the most important houses. Under the neat gray permanent wave, her intelligent cheerful face, so like that of her famous son, was as fresh in color as ever. Frau Bella dressed simply but with care. She favored dark-gray silk in winter and pearl-gray—the color of the outfit that Frau Bella had so much admired on the general's wife the day of Hendrik's wedding—in warmer weather.

Frau Bella was heartily sorry that the general's wife did not come to the Grunewald villa. "I would so gladly receive the old lady," she declared, "despite the fact that she might have some Jewish blood. We could overlook that—don't you agree, Hendrik? But she has never taken the trouble to leave a card. Are we still perhaps not distinguished enough for her?" Frau Bella shook her head. "She doesn't seem to have much money left," she said in a tone of annoyance mingled with sympathy. "She should be glad that a decent family still wants to have something to do with her."

Unfortunately, Hendrik's father was not quite as presentable as Frau Bella. Köbes Höfgen had become an eccentric who wandered around in a worn flannel jacket reading railway timetables. He tended a little collection of cactuses on his windowsill; he very seldom shaved and hid himself when guests arrived. His Rhenish high spirits had totally deserted him. He spent most of his time sitting, staring ahead of him with a vacant expression on his face. He was homesick for Cologne, although the process servers were installed almost permanently in his house and his business enterprises had come to a nasty end. Struggling for existence had suited him better than idleness by the hearth of his successful son. Hendrik's fame and glamour were an object of perpetual amazement, almost of alarm for the old man. "No, how can that have happened?" he would murmur, as though a misfortune had landed on the household. Every morning he gazed with consternation at the pile of letters which had been sent to his offspring.

When Johannes Lehmann was too overloaded with work, he sometimes asked Father Höfgen to help him out with some small task. The old man spent many a morning signing his son's photographs, for he was better than the secretary at copying Hendrik's handwriting. When the director was in a particularly winning mood he would sometimes ask, "How are you, Papa? Sometimes you look so downcast. Is there anything you would like? You aren't bored in my house?" "No, no," his father would grunt, blushing under his unshaved stubble. "I have so much to keep me busy—with the cactuses and the dogs." Only he was allowed to feed the dogs. He let no servant near them. Every day he went for a long walk with the beautiful greyhounds, whereas Hendrik would only allow himself to be photographed with them. The greyhounds loved Father Höfgen, but they were wary of Hendrik, who was in fact secretly afraid of them.

His sister Josy had a prettily decorated apartment on the upper floor of the villa, but she did a great deal of traveling and often left it empty. Since her brother had been elevated to membership in the ruling clique, Fräulein Höfgen was constantly being invited everywhere to sing on the radio. She specialized in lively songs in a Rhineland accent. Her pert face was seen in all the radio magazines, and she often had an opportunity to become engaged. And become engaged she did; naturally, now it was not just anyone who could ask for her hand. She could consider only attachments appropriate to her station in life. Her preference was for young gentlemen in SS uniforms, and their decorative figures enlivened Hendrik Hall.

"I am really going to marry Count Donnersberg," Josy announced. Her brother appeared skeptical and Josy wept. "You always tease me," she declared. Her mother consoled her. Everyone assured her that she had become beautiful. Certainly, she looked much more attractive than she had when Barbara had first met her on the station platform of the south German university town. It was partly perhaps that she could now dress herself more expensively. The freckles on her saucy nose had been almost entirely removed by a complicated cosmetic treatment. "Dagobert threatened to break off the engagement if the freckles didn't disappear," she said.

Dagobert von Donnersberg also had his moods. Hendrik had met the count in the house of Lotte Lindenthal, who liked to surround herself with aristocrats. Dagobert was handsome and impecunious, stupid and spoiled. He was promptly invited to Hendrik Hall. Josy proposed that they should go riding together; Hendrik gave his beautiful horses too little exercise—his time was precious and, besides, riding gave him no pleasure. He had learned to ride with difficulty for his film career, and he knew that he had a bad seat. He kept up the stables only because horses looked impressive in the picture magazines. And in an altogether covert manner, which he did not even admit to himself, horses were perhaps like little Böck—a late and desperately pointless way of taking revenge on Barbara, who had so often annoyed him with her morning rides.

Josy and her Dagobert rode across the countryside. The young count fell a little in love with his vivacious companion. When she

233

seemed to take this seriously, he went so far as to become engaged to her, without, of course, letting this interfere with his search for ladies who were in a position to pay a higher price for his title. But for the moment he was in no hurry to leave the little Höfgen girl and considered it unwise to offend a family that enjoyed close personal relations with the prime minister. Besides, Dagobert found life very amusing at Hendrik Hall.

The director wanted his house run along English lines. Frau Bella ordered whisky and marmalade directly from London. A great deal of toast was eaten; everyone enjoyed sitting in front of an open fire; tennis and croquet were played in the garden; and on Sunday, if the host had no performances, the guests gathered before lunch and stayed on well into the night. After dinner there was dancing in the hall. Hendrik put on his tuxedo, declaring that in the evening he felt more at ease if he changed for dinner. Josy and Nicoletta dressed up, too. Every now and then the small circle would suddenly be seized with mad impulses. In the late afternoon they would drive in three cars to Hamburg to wander in the St. Pauli night-club district. "There are certainly enough cars here," said Count Donnersberg a shade resentfully. It annoyed him that the actor was swimming in money, while he, the aristocrat, had none. (The director possessed three large cars and several smaller ones. The most beautiful machine—a giant Mercedes with glittering silver bodywork—was a present from the prime minister. The corpulent donor had been obliging enough to bring the splendid vehicle to Grunewald when Hendrik moved into his new home.)

It was rare for the director to give large receptions and he did so without great pleasure, but he liked to gather a few people informally at Hendrik Hall. Nicoletta was completely a member of the family. She appeared unannounced at meals, discussed theatrical matters with Hendrik and, over the weekend, came carrying a suitcase. It was a voluminous piece of luggage—too voluminous to contain only an evening dress and pajamas. Josy, devoured by curiosity, looked furtively to see what else might be hidden inside it. To her astonishment she found a pair of high boots made of bright red patent leather.

Nicoletta was in the process of divorcing Theophilus Marder. "I am an actress once again," she wrote to him. "I love you still. I shall revere you for the rest of my life. But it fills me with delight to be able to work once again. Everywhere in our new Germany one feels a new vigor, an enthusiastic will to work of which you in your complete isolation can have no idea."

One of the first duties of Director Höfgen had been to sign Nicoletta up with the State Theater company. She had not yet had a success that could match her Hamburg triumph. However, she was gradually losing her stiffness. Her voice and gestures were becoming more appealing and lively.

"Look—acting is coming to you again," said Hendrik. "Strictly speaking, no one should have allowed you back again on any stage, you mad creature. What you did in the old days in Hamburg was positively criminal—not where poor old Kroge was concerned, of course, but against yourself."

The truth was that Nicoletta could have been an extremely poor actress and still have been treated with marked respect by her colleagues and the press, for she was known to be the girlfriend of the director and it was clear that she possessed influence over the great man. On ceremonial occasions she appeared at his side, jangling in the armor of her metallic evening gown. What a couple they made: Hendrik and Nicoletta—two vaguely sinister but attractive gods of the Underworld, both equipped with a charm that had something disquieting about it.

It was the poet Benjamin Pelz who had the idea of calling them Oberon and Titania, as though the racist dictatorship of fascism was a kind of bloodcurdling version of *A Midsummer Night's Dream*.

"You lead the dance, you subterranean potentates," raved the poet. "You cast a spell over us with your smiles and your marvelous eyes. Ah how gladly would we entrust ourselves to you! You would lead us under the earth into the depths, into the magic cavern where blood streams from the walls, where warriors copulate and lovers kill themselves, where love, death and blood are mingled in orgiastic communion . . ." This was the new German ballroom small talk in its most exalted form. Benjamin Pelz had exactly the right tone. In the past he had been rather unworldly, but now he became more and more sociable and talkative. He quickly grew accustomed to mixing in the most fashionable circles to which his highly modern taste for the lower depths, the magic cavern and the sweet smell of decay gained him ready access. He was now vice president of the Writers' Academy, of which Caesar von Muck was president, and was one of the regular visitors to Hendrik's villa, along with Herr Müller-Andreä, Dr. Ihrig and Pierre Larue.

235

All these gentlemen considered it an honor to kiss the hand of the distinguished Frau Bella and assure Fräulein Josy of how charming she looked. Pierre Larue flirted a little with Böck, which was looked upon with an indulgent eye. There were particularly happy hours when the character actor Joachim arrived with his amusing wife and drank a great deal of beer. His fleshy face set in deep wrinkles of sincerity, Joachim announced that no matter what anybody said, nowhere in the world was so beautiful as Grunewald. From time to time he would take people off into corners to assure them that where he was concerned, "My hand on my heart—everything is in order." And his eyes would snap as he added, "A few days ago I once again had to have someone locked up for saying this wasn't so."

Sometimes Angelika Siebert put in an appearance. She now had another name, for she had married her film director. The young husband was a handsome man with chestnut-brown hair and large, serious deep-blue eyes. He alone in this somewhat degenerate circle looked like a child's idea of a German hero, a young knight without fear and without reproach. But it was he who to everyone's surprise had rebellious tendencies; he had for some time been unable to come to terms with everything that was going on in Germany. In earlier days, he had been enthusiastic about the Nazis, which made his present disenchantment all the greater.

He approached Hendrik, whose talent he sincerely admired, with grave and urgent questions. "You have a certain influence in the highest places," said the young man. "Isn't it possible for you to prevent some of the more flagrant atrocities? It is your duty to inform the prime minister about what is going on in the concentration camps." The shining honest face of the young knight flushed with zeal as he spoke.

Hendrik shook his head helplessly. "What do you expect, my young friend?" he said impatiently. "What do you want from me? Am I going to hold off Niagara Falls with an umbrella? Do you think that would have any hope of success? No. So there it is!" Hendrik spoke in the triumphant tone of one who has overwhelmingly won an argument and convinced his opponent.

Sometimes in his villa the director liked to play a role with more candor. He would suddenly drop all justifications and excuses and, his face suffused with a nervous flush, would wander through the rooms shaking with cynical laughter, and declaring in a voice both plaintive and exultant, "Am I not a bastard? Am I not an altogether incredible bastard?" His friends enjoyed this hugely. Josy would clap her hands with pleasure, but the fearless young knight would look severe and unamused. Angelika would gaze with grief and dismay at the friend on whose account she had wept such bitter tears.

Naturally, Hendrik spoke neither of the force of Niagara nor of his own evil character when guests were present who were too close to the regime. Even in the presence of Count Donnersberg the director curbed his tongue. But he knew how to combine the utmost discretion with beaming hilarity when Lotte Lindenthal honored him with her presence.

The blond, motherly actress often appeared in Hendrik Hall for a table-tennis party or to dance with the master of the house. And what a party they put on for her! Frau Bella brought out everything that was finest in the larder; Nicoletta delivered sharply enunciated compliments about the violet-blue eyes of the great lady; Pierre Larue neglected little Böck; and even Father Höfgen looked through the crack of the door at the full-bosomed lady, who filled the room with her silvery laughter. When the prime minister arrived in his giant limousine to fetch his Lotte and at the same time to wish good evening to his Mephisto, the gathering suddenly froze with awe. Lotte flew to him and hung around his neck. Frau Bella, almost sick with pride and agitation, managed to bring out in a voice that sounded like a moan, "Excellency—Herr Prime Minister—may I offer you something? A little refreshment? Perhaps a glass of champagne? . . ."

Many people met in Hendrik Hall, drawn by the fame and good nature of their host, the impeccable cuisine, the wine cellar, the tennis court, the carefully chosen gramophone records and the overall luxury of the villa. There were actors, generals, poets, senior bureaucrats, journalists, exotic foreign diplomats, actresses and kept women. However, a few people who in the past had been very close to Hendrik Höfgen took no part in the festivities. The general's wife did not put in an appearance; Frau Bella waited in vain for her visiting card. The old lady had been forced to sell her country estate and now lived in a small apartment close to the Tiergarten. More and more she lost contact with the Berlin society in which she had once played such a brilliant role. "I do not wish to go into houses where I am likely to meet murderers, perverts or madmen," she declared proudly.

Someone else who kept away from the director's residence was

Otto Ulrichs. He was not invited, and even if such an invitation had reached him it would almost certainly have been refused. Ulrichs was very busy, and busy in a way that called upon great physical and spiritual reserves of strength. Besides, he had begun to revise the image of his friend Hendrik which he had harbored in his heart for so many years with such loyalty and patience. Ulrichs had been an amiable, even tender-hearted man, despite his revolutionary commitment. He had placed a great and unshakable trust in Hendrik. "Hendrik belongs to us," he had said in his warm and reassuring voice to anyone who expressed a doubt as to the moral and political sincerity of his friend. Hendrik belongs to us! Now Ulrichs had lost many illusions, and among them those that concerned Hendrik Höfgen. He was no longer amiable, no longer tender-hearted. His gaze had developed a threatening gravity.

Otto Ulrichs was now a man poised between caution and boldness, between attack and flight; he was playing a perilous game.

He had remained a member of the State Theater, but he used his position as a cover to protect him from too close a scrutiny by the Gestapo. At least this was his hope and aim. Perhaps he was too optimistic. Perhaps he had been watched from the very start and was only allowed to have his way for a short time so that the Gestapo could lay their hands on him all the more devastatingly later, sure of finding him in possession of a damaging amount of material.

The members of the company, who to begin with had looked on him with distrust, now treated him with cheerful camaraderie. He succeeded in winning them over by his manly simplicity and easygoing nature. For he had learned the art of deception. His fanatical will power, fixed on one target and ready for any sacrifice, had made him cunning. He was even capable of joking with Lotte Lindenthal. He assured Joachim that he had not the slightest doubt about his racial purity. He greeted the stagehands enthusiastically with the prescribed salute: the "*Heil*" followed by the hated name of the dictator. When the prime minister was sitting in his box, Ulrichs announced that his heart was beating with excitement at the privilege of playing before the great man. Often, in fact his heart would be pounding because of a very different kind of agitation. For as he left the stage after his scene, the stagehand in charge of the curtain, who was one of his underground contacts, would whisper a few words about a secret meeting. Almost under the eyes of the fat giant, the almighty executioner, this small-time actor who had known the terror of the torture chambers and the concentration camps ventured to pursue his work of subversion against the regime.

His encounter with terror had blunted his resolve for only a short time. In the first weeks after his release from the inferno, Ulrichs had been in a state of paralysis. His eyes had seen what no human eye can look upon without clouding with despair. He had seen evil naked and uncontrolled and organized with a horrible meticulousness. He had seen absolute and total baseness, which even as it tortured helpless victims glorified itself as a patriotic enterprise.

"One would rather have nothing more to do with mankind when one has seen it in that state," said Ulrichs. But he loved his fellow men nevertheless, and he retained an unshakable belief that one day something decent could come of them. He overcame his despairing apathy. "When you have witnessed those horrors, you have only one choice," he said. "You can either kill yourself or go back to work with greater dedication than before." He went back to work.

Getting in touch with the illegal opposition presented no difficulty. He had many friends among the workers and intellectuals whose hatred of fascism stemmed from such a deep conviction and revulsion that it managed to survive even in the extremely dangerous and seemingly hopeless conditions of the day. Ulrichs took part in clandestine operations against the regime: secret meetings; distribution of forbidden leaflets and newspapers; acts of sabotage directed against factories, public ceremonies, radio programs and movie performances.

He took these demonstrations of resistance to fascism very seriously and had a high opinion of the psychological impact they could have on a public opinion which was paralyzed with fear.

"We are making the rulers uneasy and we are showing millions of people who have remained hostile to dictatorship but hardly dare to make their feelings known that the flame of freedom still burns and can show itself despite an army of spies." It was in this vein that Otto Ulrichs thought, spoke and wrote. The objective was to gather together the dispersed forces of the Resistance, to weld into a single movement an opposition composed of mutually antagonistic ideals and social backgrounds, to found and activate a united front against dictatorship. "That's what it's all about—and only that," said Otto Ulrichs.

And so he spread the net of the conspiracy wider than his close party comrades. He was much more anxious to contact opposition Catholics, former Social Democrats or independent republicans. At first the Communist encountered distrust in middle-class liberal circles. But his ardent eloquence generally succeeded in dispelling doubts. "But you are just as much against freedom as the Nazis," protested the democrats. He answered, "Look—we are all for the overthrow of tyranny. We can all come to an agreement about the kind of order that should be set up afterwards."

"You have no patriotism," declared the republicans, and Otto Ulrichs answered, "If we didn't love our country, how could we have such a hatred for those who degrade and corrupt it? And would we risk our lives daily to liberate our fatherland?"

In the early weeks of his illegal activity Ulrichs tried once to confide in Hendrik. But the director appeared anxious, nervous and irritated. "I don't want to know about these things," he said hurriedly. "I *must* know nothing about them. Do you understand? I'm closing my eyes to what you are doing. But I must on no account be let into the secret."

After he had made absolutely sure that they were not being overheard, Hendrik told his friend in a choked voice how hard and painful it was for him to dissemble his real feelings so consistently and over such a long period. "But I have finally committed myself to this strategy because I consider it to be the best and most effective one," whispered Hendrik with an attempt at his old conspiratorial glance, which no longer drew a response from Ulrichs. "It's not a comfortable strategy, but I must persevere with it. I am now in the middle of the enemy's camp. From the inside outwards I am undermining his power . . ."

Otto Ulrichs had difficulty hearing him out. Perhaps it was at this moment that his illusions fell from him and he knew Hendrik Höfgen for what he was.

How brilliantly the director dissembled! It was a performance truly worthy of a great actor. One might almost have thought that Hendrik Höfgen cared only for money, power and fame instead of the undermining of the regime.

In the broad shadow of the prime minister he felt so secure that he was tempted to flirt with danger as a facetious way of exorcising his fear of catastrophe. During a telephone conversation with a theatrical producer in Vienna, from whom he wanted to borrow an actor, he said in a melancholy drawl, "Yes, dear fellow—in a few weeks I may perhaps pop up in Vienna. I don't know if I can hold out much longer here. My health—you understand what I mean?—has deteriorated so terribly."

In fact only two things could bring about his downfall: either the air force general could withdraw his favor, or the air force general himself could fall from power. But the fat leader's affection for his Mephistopheles was a fidelity so uncommon in National Socialist circles that it caused widespread astonishment. Moreover, the star of the fat giant was still in the ascendant: the man who loved executions and blond actresses continued to accumulate more titles, more wealth and more influence over the leadership of the state.

As long as the sun of the fat man shone on him, Hendrik did not have to worry too much about the malicious attacks of the propaganda minister, who dared not proceed openly against the theatrical director. On the contrary, he considered it important to appear in public with Hendrik whenever an occasion presented itself. Besides, he was not without a certain intellectual affinity with the actor. If Hendrik had learned to fascinate the air force general with his cynical, amusing wit, he could also get on very well with the propaganda chief, "the old doctor," for they not only spoke the same Rhenish dialect, which gave their conversation an air of affectionate intimacy, but they employed—and misused—the same political terminology. Given a chance, Hendrik could talk incessantly about the "revolutionary dynamic," "the heroic life-force" and "the antirationality of the blood." He had many lively discussions with his arch-enemy—which, naturally, did not prevent the propaganda minister from continuing to intrigue against him.

Caesar von Muck, who had returned home from his enjoyable foreign tour, did everything he could to spread the story about a certain black woman to whom Hendrik was linked in a thoroughly sick sexual way and who was leading a brilliant and scandalous life in Paris at Hendrik's expense. Hendrik—so the rumor now went—still had secret meetings with this woman, not only to indulge in further racial profanation but also to use her as a link with the darkest and most dangerous elements among the refugees. And the reports stressed the fact that Hendrik's former wife, Barbara Bruckner, whom he had divorced only as a matter of form, played a leading role in these circles.

The main subject of conversation at the State Theater was the director's black mistress. In the most important newspaper offices and the centers of officially inspired gossip, everyone knew about the dark lady who was surrounded with all the glamour of the great Parisian Babylon. "She keeps three monkeys, a young lion, two adult panthers and a dozen Chinese coolies" was one version of the story. And she wove plots against the Nazi regime with the French military high command, the Kremlin, the Freemasons and Jewish financiers.

The situation began to be uncomfortable for Hendrik. He decided to curb the unpleasant rumors by marrying Nicoletta. The prime minister was very pleased with this decision of his cunning protégé and delivered a severe warning to those who would continue casting suspicion on the director. "The enemy of my friend is my enemy," he threatened. A notice was posted up on the State Theater blackboard, just by the entry to the stage, announcing that it would henceforth be a treasonable offence to spread or even to listen to rumors about the private life or the past of the Herr Director. Everyone was frightened at the thought of Hendrik's private spy network, so perfectly organized that the Gestapo could have taken lessons from it. It was impossible to hide anything from this dangerously wily man: he had a little army of informers which told him everything he needed to know.

Even Caesar von Muck was worried. The writer of the Tannen-berg dramas felt it advisable to pay a visit to Hendrik Hall and to converse with the master of the house in his sincerest Saxon manner. Nicoletta sat down beside the two men and immediately began talking in a high taunting voice about Negroes. Herr von Muck managed to retain his composure when she announced that she and Hendrik had a positive horror of black people. "It makes Hendrik positively sick to see even in the distance a member of the loathsome black race," she exclaimed and fixed her cheerful shining eyes on Caesar. "Even the smell of these people is altogether unbearable," she said defiantly. "Yes, yes," declared Herr von Muck. "That's true. Negros stink." And suddenly they all three burst out laughing—long and heartily.

No, this Höfgen was not to be caught. Herr von Muck realized it; the propaganda minister realized it, too; and they decided to be on the friendliest terms with him until the happy day arrived when fate would give them an opportunity to destroy him.

The fat man had arranged for Hendrik to have an audience with the dictator, for the rumors about Princess Tebab had reached even the ears of this illustrious personage, who had reacted with violent disgust: "Can a man who has relations with racially inferior people possess the moral maturity to occupy an administrator's post?"

Now Hendrik had the task of using his flashing eyes, singing voice and noble profile to convince the Führer of his moral fitness to command the German theater.

The half-hour that Hendrik was able to spend with the Messiah of all the Germans was harrowing. The conversation was difficult. The Führer did not have much interest in the theater; he preferred Wagnerian operas and propaganda films. Hendrik did not dare speak of his opera productions in the bad old days of the "system" for fear that the Führer might recall the devastating verdict of Caesar von Muck on these demoralizing and Semitic-influenced experiments. Hendrik did not exactly know what he should talk about. The living presence of power confused and frightened him.

Power incarnate had an insignificant receding forehead, over which fell the legendary greasy strand of hair, and dead staring eyes. The face of Power was putty-white, bloated, porous. Power had a very ordinary nose—a vulgar nose, thought Hendrik, in whom awe was now mixed with repulsion, even scorn. The actor noticed that Power had no back to its head. Under the brown shirt swelled a flabby stomach. Power spoke softly to save its hoarse voice. Power used long words to impress the actor with its "education." "The interests of our Nordic culture require the positive commitment of an energetic, racially self-assertive and target-oriented individual," Power said, trying to suppress its South German accent as much as possible and to speak in a refined High German. The result was like a zealous schoolboy's lesson carefully learned by heart.

Hendrik was bathed in sweat when he left the palace twenty-five minutes later. He had a feeling that he had been in miserable form and had spoiled all his chances. But the same evening he learned from the air force general that the impression he had left with Power was not at all bad. In fact, it had been the timidity of the director that had come as a pleasant surprise to the dictator. The Führer considered it an impertinence when someone attempted either to impress him or to be natural in his presence. Faced with Power, one was expected to maintain an awed silence. A brilliant Hendrik would almost certainly have aroused the anger of the Messiah of all the Germans. On the anguished actor the all-powerful passed a mild judgment. "A very good man, this Herr Höfgen," declared the dictator.

The prime minister, who collected titles as other men collect stamps or butterflies, thought that his friends would be equally delighted with such honors. He made Hendrik a privy councillor; he promoted him to senator. The director had a place of importance in all the cultural institutions of the Reich. With Caesar von Muck and several gentlemen in uniform he belonged to the governing board of the Senate of Culture. The first social gathering of this institution was held at Hendrik Hall. The propaganda minister was there and grinned from ear to ear when Fräulein Josy sang one of her popular folk songs, accompanied at the piano by no less a performer than Caesar von Muck. The catering was of deliberate simplicity. Hendrik had asked his mother to serve only beer and sausage sandwiches. The uniformed gentlemen were disappointed; they had heard a great deal about the fabulous luxury enjoyed at the director's villa. What was the use of the liveried lackeys if they only handed around the kind of snacks one had at home? The whole Senate of Culture would have fallen into a state of peevishness had not the propaganda minister warmed the atmosphere with his customary cheerfulness. The only difficulty was that nobody knew what to talk about. Culture was altogether unknown territory for most of the senators. The uniformed members of the board were proud of the fact that since their boyhood they had never opened a book; and they could claim to be in good company, for the same could be said of the universally revered field marshal, the president of the Reich, who had lately died and been buried in the presence of the Führer.

When an aged novelist, whose books were so paralyzingly boring that they were left on the booksellers' shelves but who was officially in good odor, proposed to read a chapter from his trilogy *A Nation on the March*, there was a small scene of panic. Several uniformed guests sprang up and reached for their pistols; the smile of the propaganda minister stiffened; Benjamin Pelz groaned as though he had been stabbed in the chest; Frau Bella fled to the kitchen; Nicoletta let out a strident, nervous laugh. The situation would have become catastrophic had not Hendrik rescued it with his flattering voice. It would be magnificent and a real joy to hear a really long chapter of *A Nation on the March*, declared Hendrik, his face transfigured by his flashing smile, but unfortunately the hour was rather far advanced and there were so many pressing current problems to discuss that the attention of the guests would not be concentrated enough for the enjoyment of great art. Hendrik proposed instead that a whole evening should be set aside for this reading so that everyone could bring to it the necessary concentration of spirit. All the senators drew a breath of relief. The old epic writer was so disappointed that he almost wept. Herr Müller-Andreä proceeded to tell scabrous anecdotes about the time he indignantly called "the years of corruption." Later in the evening it emerged that the actor Joachim could very amusingly imitate the baying of a hound and the clucking of hens. And his imitation of a parrot made Lotte Lindenthal laugh so much she almost fell off her chair.

Before the party broke up, Baldur von Totenbach, a senator who had made the journey from Hamburg specially to be present at this gathering, proposed that everyone stand and sing the *Horst Wessel song* and for the hundredth time pledge allegiance to the Führer. Everyone found this a little embarrassing, but it obviously had to be done.

The press reported at length on this intellectually stimulating social evening of the cultural senators in the director's house. Daily, the newspapers lost no opportunity of informing the public about the artistic and patriotic doings of Hendrik Höfgen. He was considered to be among the most distinguished and active "champions of the German cultural drive" and he was almost as much photographed as a minister. When the leaders of Berlin life turned out for the Winter Aid charity collection in the streets and cafés, the director was almost as much in demand as the gentlemen of the government. But while they were so surrounded by armed detectives and Gestapo agents that the people with their small alms could hardly push their way through to them, Hendrik could move around without any protection. Admitttedly, he had chosen to report to duty in an area—the hall of the Hotel Adlon—where there was little danger of coming into contact with the rough proletariat. He insisted on going into the kitchens, where every scullion had to drop his coin into the box in which Lotte Lindenthal's delicate fingers had just pressed a hundred-mark note. The director had himself photographed arm in arm with the plump Adlon chef. The picture appeared on the cover of the city's biggest picture magazine.

It goes without saying that the press was deluged with Höfgen pictures when the director married Nicoletta. Müller-Andreä and Benjamin Pelz were the witnesses. The prime minister sent as his present a pair of black swans to decorate the small lake in the park of Hendrik Hall. A pair of black swans! The journalists waxed ecstatic over the originality of the gift. Only a few very old people, such as the general's wife, recalled that once, a while back, a highly placed friend of the arts had bestowed on his protégé the same gift—so had the Bavarian King Ludwig II honored the composer Richard Wagner.

The dictator himself sent a cable of congratulations to the young pair. The propaganda minister sent a basket of orchids, which looked so poisonous that one might well have imagined the recipient dying after breathing in their perfume. Pierre Larue composed a long French poem for the occasion. Theophilus Marder sent his curse. Little Angelika, who had just given birth to a child, wept one last time over her lost love. In all the newspaper offices the material collected on Hendrik and Princess Tebab was hidden away in the remotest, most secret drawers. Dr. Ihrig dictated to his secretary an article in which he referred to Nicoletta and Hendrik as "in the most beautiful and profound sense of the words, a German couple." He also hailed them as "two people endowed both with the freshness of youth and with maturity, who are of pure race and the most noble composition and who serve the new society with all their strength." Only one newspaper—which was said to be particularly closely linked to the propaganda minister—dared to refer to Nicoletta's dubious past. The young actress was congratulated for having deserted the "emigrant, Jew-disciple and cultural Bolshevist Theophilus Marder" to take once again an active part in the cultural life of the nation. Marder's name was a false note in the beautiful concert of congratulatory press articles.

Nicoletta moved from the Reichskanzlerplatz to Grunewald with trunks and hatboxes. The housemaid who helped her unpack was a little alarmed when she found the long red boots. But her young mistress explained in a ringing voice that they were part of an Amazon costume. "I shall wear them as Penthesilea," declared Nicoletta in a strangely triumphant voice. The maid was so taken aback by this exotic-sounding name and the blazing eyes of her mistress that she asked no further questions.

That evening there was a large reception in Hendrik Hall. How modest the festivities in the house of the privy councillor for Hendrik's first marriage now seemed compared with this stately celebration! Oberon and Titania glowed as they moved among the dense throng of their guests. He held his chin up. She nonchalantly lifted the glistening, tinkling train of her metallic evening gown. In her hair were large fantastic glass flowers, and her face shone with bright makeup. Hendrik's face looked phosphorescent in its greenish paleness. Smiling obviously caused them both great effort, even torment. Their gaze seemed to go straight through the people they greeted and fix on something beyond. What was it that caught their eyes, so glazed under half-closed lids, and froze the smiles on their lips?

Perhaps it was the searching eyes of Barbara which stared at them from the shadows—Barbara who had been Nicoletta's friend and now, doing her grave and hard duty in a foreign land, was separated from them by a gulf that could never again be bridged. Or perhaps it was the grotesque martyred face of Theophilus Marder, who—half blind and half wise, haunted by a thousand terrors through which he expiated all his sins of pride and egotism—gazed at Nicoletta, who had deserted him. But perhaps they saw not any particular face, but the dim yet overwhelming synthesis of everything they could have become but had not. Perhaps they saw the shameful, dreary chronicle of their decline, their degradation, which a stupid world saw as an ascent. Now they belonged to each other forever. This glittering, smiling pair belonged to each other forever—like two traitors. The link that bound them would not be love but hate.

While the Senate of Culture organized social evenings, while the great of the land rattled collection boxes in hotel lobbies, soliciting "charitable gifts" for their needy countrymen which would be used to finance the propaganda of the Third Reich abroad, while marriages were celebrated, lieder were sung and an endless number of speeches were delivered, the regime of total dictatorship continued its ghastly way and the pile of bodies mounted beside its path.

Foreigners—English lords, Hungarian journalists, or Italian ministers—praised the impeccable cleanliness and order. They saw cheerful faces everywhere and found that the Führer was loved—he was the darling of the whole nation.

In the meantime, the opposition had grown so strong and threatening in the heart of the party itself that the terrible triumvirate

—the Führer, the fat giant and the limping dwarf—was forced to take prompt action. The man to whom the dictator owed his private army, at whom the propaganda minister had grinned dazzlingly only the day before yesterday and whom the head of state had called his "most loyal comrade" was turned out of bed one night by the Führer himself and shot a few hours later. Before the shot rang out there was a scene between the Messiah of all the Germans and his most loyal comrade which was hardly of a kind one would expect between eminent gentlemen. The most loyal comrade shrieked at the Messiah, "You're the blackguard, the traitor—you're the one!" He had the courage for such frankness, for he knew that his last hour had come. Hundreds of seasoned party members died with him because they were too unmanageable. At the same time several hundred Communists were slaughtered, and because they were killing on the grand scale, the fat giant, the limping dwarf and the Führer liquidated anyone against whom they had a personal grudge or from whom they felt they had something to fear in the future—generals, writers, former prime ministers in retirement. No distinction was made, and sometimes wives were shot with husbands. Heads must roll—the Führer had always said so—and now the hour had come. A little "cleansing operation" was announced after the event. The lords and the journalists found the energy of the Führer quite wonderful. He was the gentlest of men—he loved animals, never touched meat—but he could watch the execution of the most loyal comrades without turning a hair. After the blood orgy the people seemed to love the Führer even more than before. Lonely and scattered were those in the country who were revolted and horrified. Theirs was the plaint of Faust: "I have to live to see insolent murderers win men's praise."

And men were murdered whose only fault was that they had not wanted to renounce their socialist principles—and yet the Messiah who had them executed called himself a socialist. But then the Messiah also declared that he loved freedom, and he had pacifists tortured and killed in concentration camps. German youth learned the word "pacifist" as a swear word. German youth no longer needed to read Goethe or Plato; they learned how to shoot and throw bombs; they enjoyed themselves on night maneuvers; and when the Führer preached about peace they understood that he was joking.

This militarily organized, disciplined, well-drilled youth had only one aim—the war of revenge, the war of conquest. Alsace-Lorraine was German. Switzerland was German. Holland was German. Denmark was German. Czechoslovakia was German. The Ukraine was German. Austria was so completely German that the case did not even have to be stated. Germany must have its colonies back. The whole country was transformed into an armed camp; the armaments industry flourished; there was a permanent state of mobilization, and the foreigner gazed spellbound at this imposing, terrifying spectacle, like a rabbit at the snake that is just about to swallow it.

Life was fun under the dictatorship. Strength through Joy was the watchword. There were nation-wide celebrations and festivals. The Saar was German—a national celebration. The fat man at last married his Lindenthal and allowed himself to be given wedding presents worth millions—a national celebration. Germany left the League of Nations and regained sovereignty over its defense—an enormous national celebration. Every breach of a treaty—Versailles, Locarno—produced a national celebration, and so did the obligatory plebiscites that followed. The persecution of the Jews was a prolonged national celebration, as was the pillorying of those women who committed "race profanation" with them. So was the persecution of Catholics, about whom one learned for the first time that they were never much better than the Jews and who were slyly brought to trial on "currency offenses" involving ridiculously small sums, while the leaders of the regime hid away enormous fortunes abroad. And finally a long-drawn-out national celebration surrounded the persecution of "reaction," a term designating nothing very precise. Marxism had been "eradicated," but was still a danger and an excuse for mass trials. German culture was now "Jew-free" but, as a result, had become so dreary that no one wanted to know anything more about it. Butter was becoming scarce, but guns were more important. On May 1st, which in the old days had been the holiday of the proletariat, a drunken doctor—a veritable corpse swollen with champagne—orated about the joys of life. Did the people not begin to tire of so many dubious carnivals? Perhaps they were already weary. Perhaps they were already groaning. But nothing could be heard above the din blasting forth from megaphones and microphones.

Whoever stepped out of line knew what he risked. Whoever spoke the truth had to contend with vengeance. Whoever tried to spread the truth and struggled on its behalf was threatened with death, and with all the terrors that preceded death in the dungeons of the Third Reich.

Otto Ulrichs had ventured far. His political friends entrusted him with the most difficult and dangerous tasks. They felt—or hoped— that his position with the State Theater would to a certain extent protect him. In any case he was more fortunately placed than many of his comrades—who were living in hiding under false names, always in flight from the agents of the Gestapo—and could take a lot of chances that they could not attempt without courting certain disaster. But he took too many chances. One morning he was arrested.

It happened while the cast of the State Theater was rehearsing *Hamlet*, with the director in the title role. Ulrichs was to be the courtier Guildenstern. When he did not turn up at the rehearsal and sent no message excusing himself, Hendrik took fright. He immediately guessed—he almost knew—what had happened. He slipped out of the rehearsal early, leaving the cast to continue without him. When the director learned from Otto's landlady that three men in civilian clothes had called on Otto early in the morning and left with him, Hendrik rang the prime minister's palace. The fat man was good enough to come himself to the phone, but he became very curt and distant when Hendrik asked him whether he knew anything about the arrest of Otto Ulrichs. The air force general answered that he had not been informed. "And it's really not my province," he said somewhat testily. "If our men have put the fellow behind bars, it is certainly because he has something to answer for. I have had my suspicions of that man from the beginning. That Stormy Petrel in the old days was a nasty place." When Hendrik then ventured to ask whether anything could be done to alleviate Otto's situation, the prime minister's tone sharpened. "No, no, dear fellow—you'd far better let this whole matter drop. It would be more intelligent of you to worry about your own affairs." That sounded threatening. And the allusion to the Stormy Petrel, where Hendrik had himself made an appearance as a "comrade," did not have a pleasant ring.

Hendrik realized that he would be in danger of losing the favor of the godhead if he tried to help his old friend any further at that moment. I shall let a few days go by, he thought. Then, if I find the fat man in a better temper, I shall very cautiously try to go back to the subject. In one way or another, I shall succeed in getting Otto out of the Columbiahaus jail or the concentration camp. But that will have to be the end of it. It's essential for my safety that the man leaves the country. His senseless rashness, his childish notion of heroism, are going to get me into appalling trouble . . .

When after two days Hendrik had still not managed to find out anything about Ulrichs, he began to get worried. He dared not try another call to the prime minister. After long deliberation he decided to ring Lotte. The golden-hearted wife of the great man immediately declared how happy she was to hear Hendrik's dear voice once again. He assured her, though a trifle hurriedly, that it was also a pleasure for him to hear her voice, but apart from that he had this time a particular reason for calling.

"I'm worried about Otto Ulrichs," Hendrik said.

"How do you mean 'worried'?" exclaimed the blond actress. "He's dead."

She seemed to find it almost funny that Hendrik had not heard.

"He's dead," repeated Hendrik softly. To the astonishment of the prime minister's wife, he hung up without saying good-bye.

Hendrik ordered his chauffeur to drive him straight to the prime minister's palace. The man of power received him in his workroom. He wore a fantastic housecoat which was trimmed at the cuffs and collar with ermine. At his feet lay a huge bulldog. Above his desk a broad serrated sword shone against black drapery. On a marble pedestal stood a bust of the Führer gazing with blind eyes at two photographs. One showed Lotte Lindenthal as Minna von Barnhelm; the other was a portrait of the Scandinavian lady who had once driven the wounded adventurer through Italy and over whose grave there now stood an immense mausoleum—a shining marble dome encrusted with gold stars with which the widower was thought to have expressed his gratitude, whereas, in fact, he had raised the memorial only to his own vainglory.

"Otto Ulrichs is dead," said Hendrik standing in the doorway.

"Certainly he is," answered the fat man from his desk. When he saw a pallor like the reflection of a white flame spread over Hendrik's face, he added, "It appears it was a case of suicide."

Hendrik staggered for a moment and gripped his forehead in his hands. It was perhaps the first fully sincere and absolutely unrehearsed gesture that the prime minister had ever seen the actor Höfgen make. Such a lack of self-possession in his smooth favorite shocked the great man. He got out of his chair and stretched himself to his full frightening bulk. And the bulldog rose, too, and growled.

"I have already given you a piece of good advice," said the air force general menacingly. "And I repeat it now, although I am not in the habit of saying things twice. Let this matter drop!" That was plain enough. A trembling Hendrik felt himself at the brink of the abyss into whose depths this obese giant could easily throw him.

The prime minister stood with bowed head. Three thick folds of flesh stood out on his bullneck. His little eyes snapped; his eyelids were inflamed and even the whites of his eyes had a reddish sheen as though a wave of blood had risen to the head and now dimmed his vision. "This is a bad case," he said. "This Ulrichs was up to his neck in shit. He had every reason for killing himself. The director of my State Theater should not involve himself too closely with a notorious traitor."

The general bellowed the word "traitor." Hendrik now saw the abyss so close that his head began to swim. To prevent himself from falling he clung to the back of a heavy Renaissance chair. When he asked for permission to leave, the prime minister dismissed him with an ungracious nod.

No one at the theater dared talk about the "suicide" of their colleague Ulrichs. However, by some roundabout secret route everyone soon learned how he died. He had been tortured to death, because he would not reveal the names of his collaborators and friends. The Gestapo was enraged, for they had found no clues in Ulrichs's lodging, either—no written word, no scrap of paper giving an address. It was less in the hope that something could be got out of him than in the wish to punish him for his obstinacy that they intensified the tortures.

"Has it affected you deeply, Hendrik?" asked Nicoletta with what seemed almost malicious curiosity. "Does it haunt you?"

Hendrik dared not meet her glance. "I knew Otto for so long," he said softly, as though he was looking for excuses.

"He knew what risks he was taking," declared Nicoletta. "When you gamble you have to be ready to lose your stake."

Hendrik, who found this conversation painful and was at a loss for something to say, murmured, "Poor Otto."

She answered sharply, "Why 'poor'? He has died for what he saw as a just cause. Perhaps he is to be envied." After a pause she said dreamily, "I shall write to Marder and tell him about Otto's death. Marder admires people who risk their lives for an ideal. He loves obstinacy. He too would be capable of sacrificing his life out of obstinacy."

Hendrik waved his hand impatiently. "Otto was in no way an exceptional character," he said. "He was simply a man—a simple soldier of the great cause . . ." Here he fell silent and a quick flush passed over his sallow face. Now that he had in this brief instant understood the weight and dignity of such words he felt that he profaned them by letting them pass his lips. He felt that in his mouth these grave words had a ring of mockery.

No one was allowed to be present at the burial of the actor Otto Ulrichs who had taken his life "freely and out of fear of the just punishment of the People's Court." The state summarily disposed of the mangled corpse, bundling it into the earth with as little ceremony as if it had been the body of a dead dog. But his mother, a pious Catholic, sent money for the coffin and a small gravestone. In a letter that grease spots and tear stains made almost unreadable she implored that her son be given a Christian burial. The Church had to refuse. No priest must stand at the graveside of a suicide.

In fact it would not have been possible for the old woman to send the money for the coffin and the gravestone, for she possessed nothing, had it not been for a friend of the dead man who sent her the necessary sum from Berlin. He had given precise instructions as to where the money was to be forwarded. "Forgive me for not giving you my name," wrote the donor. "You will certainly understand and approve the reasons that compel me to show caution."

The old woman understood nothing at all. She wept, shook her head in bewilderment, prayed and sent the money that came from Berlin back there again.

So the coffin and the gravestone were paid for from the high salary that the theater director received from the National Socialist state. This was the last and only thing that Hendrik Höfgen could still do for his friend Otto Ulrichs—or the last affront he could inflict on him. Hendrik felt relieved after he had sent off the money to

Otto's mother. Now his conscience was a little more at peace, and on the page in his heart where he listed "insurance" there was once again a credit balance. The tension in which he had been living during these dreadful days relaxed, and he was able to concentrate all his energy on *Hamlet*.

This role presented some unexpected problems. How lightly back in Hamburg had he improvised the character of the Danish prince! Old Kroge had been furious and even at dress rehearsal had wanted to cancel the whole production. "I won't tolerate such shit in my theater," the old veteran had roared. Hendrik couldn't help smiling at the recollection.

Now there was no one who dared to speak about the "shit" in his presence, but when he was alone, with no one to hear him, Hendrik would groan, "I'll never make it." With Mephisto he had known from the very first minute exactly what gestures he should make and the exact intonation to give every word. But the Danish prince was difficult, he kept slipping away from him. Hendrik fought. "I won't let you get away!" he cried. But Hamlet turned away from him and said, "You're making the character the kind of man you understand. Not Hamlet."

"I've got to play you. If I fail at playing you, I'll have failed everything. You're my ordeal by fire; I've got to pass. My whole life, all the sins I've committed, my great betrayal, all my shame can only be vindicated by my art. But I'm an artist only if I can play Hamlet."

"You are not Hamlet, you don't have the nobility that only suffering and experience can give. You are merely the monkey of power, a clown to entertain murderers. Besides, you don't even have the physical attributes to play Hamlet. Look at your hands—are those the hands of a man ennobled by suffering and experience? And you're too fat. I regret to have to say this, but a Hamlet with hips like yours —sheer disaster." The prince laughed.

"You know perfectly well I can always look thin on stage. I've had a costume designed in which not even my worst enemy could see my heavy hips. Why must you bring that up when I'm already so nervous? Why are you doing this to me? Do you hate me that much?"

"I do not hate you at all. You are simply not of my kind. You had the choice, my dear fellow, between nobility and a career. You made your choice. Be happy with it, but leave me in peace."

The slender silhouette was beginning to fade away.

"I won't let you go," the actor cried and stretched out his hands, but they closed on empty space.

"You are not Hamlet," the proud voice echoed! . . .

He wasn't Hamlet, but he played him like the consummate actor he was. "It'll be magnificent," the stage manager and his fellow actors all said to him, through either a lack of discernment or a desire to flatter. "Since the time of Kainz, such a performance hasn't been seen on the German stage."

Yet, he himself realized he wasn't expressing the real content, the poetic mystery of Hamlet. His interpretation remained on the level of rhetoric. Because he felt so unsure of himself, he experimented: with nervous intensity he fleshed out his performance with little surprise effects which lacked internal coherence. He had decided to emphasize the virile, energetic aspects of the prince's character. "Hamlet wasn't a weak man," he said to journalists when interviewed. "There was nothing weak about him. Generations of actors have made the mistake of viewing him as a feminine character. His melancholy wasn't hollow but came from real motives. The prince wants to avenge his father. He is a Renaissance man—a real aristocrat and something of a cynic. I want to strip him of all the melancholy traits with which he has been burdened by conventional portrayals."

His colleagues and the journalists found this original, bold and interesting. Benjamin Pelz, with whom the actor had long discussions about Hamlet, was full of enthusiasm for Hendrik's conception. "It is only as your genius has fulfilled and interpreted him that we cynical men of action today can find Hamlet at all bearable."

Hendrik played Hamlet as a slightly neurotic Prussian lieutenant. All the effects he used to obscure the emptiness of his performance were excessive and shrill. At one moment he stood stiffly to attention; at the next he fell noisily to the ground in a dead faint. Instead of lamenting, he shrieked and raved. His laugh blared. His movements were convulsive. The deep and mysterious melancholy that had been so much a part of his Mephisto—without its being intended or contrived—was missing from his Hamlet. The great soliloquies were recited with exemplary professional skill; but they were only recited. When he came to

> "O! that this too too solid flesh would melt,
> Thaw and resolve itself into a dew"

the music and the harshness were missing, the beauty and the despair. There was no feeling of what had been thought and endured before these words were uttered.

Nevertheless, the first-night performance was a triumphant success. The new Berlin public judged actors less by the quality of their performances than by their relationship with those in power. Besides, the whole production was arranged to impress this audience of high-ranking officers and bloodthirsty professors and their no less heroic wives. The producer had crudely and insistently underlined the Nordic character of Shakespeare's tragedy. The massive sets might well have been used as a backdrop for the epic heroes of the *Nibelungenlied*. The lighting was a somber semidarkness filled with the rattle of swords and hoarse cries. Amid his uncouth companions Hamlet moved with exaggerated foppishness. At one point he allowed himself the indulgence of sitting motionless for minutes on end at a table, showing only his hands to the hushed audience; his face remained in shadow. His hands, painted chalk-white and harshly lit by a spotlight, stood out against the black tabletop as if they were precious relics. This he did out of insolence—to see how far he could go—and to torment himself a little. For he truly suffered from this exhibition of his broad and all too ordinary hands.

"*Hamlet* is the exemplary Germanic drama," Dr. Ihrig proclaimed in his introduction, inspired by the propaganda ministry. "The Prince of Denmark is one of the great symbols of the German people. In him we find expressed part of our deepest being. As Hölderlin exclaimed, 'For you Germans, you too/Are poor in deed and rich in thought.' Hamlet is therefore a danger for the German people. We have him in all of us and we must get the better of him. Providence, which has sent us the Führer, commits us to action in the defense of the national community from which Hamlet, a typical intellectual, withdraws into a brooding isolation."

However, the general opinion was that Hendrik had managed to make his Hamlet an embodiment of the tragic conflict between the demands of action and of thought, which so interestingly distinguished the German from other men. For he played the Prince as a swashbuckling hero who was subject to nervous fits, and he did so before a public that fully appreciated both the bravado and hysteria.

The director, who was dressed so artfully for the part that he really did look youthfully slender and lithe, was called out in front of the curtain again and again. At his side was his young wife Nicoletta, who, as Ophelia, had been somewhat strange and stiff but, especially in the mad scenes, very impressive.

The prime minister, shining in purple, gold and silver, and his Lotte, softly radiant in sky-blue, stood side by side in their box and applauded loudly. This was the reconciliation of the potentate with his court jester: Mephistopheles/Hendrik acknowledged it with gratitude. Handsome and pale in his Hamlet costume, he bowed low to the exalted couple. Lotte is in love with me again, he thought as he raised his right hand to his heart in a gesture that revealed his exhaustion but still had a certain beauty. Under the black arches of his eyebrows his eyes flashed seductive glances around the hall. The sorrowful look of strain about his temples ennobled his face and gave it a touching quality. Now the air force general's wife waved to him with a little silk handkerchief that was the same sky-blue color as her dress. The general grinned. I have been forgiven and am back in favor, thought Hendrik, relieved.

He refused all invitations, excused himself with an air of intense weariness and had himself driven straight home. Once alone in his study, he felt that sleep would be impossible. He was depressed and agitated. The ovation in the theater did not let him forget that he had failed. It was good and it mattered greatly that he had won back the fat man. But even this considerable victory could not console him for the defeat inflicted that evening on his higher ambition. I was not Hamlet, he said to himself miserably. The newspapers will assure me that I was every inch the Prince of Denmark. But they will be lying. I was bad—I still have enough judgment to know that. When I think of how I delivered "To be or not to be . . ." I feel sick.

He sank into an armchair that stood in front of the open window. He had snatched up a book, but now he listlessly laid it aside. It was Baudelaire's *Flowers of Evil*, which reminded him of Juliette.

The window looked out on the dark garden; the scent of flowers and trees rose up to him on the damp night air. Hendrik shivered. He drew his dressing gown closer about him. What month was it? April—or was it already the beginning of May? It struck him suddenly how dreadfully sad it was that he had for so long not noticed the approach of spring and its beautiful transition into summer. This damned theater, he thought angrily. It devours me. Because of it life is passing me by.

257

He was sitting there with closed eyes when a rough voice called out, "Hey, Herr Director."

Hendrik leaped from his chair.

A man had just pulled himself up from the garden to his window, which was no mean acrobatic feat because there was no trellis to provide a foothold. His head and shoulders were framed in the window. Hendrik was terribly frightened. For a few seconds he wondered whether it might be a hallucination, a product of his frayed nerves. But no, the man in the window seemed real enough. He wore a gray cloth cap and a dirty blue denim blouse. The upper part of his face lay in deep shadow. His jaw was covered with a reddish beard.

"What do you want?" cried Hendrik, groping behind him for the bell on the writing table.

"Don't shout like that," said the man, whose voice was not without a certain rough friendliness. "I'm not going to hurt you."

"What do you want from me?" repeated Hendrik more quietly.

"I've just come to bring you greetings. Greetings from Otto."

Hendrik's face was as white as the silk scarf around his neck. "I don't know what Otto you're speaking about," he whispered.

A sinister laugh came from the window. "Well, I never! What shall we bet that your memory will improve as we go along?"

Then the voice became intensely serious. "In the last note I had from Otto he said I should give you his regards. Don't think it's any fun for me to be here. But I have to respect Otto's wishes."

"If you don't leave immediately, I'm calling the police," Hendrik muttered.

With that, the laughter of the man in the window became almost friendly. "Just the sort of thing you would do, Comrade," he said cheerfully.

As surreptitiously as he could, Hendrik opened a drawer of the desk and slipped a revolver into his pocket. He hoped the visitor had not noticed.

With a contemptuous gesture the man pushed his cap back from his eyes. "You could have left that thing in the drawer, Herr Director," he said. "There's no point using it—it would only cause you trouble. What are you afraid of? I've just said that I wasn't going to do anything—this time."

The man was much younger than Hendrik had thought at first. This was clear now that the shadow of the peaked cap no longer hid his brow. His face was handsome, with broad Slavic cheekbones and striking light-green eyes. His eyebrows and lashes were red, like his thick, stiff beard. His skin had the ruddy well-tanned look that comes from working all day in the open air or sunbathing.

Perhaps he is mad, thought Hendrik, and this notion, although it suggested the most alarming possibilities, was somehow reassuring. I think it's very possible he is mad. If he were in his right mind, he would not have paid this idiotic call on me, which might quite easily have cost him his life, and is of no advantage to anyone. It's scarcely conceivable Otto really gave him the message. Otto had no leanings toward eccentricity. He knew we need to conserve our strength for more serious things.

Hendrik had moved closer to the window. Now he addressed the man as one would a sick person, all the time holding the handle of the revolver in his pocket. "Get out of here, my boy. I'm warning you for your own good. A servant could see you from down below. It's possible that at any moment my wife or my mother may walk into the room. You're putting yourself in terrible danger for absolutely nothing —nothing at all!" The figure stayed motionless in the window frame. Hendrik's voice rose to an exasperated shriek. "Come on, get out of here!"

The man responded in a perfectly calm voice. "Tell your friends of the regime the message that Otto passed on to me one hour before he died—'I am more convinced of our victory than ever before in my whole life.' There he was, his body battered all over and his mouth full of blood he could hardly speak."

"How do you know that?" asked Hendrik, whose breath was now coming very fast.

"How do I know?" The visitor again gave his sinister, cheerful little laugh. "From an SA man, who was close to him until the end, who happens to be one of ours. He wrote down everything Otto said to his dying minute. 'We shall win,' he said over and over again. 'When you're as far gone as I am now, you're no longer mistaken.' That's what he said—'We shall win!'" The visitor, both arms resting on the windowsill, leaned forward and scrutinized the owner of the house threateningly with shining green eyes.

Hendrik recoiled from this gaze as though seared by a flame. "Why are you telling me all this?" he gasped.

"So that it will come to the ears of your important friends." The man was shouting now and there was a note of triumph in his hoarse voice. "So that the big shits learn about it! So that the prime minister learns about it!"

Hendrik began to lose his nerve. He made strange convulsive gestures. His hands flew up to his face and then fell to his side again; his lips twitched and his eyes rolled. "What does it all mean?" he murmured. A little spittle appeared around his mouth. "What exactly do you hope to achieve from this theatrical joke? Are you trying to blackmail me? Do you want money from me? Here take this!" He groped absurdly in the pocket of his silk dressing gown, but there was only the revolver and no money to be found. "Or are you just trying to intimidate me? You won't succeed. You may think I'm trembling at the thought of the moment when you get the upper hand— for naturally, you are going to get the upper hand one day." The director's words came from white shaking lips as he moved, almost bounded across the room.

"On the contrary," he shouted shrilly, coming to an abrupt stop. "That's when I'll really be great. Don't you think I've made provisions for that?" The director had worked himself into a state of hysterical elation. "I'm on the very best terms with your people. The Communist party appreciates me—they are greatly indebted to me."

A sarcastic laugh answered him. "That's really great," exclaimed his tormentor at the window. " 'The best terms with our people.' You'll find, my friend, we won't make life easy for you. We have learned how to be ruthless, Herr Director. And I climbed up here just to tell you that. We've learned to hold grudges. Our memory is good, my friend—it's really brilliant. We don't forget anyone! We know exactly who we should hang first!"

Hendrik could only scream, "Go to hell! Get out! If you're not out of here in five seconds I'm calling the police. We'll see which of us hangs first."

Trembling with rage, he tried to throw something at the intruder. But all he could do was pull his horn-rimmed spectacles from his nose. With a strident cry he hurled them toward the window. The pathetic weapon missed the enemy and broke with a light clatter against the wall. The intruder was gone. Hendrik ran to the window to shout after him. "I am absolutely indispensable!" yelled the director into the dark garden. "The theater needs me. Every regime needs the theater! No regime can get along without me!"

There was no answer. The red-bearded visitor seemed to have been swallowed up in the gloom. And now there was nothing to be heard but the rustlings of the night. The garden exuded its scents and cool breezes. Hendrik wiped his damp brow. He bent down to pick up his spectacles and realized with distress that they were broken.

He wandered around the room, fumbling at the furniture like a blind man.

As he sank down in one of the large armchairs a wave of complete exhaustion closed over him. What an evening! He thought of all that he had gone through. Surely such ordeals overwhelmed even the strongest men, he thought self-pityingly. And I'm certainly not the strongest. He pressed his sweating face into his hands. He would have liked to have cried a little. But there was no point in shedding tears that nobody would see. After all the terror that he had survived, he felt that he had a right to the consoling presence of a loved one.

I have lost them all, he whispered. Barbara, my good angel. And Princess Tebab, the dark source of my strength. And Hedda von Herzfeld, my faithful friend. And even little Angelika. I have lost them all.

The dead Otto Ulrichs was to be envied—there was no more anguish left for him to bear. And his last thoughts had been of faith and a proud trust in the future. Was not even Miklas enviable—Hans Miklas, that defiant little enemy? All of them were to be envied—all who could believe in something, and doubly to be envied were those who in the sweep and thunder of faith had given their lives . . .

How was he to weather this evening? How was he to recover from this hour of total helplessness, full of fear and yearning and despair? Hendrik felt that he could scarcely endure another.

He knew that above him in their bedroom, his wife Nicoletta was. waiting for him. No doubt she was wearing under her light silk gown the high boots of supple brilliant red leather. The whip that lay on the dressing table among the makeup bottles and jars was green. Juliette's whip had been red, and her boots green . . .

Hendrik could go to Nicoletta. She would twist her sharp mouth into a greeting. She would make her cat's eyes as bright as possible and say something facetious with impeccable diction. No, that was not what Hendrik wanted now or what he needed so desperately.

He let his hands slip from his face. His troubled glance tried to find its bearings in the half-dark room. With difficulty he succeeded in picking out the bookshelves, the large framed photographs, the carpets, bronze busts, vases and paintings. Yes, it certainly looked distinguished and elegant. He had come a long way—no one could deny that. The director, privy councillor and senator, fresh from the dazzling reception of his Hamlet, relaxes in the comfortable study of his lordly dwelling . . .

Hendrik groaned again. Then the door opened and his mother entered.

"I could have sworn I heard voices here," she said. "Have you had a visitor, dear?"

He slowly turned his stricken face in her direction. "No," he said softly. "There was no one here."

She smiled. "How mistaken one can be!" Then she moved closer to him. Now he noticed for the first time that she was working at something with her hands as she went. It was a large woolen object— probably a shawl or a sweater. "I'm so sorry that I couldn't be at the theater tonight," she said, her eyes on her knitting. "But you know what my migraines are. I didn't feel at all well. How did it go? I'm sure it was a great success. Tell me . . ."

He answered mechanically, staring at her with eyes that seemed to look straight past her and yet with a strange distracted craving to devour her, "Yes, it was a success."

"I was sure it would be." She gave a gratified nod. "But you look worn out. Is something wrong? Do you want me to make you some tea?"

He shook his head silently.

She sat down beside him on the broad arm of the chair. "Your eyes are so strange." She studied him, worried. "Where are your glasses?"

"Broken." He tried to smile. The attempt failed. With the tips of her fingers Frau Bella soothed his bald head. "Why, what's the matter?" she said gently.

Then he began to cry. He threw himself forward, sinking his head in his mother's lap. His shoulders began to heave with sobs. Frau Bella was accustomed to her son's nervous spells. But this time she was alarmed. Her instinct told her that these sobs sprang from a different source, something deeper and more serious than the little breakdowns that he indulged himself in every so often.

"What is it, then . . . what is it?" she said. Her face was close to

262

his. She felt his tears on her hands. He seized her neck with an impulsive gesture as though he wanted to bind himself fast to her.

As she listened to Hendrik's moaning, her heart brimmed with pity. She understood everything, the whole story of his guilt, his great failure, and the despairing inadequacy of his remorse and why he lay there and wept. "But, Heinz!" she whispered. "But Heinz—quiet now. It isn't as bad as all that. There, there, Heinz . . ."

At the sound of the name of his childhood—the name that his ambition and pride had rejected—his weeping first became more violent and then began to subside. His shoulders stopped shaking.

Minutes passed before he slowly raised himself. Tilting back his exhausted tear-stained face, he extended his arms in a fine grieving gesture and cried, "What do men want from me? Why do they pursue me? Why are they so hard? All I am is a perfectly ordinary actor . . ."

FOR THE BEST IN PAPERBACKS, LOOK FOR THE

In every corner of the world, on every subject under the sun, Penguin represents quality and variety—the very best in publishing today.

For complete information about books available from Penguin—including Puffins, Penguin Classics, and Arkana—and how to order them, write to us at the appropriate address below. Please note that for copyright reasons the selection of books varies from country to country.

In the United Kingdom: Please write to *Dept. JC, Penguin Books Ltd, FREEPOST, West Drayton, Middlesex UB7 0BR.*

If you have any difficulty in obtaining a title, please send your order with the correct money, plus ten percent for postage and packaging, to *P.O. Box No. 11, West Drayton, Middlesex UB7 0BR*

In the United States: Please write to *Consumer Sales, Penguin USA, P.O. Box 999, Dept. 17109, Bergenfield, New Jersey 07621-0120.* VISA and MasterCard holders call 1-800-253-6476 to order all Penguin titles

In Canada: Please write to *Penguin Books Canada Ltd, 10 Alcorn Avenue, Suite 300, Toronto, Ontario M4V 3B2*

In Australia: Please write to *Penguin Books Australia Ltd, P.O. Box 257, Ringwood, Victoria 3134*

In New Zealand: Please write to *Penguin Books (NZ) Ltd, Private Bag 102902, North Shore Mail Centre, Auckland 10*

In India: Please write to *Penguin Books India Pvt Ltd, 706 Eros Apartments, 56 Nehru Place, New Delhi 110 019*

In the Netherlands: Please write to *Penguin Books Netherlands bv, Postbus 3507, NL-1001 AH Amsterdam*

In Germany: Please write to *Penguin Books Deutschland GmbH, Metzlerstrasse 26, 60594 Frankfurt am Main*

In Spain: Please write to *Penguin Books S. A., Bravo Murillo 19, 1° B, 28015 Madrid*

In Italy: Please write to *Penguin Italia s.r.l., Via Felice Casati 20, I-20124 Milano*

In France: Please write to *Penguin France S. A., 17 rue Lejeune, F-31000 Toulouse*

In Japan: Please write to *Penguin Books Japan, Ishikiribashi Building, 2-5-4, Suido, Bunkyo-ku, Tokyo 112*

In Greece: Please write to *Penguin Hellas Ltd, Dimocritou 3, GR-106 71 Athens*

In South Africa: Please write to *Longman Penguin Southern Africa (Pty) Ltd, Private Bag X08, Bertsham 2013*